BY ARTHUR CAVANAUGH

Missed Trains
Leaving Home
The Children Are Gone
My Own Back Yard

MISSED TRAINS

A NOVEL BY

Arthur Cavanaugh

SIMON AND SCHUSTER · NEW YORK

Copyright © 1979 by Arthur Cavanaugh
All rights reserved
including the right of reproduction
in whole or in part in any form
Published by Simon & Schuster
A Division of Gulf & Western Corporation
Simon & Schuster Building
Rockefeller Center
1230 Avenue of the Americas
New York, New York 10020
Designed by Edith Fowler
Manufactured in the United States of America

1 2 3 4 5 6 7 8 9 10

Library of Congress Cataloging in Publication Data

Cavanaugh, Arthur.
    Missed trains.

    I. Title.
PZ4.C3767Mi   [PS3505.A899]   813'.5'4   78-24535
ISBN 0-671-22479-4

ACKNOWLEDGMENTS

Writing is a solitary occupation, yet in this instance it was shared by many, whose help I wish gratefully to acknowledge. To Michael Korda, my editor, for his support during the long haul, and to John Cushman, my agent, and William Peter Kosmas, my attorney, for theirs; Dale Engle, Gladys Hurlbut, Bill O'Brien, Sherry Bennett Salisbury, for sharing their memories of road tours; Ida Kaul, whose recollections of small Kansas towns made real for me the fictional town of Clarion; Jerry Van Meter, railroad man, who put up with my queries about the Santa Fe and the Superchief while we traveled that illustrious route; M. Bloom, manager of the Wilbur Theater in Boston, who allowed me to roam the playhouse used as a setting in these pages; Jeanne Marie Fox, for guiding me around Chicago to the places Maggie and Christopher might have known; Sandy Giallorenzi, for manuscript typing best described as heroic; to Walter Mintz, Donald Cecil and Michael Victory, who generously offered the use of their offices, where this book was begun; and by no means last, to John Krol, for coming along at the end, when he was needed . . . to these kind people, I shall always be indebted.

Arthur Cavanaugh
July, 1978

PROLOGUE

Janya

1935

1

Every Sunday afternoon after dinner, they went for a walk, she and Papa.

Janya?

Yes, Papa?

You comin' or not?

Oh, yes, Papa, wait, I'm comin'.

Most Sundays, that is. Most of the time, they went for a walk. It could depend on various factors—the weather: rain, snow, or fiery Kansas hot—but most often it depended on Papa, on what inclination he was in.

Maybe yes, maybe no, you could seldom predict. It was a mistake to do any begging, that was almost sure to nix it. You had to just wait, that's all, and judge his inclination. It could take up the better part of the day.

Sundays began, as did this particular one . . . this particular Sunday in early November, when the train stopped in Clarion that was to set in motion the course of Janya's life . . . as always, it began with Mama waking her in the one-story maize-brick house on Dakota Street. A hall ran down the middle of the house dividing the sleeping from the living quarters. Three bedrooms, Mama and Papa's in front, a second for renting out, if they could find a boarder, which thus far they hadn't, then the bathroom, then Janya's sliver of a room tacked on at the back, opposite the kitchen . . . from which now came the bang of the oven, the clatter of the fry pan on the stove.

Eight o'clock. Janya hopped around, shivering, in undershirt and panties. She had felt the cold creep under the blankets even before Mama had come to fondle her awake. She sat on the spindle chair by the chest of drawers —the room's size permitted no furnishings other than the bed—and pulled on her lisle socks, turned them neatly at the knees. She put on her shoes and tied the laces in graceful bows, her breath forming cloudy vapors. She thought of winter and the poem Miss Foster had read in class. *When icicles hang by the wall* . . . Poems told of what the eye could not behold by itself, and made the cold into a friend. Well, almost.

It pinched icy fingers at her, all the way down the hall into the bathroom. The cold in the house was on account of the Depression; Papa kept the furnace turned on six hours a day, half the usual amount. The Depression, thought Janya, cupping the trickle of tepid water from the faucet to splash on her face, meant slicing things in half, like the hall sliced the house. Half the coal, half the food money, half the clothes, and unless a boarder turned up for the spare room . . .

On the washstand she observed something that swept other thoughts from her head. It was Papa's shaving brush, and its bristles were wet, which indicated that he was already up and shaved. It was a good sign, for if he didn't choose to remain in bed until the last possible . . . Janya scrubbed her face hard with the soap rag, neck, ears, behind the ears . . . she liked the feel of soap and water. *Scrub-a-dub-dub.*

She was eight years old and her proper name was Virginia. Virginia Ruth, but everybody pronounced it Janya, Kansas-flat and twangy, *Jaaaanya* like a banjo string. It wasn't a name to admire, like Rosalind or Guinevere or Ramona, names she read in storybooks, but to have a beautiful name might be worse, if the face that went with it—? She scrubbed her face, wiped it squeaky-clean. She combed her hair . . . her wispy dandelion hair.

It was while she was putting on her dress, back in the bedroom, that she commenced to seriously contemplate the Sunday walk. Thoughts of the future, of glorious changes and events, are beyond the grasp of an eight-year-old. Only the present is of acute concern, and she proceeded to weigh the different pros and cons. The weather was in her favor—a glance out the window showed that the azalea tree in the back yard barely stirred in the wind, and that the sun in the overcast sky was doing its best to shine. The shaving brush was in her favor, and the weather, but what about the Sunday dress? That could weigh against her.

Janya had two Sunday dresses, which her mother alternated from week to week, and of the two dresses Virginia had a decided preference. She was not talking of her all-time favorite, the yellow dress that she wore in summer, with the white rickrack and the sash that tied so as to make the skirt fluff out. Janya considered she looked near to pretty in that yellow dress. She would have been content to wear it the year round, in fact forever, until she was old and stooped. But of the two winter dresses, only the blue could be said to pass muster. Blue, with little bunches of violets on it, like Mama's seed packets, pleasing to look at.

This Sunday, however, was unblessed. It was the brown dress's turn, just like in a spelling bee in school. Janya gave a deep sigh as she slipped it over her head; she smoothed the white collar, pulled and yanked at the skirt in a vain effort to fluff it out. Ugly brown, with hateful rust-colored specks, it made her look . . . there was a nickname Papa sometimes called her by, and it could be that the sight of her in it . . . Why was the Sunday walk so important?

She hurried down the hall and into the kitchen, lest Papa should already be at breakfast and she would give cause for complaint. But the chairs at the oilcloth table were vacant, there was only Mama at the stove. Janya went flying over to her.

"Mama, y'know this here brown dress?" She tugged at the skirt. "I don't believe it fits no more."

A hearty laugh bubbled from Ida Belton, who stood at the stove, melting lard in the fry pan while the coffee perked. Ida's ample proportions were girded into the high-necked black bombazine that she deemed appropriate for church, over which a sleeved apron was tied in protection. "Why, you little fibber." She turned to hug the brown head that reached barely to her waist. "I don't reckon you growed s'much as an inch since last year." Ida reached for the bowl of eggs on the counter next to the stove. "Not fit you, indeed."

Virginia's arms encircled the aproned waist. How nice her Mama was, how warm even in the cold house, and sweet-smelling, she was. "Half a inch?"

"I hear no mention of the blue dress being too small. Well, do I?"

Janya laughed in reply and carried the jelly jar of knives, forks and spoons to the kitchen table, where, with the exception of Sunday dinner, all meals were taken in the Belton household. She ran her hand over the daisy-patterned oilcloth, which she knew Mama had chosen out of her love for flowers. It was a passion of Ida's, thwarted by the Kansas droughts. In the back yard the azalea tree survived the seasons, but little else did and so Ida expressed her passion by the iris wallpaper in her daughter's room, the daisy oilcloth and rosebud china, and the seed packets—hollyhocks, lily-of-the-valley, gladiola—that were tucked above the sink. Janya laid out the knives and forks and thought that, as much as Mama loved flowers, she loved her mother that much more. She set out the rosebud plates and reflected that it was needless to have hurried, Papa was always last to the table, whatever time he awoke.

But then, looking up, not hearing his steps, she saw him in the doorway, doing battle with his starched collar, and she ran to fetch his cup and saucer. Mama had told her that in his heyday Papa had been the town dandy, the envy of Clarion's young manhood for his manner of dress and stylish ways. "Mornin', Papa," she ventured from the cupboard. "Seems like a nice enough day."

Having attached the collar, George Belton ran the stiff moire tie under it and expertly tied it in a Windsor knot. His shirt was distinguished by French cuffs as well, which he snapped as he strode to the kitchen table. George's face was an assemblage of sharp planes cut by a thin, clipped mustache, ginger-colored, as was his thinning hair. It was a face that had possessed a youthful slickness, long gone, but it retained one uncommon feature. George Belton's deep-set eyes, thick-lashed, dark as sable, had caused flutterings in many a maiden, as Ida Belton could attest, but in those eyes now was a hard glint, chill as the house, narrow as its rooms.

A short man, he seated himself at the table with military erectness. Janya set a cup and saucer at his place, Ida hastened from the stove with the coffee and a platter of fried eggs. He speared eggs onto his plate, signaled that his cup was sufficiently full. "Fortune in coal bills . . . damned cold in here," he said. "Noon, before that furnace takes effect."

"Sun'll be comin' out," Janya said, taking her chair. "Sure is tryin' to." She nodded at the window. She shouldn't have said that, it might sound . . .

"Now, George," Ida Belton soothed, traveling back and forth from the stove. "Most houses have a mornin' chill on 'em." She opened the oven, warm from the rack of toast. "There, that'll help."

"Need more'n that to help." George cut into his eggs. "Pot of gold in the cellar, maybe. A boarder for the spare room."

"High school's due for a new teacher next term, might be wantin' a room. Or a new nurse over at the hospital."

George spread jam on his toast. He was the reason the spare room went empty, his refusal to grovel or kowtow to the scant few who came to inquire. "Tell you what," he said. "I'd settle for havin' Sunday to call my own. Sleep late as I damn please."

Ida *tssked* in sympathy and sat down across from her husband. She flinched at the groan the chair emitted—George disliked corpulence in a person. Still, she forgave him his grumpiness. Church was Ida's abiding comfort, but Sunday was George's one day in the week to stay abed, and unfortunately, Mr. Carewe, who was president of the bank, was also a warden at First Methodist, and while he didn't force his employees to attend . . . Ida forgave George his resentment, as she did a heap else, but, oh, my, she did wish he'd take notice of the other little soul at the table. Pitiful, the glances that kept darting his way.

Janya pushed wisps of hair from her brow—silky-fine as a baby's, Mama had said, although Papa had joked it was dandelion fuzz—and concentrated on her eggs. So far, it wasn't going too well. Not the worst it could be, but not good either. She forced her eyes to her plate, sopped up the yolk with a piece of toast. Food cost money.

"Man's entitled to rest on Sunday."

"Let me get you more coffee, George."

Janya drank her milk to the last drop. Under the table she crossed her fingers—sometimes it was the most a body could do, Mama decreed, to cross your fingers and hope for the best. Glance lowered, she rested her glass on the oilcloth. Then, unable to control herself, she looked up and her heart thudded, skipped a beat.

"Yes, Papa?"

He was smiling at her. Had spoken to her. "Cat got your tongue?" He leaned across the table, but she was powerless to reply. When Papa smiled, his face changed; one person disappeared and was supplanted by another, the secret person she had come to know from the Sunday walks.

"How's the day treatin' you?" he asked.

"Fine, Papa." She scraped her fork over her plate, though no scrap of egg remained, and smiled back at him with the enormous sable eyes, set in the thin, pinched face, that were George's gift to her. It was going good. If church services went all right, if the sermon didn't irk him and was not overlong; if, when they returned from church, Jezbo's had delivered the Sunday *Star* to the doorstep, and Papa could relax with his paper in the parlor and Sunday dinner was to his liking—

If, if . . . why was it so important?

By three that afternoon, dinner was over and Virginia stood in the sacrosanct, once-a-week dining room, clearing the remaining dishes from the table. The dining room was separated from the adjacent parlor by sliding oak doors, which were closed. As she gathered the dishes her eyes kept appraising the closed doors. Papa had gone back in there, with not a mention of a walk.

Mama had done her best to help. After the rice pudding, when he'd risen from the table and complimented her on the dinner—"Ida, the pork was delicious"—she'd tried to divert him from his mission.

"It's the apples give it flavor. Say, George—" as he'd moved toward the sliding doors "—with all that food inside, you could do with some exercise."

He'd stretched lazily and appeared to consider it. His trousers were creased razor-sharp and elastic bands held up his shirt sleeves, to protect the French cuffs. He wore the French cuffs only Sundays, but then, few men in Clarion wore them at all. He slapped his hard, flat stomach. "Exercise?"

"Lord knows, the way you keep after your figure . . ."

Perhaps that was Mama's error. He'd swung his glance over the spreading girth that strained the black dress. "Not like you, eh, Ida?" and it must have stirred up other thoughts. "Damn one-horse town, what difference does it make?"

Then, sliding the doors closed behind him, Papa had retired into the parlor.

Virginia stacked the dessert dishes, not yet abandoning hope. Papa's other Sunday rite consisted of reading the Kansas City *Star*. He went through it section by section, and she was a poor rival to it. It was a beautiful name for a newspaper. *Star light, star bright* . . . she sighed at the knowledge that she was stuck with the name she was born with, unless she got married someday. Otherwise, she was stuck with Virginia Ruth Belton, same as with her eyes and nose and face. Not a mite to be done about it. *Nothing.*

The word clutched at her, so that she was unaware of the dishes in her hands, the room, the November light from the window, falling across the table. It was a scary word—*nooothhiiing*—like a stone falling in a well. Janya gazed at the sliding doors to the parlor. Scary, because take for instance this moment right now—here she waited on one side of the doors, while to Papa, on the other side, she might as well not be there.

It angered her that the walk was of such importance. Let him read his Sunday paper, who cared? She carried the plates into the kitchen, and her anger ebbed at the sight of her mother. Why wasn't Janya like her, sensible, instead of filled with fancies and dreams? If she could pick someone to be like, it would be her mother.

"Sweetness?" Ida Belton was bent over the sink, washing dishes. As her hands dipped in and out of the suds she accompanied herself with a favorite hymn. *Come to the church in the wildwood, come to the church in the dell.* Ida was active in the sundry functions of Clarion's First Methodist Church, its cake sales, bazaars, raffles, in return for the solace she drew from the Lord.

She rinsed the dishes under the faucet. "Daddy still cooped up with his paper?"

"I don't care one bit," Janya said. She went to the sink, nodded at the seed packets tacked on the wall. "Mama, tell me about . . . you know."

" 'Bout my garden? Sure had my heart fixed on growin' me a garden, but the Lord"—she wiped her hands and gestured at the packets—"didn't intend delicate blooms for Kansas. Until, that is," she turned and beamed, "He sent me the fairest flower of all."

"Honest?"

Ida frowned, recalling how she'd yearned for a brother or sister to present to her child. To Ida, the tragedy of the spare room wasn't that it stayed empty for lack of a boarder. But if George had had his way, there wouldn't have been . . . "Honey, you mustn't mind about your Daddy."

"I don't," Janya said. "I was thinking we'd get out the Sears Roebuck."

Funny little soul, Ida thought, to care so deeply about a Sunday stroll. "He gets to worryin' about the Depression, and that job he hates at the bank. Town like Clarion wasn't meant for George, wantin' what's beyond him."

Janya's mouth trembled. "We'll get out the catalogue and look at the pretty dresses . . . and you can tell me 'bout Kansas City, when Grandma took you to the department store."

Ida deliberated a moment, then lumbered toward the cupboard. She removed her sewing basket from a drawer, rummaged among its contents. "Just as I 'spected," she sighed. "That sampler I'm making for the church sale? Left it plumb in the parlor last night. Run fetch it for me, honey."

Janya stared at her mother. "I couldn't. Papa's in there."

"Well, now, just you march y'self in—"

"But the doors."

"Don't fuss about the doors."

"When Papa closes them doors—"

Ida put a sheltering arm on the thin shoulders. "Truth is, Daddy forgets about the walk, so you got to remind him. A ladylike *tap-tap* on them doors and—"

Janya twisted at her hair. She couldn't ever—the doors were Papa's Do Not Disturb sign, trespass who dares. When Mama sent her in to announce Sunday dinner, often her hands would reach to slide the doors back and then would not obey. It was the picture she had of herself standing there, invisible to Papa, exactly as if . . .

"I couldn't," she reaffirmed. "Why, I'd—"

"Well, if openin' them doors is what prevents you from—"

She was not required to, the day was in her favor after all. She listened as Papa called from the hall, "Janya?"

She didn't breathe. "Yes, Papa?"

"You comin' or not?"

She stood there dumbly, then her legs sprang of their own volition. "Oh yes, Papa, wait, I'm comin'," she cried, and ran to the front hall . . .

"Shake a leg, slowpoke."

"I am, Papa."

He'd left the front door open; the wind gusted in, and he was shouting at her from the sidewalk. In a frenzy of haste, she searched among the hangers in the closet for her coat. So twitchy-fingered was she that Mama had to help her on with it. The coat was an extra size large, purchased with the idea that she'd grow into it; after a year's wear, it still hung below her knees and the sleeves had to be rolled back. As for the knitted cap, she would have left it gladly on the hook. Worst sight ever, shaped like a mushroom, always sliding over her eyes . . . but Mama had knitted it for her.

"Easy does it," Ida soothed, and slipped a nickel in the coat pocket, whispering, "Treat y'self at Jezbo's if you can." She pulled the cap over Janya's ears. "Wished I knew what's so special about these walks."

"Oh, Mama, Mama." Janya hugged her.

"Scoot, now."

"I'm comin', Papa."

She ran out the door, onto the little gabled porch. Her father stood on the sidewalk, below the steps that led down from the front walk. He opened his arms as she raced toward him, and with a joyous laugh she went flying over the steps into his embrace. "Caught you," he said.

"Yessir, you did."

In defiance of the November rawness, George Belton wore no overcoat over his mustard tweed suit. He squeezed his daughter tight and felt an odd resentment that she should have inherited his eyes, a resentment at the shining luster of them. "Caught Miss Mouse," he said with a laugh.

"Papa, please don't . . ." She verged on asking that he not call her by that nickname. She'd seen a mouse up close, a poor scurrying brown thing, and did not enjoy the comparison.

"Please don't what?" George blew at the wisps of hair that escaped from the knitted cap. He envied the luster of her eyes, which his had lost. "Careful, your dandelion fuzz'll clean blow away."

"Papa."

Plain as a brown hen, except for the eyes. His eyes. George smiled then at the thought of what else she'd inherited from him. "Well, where'll it be today?" he asked.

Janya linked her arms around his neck. He was smiling, the sun had emerged from behind the clouds, glinting on his ginger mustache. "Yes, where?" she challenged ecstatically.

"Up to the young lady."

Virginia put a delighted finger to her mouth. The other person had vanished; in his stead was the Papa who was different from everybody else in Clarion. "Let's see . . ." she made as if to deliberate. They shared a secret between them, concerning these Sunday walks. She'd told it to no one, not even Mama, because Papa had cautioned, "Want the whole town hootin' at us? Two crazies ready for the asylum?"

"Can't make up her mind?" George Belton shifted her in his arms. "Shall I get out the Atlas?"

Janya pondered. So many countries to choose from. They could go out South Road to the old deserted farmhouse, which, under her father's spell, became a ruined castle in Scotland; the farmhouse boasted a rooftop porch, and stationed there they were a Lord and Lady, rulers of all they surveyed. Or they could take the highway out to Scroggin's greenhouse, stroll among the hothouse rows, the exotic gardens of Shalimar in India. Or to the footbridge over the dried-up creek, which became not a footbridge but a drawbridge, to an abandoned mill which became a Chinese fortress. "Wellll," she said.

That was their secret: On their Sunday walks Virginia and her father did not traverse the streets of Clarion or its environs. Their feet might tread those pavements, but they themselves walked in other lands.

"Well, Miss Mouse, quick about it."

Already she sensed a growing impatience in him. "S'pose we—" She had read of foreign lands; Clarion's streets had faraway names—Wyoming, Colorado, Oregon—but when Papa was a doughboy in the war he'd actually traveled to a foreign shore. "What about France?" she proposed.

"Where in France?"

"Paree?" she asked, and his face lit up. "Your heart's desire, you said it was."

"*Paree.*" He tasted, savored the champagne sound of it, reluctant to have it disperse. Stinkin' cattleboat from New York, two weeks heavin' his meals from the roll and pitch. Stinkin' PFC in the mud in Vincennes, then . . . then the Armistice and Paree. Oh, God in hell, that gorgeous city, best time of his whole life, God in hell, the parades and cafes and wine and mamzelles . . . He deposited his daughter on the sidewalk and rewarded her with a broad grin. "Best idea I ever heard," he congratulated her. "Which part a' the city we head for first?"

"What about—" Janya wriggled with excitement "—the Champs Elsie?"

George seized her hand and they started off down Dakota Street. "Most beautiful street in the world, take it from me," he enthused. Clumps of weed poked up between the cracks in the sidewalk, and the irregularly spaced houses they passed were drearily alike, sawed-off little one-story houses, some with *For Sale* signs or boarded-up windows, interspersed with weed-choked empty lots begging for buyers. But this was not what George Belton saw.

Not once did George's glance rest on spurious details. To the plain-garbed neighbors who passed, he gave merely a formal nod; he did not, had never, belonged among them. A lone Model-T chugged by, and for a moment he remembered the snappy 1928 Chevrolet roadster of which he'd been the proud owner, the two-story house he'd set his eye on, the . . . Depression, repossession, it rhymed. Images of the beautiful city of Paree replaced grim reminders of reality. He was striding along a boulevard, twirling a cane.

"Let's see," he mulled. They'd reached the corner of Third and Dakota and his glance took command of the drab side street. "This looks like the Rudy Rivoli to me, don't it to you?"

"I do believe it is," said Janya.

"Over there"—he brandished the imaginary cane—"over there is the Loover museum." He wished he could pronounce French correct, his tongue never could get the knack of it. "It's where they got the Mona Lisa," he said.

"What's that?" Certain questions were required to be asked, it was part of the game.

"Why, it's the world's most priceless piece of artwork," said George. With jaunty but military bearing, he stepped from the curb. "To get to the Champs Elsie, we follow the Rudy Rivoli," and they walked up Third Street.

To keep pace with her father, Janya was forced to take quick hoppity-skips, but she didn't mind. The game was underway. She didn't play it near as well as Papa. She accepted that Paree was a city across the ocean in France; he'd told her so and showed her on the map, but in fact none of it was real to her. Only Clarion was real, the town of Clarion, population 9,000; seventy miles northwest of Wichita; forty miles west of Hutchinson. The people and streets and houses, the dust and wind, furnace of summer ... only the town and the flat plains of Central Kansas that stretched beyond sight to the horizon were real to Virginia. All the rest, what Papa talked of, was not real, was made up, like the storybooks in the library or the movie pictures at the Alhambra. It didn't lessen the enjoyment of the game, she infinitely preferred it this way. The knitted cap, the brown dress, the dandelion hair were real, and what wasn't to be preferred over them? "Will there be music in the cafes?" she asked, pushing up the knitted cap, encumbered by the oversized coat, trying to keep pace.

They reached Montana Street, and for both of them it too represented an unreality. On the two blocks of Montana between Second and Fourth Streets were the homes of Clarion's affluent citizens. Large, comfortable houses, they were set on wide lawns under spreading trees, and were separated by privet hedges and trellised arbors rather than by weed-wild vacant lots. For George, these blocks exerted both a pull and a repulsion. The fine mullioned Tudor house was the property of Harlow Bates, Doc Bates, folksy as a country minstrel while squeezing the last nickel from the town for services rendered. Folksy grins and chucking babies under the chin, but try lettin' a bill go unpaid. Tudor mansion from his earnin's, and got county funds to build Bates Hospital but owned it lock, stock and barrel, him and the board. Folksy, friendly Doc Bates.

And neighbor to Doc Bates's Tudor in more senses than one was the rose-brick, white-pillared residence that most compelled George's attention. His gaze lingered on the Pierce-Arrow that idled in the Carewes' graveled drive. Thornton Carewe, soft-spoken and benevolent, handshake like an iron vise. Courtly and genial, pious warden of First Methodist, mortgage-holder of Vida County, president of Title & Guaranty. Fatherly to all, benignly concerned for his employees' welfare. *See you at services tomorrow, George? It's a man's Christian duty.* Every Saturday at noon when the bank closed for the weekend, that parting question had been directed at George Belton. Every Saturday, for thirteen years, at assistant teller George Belton. *Thirteen years assistant teller . . .*

"Papa?" Virginia asked. Her fancy was captured, as always, by the green-clapboard Victorian house at the corner of Second, where her mother had come, a farm girl, to work for the Cogswells. As a baby, Mama had taken her to the turreted, gingerbread-porched house to show her off to Mrs. Cogswell. Every July birthday Mrs. Cogswell invited her and Mama for lemonade and iced cupcakes in the parlor. It was in winter that Janya best liked the Cogswells' house, sturdy and solid, smoke curling from its three chimneys, so that she could not conceive of the cold invading it on frosty mornings that turned her own lips blue. At night she'd walk out of her way just to see the Cogswells' house with the windows all lighted, sending forth a warmth that seemed to reach out and enfold her as she went by.

"Papa, what street in Paree is this, with these fine houses?" she asked—which was a mistake and prompted George to glare and stump along up Third, without reply. She hurried to catch up, fell into breathless step. "I mean, the Champs Elsie, Papa. Where's the Champs Elsie? Will there be music and cafes? Show me, Papa."

She clasped her father's hand and, relenting slightly, George resumed the game. "Music? Cafes? Why, just look at that fab'lous bouleyvard."

"Tell me about it, Papa."

"Got eyes of your own, don't you? Well, then . . . carriages with beautiful ladies. Flower stalls. Violins in every cafe . . . right fine, don't you think?"

It presented a not-inconsiderable challenge, to transform the grubby frontage of Main Street into the Champs Élysées. Running between the Vida County Courthouse at the eastern end and the steep-pitched shingled roof of the depot at the western end, its four blocks were an assemblage of ragtag one- and two-story commercial buildings—Garver's Hardware, Friedman's Fine Furniture, Hepple's Pharmacy, J. C. Penney, Holzman's General. On many store windows signs were pasted, *Must Sacrifice, Free Offer, Prices Slashed*, but contributing a more ominous note were the vacant storefronts, abandoned as if by stealth of night. Dusty twirls of crepe paper, display remnants, strewed the vacant windows; in one, the severed limb of a clothes dummy lay among scraps of tissue and shoe boxes.

Why had he come back? George Belton wondered, surveying the straggle of storefronts. *He'd had the chance to stay away, across the ocean there in France, or New York if he'd wanted . . . Chicago, St. Louis, K.C. He could've stayed and taken his chances instead of . . .* The stores looked as if they too had raised the white flag of surrender.

"Where's the cafes, Papa?" Janya could sense that the

game was winding down, like a Victrola in need of cranking. The game wasn't going well, she had to help him. "I see the cafes," she avowed, gesturing at the drab lineup of stores. She remembered the nickel in her pocket and debated whether to suggest a visit to Jezbo's, which was right there on the corner. Jezbo's! Soda fountain and candy bars, toys, magazines, games—Jesse Bozeman was the proprietor, known to one and all as Jezbo, not a jollier, fatter, nicer man in town. Could get her smiling out of her shyness quicker than anybody, didn't fuss no matter how long she dawdled at the candy-bar shelves. Oh Henry, Baby Ruth, Root Beer Barrels, Milk Duds, Chocolate Sponge, *which, which?* The worst agony, and convinced she'd choose wrong and regret it. A nickel for a Hershey, a nickel for a Mounds, a nickel for . . . Papa would get mad if he knew Mama had given her a hard-earned nickel to squander. No, she'd better not make like Jezbo's was some Paree cafe.

"Janya," Papa said, "maybe it's too late this afternoon to—"

Shifting direction, her eyes spied a diadem of lights winking on and off. Orange and blue light bulbs chasing around a marquee, suffusing the sidewalk in front with rainbow colors. "Look, there's our cafe," she cried, and took off from the curb. "There's our music," and she ran toward the Alhambra.

But it wasn't really necessary for Janya to pretend about the Alhambra. The orange and blue twinkling lights broadcast a make-believe of their own, luring her over the pavement. Second to the library, no, second to none, the movie-picture house was her favorite place in all of Clarion.

On the marquee, banded by the dazzle of orange and blue, was spelled *C. Gable & J. Crawford in Dancing Lady.* She went diving under the marquee to inspect the posters. A big colored one showed Joan Crawford and Clark Gable locked in an embrace, while swirled around them was emblazoned the gaudy heading, *Dancing Lady.* Janya studied this large poster intently, then transferred her scrutiny to the stills, which depicted scenes from the movie. Joan Crawford was shown in a sequin dress; a stage full of chorus girls kicked their legs in spangled tights; Clark Gable was seated at a piano, his sleeves rolled up and a lock of hair over his forehead . . .

She carefully studied the stills, although it was beyond her to figure it out yet about movies. Take, for example, these chorus girls . . . inside, on the Alhambra's screen, you'd actually be able to see them dance. Joan Crawford would really talk, and Clark Gable would actually put his arms around her . . . *but how?* It was only in the last year that Janya had attended the movies, and each time it baffled her. Movie pictures . . . pictures that moved on a screen; people talked and danced, rode horses, fired guns . . . then the lights came on and the screen was blank. *What had appeared to be real proved to be . . . a blank screen. Not real.*

"Gettin' cold, Janya. I think we might's well—"

She darted from the marquee and took her father's hand, before the game fizzled out completely. He hadn't been interested in the Alhambra, and she'd idled there, trying to figure it out about movies. They continued along Main Street and she concluded that movies were like these Sunday games, unconnected with what was real. They were made up, like storybooks.

They neared the next corner, which was occupied by the Title & Guaranty, and she knew she must hurry him past it. If he started to think about . . . she pressed her father's hand and made a wish for him. She wished that someday he'd never have to work at the bank any more, that the three of them, Mama, Papa and her, would leave Clarion and . . . "I guess the Champs Elsie is everybody's heart's desire," she said, striving to continue the game.

George Belton ignored her chatter and blankly regarded the brass-plated bank doors, to which he would report tomorrow morning at 8:30. *Four minutes past the half-hour, George. Promptness is a virtue we must strive to achieve. "A day's work for a day's wages" is a fair maxim, I think.*

George's mouth, under the clipped mustache, was a thin line.

"Papa—" Janya tugged at his sleeve, knowing it was no use, the game was over, but at that very instant, rescue came. Far beyond the town, a train whistle sounded its haunting cry.

It was a deliverance, and she seized upon it. She looked up at her father, pushed at the sliding knitted cap. "Shall . . . shall we go down to the depot and watch the Chief go by?" she asked. "It's about time for it, isn't it?"

The whistle faded, and George consulted his watch. Clarion was situated on the mainline tracks of the Atchison, Topeka & Santa Fe, and consequently trains were a daily feature of the town's life. Day and night, whistles sounded and wheels clacked over the rails, sending their reverberations up and down the streets. At almost any hour, a puff of engine smoke would go spiraling into the sky above the prairie, wisps of it lingering to mingle with the clouds. Of this mighty commerce, however, few trains stopped at Clarion. The Dodge City–Wichita–Kansas City Local each morning, and its return counterpart each night, carrying passengers and mail. Freight trains, which would unhook cars onto the siding, reclaim them after unloading. Clarion was not a flagstop town, and its few citizens who embarked on long-distance train trips were compelled to board at Hutchinson or Dodge City. The daily Local and freight; but apart from these the trains ignored Clarion. The crack long-distance expresses went thundering past, relinquishing not a moment's pause in their proud pursuit of the miles.

The town had its quota of train buffs, but George Belton was not among them. Train-watching for him was a painful reminder of lost opportunities, wrong choices . . . but there was one train, preeminently the grandest of them all, whose swift and powerful passage gave him a thrill to observe, when he elected to avail himself of it.

He checked his watch as, rapidly, the dank thoughts of tomorrow receded. "Correct," he complimented his daughter. "Chief goes by in another ten minutes. Shall we hotfoot it on down to the depot?"

"Papa, let's."

"C'mon, then, Miss Mouse."

Joining hands, two crazy people, they lit off down the sidewalk, bound for the steep-roofed building at the foot of Main Street.

3

The Chief went flashing by every day of the week, but watching it go by on Sundays was a popular diversion in Clarion, having the virtue of not costing a penny. Onlookers would be grouped at various junctures along the route—rail crossings, the highway, cow pastures, cornfields, waiting to cheer the train's brief and hurtling presence among them. The day's increasing chill and fitful sun, however, had brought only a handful of spectators to the depot.

George came onto the wooden platform with his daughter and took inventory of the regulars, Dan Jensen, Clyde Filmore, Ev Durkin and the like, who'd turned out. These were the buffs, who could recite the Santa Fe timetables, the numbers assigned to each train—the Chief was No. 19-20, the odd number denoting westbound passage, the even number indicating that it was bound east. Baldwin 4-8-2 engines, Baldwin Pacific 2-4-4-6, 1700 class—the buffs could talk you deaf with statistics. If you let the fools jaw at you, that is. George exchanged brief nods with the men and escorted Janya from their midst.

He consulted his pocket watch as they moved down the platform. "Made it in two minutes. Not bad for a middle-aged geezer."

"Oh, Papa," Virginia demurred.

In their mad race down Main Street, the other game had been forgotten, although this new pursuit was in fact an extension of it. Behind them, the depot waiting room lay in a dusty vacuity of silent benches and shuttered ticket and freight windows; that no commerce was transacted at the depot on Sundays was prime evidence of the town's vagrant rail activity. The potbellied iron stove in the middle of the planked floor spread no rosy-embered warmth and would not do so until morning. The ticking of the wall clock above the rack of timetables, train brochures and bulletin notices provided the only note of animation in the waiting room.

"Can't beat fools," George said, proceeding to the far end of the platform, where it extended beyond the roof. "Gobble up information like hogs, but them experts still don't know where the best viewin' spot is." He was asserting his natural innate superiority.

The advantage was minimal, but to stand at the far end afforded a view of the platform's length and the rails that ran alongside it: to watch the Chief thunder past the stationary platform made its passage appear even swifter and grander. North of the platform the tracks withdrew in a long perpendicular that sliced over the table-flat land to where, two miles distant, they made a sharp curve eastward and passed from sight. The flat monotony of the land was broken by a barn or silo, a farmhouse under a clump of cottonwoods, a windmill; but at the point where the tracks curved east, the enormity of sky was punctuated by two immense granaries, and it was to these that George directed Janya's attention.

"Tracks go out of sight, but keep your eyes fixed on them grain elevators," he instructed. "It's right there you'll catch your first glimpse a' headlight." With the authority of a traveler to France, he leaned an arm on the wooden rail of the platform, disregarding the chill that penetrated his tweed suit. No other man was coatless, only George Belton. He gestured toward the distant granaries. "Keep lookin'. Any second now. Santa Fe's number-one prestige train, none finer on the *en*tire continent, in my opinion."

The wind plucked at the knitted cap, forcing Janya to

anchor it with her hand. She didn't understand about trains; it was like Papa's talk of faraway lands, to be enjoyed if not comprehended. Only Clarion existed: she had traveled twice to Hutchinson and once to Wichita, but the latter was when Papa had the Chevy and she'd been little more than a baby. Really, she knew only about Clarion: the trains, where they traveled, to what mysterious places . . . she was unable to imagine.

"The grain elevators. Keep watchin'."

She clamped the hat against the wind. "I am, Papa."

The seconds ticked by, there was much checking of watches by the experts; the suspense mounted, a stir of anticipation circulated along the platform. Every gaze was riveted on the same distant point of the two granaries.

"*There*," shouted George Belton, "there she comes, tiny speck of headlight, see her?"

Virginia strained her eyes. She stared mightily at the distant granaries but could glimpse no speck of light. A whistle blew, far off, mighty and resounding over the plains, and . . . wait . . . yes, she thought she could see it. A beam of light between the granaries, a smudge of black. It grew larger as she watched, and then it wasn't a smudge any more, it was a locomotive. With every second, it grew larger and took on definition. It rounded the distant curve in the tracks and charged fully into view. Onward, the locomotive coursed, pulling behind it a line of cars so long that some had yet to round the curve. "I see it!" Janya jumped up and down. "Here comes the Chief. I see her!"

On the platform, a general whoop of excitement went up as the great train revealed itself, but George held his emotions in check. "Lookit her come," he whispered in a kind of sing-song. "Costs extra just to ride the Chief, y'know that?" he asserted. "You have to pay extra fare, and there's no coach section. No sit-up, nossir. It specifies in the ads—one-hundred-percent Pullman deluxe," he whispered the litany to himself.

Still a mile up the tracks but splendidly revealed, the Chief thundered toward them. High above in the leaden sky, the gray clouds shifted and a golden ray of sun shafted down, as if to herald the train's approach. The sun glinted on the orange streak behind the locomotive, which proved to spell *Santa Fe* across the coal cars. The mail and baggage cars were clearly distinguishable; behind these stretched the fleet of Pullmans, of such royal length that only now was the rear observation car in view. Briefly, the sun shone on the black, iron-jawed locomotive and its imperious stab of headlight. A puff of steam went skyward, the wheels and pistons churned in pulsating rhythm along the rails and sent ahead a steady clacketing over the bands of steel.

The impossible, the unheard of, happened then. The group on the platform was watching in awed delight, and George had steered his daughter away from the platform's edge, up against the depot shingles. "Stand back," he cautioned, shielding her with his arms. "The way she comes roaring past—"

But the Chief didn't roar past. A mile up the tracks its churning wheels commenced to slacken their onward race. The whistle sounded a series of short warning blasts, this in itself unprecedented. Then the unimaginable, the impossible happened, and the air was charged with a grinding of brakes.

"By God, she's slowin' down," came a voice of disbelief.

"By damn, she's *stoppin'*," cried another, in the slowly darkening afternoon.

There followed a profound silence among the onlookers, as at the advent of some supernatural occurrence. Incredibly, the mammoth engine rolled down the platform, close enough to touch; the orange-lettered coal cars clacked past, followed by the mail and baggage cars . . . several hundred yards down the tracks, the engine slowed to a halt.

There was a stampede to the platform's far end, where George and his daughter stood. The buffs looked on knowledgeably at the two men in striped overalls, who clambered down the ladder from the locomotive's cab. While the engineer and fireman crouched down to examine the locomotive's underbelly, a third man, the flagman, posted himself on the tracks with lantern and flags. The sharp clang of wrench on iron echoed up the tracks. Another man, the conductor, was hastening along the tracks to the engine. He crouched down and conferred with the engineer.

Let the others goggle and gawk. George pushed away from the rail with Janya. "Some minor adjustment, prob'ly," he said, striving to suppress the excitement that tingled through every fiber and nerve. All the times he'd watched the Chief go by, and here the mythic creature was, parked on his doorstep, so to speak. The real thing, but it was more painful than enjoyable. "Sure enough is a sight," he said, listening to himself, his speech that was like any small-town yokel's, same as he couldn't learn to pronounce French. He held his daughter's hand and indicated the long funnel of cars that stretched along the platform and up the tracks past it. "Feast your eyes," he said. "Only chance you'll get, for sure."

Directly across from them, towering above the platform, was a car such as Virginia would not have thought to exist on a train. She sucked in her breath at the wonders it revealed, but at the same time was utterly bewildered by them.

Take the windows, to start with. Rather than parched green shades, the windows of this particular car were fitted with tieback curtains. The prettiest curtains ever, of rich material, with little palm trees woven on them. The usual coach seats—there were none. Instead, a table was placed at each window, a dining table with chairs and a snowy cloth set with china, silverware and sparkling glasses. Each table had its own little lamp with a pleated pink silk shade, and a silver vase from which arched a single red rose. A rose in a silver vase on every table, if you could imagine it.

"Papa, look," Janya nudged, calling attention to the lady and gentleman who were seated at one of the tables, framed by the tieback curtains. "Look—" She tugged at her father's sleeve, wide-eyed and solemn.

"That's the Fred Harvey dining car," George informed

her, beginning to take pleasure in the Chief's presence. "It's where the passengers luxuriate and dine on banquets," he said.

Janya pushed at the knitted cap. She'd ridden the Local to Hutchinson, and for lunch the passengers had unwrapped sandwiches from paper bags—it was how you ate on a train. She observed the lady at the table lift a silver fork delicately to her lips; the gentleman sipped at some ruby liquid from a long-stemmed glass.

"What are they eating? Drinking?" she asked. "I declare . . ."

George watched with an awe equal to his daughter's but mixed with a more troubling emotion. "Wine and Christ knows what else," he sighed. "The Chief's got as outstanding a menu as—" he searched for a worthy comparison "—as the Muehlebach Hotel in K.C.," he vowed. "Any and every type of food you request. Pheasant, T-bone steak, lobster."

Virginia stared at the lady and gentleman, who were conversing and as yet had not glanced from the car window. The lady wore a string of pearls. "What's lobster?" she asked.

"Money . . ." George answered slowly. "It's money . . . shipped on cracked ice." He pulled at the jacket, conscious of its age: *three, four, how many years old?* The clang of the iron wrench resounded along the rails, indicating that repairs were still in progress; he took Virginia's hand and moved along the platform.

"Those there are the sleeping cars." He nodded at the next set of train windows, which disclosed a vista of what resembled rooms, little rooms with built-in sofas, cushioned chairs, burnished paneling, mirrors, light fixtures. "Private sleeping compartments," George explained. "During the day, you relax yourself on a nice sofa, then at night the porter converts it into a—"

But there his description ended, for another wondrous sight overtook father and daughter. The door of one of the Pullmans was opening. A black-uniformed Negro porter descended with an iron footstool and placed it below the car's steps. The porter reached up his arm, and *then*—!

Assisted by the porter, a covey of passengers alighted from the Pullman. They were of a breed Virginia had never set eyes upon, and as they came forward she instinctively backed away. The ladies were dressed in clothes that no Sears-Roebuck catalogue depicted—fleecy coats, fur wraps, silk prints, satins; jewels glittered at throats and wrists. The ladies wore their hair sleek and curled, like fitted caps; even their walk, the way they held themselves, was different. Like butterflies in November, they drifted about the rough wooden platform, not seeming to set foot on it. They hugged their coats and furs against the wind; laughed, chatted in unheard-of accents; glanced about in bright, rueful amusement . . . and the men with them were no less beautiful. Some were darkly tanned, teeth gleamed white as they laughed and chatted with the ladies. One man wore a jacket with gold buttons, a white silk scarf knotted at his throat. One of the ladies took a cigarette from her purse, and a silver-haired man instantly held a thin square of gold to the cigarette; a flame leaped magically.

Of its own accord, Virginia's hand inched to the mushroom hat and removed it. She looked at these favored beings and wished it was summer and that she was wearing her yellow dress, the one with the rickrack and sash, that made her look near to pretty. *Wished, wished . . .* who *were* these persons from the train? She thought of the Champs Elsie, her father's descriptions of the cafes and music and ladies in carriages—and the realization came jolting her; these were the people from Papa's dream world . . . except they were real.

"That's your upper crust," George told her of the strolling, chattering group. "Your swells." At that moment the silver-haired man turned, their glances met, and George gave a slight bow, as when Mr. Carewe approached him at the bank. George bowed at the silver-haired man and cursed himself for it; he yanked Virginia away, only to stumble upon an even more incredible sight.

As they left the group of passengers and advanced along

the platform, George pulled back, jabbed wordlessly at his daughter. Recovering his speech, he urged, "Next Pullman, look who's comin' down the steps. Look who it is, by God."

Images, impressions, swirled dizzily in Janya's mind. She saw where her father pointed, but she did not in the least recognize the lady whom the porter was assisting down the steps. Despite her father's prodding, she made no connection whatever.

"Goddammit," George snapped, "you were gawkin' at her picture not ten minutes ago. Use your eyes, dummy. Can't you recognize a movie star when you see one?"

Virginia's mouth fell open. The lady, having descended from the train, was pacing up and down the platform. A mink coat was draped over her shoulders, a bracelet glittered at her wrist, and in her arms was a tiny fluffy dog. She stroked its ears as she paced back and forth. She herself was not tall, but her high-heeled shoes, together with some quality in her manner, made her appear very tall indeed. Her reddish hair was swept back, the large expressive eyes in the boldly drawn face seemed to give off sparks. Where a moment ago she had been a solitary figure, a small crowd had quickly formed around her. The lady held the fluffy dog and smiled graciously as slips of paper were offered for her signature. It dawned on Virginia who she was. Unmistakably, she was the poster lady from the Alhambra.

"Take a good look," George advised. "Only movie star you'll ever see. Goddamn, she was something in that *Grand Hotel* picture. Had on this blouse, y' could almost . . . Look at Clyde Filmore push right up to her. Me, I value my dignity more."

Virginia was close to tears. She jammed the knitted cap back on and shook her head. First these other dream people, and now . . . She stared at the lady from the poster and said, "It can't be."

"What can't? What're you talkin' about?"

She nodded tearfully at the beautiful lady, who was smiling and signing the slips of paper. "They're only pictures," she said, fighting the tears. "After the movie is over, the lights go on, and . . ."

"An' what?"

"The screen is blank," she insisted. "None of it is real—it's only pictures that move."

George digested this unlikely information in stupefied amazement. He had never, with the exception of the eyes, which were his, credited his daughter with looks—how to give credit where none was due?—but apparently she was also deficient in the brain department. "A course, pictures," he said. "*Movie* pictures, and where you think they make 'em?"

"It's just pictures that . . ."

"Where do you think the Chief's headed?" George demanded. "How come Miss Joan Crawford's on it—to get to Peoria?"

"I don't know." The tears sprang afresh. She wished she'd worn her yellow dress, summer or not. From now on, she'd wear it every day. "I don't understand about it," she acknowledged. "Not any of it."

"Well, permit me to inform you, Miss Mouse—"

From down the platform, the conductor's whistle sounded a series of piercing beeps, and as quickly as the scene had materialized, it proceeded to dissolve. The news was circulated by the buffs—air leak in the engine was fixed, the flagman had scurried back from his post on the tracks. "Allboooarrd," the cry rang out. "Allboooard," and in an instant, it seemed, the passengers had dissolved from the platform. They were absorbed, laughing and chatting, into the Pullmans. Porters whisked away the footstools, steel doors were clanged shut. Whistles blew, the conductor waved a lantern, and was answered by another lantern far down the tracks.

Except for the handful of spectators, the wooden platform was deserted. The last of the afternoon light drained from the sky, turning the Pullman windows into bright yellow squares. The passengers could be seen reassembled on sofas and lounge chairs, as if they had never left them.

In the dining car, the lady and gentleman sat at the snowy table, occupied with their dinner, which they had not interrupted.

"Look at that pair." George Belton thrust his jaw at the dining car. A tremor ran through him that had nothing to do with the raw wind or his lack of an overcoat. "Can you beat it? Never stopped eating once."

Janya stared at the pink-shaded lamps, the silver vases of roses, one for each table. Mama would be happy with the roses, the way she favored flowers and all. She tried to imagine what it would be like, Papa and Mama and herself, dining amid such grandeur. A wild and reckless notion seized hold of her; she gripped her father's hand. The Chief hadn't departed yet, it was still in the depot . . . why not get on? They'd simply get on, Papa and her . . . and ride wherever the train was going. Afterwards Mama would join them and in this other place Papa would find a job he liked. They'd buy a nice house, with maybe roses growing in the back, Mama would buy a silver vase and every night at dinner . . .

"Alllboooard," rang a final cry; a final beep of whistle. Up the tracks, the engine whistle blew, there was a lurch, and the train wheels began to revolve. Janya nestled close against her father. Not this time, they wouldn't ride off, but maybe . . . She hung on to her Papa and wished . . . *wished* . . .

George Belton had not lifted his gaze from the couple in the now-moving dining car. "Never looked up once," he said, and the tremor swept through him, colder than any wind. It swept away the golden visions of the Champs Élysée, the days when he'd been young and free, before he'd returned to Clarion and set his foot in the bear-trap of responsibility. Miserable bank, miserable sawed-off house, kid he never wanted, Ida fat as a sow, while he, George Belton . . . "Who'd bother to look out the window at Clarion?" he said aloud to the dining car as it trundled away.

"Papa, listen—" Janya wanted to tell him of her notion, but he was staring at the train.

The Pullmans rolled past in lordly procession, one after another, gathering momentum. The yellow windows threw slats of light across father and daughter, and glancing down at his hands, George saw that the train soot had blackened his French cuffs. "You know why nobody'd look at Clarion?" he asked, clenching his fists. "You know why?"

A shiver went through her. Papa was starting again. She must tell him of her notion, explain to him that—

"Because it's nowhere," George angrily answered his own query. The bars of light hit his face, the rear observation car shuttled past, with its open platform and tailgate sign, *The Chief*. The train was gone, unraveling a spool of track in its wake. "Who'd be crazy fool enough to come back to nowhere?" George asked as the other men shuffled from the platform.

"Papa?" Virginia tugged at her father's sleeve. "It really happened, didn't it?" she said. "The Chief didn't go past, it really stopped . . ." She was doing a poor job of explaining what she meant, which was that the Chief might stop there again someday, and . . . "Oh, Papa, it was the best Sunday," she said, and turned, gestured at the spools of track beyond the platform. "Look, you can still see it," she urged. "It's not gone yet."

She ran to the wood rail at the far end, clamped hold of the mushroom hat, fighting the wind. She peered into the dark and followed the span of the rails to where, across the plain, the Chief's windows strung tiny yellow lanterns in the night. At which window, she speculated, was the poster lady seated with her fluffy dog? She couldn't figure it out, how you could be a lady on a poster, pictures moving on a screen, and at the same time be real?

"There it is, Papa, wave." She climbed onto the rail, leaned out, and waved at the string of yellow lanterns in the far distance. "Papa, see?"

There was no reply, and when she could no longer glimpse the lanterns and had climbed down from the rail, she saw that the platform was empty. She backed against the rail and searched the deserted length of the platform.

Her voice echoed queerly over the wood planks, *"Papa?"*

She ran into the depot waiting room, thinking that perhaps she would find him there. Fear nudged at her; she scanned the empty benches, the shuttered ticket window, the black potbellied stove. She listened to the clock ticking on the wall, and the same panic seized her as when . . . when Mama sent her in to announce Sunday dinner and she would stand at the sliding doors that closed off the parlor, afraid to open them, because often Papa would glance up from his newspaper and look at her as if . . . not just as if she was Miss Mouse, but worse than that. It was what frightened her now in the empty waiting room, while the clock ticked loud as cannon shots.

He had walked off, left her behind, in the same way that he'd glanced at her through the sliding doors . . . The word was a stone falling, falling into a well. *Nooothhiiing,* he looked at her as if she was nothing, and coupled with this image she heard again the other scary word he'd spoken on the platform, *noooowhere . . .*

"Papa," she called. "Papa."

She fled from the ticking clock, out of the depot. *Nooothhiiing, noooowhere . . .* she stood at the foot of Main Street and looked at the low, converging line of stores that was silhouetted against the crimson-streaked sky. The street lamps made sickly daubs on the stretch of dark, deserted sidewalk. Only the twinkling orange-and-blue glow of the Alhambra's marquee fought against the night on Main Street. In the light that it shed, she glimpsed, at the corner of Second, a man's figure.

"Papa, wait." She ran through the darkness, swallowed the fear inside her, of what she was. She ran as if her life depended on it, but when she caught up with her father she gaily took his hand, as though this were one more extension of their Sunday game.

"Magic disappearing act, you had me fooled," she laughed, gasping for breath on this November Sunday that was to affect the course of her life. "Honest, you had me fooled," she said, clasping his hand.

"Awful damn cold. C'mon, we'll head down Second."

She swallowed the lump of fear . . . *nooothiing, nooo-where* . . . and they started down Second Street. She looked through the dark toward Montana Street, the lighted windows of the Cogswell's house, and told herself it was all right, she needn't be afraid.

She was Virginia Ruth Belton, age eight and a—no, she was Virginia Starr, walking home safe in the night with her father, who loved her.

PART ONE

Christopher
1948

CHAPTER **1**

We cannot know, ever, what the course of our lives is to be, nor even with certainty where the next moment from now will take us.

It is subject to change.

In October of 1948, six months before I met Maggie Jones—the name she was called by then—I climbed on a bus in Glens Falls, New York, the second time in that number of years that I was bound again for home.

The sun was mounting the hills, suffusing the sky with a pale opalescence, when the bus chugged out of Glens Falls. I sat by myself in the rear, in the clothes that had been given me; the undersized jacket, denim shirt and baggy pants might have been the garb of an itinerant farm worker, or of a refugee of indeterminate origin. Slung on the baggage rack overhead, the cardboard suitcase, also donated, jiggled with the motions of the bus. We made detours into tidy industrious Hudson towns to discharge and pick up passengers, but mainly we kept to the highway that stitched and wound through the hills—and mainly I stared out at the green-gold, russet- and scarlet-tipped trees that went by in a blur of autumnal colors.

Homecomings are alike in that they are either joyous or sad or a mixture of both, in varying degrees; in this instance the contrast with my last such journey was notable. From the bus window I saw, not the blur of trees, but the train that, after maddening delays, had carried me and several hundred other ex-servicemen into Grand Central

Station in New York. There wasn't a brass band on the platform, but the air had seemed to split with the blare of coronets, the swirl of drums, as the swarm of whooping, hollering men had surged up to the gates and the shouts of "Look, there's Billy!" "Ralph, here we are!" "It's Tom, yes, it *is!*" The war was over, a new life waited beyond the gates. Screams, sobs, embraces, as wives, sweethearts, parents, were reunited with Billy, Ralph, Tom, Eddie, Joe. A new life, a new start, and for me, caught up in the swarm, there was a glimpse, a half-formed, just-out-of-reach glimpse of . . .

I turned from the bus window and the blur of trees. My stomach gave a rude growl, diverting me to thoughts of food. Maybe at the next stop they'd have a candy machine. Boy, could you tie that? Twenty-two years old, come December tack on another, and not yet graduated out of candy bars. Terrific, if someone asked what the hardest deprivation of the past months had been, and I'd said candy bars.

The bus rolled into the Trailways terminal in Manhattan at two-thirty, fifteen minutes behind schedule. I waited for the other passengers to file out, then hoisted down the cardboard suitcase and pushed up the aisle, the last to leave.

But I wasn't the last.

The old man in the plaid mackinaw and earmuffs was still marooned in the seat behind the driver's. He'd gotten on south of Albany, hauled on bodily by a stout, fiery woman in a babushka, who'd scampered off to a car waiting at the roadside. He sat now, clutching a thorn cane and a mesh bag of apples, muttering to himself.

"Hey, Gramps." The driver poked his head in the door. "End of the run, everybody out. You, too, pal."

"That so?" The old man brandished the cane at him. "S'pose you tell that to my arthritis. Durn leg twisted up, might as well chop it off."

The driver loped off; I went up the aisle to where the muttering had resumed. "Excuse me, but I'll be glad to give you a hand," I said.

The grudging inspection he treated me to didn't bring him much reassurance. "No, thanks, sonny. Edna June, my daughter-in-law, where the hell is she?" He mulled it over, reconsidered. "Well, if it ain't burdenin' you none . . ."

I collected his suitcase, which was as dog-eared as mine, and gave him my arm. Even with that and the cane for support, it took several minutes to negotiate the ramp to the waiting room. He clung to my arm, though, and stumped along with a tenacity that made me appreciate his doughty presence.

"What's yer name?" He stabbed the cane on the cement.

"Casey. Christopher Casey."

"Amos Feather here. Soon to be eighty-seven and don't recommend it a whit. Where yuh comin' from?" Jaws working, he steered across the waiting room and, by cautious degrees, lowered himself onto a bench in the corner.

"Thanks, young feller. Go along."

I set the suitcases down. "Hadn't you ought to look for your daughter-in-law?"

"Let Edna June find me, her eyesight's a dang sight better. Run along now."

I sat down next to him. "I could wait with you. I mean, if you want me to."

"Suit yourself." He edged away, appeared to think better of it. "Here, have a McIntosh." He proffered the mesh bag. "Go ahead, help y'self."

"Thanks." I took an apple, I polished the firm, round redness on my sleeve. "I'm not just out of prison, if that's what's worrying you."

The statement failed to disconcert him. "I admit it crossed my mind—awful scrawny, you look, and them hands—" he nodded, "been doin' heavy labor, but I shoulda seen . . ."

The din from the street sounded strange and alien. "Seen what?"

"Go on, bite in, apples is sustainin'." He watched me bite into the tart, juicy flesh. "I shoulda seen right off you don't have prison eyes." He shook his head in self-reproach. "Ain't like me to be suspicion-minded. Once, I'd a' gived you a hand same as you done me, and not a question asked."

"A total stranger—you couldn't be sure."

"Take it from me, age don't improve a person." The watery but lively, inquisitive eyes appraised me. "Say, I don't know beans about you, but it'd sure be funny if we was both up to the same trick of hidin' out."

"Hiding out?"

He grinned, the seamed face alight with mischief. "Last person off a bus . . . gen'rally don't want to leave that bus. Me, I'm on the hideout from Edna June."

I grinned back at him. "Your daughter-in-law?"

"Yup, the very same." He gripped the cane and ruminated in silence. "They pass me around, y'see. Wilma gets fed up with me up home and ships me down here to Lucas in Mineola." The gaze dimmed; the gullet bobbed in the turkey neck. "Home, where's that?" he asked quietly, then straightened up. "So what I do to keep myself goin' is stir things up. Ought to try more of it y'self, sonny."

He swiveled around, fastened the watery gaze on me. "Not to pry, but are you headed for home, and not aching to get there?"

"I—I suppose not." I hesitated a moment. "I've been away a year, largely a wasted year—"

"Don't talk of wasted." He stamped the cane for emphasis. "Good and bad is all mixed together in life. You won't learn to sort which from which till you're old as I am. Meanwhile, take my advice and stir things up. Yessir, pitch right in and—"

"Why, Grandpa, you sly devil," reproved a large female in slacks and hair curlers, swooping down upon the bench. "Waitin' forever by Information, like I specified, and here you sit the whole blessed while, parkin' lot eating up my last dollar."

Amos Feather squinted up at her; he cupped a hand to his ear. "What's 'at? Speak up, I'm deaf as a post."

"When you choose to be, y' mean. Wearing them earmuffs for spite." Hair curlers trembling in indignation,

Edna June took hold of the suitcase and derricked its owner up from the bench. "Not another peep out of you," she scolded, propelling him across to the street doors. "Had enough of your antics, I warn you fair."

"What's 'at?" shouted Amos, stirring things up. "Speak up, Edna June. Put on some poundage, have yer?" At the doors he yanked free of her and turned back. "Take my advice—and good luck, young feller," he called across the room.

"You, too," I called back, before he was herded out by Edna. "And thanks . . . for the apple."

I watched until he was swallowed up in the sidewalk crush. I picked up my suitcase, bought a copy of *The Times* at the newsstand, by way of a reintroduction to the world I'd been away from. I invested as well in some Baby Ruths, then, readier than I had been, I walked out into the alien and strange-sounding noise of the city.

An hour later, when I got off the El at the Richmond Hill stop in Queens, it was with a picture of Amos Feather fixed in my mind. Deciding to do him proud, I went down the El stairs actually swinging my suitcase. Swagger was out, not to mention inappropriate, so I settled for a jaunty informality as I turned off Jamaica Avenue and onto the street of my birth.

It was a classic Queens street composed of rows of brick, stucco and frame houses, detached and semidetached, with Band-Aid driveways and postage-stamp lawns adorned with cement birdbaths. School was out, squads of Queens kids whizzed past me on roller skates and bicycles. They paid me a glance or two, but it was the windows I was aware of, the lack of activity at the windows. No speculating eyes peered out to witness my return. Midway up the block I paused and shifted the suitcase, to get a grip on my jauntiness. I stood in front of the house, the cream-painted two-family house where I was born. Originally we'd occupied the ground floor, but when I was seven my father had . . . he'd died, and since the lower floor fetched more rent and the top floor was vacant, we'd moved upstairs, Mama and I . . .

I gripped the suitcase, turned in at the walk, and "*Psst,*" I heard from an upstairs window. Glancing up, I saw my mother's head poke out. She was making frantic signals, in an apparent effort to elude public notice.

"Hi," I called up to her loudly, in a tribute to Amos Feather. "Why all the sign language? Can't be the neighbors, can it?"

Instantly, her head shot in, as if every curtain on the block had parted, and she pantomimed that she'd be down to let me in. Keys were among the earthly possessions I'd left behind a year ago . . .

I went up the steps onto the porch and into the small vestibule with the umbrella stand, which gave access to the upper and lower apartments. I prodded at the door to the upstairs flat, which swung open . . . and at the foot of the hall stairs, a distance between us as always, was my mother.

"Mama."

"Christy . . ."

She kept to the bottom step, held back by the implacable reserve that was her trap for as long as I could remember. She twisted at a dust cloth, Agnes Theresa Casey, née Lenihan. A young girl's prettiness clung to her still, despite the haggard lines, the whitening hair; the summer-blue eyes had long given up trying to comprehend the blows that life dealt out, the turns it took, such as this now.

I set down the suitcase. "Wow, the commotion when I came up the street. I take it you didn't broadcast the news."

"Why go doing that when they'll find out on their own— and not understand?" The hands plucked at the dust cloth.

I pulled at my jacket sleeves. "Well, say something," I joked. "It's not every mother whose son goes off to the monastery—and surely not every day that he comes home. A one-time event, after all."

She spanned the carpet to me. "Christy. Christy." Her hands smoothed the black, tangled hair and felt of me. "So thin—and that poor jacket with the wrists stickin' out."

"Best available." I pulled her to me. "No well-dressed novices lately. Slim pickings."

"Did you think to pick up a meal at one of the stops? No, I bet. Never a practical thought in your head."

"Baby Ruth bars—and an old man on the bus gave me an apple."

"Apples! Candy bars! Typical!" She laughed and, on the pretext of inspecting me in closer detail, extricated herself from the embrace. Physical intimacy was not Agnes Theresa's forte. "Well," she said, and made a dive for the suitcase. "Well, let's get you upstairs."

My voice had an edge to it as she started up the stairs. "No questions?"

She tested me with a playful smile. "Scarcely in the door, I'd think you'd want to—"

"Mama, you could've told the neighbors," I cut in. "You see, there's hardly anything to tell. No scandal or disgrace, no sneak visits to town or flouting of the rule."

"Why, Christy, as if for one second—"

"Hardly anything to relate." I spoke partly to dismantle the silence that walled between us, partly out of another motive. "The Abbot called me in last week. Nice having me there, nice kid, but no vocation for the religious life."

My mother's eyes lifted reluctantly from the suitcase. "Seems to me . . . he might've broke it to you gentler."

"No, he was being truthful—all summer I'd been thinking it myself. That I didn't belong there, that it was a mistake. Home from the war and settled down to college—then off to Mede's to turn into St. Francis chatting with the birds. A mistake."

The hand twisted at the suitcase. "Well, it's behind you now. You're home to start anew." She looked at me and in her glance for a moment was a recognition of what we had passed through together, mother and child; what we'd come through . . . or had we? She fetched a perky smile to ward off further discussion, and turned to go up the stairs. "Come, dear. Your old room's waiting to greet you like an old friend."

"How's Cash?" I remained below on the carpet; delay

being my other motive for the rush of talk. "How's the queen of Macy's switchboard?" Cash was my mother's sister, the third member of the household.

"Same old Cash, buzzing me every ten minutes from the board to learn if you got here." Pause. "Shall we go up?"

I made no move to do so. "I—I was thinking I'd take you and Cash out to dinner tonight. It's not exactly an occasion to celebrate, but—"

"Go out, when there's lovely veal cutlets for supper?" She started up the narrow, dim stairs. "Come, dear."

"Right behind you." I glanced up at the landing, envisioning the rooms that admitted no passage of time. Agnes Theresa's museum, dusted and waxed and polished.

"Christopher?"

"Coming." I followed her up the stairs.

I fared better than I'd anticipated.

There was the obligatory tour of the museum—"I hear these women at Bohack's go on about new this and new that," said Agnes Theresa, resting the suitcase on the landing. "Don't they know the comfort of old things?" she demanded, with a gesture at the mottled brown-plush sofa, the fringed lamps, doilies, cut-glass bonbon dishes, the lurid sunset oil framed in gold over the imitation fireplace, and the big sausage-armed chair that comprised the living room decor. Her sister had once remarked that it had the cozy warmth and charm of Lawlor's Funeral Parlor. We'd had occasion for comparison.

"What's important," I said to the museum's curator, "is that it's a comfort to you."

"Ah," she beamed, as though it were the setting of joyous happenings only. "Not such a bad prospect, coming home," and she led the way through the arch into the dining room.

I carried the suitcase after her, past the fumed-oak table and the cone-shaded light above it, which for weeks one winter had been the only light kept on at night after supper.

"Cold lamb waiting in the fridge." Agnes gave a wave at the black-and-white-tiled kitchen as we went by. "Your favorite sandwich, I seem to recall." Then we were in the hall, the back hall that sliced the rear of the flat in half. The faucets of the tub in the bathroom still leaked; you could hear the steady drip of water. *For weeks that same winter I'd fought against the nightly bath, declining to state why, which was that the shape of the tub had reminded me of . . .*

"Here we are," trilled the curator, turning in at a doorway. "Spent the whole of yesterday airing and cleaning, everything in order."

Really, better than anticipated. Barely a moment's reluctance, and I marched into the room of my childhood. At the time of the move upstairs, the furnishings had been transplanted intact from an identical room below.

With admirable equanimity, I surveyed my meticulously preserved child's belongings, the Yankees pennant on the wall over the maple desk, the maple bookshelf with its trove of juvenile titles, the maple chest of drawers with the faded brown photograph reposing on it. There was still a crack in the glass.

"Well, say hello back." My mother smoothed her apron, the only betrayal of anxiety.

I swung the suitcase onto the bed that had replaced the youth bed of earlier days, the one acknowledgment of my growing up. "Hello to who? What?"

"Why, to your old friend, the room."

"Mama, you don't really think I'm going to stand here and . . ." I untied the twine on the suitcase, took out the few books and articles of clothing I'd brought back. I added the books to the shelves. On the wall above was my aunt's contribution to the decor. It was a theater poster, circa 1939. *Max Jacobs presents THE PUMPKINS*, it read. My name was featured on it, the stage name I'd used during my days as a child actor.

My mother was occupied with the chest of drawers. One by one as she opened them the drawers gave off the sharp odor of camphor. Proudly she displayed the stacks of freshly ironed shirts, pajamas, underclothes, rolled balls of socks. "You see how everything's ready for you? Other than some new suits—it shows your sincerity, giving away the old ones . . ."

I was not doing so well at the moment. She closed the bottom drawer, got up, and in reaching for the dust cloth on the chest, knocked over the framed photograph. With a little cry, she righted it. "He had gentle eyes, didn't he?" she said. "As gentle as yours, till the hard times came." Then, "To stay on in this house . . . the only way, y' see, was to make a friend of it. Shall I fix you a sandwich?"

"Mama, listen." I intercepted her as she started for the door. "You mustn't mind if I'm tense or edgy. Mede's was about the only plan I ever came up with for the future . . . and now I'm back at the starting line, sort of like Parcheesi. . . ."

"Why, you'll go back to college, of course."

"Yes, probably, but—"

The phone rang at the front of the flat. I went back along the hall, knowing who it was likely to be. I picked up the phone on the table at the landing and said, "William Morris office. Sorry, we're not booking tap and toe."

"Lover?" My aunt hollered in delight from her Macy's switchboard at the other end. "Is this my lover boy I'm talkin' to?"

"Depends," I growled from the side of my mouth. "This the former Kitty Lorraine I'm addressing? See, I just blew into town, and this drummer I happened to run into in Toledo—"

"Sells girdles, snappy dresser?" Cash joyously took up the routine. In her salad says she had been a dancer in vaudeville, billed as Kitty Lorraine. "So Fred told ya to look me up?"

"You bet, sweetheart." I gripped the phone, taking refuge as I had so often in my aunt's rowdy, freewheeling warmth. "What I was wondering is if you're footloose and fancy-free tonight—"

54

"Jeez, baby. Jeez, how I've missed you."

I pushed away the vision of the child's room waiting, waiting. "It's the start of a whole new ball game, right?" I said into the phone. "That calls for dinner out, doesn't it?"

"Damn tootin', baby. Name the spot."

"The Triangle at six?"

"I'll be there. With bells on."

I hung up the phone. The museum living room languished before me in the fading afternoon light. It held no claim on me any more. "Christy," sang Agnes Theresa from the kitchen. "Mr. Sandwich and Mrs. Milk are waiting for you."

"Coming," I chorused back, challenging ghosts, refuting them, and strode past the dining table and its cone of light, into the kitchen.

I wasn't doing badly, not badly at all.

Not badly if I could locate the light switch, that is.

To the right. Unsteadily, I groped over the wall to the right of the door. Oughta know where the damn switch was.

"Watch it, baby," Cash laughed from the hall. "One too many, I think. Smashed."

Located the switch, *flick*, and the room leaped out of the shadows. "Def'nitely not smashed." I turned to my aunt, who was none too steady herself. The ostrich-plumed hat was squashed down tipsily on the Kewpie-doll face. Agnes Theresa, I noted, had fled to her chamber. Home from the monastery, was her son, and staggering up the street bawling out show tunes the very same night.

"Am merely in a state of euphoria, reached with the slight assiss'ance of Bushmill's," I said, enfolding the generous proportions of Cash, née Kathleen, Lenihan in my arms. "Hey, where *is* the state of euphoria?"

"Search me, baby. South of Georgia, maybe?" She hugged me to her bosomy girth. "Sure you don't want company a bit more?"

"Perf'lcly able to cope." I steered her in the direction of her bedroom. "See you tomorrow."

"Whole new ball game, kiddo." She turned in her doorway, swatted at the droopy ostrich plume. "If I was you I'd take a few days to get in step."

"Tomorrow. Bright and early tomorrow."

She swiped at the ostrich plume. "A' course, skipping the monk stuff, the puzzle to me is why you ever quit . . ." She put off for the moment the often-asked question. "Great havin' you home, baby."

"Great being home."

She went into her room. I closed the door and switched off the light. In the dark I shucked off the old gabardine that had been discovered in the attic. There was something I had to do before I could get tomorrow in shape, and the dark would help me accomplish it.

Naked, I pulled on the bottoms of the camphor-scented pajamas that were laid out at the foot of the bed. I tied the drawstring, then crossed in the darkness to the chest of drawers. A chink of street light, slanting in the window, fell on the photograph and glinted on the crack in the glass.

There was no use staving it off. I would have no peace until I faced it once again. Before the photograph, however, another museum piece required attention if the ritual was to be carried out.

I reached for the copperplate that was propped against the mirror of the chest. I held the blackened plate to the mirror and it reflected in reverse the flawless Roman script of a birth announcement, engraved by my father to herald my advent. *Mr. and Mrs. John F. X. Casey . . . announce with joy . . . the birth of . . . Christopher Kerry.*

I deciphered the thin, fine tracings in the mirror, then rested the plate against it. Then, groggy from the whiskey and the long day's exhaustion, I lifted the photograph from the dresser scarf.

The faded brown image was that of a young man, darkly handsome and serious of mien. He was stiffly posed, and

the smile that the photographer had coaxed from him con-
spired instead to heighten the gravity of his face. A printer
by trade, he was to sail from Queenstown in a month's
time, which perhaps accounted for his seriousness, the look
in the gentle eyes that questioned what his fortune would
be in the new land.

I heard loud in my memory the sound of rain. I held the
photograph to the chink of light and traced a finger over
the crack in the glass, remembering the day we'd moved
upstairs, when it had got broken . . .

CHAPTER **2**

"Where'd I put 'em?" I heard my mother query herself. "Where'd I put the carton with your books?"

I stood, seven years old, at the bedroom window, looking down at the alley that ran between the houses to the street; I stood listening to the rain while my mother rummaged among the cartons that were stacked like alphabet blocks on the floor.

"Where'd I . . . ? It's the same room, Christy, the very same, d' y' see? Only it's up a floor."

A floor up, you had more of a view of the street, but the slope of the roof cut off the front porch, where I'd run after my father that last morning. Which morning? I listened to the rain that had been falling all week, since the day of the funeral, which meant that today was . . . I didn't know. I didn't know one day from another any more.

"Here the rascals are," exclaimed my mother. "Look, Christy darlin'. The lovely books he gave you, waitin' to be put in the very same bookcase as before."

I bit down hard, unable to distinguish between the blur of tears and the rain on the window. I turned to my mother, who was smiling and holding out the books. Dirt smudged her chin, her soft chestnut hair was slipping untidily from the bun at the back, giving an eeriness to her smile. I took the books from her and went to the bookcase that Uncle Ed had placed catercorner to the desk, same as downstairs. I knelt down to put the books on the shelves:

Jungle Tales, Oliver Twist, Hans Brinker, or *The Silver Skates* . . . every birthday and Christmas he'd add a new book to the shelves, so that when I'd learned to read good at St. Rose of Lima's I'd have a whole library to choose from.

"But I don't have to wait, Papa. Not with you to read to me."

"Me? Ahhh, my lack of schooling sticks out like a sore thumb, when it comes to books."

"No, it don't. You read terrific, I sure can tell you. Just a chapter before bed? Please?" And I would race into the bedroom, race back with the current selection from the shelves. Climb onto his lap in the big sausage-armed chair by the fireplace in the living room. Always he made a ceremony of it. He sat back while I opened the book to the title page, at which point we both examined the bright-colored frontispiece and discussed its place in the story.

He then, in a measured voice, read aloud the title and author of the book—"*Oliver Twist,* by Charles Dickens"—then turned to where he'd inserted the bookmark from the previous session.

Slowly at first, taking care with each word, he began to read, and as he did the caution would vanish, his voice change, caught up in the excitement of the story, till he *became* Oliver Twist and Mr. Bumble, the Artful Dodger, Fagin and Bill Sikes. Turned *into* the characters, right as I sat on his lap.

"Take my word for it, Papa. Nobody reads as good as you. You're twice as good as Sister Marietta at school."

"Why, thanks, son." He reached to turn a page, and as I listened to him read, my head nodding back, I puzzled over the person who was my father. He was two different persons, but on account of his quietness, his shyness, not many people, including my mother, saw this other side of him. According to Aunt Cash, the occasion was rare that my father revealed his true self. Once at the Kerrymen's St. Patrick's Day Ball I'd watched him take part in the men's reel. Cash had to push him onto the floor, but as the pipes skirled and the fiddler sawed, his feet had tatooed the floor faster than any man's and his eyes had shone dark in his face, with a flame leaping from them. "Look at him," said Aunt Cash. "It's the shyness holds F. X. back. He just needs someone to start the music, is all."

What other printer, the night his child was born, had raced straightaway to his shop, got out the copperplate he'd held in reserve, and not left till the engraving was done and the birth announcements run off? What other man thought to say of the event, "That was the year Christmas came early for Ag and me."

He took me for Sunday walks in Forest Park, the two of us strolling the leafy paths or sitting on a hillock—and there I'd learned how to get past his shyness. Start the music going, as Cash put it. The grassy green hill, the green slopes spread below . . . "Does it remind you of Ireland, Papa, up here in the park?"

"Well, the greenness a bit . . ." He'd talk, gropingly at first, of County Kerry, where he was born. He'd bring alive the green-bursting hills, the craggy rocks, the emerald-blue sea crashing against the cliffs. "It's the rain makes it so green. A land of contradictions if ever there was one."

"Contradictions, Papa?"

"The endless rain, yet from it springs the greenness. The dreary poverty, yet from it the Irish spin dreams." He shook his head. "Dreams, not potatoes, are the leading produce. It's almost a curse. The good fortune I've had in America—my own shop, my own house with a tenant upstairs, yet I can't shake the fear . . ."

"Yes, Papa? What?"

"The curse of dreams is that they get broken." He'd turned to me, a smile banishing the dark, helpless frown. "Cheer up, is what I should do. The Depression can't last forever. Year or two, we'll be on top of it. House free and clear, the shop thriving, then one summer I'll close up and—"

"I know," I chimed, for he'd spoken of it often. "We'll sail to Ireland, you, Mama and me. You'll take us to the county I was named after."

60

"I'll take you to Kerry and what a time we'll have, visiting old friends and old places. It'll work out, Christy, never you fear."

Never you fear . . .

I slid the last book onto the shelf and went for another armful. My mother was shuffling through the cartons; her hand kept darting to fasten the bun of hair. "The linen," she said. "Wherever did I put the linen to make up your bed? It's in the very same corner as downstairs, you'll notice."

The tattoo of rain beat louder at the window. I lifted the remaining books from the carton. The funeral was Thursday, today was Saturday . . . which made it Monday that he'd left the house, forgetting his coat in his zeal to get to the printing plant for a place at the front of the line.

The rain drummed louder, the rain that had splattered the coffin as it was lowered into the ground. I knelt at the bookcase, fumbling with the volumes that skidded from my hands. *Papa, papa, where are you, where did you go?*

It hadn't worked out as he'd hoped that Sunday in the park. Nor was he, as I'd thought, only two different persons. There was a third person in my father, whom I'd never seen until last summer. The shop on Jamaica Avenue was closed by then, the presses carted away by some men named Creditors. Slowly in the months that followed, when he could find no more than a few days' work, often none for weeks at a stretch . . . slowly he had changed into this third person, who sat at night in the sausage-armed chair, with staring eyes that looked through me.

"Papa? *Papa?*"

He'd blink, jerk up. "Yes? Yes?"

"Nothing, Papa." And, hiding the book I'd brought to be read, I ran back down the hall to my room.

In November, in the middle of the night, the upstairs tenants had made off, leaving behind a few sticks of furniture in lieu of the rent they owed. My father had paced back and forth through the empty flat. "Ah, well, Charley Fox was up against it as bad as me." I followed at his feet, stopped when his pacing halted. "The downstairs flat

61

fetches ten dollars more. We could rent it out instead. Agnes?" He strode to the stairs. "Agnes?"

"Papa, wait," I called, running after him. "Wait, you forgot me."

It was December then, my birthday and Christmas were approaching, and Mama had a talk with me. She said it wouldn't be the same as other years, and I mustn't be disappointed. All the worries on his mind, Papa might even forget my birthday, so I wasn't to mention it, no hints or anything of the kind, was it understood? Yes, I said. I understood.

When I woke up the morning of my birthday, he'd already left to look for work. He'd already left, but on the chest of drawers was his gift, wrapped in tissue. It was the copperplate he'd engraved the night of my birth. I held the reversed script to the mirror. *Mr. and Mrs. John F. X. Casey announce with joy . . .*

"Papa? Papa?" I ran down the hall after him, but he'd left. He'd already left.

Vanished, like the upstairs tenants . . . and in January the father I scarcely recognized grew even stranger.

One night in January he'd rushed in from the porch, wild and elated, shouting to my mother in the kitchen. "You won't believe it, Ag. The bargain of a lifetime! I was passing a travel agency today, and for the mere sum of one hundred and ninety dollars—"

"Travel agency, John?"

"Three fares tourist class on the . . ." He dug a steamship folder from his pocket. "The S.S. *Franconia*, sailing twice monthly for Queenstown. Think of it, Agnes. A mere hundred and ninety dollars."

"John . . . supper's on the stove. Supper's ready. Why don't you hang up your coat and—"

"That's your response?" He stared wildly at her, anger and rage sending the blood to his face. "God help me, but I could never talk to you. A stone is what you are, behind that prettiness. The things inside a man . . . it's like ramming against rock, like . . ."

He'd stood in the kitchen doorway, the anger draining as suddenly as it had erupted. Mumbling, a blankness stealing over his face, he'd gone to the closet to hang up his coat.

Then it was February, and some printer friend had alerted him to a plant in Bensonhurst that was hiring jobbers, provided you got there early. At breakfast he was his old self, the person I knew best, the flame kindling behind the shyness, the dreams stirring in him: schemes for starting afresh, a new shop, a new business, new tenants, a loan at the bank to pay his debts and tide us over.

"Matt says it's a cinch today, so long as I get a place at the front of the line. Well, if I can find enough piece work to show them at the bank that—"

"John, you haven't touched your oatmeal. It's warm and filling on a cold morning like this."

"What the hell substitute is oatmeal? It's hope I need from you, a miserable grain of hope."

"It's . . . past seven, John. If you want to make the front of the line."

"Yes, Agnes. Yes, you're quite right." He held a spoon to the steaming bowl. The blankness in his eyes, he spooned down the oatmeal until the bowl was empty. He shot up from the table. "Must hurry if I'm to be first," and he shouldered through the arch to the living room. "Must be off, not a minute to waste."

"John?" My mother hurried to the arch as the front door thudded shut. She clawed at the closet. "Love a'mighty, freezing out and the man forgot his coat."

"I'll take it to him."

"Quick then, Christy. Hurry, run after him."

I took the coat from her, ran out the vestibule onto the porch. He was halfway down the front walk. The icy wind swooped up my voice as I called to him.

"Papa, wait! Wait, you forgot your coat."

He turned on the walk. The ragged black hair curled thick around the haunted face. "Well, no wonder I felt the cold nippin' extra sharp," he said. "Well, fancy that."

I ran down the walk to him and stood while he pulled on the frayed coat.

"Papa?" I wanted to tell him . . . I wasn't sure how you gave someone a grain of hope. "What's that?" I nodded at the paper he'd taken from his pocket.

The wind whipped at the steamship folder gripped in his hands. "Sailing schedule . . . for Queenstown," he said, and the expression on his face sent an icy wind blowing inside me.

"We'll get there, Papa," I said. "Next summer for sure, I'll bet the world on it."

He pulled at the coat collar. "Run inside, you'll catch your death of pneumonia."

"Papa, are you all right?"

"Run. Get a move on." He pulled at the collar, then as I turned to go up the walk: "Thank you, Christy."

"For what?" I turned back to him. "For bringing the coat out?"

"No." He reached out, touched his cold hand to my face. "No, for being my son," he said, then yanked up his collar. "Run, now. Back in the house with you."

"Papa, I—"

"Run, I said. *Run.*"

I ran up the porch steps and watched from the rail as he went down the street. The coat collar was pulled over his chin, the wind hit at him, but his stride made me think of the Kerrymen's Ball and the proud rise of his head when he'd danced the reel. I ran down the steps to call to him, *call what, to bring him back?* It was too late, he'd turned the corner at Jamaica Avenue, was gone under the pillars of the El that shunted overhead.

It was the last that I ever saw of my father.

"Have you the books put away, Christy darlin'?" my mother asked. "See how I'm getting your bed snug and ready for the night?"

I turned from the bookcase, but no sooner had she spread the sheet unevenly on the mattress than she abandoned it for other tasks. *We've lost our Johnny, she'd said to the callers at the funeral parlor, twisting at the black-edged hankie. Johnny's gone from us, we've lost our Johnny.*

"It's far the best idea, havin' the downstairs to let," she went on, dipping once more into the cartons. "It's what John intended, had we not lost him."

Lost, but where? Gone, but where to?

I listened to the rain that had hurled onto the coffin as it was lowered by ropes into the dug-up earth. Gone there, into the ground with the rain lashing down on him? My father, spaded over with earth, like the Kranzes' poor dog buried in the yard next door? Who'd do a thing like that to him? No, no, he hadn't gone there.

Then, as my mother's wandering hands drew another random possession from the cartons, I thought of the steamship schedule. I chased the sound of the rain from my mind, saw again the folder he'd taken from his pocket the last morning.

"Christy darlin'," my mother said. "Look what I have, to keep for your very own. Christy dear?"

The steamship folder, the wind blowing at it while he examined the schedule of sailings. "I'm sorry, Mama," I said and felt myself sway, as from dizziness. "What did you say?"

"Why, what a shame," she clucked, as she set the framed photograph on the chest of drawers. "Look, the glass is cracked. In the move upstairs, it must've got broken . . ."

The aftertaste of the whiskey was sour in my mouth. I rubbed my eyes blearily and returned the photograph to the chest.

I crossed to the bed, slid between the camphor-scented sheets. The soft give of the mattress felt luxurious compared with the straw pallet I'd slept on at Mede's. I ran a hand along the side, remembering the bars that had protected the bed that had been moved upstairs.

A youth bed, my father had called it, but why the bars? Wasn't I big enough at seven to pick myself up and get back in if I fell out? If I was a youth, then why the bars? Those nights after the move upstairs, lying there at night with questions spinning in my head, it had felt as if I'd fallen out for sure, bars or no bars.

Questions spinning round, and fear plucking at me in the dark, a new and different fear, having to do with my mother and what was happening to her.

It was her I had to think of, not steamship folders and sailings to Ireland. With each day that fled behind us, she grew vaguer and more forgetful, just as my father had done. Like him, she began to get mixed up in her actions. The phone would ring, and she would appear not to have heard it. *Brrnng, brrnng*, then she'd hurl around—"Someone to look at the flat"—and hurry to the landing to press the door buzzer.

"It's the phone, Mama."

"What?" She'd take her hand from the buzzer, reach for the phone. "Oh, yes . . . so it is."

Sometimes in the midst of a household chore, dusting the furniture or waxing the floor she'd waxed yesterday, she would go motionless as a statue (*stone, he had said*) and stare puzzled at the mop or broom until she recalled why it was in her hand. Always I'd walked the few blocks back and forth to St. Rose's by myself, but it started to be that, after the three-o'clock dismissal bell, when I filed into the yard with the lines of children . . . a black-coated figure would hover at the fence.

"Thought I'd surprise you," she greeted me the first time it happened. "Just this once," she said; but a few afternoons later she was at the fence again, then it was every afternoon . . . and it wasn't forgetfulness that brought her there. It was that she was afraid of being alone in the cream-painted house. She'd chat about school with me, but as we drew nearer the house her hand tightened on mine . . . then she'd scurry up the front walk, past the FLOOR TO LET sign that was still nailed on the porch. In the vestibule she couldn't locate the keys in her purse. When she had, we'd go up the narrow stairs to the landing, where she'd move to switch the light off.

"There I go, forgettin' to conserve on electricity. Soon I'll have to be pinning notes to myself."

Those winter afternoons, with the lights turned off, the apartment grew dark in a hurry. After supper, when the dishes were washed and the kitchen tidied, the only light was that from the cone-shaded fixture above the table in the dining room. I did my homework at the table, and each night, after she'd washed the dishes and spread the damp cloth to dry on the drain board, my mother joined me at the table.

"Like a bit of company?" She sat in the chair opposite mine, with her mending basket. "How's the arithmetic going?"

"We're starting on fractions."

She unwound thread from a spool. "Now you're the man of the house, you'll need to know about fractions. You mustn't worry, we'll do all right."

"I know, Mama."

"No shame to having soup for supper. It's very nourishing. Did I tell you—" The thread slipped from the needle eye. "I went to Schierman's bakery this mornin'. That early, and they'd already hired a counter woman." She moistened the thread with her tongue. "I'm thinkin' of placing an ad in the *Leader-Observer*, for housework. You mustn't worry, do you hear?"

"I don't, Mama. I don't."

Night after night we sat there in the yellow cone of light, I with my schoolwork, my mother with her mending basket and garbled talk. Each night sooner or later her hand would stray to the letter she kept guarded in her apron pocket. Inch down, then pull back . . . and I would become afraid, too. Afraid of the ticking silence and jabbing needle, afraid of the darkness that lapped closer under the cone of light. And on nights when it was especially bad, when the darkness lapped like water and I crouched over the copybook, pencil rigid . . . I waited, listened for the downstairs buzzer to ring.

On the nights that it rang, I leapt from the table, and

my mother's face would brighten, too, as I raced to the landing to press the door release.

"It's her, I bet. It's Aunt Cash."

And, grinning, I squatted down on the landing so as to observe the progress of the copious, jiggling poundage, the feathers, bracelets and glass beads, of my aunt toiling up the stairs.

"Hiya, kiddo. Feel like chop suey? I picked up some at Loo Fong's." Bracelets jingling, hips swinging, laughter gusting from her. "Jeez, this climb is worse than Mount McKinley. Well, kiddo, how's the widow and orphan tonight?"

"The widow and orphan" was Aunt Cash's term for us, but she made it sound jolly rather than sad. She made everything sound jolly. Cash worked as a telephone operator at Macy's—"Queen of the switchboard and lemme tell you, baby, when I plug in, it's show time." She lived in a rooming house on Lefferts Boulevard, which was the berries, she said, since it reminded her of her vaudeville days. Cash used to be a hoofer in vaudeville, until she'd injured her ankle in a fall while appearing on the Pantages circuit. "Hell, I still live out of a trunk."

Cash was short for Kathleen. Kathleen Lorraine Lenihan, also formerly known as Kitty Lorraine—"Spiffy, huh? For the stage you gotta have a name that catches the eye." Before February, although her rooming house was ten minutes away, it was like pulling teeth to get Cash to visit us. "Thanks, Ag, but no thanks. You and F. X. and the kid don't need me horning in on the act." It was only after February that she took to showing up two or three nights a week, with no prior announcement.

Bzzzz. Bzzzz.

"It's her, I bet. It's Aunt Cash."

"Hiya, kiddo." Slamming, swinging, laughing up the stairs. "Jeez, you look like one of them Hundred Neediest Cases. Here, dig into this knockwurst I picked up at the kraut's."

She brought toys for me, Macy's rejects, dented tin soldiers, a wind-up policeman that worked if you knew where to bang it. She brought cheer and gusto, wisecracks and talk of her vaudeville days that transformed the dark flat into a theater rosy with lights and a stageful of acrobats and magicians. But it was in another connection that my aunt gave me the best reason for listening for the buzzer to ring.

It was in connection with, of all things, candy bars.

For, tucked invariably among the wonders from Loo Fong's or Macy's, stashed away in the rhinestone-clip purse, was a selection of candy bars. Three or four kinds usually; but Aunt Cash didn't just hand them over, not before some serious comments.

"Now, pay attention, Christy. I could be wrong about you, although I don't think so. Now here's a Fruit Chunky and here's a Three Musketeers. Now this is a test, so are ya listenin' careful?"

"A test of what?"

"For the time being, *I* ask the questions. Now I want you to eat these two items at your leisure an' next time I come you're to give a report on your findings."

"Findings?"

It was thrilling, is what it was. The findings consisted of which candy bar I rated superior, the Fruit Chunky or the Three Musketeers. On her next visit I raced to the landing with the news that Three Musketeers was superior.

"Why is it? Well, the Fruit Chunky, despite it's got chocolate and raisins—the taste don't hit me like a Three Musketeers."

"No, huh?" She hoisted her poundage onto the landing and delved in her purse. "I could be wrong about you, kiddo. It's sort of exclusive, the club is, and not everybody qualifies."

"Club? What club?"

"Sorry, I can't reveal more at this point. Now it gets tougher. I have in this hand a Mounds and in this an Almond Joy . . ."

It took weeks before I learned about the club and what

qualified you to belong to it. Two entire weeks of comparing Mounds versus Almond Joys, Oh Henry versus Baby Ruth, Mars versus Milky Way—thrilling weeks of tasting and comparing and reporting my findings. Cash said that my chances for the club shot way up when I was able to specify that Walnettos were the bottom worst of any item yet tasted. But it was when I reported my findings on the best of the lot that Cash elected me to the club. I spent the whole day at school concentrating on it, and that same evening the buzzer sounded from downstairs.

Bzzz. Bzzz.

Up from the table, zoom to the landing. "I got it, I got the answer for you. Whew, you were right, it's even harder than picking the worst. I didn't think of a single other thing at school all day."

"Quick, I can't stand the suspense. Out with it."

I gulped excitedly for breath. "Well, it was on account of school that it came to me. Honest, it was rotten. It really stank, Aunt Cash. Sister Donna Catherine was going on and on about verbs, hollerin' if you moved an inch—I sat there and tried to think of what would make the day better than it was. Make it into terrific, even."

"Yeah?" Cash prompted softly and knelt before me on the landing. "I'm listenin', kiddo. What'd you figure would do the trick?"

I licked at my mouth, getting nervous and unsure of myself. "I figured of anything . . . a Milky Way would do it," I said. "So that must mean it's the best."

My aunt shook her head. "It means you're elected to the club," she said, very solemn.

"It does?" I gazed solemnly back at her. "How, though? What qualifies me?"

"It's like you said about school. You gotta know about hard times," she explained, and brushed at the unruly tangle of my hair. "Cranky nuns, for instance . . . or losing F. X. like you did. Hard times."

F. X. was what she'd called my father. She'd used the same word about him as my mother had. If something was lost, didn't it mean it could be found? "Cash. Aunt Cash?"

I grabbed on to her. "About my father, when he left the house that last morning . . ."

"Yeah, baby? What about it?"

Why was it always my *left* leg that shook, never the right? I wanted to ask her what had happened to my father that he hadn't come home. I knew what she'd answer: he'd met with an accident and was taken from us. *Lost*, that word again.

"Hard times,'" I said. "What's that got to do with the club?"

"The candy-bar club?"

"Is that what it's called? Gee, that's a neat name for a club."

"It means you're a special-type person." She brushed at my hair, her Kewpie-doll eyes shining. "It means you're not afraid, that nothing can keep you down for long," she said, "because any minute a Milky Way might be coming up to make things better."

"And I'm a member?"

She smiled at me. "You bet you are, sweetheart. Top of the heap."

"Oh, Cash." My voice turned blubbery and I threw my arms around her. "Cash, I'm so glad you took to ringing the buzzer. Why didn't you before? Why did you wait till we lost F. X.?"

Cash was short for Kathleen, Kathleen Lorraine Lenihan, but it spelled much more than that. It spelled the part that was over, the nights under the cone of light with the darkness lapping closer; and the part that was about to begin.

"It never struck me before," said my mother, steering in from the kitchen on a night shortly after my election to the club. My aunt had arrived with egg rolls and pork-fried rice from Loo Fong's; her sister had made tea to accompany the feast.

"It never struck me"—Agnes Theresa steered with a tray into the cone of light—"that the Irish and Chinese share any traits in common, but we do."

She set the tray down, transferred the cups and saucers

onto the table. "We share a fondness for tea. It's such a treat when you drop by, Kathleen. It makes for such a nice change. Some nights we sit here, Christy and me, my goodness—"

The nervous prattle cut off; the cone of light outlined the thin, bent figure suddenly turned statuelike. "No spoons," she *tssked*. "Where's the spoons? I swear I'll soon be havin' to pin notes to myself. What was I sayin'? Oh, yes. Such a treat, Kathleen, to—to—"

My aunt was marching around the living room, switching on every light she could lay hand to.

"Kathleen, what in God's name—"

"Relax, Ag." On went the floor lamp at the armchair. "I paid Con Edison yesterday, relax, the bastards aren't shutting off a damn thing."

"Off? Off?" The statue leaned over the table, stole a hand to the apron pocket; jerked it away as from burning coals. "Spoons," she gasped. "Where's the spoons for the tea?"

"While we're at it"—Cash went toward her—"let's have a peek at that billet-doux you keep hiding in your apron. From the bank, is it?"

The statue swayed and clutched at the table. Made of stone, my father had said, but now the stone was shattering, strangled animal cries were tearing from it.

"Agggh," the cries tore out. "Agggh. I watched him go under and couldn't help. I was the wrong person for John. Wrong clean through. The mortgage. God, God, oh, God."

"Ag." Cash struggled to calm her.

"We're losing the house. God, oh, God, God."

My aunt grappled with the swaying, keening figure. "Christy, go to your room," she ordered. "Ag, listen to me. I'm here, you don't have to fight this alone. Ag!" She seized the flaying arms that wrenched free. "Your room, Christy."

Horror paralyzed me. *Run, he'd said the last day. Run, run.* I stumbled from the dining room, the cries pursuing me down the hall. I shut the door of my room but the cries still followed. I lurched in the dark to the chest of drawers, took down the photograph, and spoke to it.

"The steamship folder. A ship was sailing, you went to Ireland." Over and over, to drown out the cries, I repeated the incantation. "To Ireland . . . but you'll come back. You'll come back or I'll go find you."

What was lost could be found, wasn't it so? "You'll come back, and till you do, I'll take care of us. I promise, I swear, if you'll only come back." I chanted my vow over and over until the cries had faded and I no longer heard in my mind's ear the rain striking the coffin the men were lowering into the ground.

I shivered, despite the warmth of the covers pulled over me. The room was stifling warm compared to Mede's. There the cold howled along the stone cloisters at night, invaded the cells like hounds with icy breath.

The steamship folder . . . you'll come back . . . I'll take care of us, I swear, I promise.

By the week following, Cash had moved into the spare bedroom, with her vaudeville trunk pasted with stickers, her wind-up Victrola and phonograph records that played wonderful tinny show songs—the Duncan Sisters, Rae Dooley, Sophie Tucker, Al Jolson, Nora Bayes. "Strictly a cash basis, Ag," she'd ruled. "Hand out eight bucks a week to that battle-ax Mrs. Schultz and not to you? Make that twelve, on account of here I get kitchen privileges. It's either cash or no dice."

Cash. Cash was how you spelled rescue . . . and it was how I got the notion of what I could do to contribute to the household. Without Cash it never would have occurred to me; I never would have dreamed up the idea at all.

It didn't come about until the fall after she'd moved in with us. By then she'd collared some tenants for the downstairs flat, the Johnsons, who had remained our tenants to the present. With rent money coming in, and a halt to the notices from the bank, the haunted look was fading from my mother's face. But in bed at night I'd hear the sisters in the kitchen. "We're makin' headway, Ag. You don't have to get scared every time you go for the mail. Okay, we're not out of the cellar yet, but we're getting there a step at a time."

Out of the cellar, what did that mean? The bottom, like Walnettos. I twisted around on the pillows, stared through the darkness at the photograph on the dresser.

How? How would I do what I'd promised? Paper route, delivery boy, magazine subscriptions? How?

Cash herself, or rather her vaudeville records, had supplied the answer. Often at night I'd flop on her ruffled bed while she cranked up the Victrola, flicked ashes from her Lucky Strike cigarette, and reminisced about the performers whose gusty songs blared scratchily from the machine.

"I was on the bill at the Oriental with her, y'know," she remarked of Fanny Brice, who was crooning "My Man" on the Victrola. "Talk about class acts. Two grand a week and worth every cent."

I'd jumped up on the bed. "You get *paid* for vaudeville? You don't do it just for fun?"

"Hell, baby, if you were a headliner . . . why, I remember in Atlantic City, that kid actor from the movies—"

I knelt back, saucer-eyed. "*Kid* actors get paid. You're not making it up?"

"Jackie Coogan, is who it was. A week at the Steel Pier, six a day, and he pulled down a cool five G's."

I'd gawked at her, awestruck. "Five G's for a kid actor? You're being serious?"

Every Friday Cash faithfully came home with her copy of *Variety*, the bible of show business. It required the weekend for her to finish perusing its fascinating pages . . . and soon I was asking for a look at it. I got to be expert at interpreting the colorful and unique language of *Variety*.

"Did you read," I'd inquire of my aunt, "where Harriet Hoctor clicked at the McVickers on her holdover? She's canceling her stix dates and opening at the Egyptian in L.A.''

"Personally, honey, a little of that twirling toe work . . . say, explain something to me."

I lowered the paper and returned my aunt's quizzical stare. "Yeah, Aunt Cash? Explain what?"

"You just did, kiddo." She came over to me, tilted up my face, and treated it to a long appraising inspection. "The bug's bit you, hasn't it," she said. "Well, Jesus, it's not like you got it from the stones in the street."

"What bug you talkin' about?"

The long scrutinizing continued. She moved my face to the left, then the right, and instructed me to stand back so she could get an overall impression.

"Kiddo, it just might be worth a try," she'd pronounced when the inspection was concluded. "I tell you what you've got going for you. Backed up by talent, it could be dynamite."

I stood with my shoulders squared and my chin jutting out. A logjam of emotion welled in my throat and my left leg commenced as usual to shake. "Y'mean, if I was to have a try at being a kid actor?" I asked. "Who can tell, maybe I could do it. I been thinking about it. Need a stage name, right? I already thought of one. We need money, right?" The words careened out of me. "I hear you and Mom talking. Still in the cellar, right? Maybe this is a way for us. I don't know nothing about it, except—"

"I do," Cash had said, and reached a hand to my face, gently, as my father had on the walk the last day. "What you got goin' for you . . . is the look of the candy-bar club," she'd said. "And in show biz, kiddo, that's a big dividend."

I threw off the covers, turned on my side. I licked at the sour aftertaste of the whiskey that sandpapered my mouth. Had I actually believed it, believed that if I kept to my promise, miraculously one day, as in a dream, my father would come back?

Through the five years of agents' and producers' offices, the auditions on bare stages, the rehearsals, the openings, the closings, the radio work, the occasional movie shot in New York; the waiting on benches, eyeing the competition, the casting sessions—"You. You. Not you. Come back tomorrow"—I had not let go of my dream. I was proficient at my newfound occupation. Acting was something I could do, like magic tricks or high-wire walking; I was good at it, and no less proficient at getting work. The crucial thing, I'd learned early on, was to manage somehow always to be at the front of the line.

But through all of it—the out-of-town tryouts, the play that ran for eight months, the one that opened on Thursday, closed on Saturday—through all of it, wherever I'd gone, wherever I was, subways, buses, train stations, Philly, Baltimore, I'd searched for him. My father was dead. Unless the cemetery earth were to be unspaded and the coffin pried open, he was not to be found—yet I went on looking for him. Faith, the nuns had taught at school, was the act of believing beyond doubt or reason, against all odds.

I had become a secret practitioner of faith; it had taken possession of me; I could not have stopped it if I'd wanted to. *Papa, Papa, wait, you forgot your coat . . .*

The curse of dreams, he'd said, was that they got broken . . . and one Saturday in June, when I was thirteen, my child's dream of him had, like the glass on the photograph, been cracked apart.

I turned over again on the pillows. The tangle of pushed-down blankets caught at my legs; I kicked free of them and got out of bed.

The poster above the bookcase glimmered dimly in the darkness. *Max Jacobs presents THE PUMPKINS*, and under the title, my name in featured billing, *Christopher Kerry.*

June, '39, winding up the long run at the Garrick. Max Jacobs was sending us on tour after the summer layoff. The contract he'd offered for the tour would up my salary to four hundred. Mortgage paid off, money in the bank, and for the layoff, Mom, Cash and I were taking a vacation. We were sailing on the *Georgic*, a Cunard steamer, for Ireland.

June, the next-to-last Saturday matinee. After the performance, Willie, the stage doorman, had knocked at my dressing room. "Dame to see you. Says she used to be a neighbor. Send her up?"

"Sure, Willie."

I did not remember Mrs. Tredder, but she had no difficulty in remembering me. "Muriel and Howard Tredder, next door to the Lindstroms?" She'd plumped down in the chair next to mine at the dressing table. "Moved to Yonkers ages ago, but the instant you came on the stage I said to myself, It's him, why, it's the Casey boy."

"Next door to the Lindstroms? Let's see . . ."

"He's changed his name, I said to myself, but who could blame him?"

I'd stared at her blankly, a round little woman in a spun-sugar hat. "Blame me?"

A white glove clapped to the small round mouth. "Dear me, I trust I'm not speaking out of turn. Did they keep it from you? Weren't you told?"

My voice was issuing from someone else. "No, I . . . later. I was told later."

"Just as well. I shan't forget the day it happened. February, wasn't it? I was coming up the street from Bohack's, and Dorothy Lindstrom came rushing over to stop me."

Stopped.

That day in the dressing room, Mrs. Tredder had achieved what I'd been unable to. The small, busy mouth had resembled an industrious snail, and when she was finished, my father had died for me. There would be no more fugitive searching of crowds, no sailing to Ireland; no more Christopher Kerry.

To Max Jacobs' abiding wrath, I had not signed the contract for the tour. I was to start high school in the fall; I'd used that as my excuse. A normal everyday school, normal everyday routine. In September I'd enrolled at Brooklyn Prep, registered under my own name, seeking my own identity, my own life.

The trouble was that I couldn't seem to find it. The old

life would not drop away; it stayed there, a silent hovering presence that followed after me, so that most of what I did turned out to be an effort to escape from it. The war, to be free of the cream-painted house where every footfall was a recapitulation of the past. Mede's, for the same unwitting purpose . . . and now once more I was back again.

Back in my child's room, with the cracked-glass frame on the chest of drawers and the chink of street light slanting in the window.

I went over to the window and opened it. The night air stirred the curtains, trailed cooling fingers across my chest; I gazed beyond the curtains, above the dark rooftops and chimneys, at the black starless unfathomable sky. For so long I had felt so alone . . . yet somewhere mustn't there be someone who'd gone through what I had and therefore would understand? Someone who'd look at me and, by just a look, would understand?

Tomorrow. Got to start thinking of tomorrow. Make plans.

A wave of fatigue suddenly washed over me and I moved back through the chink of light to the bed. I lay in bed, the covers pulled up, and wondered how Amos Feather was faring with Lucas and Edna June in Mineola. Who was Amos that I'd made it a point to help him from the bus, sat by his side in the waiting room, would have forever if he'd asked. How many surrogate fathers over the years? Max, don't forget Max, what you did after Mrs. Tredder had departed from the dressing room with a gay wave of the white glove . . . and today, Amos Feather.

Dear Christ, it hadn't ended: I was looking for him still.

Tomorrow, had to get started again tomorrow. Letters to colleges to apply for next semester . . . in the meanwhile, a job to keep me going, keep me busy.

Papa, Papa, wait . . .

As of old, the darkness lapped closer and ghosts flapped in it. "Help me," I whispered aloud in the dark to no one, and after many turnings fell asleep.

• •

We cannot know, ever, the course of our lives; nor even with certainty where the next moment from now will take us.

It is subject to change.

In April, out of the days that had been going nowhere, I met Janya, who by then was called Maggie Jones.

CHAPTER 3

I didn't intend that the days go nowhere—who intends it? But it was how it worked out.

"Are you up?" chirruped Agnes Theresa from the kitchen the morning after I'd come home. "Is that you, Christy?"

"Yeah, at least I think so." The gaunt, black-stubbled reflection in the washbasin mirror might have been a stranger's, cheekbones like knife slashes, no wonder Amos Feather had suspected recent incarceration.

"I was thinking of a big hearty breakfast," my mother chortled down the hall, "to put some meat back on those bones."

"Sounds great." I churned up a thick foamy lather in the soap mug, swabbed it over the rough, black stubble, and with the first stroke of the razor willed my former self to be gone.

Orange juice, bacon and eggs, toast and marmalade, coffee and cream; then in the old tan gabardine, restored by Agnes Theresa's iron, I rode the El to the city.

The noise and swarm of the city weren't as jarring or alien as yesterday. Fifth Avenue was a bright panoply of shops and department stores, double-decker buses and streams of pedestrians aflow in the warm October sun. I'd always bought my clothes at Browning King; this time I took myself round the corner to Roger Kent. Charcoal-gray suit, herringbone jacket, flannels, trench coat with zip-in lining—ready for pickup next Monday, the salesman said.

"Fine," I said, and wrote him a deposit from the checking account I'd assigned to my mother when I'd entered Mede's. The balance was unchanged . . . had she anticipated I'd be back?

It didn't matter; what mattered was what I did about being back.

I went that same morning to Gray's, an employment agency on Sixth Avenue. I walked along in the sidewalk flow, enjoying the pretty girls, slim and alive, breasts jouncing from the quick, easy strides. Thinking about girls was about as far as I'd gotten, even before Mede's. Well, it was that much more to get started on.

Gray's was located in an office building at Sixth and Forty-sixth. *Use Stairs for Gray's*, advised a sign at the elevators in the dingy lobby; I climbed the well-worn flights to the second floor, filled out an application at the stand-up desk in the fish-tank-green office, joined the lineup on the benches, and waited to be summoned into one of the cubicles by the interviewers.

Mr. Ferguson was my interviewer. He motioned me into the four-by-four, file-crammed space, ran a practiced eye over my application.

"This Saint Mede's—never heard of it."

"It's a . . . small institution in upstate New York. Not many have heard of it."

"Let's say it don't ring a bell like Harvard or Yale." He tapped a pencil on the application. "You didn't indicate."

"Excuse me?"

"Whether you're permanent or temporary. We handle both."

"Oh. I see. Well, it's just till I go back to college in January."

"That makes you a temp." He checked a square on the application, thumbed through a metal index box. "How's your typing? I can send you to Speed-O, direct-mail outfit, typing envelopes. How's that strike you?"

"Fine. Strikes me fine." I took the card he wrote out, thanked him, and backed from the cubicle. "As I say, it's just until January."

Mr. Ferguson looked up at me from a batch of applications. "Sure, Casey," he said. "Sure it is. When Speed-O's finished with you, drop back. I'll be here."

"Thanks. I will."

Speed-O operated out of a loft on Nineteenth Street pounding with the thump and clatter of Addressographs, Multiliths and typewriters. I was given a desk in a row of desks, lists of addresses, boxes of envelopes and an ancient carriage-clanging Underwood on which to turn out the envelopes. You were expected to produce seventy per hour. Mr. Peisky, the foreman, patrolled the aisles, checking on output.

I averaged fifty-eight the first day.

Sixty-four the second, and by then I'd gotten letters mailed off to the Universities of Wyoming, in Laramie, Montana, in Missoula, and Reed College in Portland, Oregon. The West. I'd never been farther west than Chicago. Different world, different air to breathe, different person.

The third day at Speed-O I averaged sixty-eight envelopes per hour.

The job lasted two weeks; bright and early the next morning I climbed the well-trodden flights to Gray's.

Mr. Ferguson was in his cubicle. "It's easily seen, Casey, you're not the usual temp," he said.

"Oh? How's that?"

"When'd you get through at Speed-O? Yesterday?" He tilted his chair back and grinned. "Just look at you this morning. Somebody sure drilled it into you to make the front of the line."

By the middle of November the replies from the colleges had come in. It was simply a question, I told myself, of deciding which to go to.

Wyoming wrote first, then Montana. It wasn't necessary to check the mail when I got home at night. If a letter had arrived, Agnes Theresa would be at the top of the stairs, waving the prized epistle, waiting with bated breath while I read it.

"Well, dear?"

"Says to mail in the deposit by December one."

"You're accepted? Same as Wyoming. Oh, how fine, Christy. If your confidence needed a boost, which of course it shouldn't—what else does the letter say?"

"I already told you." I slid the forms that were to be filled out back in the envelope, tossed it on the table. "Plenty of time to decide." I hung up my trench coat, headed through the dining-room arch with the paperback of James I'd picked up.

"How did your day go, Christy? The, what is it, deodorant survey?"

"This week it's chewing-gum samples," I said. "New flavor they're testing, Mango Lime."

"Well, you're certainly acquiring interesting experiences. Since you're going to your room"—she fetched the letter from the phone table—"why not keep this on your desk as a reminder."

"Look, stop worrying, Mama. It's just a question of deciding." I took the letter from her, glanced at it a moment. "Reed ranks the highest academically, wouldn't you agree I ought to wait till I hear from them?"

"Yes, of course you should." Then, as I started past the dining table: "Cash phoned. She says if you'd like to catch a show in the city tonight—"

I knew what that was about: the former Kitty Lorraine's pitch for my future did not center on college. "Like to, but I'm sort of bushed," I said to my mother. "Handing out samples of Mango Lime might not be executive training, but it's rough on the feet. I—I thought I might read, or lie down before supper."

"Yes, dear." On her face as she looked at me was a queerly familiar anxiety. "Shall I get you up when supper's ready?"

"I said I might read." I hesitated, went past the kitchen

to the back hall. Home over a month, where were the days going? "But if I do lie down, wake me," I said and went down the hall.

The letter from Reed College arrived a few days later. It was a conditional acceptance, based on my retaking the college boards. It joined its companions on the desk, the sturdy maple desk in my sturdy child's room; and it was several days before my mother made any reference to it.

Then at supper one night she laughed and exclaimed, as she passed the pot roast, "My goodness, I was handed a shock when I glanced at the calendar this morning."

I helped myself to the pot roast. "A shock of what type?"

"Well, I'd no idea—" she laughed and passed me the turnips—"that December's almost upon us. Tuesday's the first, if you can believe it."

I threw down my napkin and got up from the table. "I haven't decided yet," I heard myself shouting at her. "Would you prefer I do it right this minute? Would that goddamn please you? Would it?"

She stared at me as if she'd been slapped. "I'm sorry," I mumbled and resumed my seat. "There's the weekend to get it done. I'll have the deposit in the mail by Sunday at the latest."

"Yes, dear." She picked up her fork, ironed from her face the anxiety that struck in me an awful chord. "Eat your supper, Christy," she said. "You . . . you mustn't let it get cold."

The way I'd always fixed the date of my birthday in my mind was by counting the shopping days left until Christmas. No shopping on Sundays, so that put it at thirteen days left, December tenth, to be exact . . . which was the evening that I returned very late to the cream-painted house, in company with the former Kitty Lorraine.

She'd taken me out on the town to celebrate, a play, supper and drinks afterward. It had required my birthday to accomplish it, but Cash had finally corralled me into a theater again.

Very late, and the two of us *shssh*ing each other as we stumbled up the porch steps . . . reminiscent of the night I'd come back from Mede's, a date that was rapidly receding into the past. But that was my trouble, wasn't it? That I couldn't make the past recede? Nor could Kitty, for what else was behind the birthday treat she'd arranged?

"Jeez, baby," she said, as I took elaborate care to close the vestibule door noiselessly. The drinks at Sardi's didn't entirely account for our inebriated behavior. "Jeez, didja have to be so almighty rude about it?"

I followed her swaying, evening-skirted poundage up the dark stairs. We were exaggerating it, like comedy drunks, which was part of the strategy. "Rude? How was I rude?" I demanded.

"We come in the lobby and there she is, Max's secretary, what'sa name?"

"Weintraub. Rose Weintraub." The play Cash had selected for the birthday treat was *Anniversary*, a comedy produced by, guess who, Max Jacobs. "Explain how I was rude to her. Explain."

The theater, to complete the surprise, was the Garrick, scene of former triumphs. "Well, migod, brushing straight past her, after she spotted you 'n all."

"Wrong, baby," I said, wearying of the drunk act. "Rose didn't recognize me from Adam."

"Lou, the ticket taker, did. He di'n' say hello only 'counta you di'n'." She gave a boozy sigh and hoisted herself onto the landing. " 'Fess up, baby." She flopped down on the telephone bench and fluffed at her fox collar. "It was swell, wasn't it?"

I groped for the light switch on the landing, *no, save on electricity, the February days, dark so early.* "What was swell, *Anniversary*? The play?"

"No, to be back at the Garrick. Jeez, all I could see on that stage was you, the bit in the second act where—"

"Wrong, baby." I switched on the light and she blinked, tired and lipstick-smeared, in its sudden glare. "You always got it wrong," I said. "All I saw tonight was the grind of those four hundred performances. No nostalgia, no nothing. You were the show-biz fan, not me."

The Kewpie-doll eyes blinked at me. "It was the money, period," I said, getting to the point of the evening. "We needed money. When there was enough of it I got out. No plans to get back in. None, so if that's what you're hoping—"

"Plans, you say?" Cash pushed at her hat, which was askew; her speech was remarkably unslurred. "Strikes me you could do with some plans at the moment."

"Perhaps so, and I appreciate your concern, but—"

She sat up on the bench. "Glad you do, baby, but what's the schedule these days? College is out, apparently, and—"

"Not necessarily. Not permanently." I turned away, unbuckling the trench coat. The museum living room lay shrouded in shadows. I threw the coat on the sausage-armed chair. "I can start in the fall. This summer, even."

"Skip the summer. What's on the docket for tomorrow? Bright and early to Gray's?"

"I call in. I don't always go in."

"Back to Gray's. Terrific."

"*Back*. Jesus, I hate that word." I started through the dining room.

"A person of your talent. The sheer lousy waste." The bench groaned as Cash lumbered up from it. "I never had talent—you can't waste what you don't have—but you, Christy. Why d'ya think you got paid that money for, nice manners and being polite?"

"I'm going to bed."

"No, you're going to listen to me." She charged into the arch and stood there. "You're lying about why you quit. Walking out on Max's tour, that stuff about high school— *lies*," she said. "You quit for other reasons."

I turned slowly around and looked at her. "What other reasons?"

She swallowed, and in the shadows her eyes glistened wetly. "What's the one topic we never get around to discussing?" she asked softly.

I kept my voice even. "What could that have had to do with it?"

"Everything else did—the name you took, your reason for trying the stage." She bit at her mouth. "I had the feeling when you quit that it was because of F. X., too," she said, with a tremble. "We didn't go into it much at the time, how he died, but maybe you took to brooding about it and—"

"How he died?" My voice sounded hollow, disattached, as it had with Mrs. Tredder. "I knew about that long before *The Pumpkins*," I said to Cash. "It's the sort of thing . . . you piece together by yourself."

"We should've talked about it more. You were so little then . . . but now you're not." Her glistening eyes shifted to the back hall. "Mustn't wake Ag, but I could put on some coffee and if you'd care to talk about it . . . okay?"

I didn't answer; she gave a little nod of encouragement, went past me toward the kitchen, teetering unevenly on her spiked heels. "I can't," I said, as she reached for the kitchen switch. "I can't talk about my father, Cash. I'm not able to. Once at Mede's I made an appointment with the Abbot. Sat there discussing Thomas Aquinas when all the while . . ." I felt my jaw tighten, the muscles clench. "Maybe someday I won't think of the rain as some terrible enemy that took him from me. Each time it rains—"

Cash put out her hand. "Sweetheart."

"Each time it's as if I'm back there and it's all still happening." A shiver went through me. "This house, each night I turn in at the walk—it all keeps happening, Cash."

"Oh, baby." She shook her head. "What can I do to help?"

"That's just it—nothing." I gestured at her in an effort to explain. "Not mailing the college deposit—I think it was because I knew it wouldn't change anything. I'd be the same, just as I was at Mede's."

The Kewpie-doll face struggled to comprehend. "The way it's been going, baby, anything would be an improvement."

"Yeah, it's been going nowhere. Walnettos. Days and nights of Walnettos, but every so often . . ."

"What?"

"Well, take the city and me. All the dopey jobs, constantly turning some damn corner or other to report at some new address."

"Baby, I'm not catching the drift."

"All those corners—" I went over to her in the kitchen doorway. "One of these days, who knows, I might turn the right corner. Sounds foolish, I admit—"

"No, just young," Cash said. "It's the candy-bar club talkin'. Listen. Listen here." She gripped my arms. "I don't worry about you in the long run. Chewing-gum samples or a glue factory—I don't give a rap, if it makes you happy. You and your somedays. Know when mine'll be?"

"When?"

She looked up at me, the rouged blowsy face a child's. "The day I'm waiting for," she said, "is when you come to me, or call me up from wherever you are, and say, 'Cash, I'm so happy I don't think I was ever alive before.' That'll be my payoff, ya big palooka," she grinned.

"I—I promise," I said. "You'll be the first to be notified. I guarantee."

"Well, don't forget." A tidal wave of a yawn engulfed her and she rubbed at her bleary eyes, started for the back hall. "Me for some shuteye, baby. Jeez, the switchboard tomorrow . . ."

The back hall, the light from the bathroom knifing the shadows . . . in her doorway, removing a shoe to massage a swollen ankle, Cash said, "About tonight, sweetie. One more comment, if I may."

"Yes?"

"You beat it out of the Garrick like it was on fire—broke into a run, practically."

Run, he'd said. "And?" I cued my aunt.

"Suppose Mr. Jacobs had been there. You owe him an apology, you know."

"For pulling out of the tour?" I could have remarked

that Max owed me some apologies. The Saturday matinee Mrs. Tredder had visited my dressing room, afterwards I'd . . . *there it was again, the past.*

"I'm just saying that if the opportunity presents itself again—" Another Grand Canyon yawn engulfed Miss Lenihan, and she padded into her room. "An apology wouldn't cost you none. Night, baby."

"Good night. Thanks for the celebration."

I sucked in my breath, grasped the doorknob, and went into my child's room. In the darkness, as I closed the door behind me, the chink of street light shone on the cracked glass.

I sagged against the door. Tomorrow was Gray's again. Back to Gray's.

Then what?

I didn't know. I didn't know.

The corner, when finally I turned it, was undistinguishable from any of the others; not a sign, a hint of its difference.

It was February by then, a month I didn't particularly relish getting through. February, cold and blustery, a light intermittent drizzle starting to fall, as I came out of Horton & Co., Publishers, on Thirty-sixth Street, and headed uptown in the dusk that was falling with the drizzle over the city.

The days had gone stumbling along, and with them the procession of jobs, a few days, a week, none of them leading anywhere, amounting to anything.

Except this last job at Horton's, which had ended today, about an hour ago, when Mr. Atwood, the office manager, said that, much as he regretted having to let me go . . . could finish out the day, he'd said, but then at four-thirty, when I was still unable to get Wally Pfeiffer at his rooming house . . .

I pulled up the collar of the herringbone jacket against the drizzle and continued on up Second Avenue. I'd left my trench coat at Horton's; I'd go back for it tomorrow.

More important that I get hold of Wally. He was in bad shape if he couldn't make it from the bed to the phone.

Horton's was the longest-lasting job yet, thanks to him, and the only job that had contained some suggestion of a future. Originally it was to have been for a week, typing and filing orders in the sales department. Wally Pfeiffer occupied the desk next to mine—a skinny little guy who wore a green eyeshade in the style of an old-time newspaper editor and was given to hopping around the office as if firecrackers were exploding under his feet. At lunch the first day he'd bought me coffee from the wagon that went *ring-a-ling* in the hall and offered to share his tunafish sandwich, dug from a paper bag and spread out on the desk.

"Well . . . so tell me, son"—pulling up a chair—"what's your impression of the publishing world?"

"Well, so far I've only—"

"Rewarding. Most rewarding racket there is."

After lunch that first day he'd conducted me on a tour of Horton's: the art and production departments, book schedules, jacket illustrations, ad copy pinned helter-skelter on the walls; the editorial department, galleys and manuscripts arranged in bins, the staff absorbed in discussions, arguments, pleadings, all having to do with books and authors. The tour wound up in the Horton library, the shelves of new titles emanating the wondrous smell of linen, glue, ink and paper stock fresh from the binder. "Best smell in creation," Wally pronounced it—and with a wink he'd ducked some bright-jacketed volumes under his coat. Out in the hall, he'd presented them to me.

"Don't have to utter a word," he'd protested, waving bony, speckled hands that were prey to a noticeable tremor. "A reverence for books is manifest in your very silence. Tell me something."

"Yes?"

"Bright young feller like you—ever consider a future in publishing?"

"No . . . but at this very moment," I'd confessed, "I'm kicking myself for not having thought of it."

"Well, son, if you want," he'd said as we went back down the hall, "I could speak to my pal Bob Atwood about lining up some . . ."

I wiped at my face, glanced up at the street sign at the corner. Forty-fourth . . . the rooming house was on Forty-ninth. Umbrellas were sprouting up and down Second Avenue; the wheels of the buses, trucks and autos were cutting a spray as they drove past. The drizzle was turning into a downpour. I burrowed under the hitched-up collar; couple more blocks, I'd be at Wally's . . . this near, maybe I ought to look in the bars I was passing. It could explain why he hadn't answered the phone.

Wally was the office drunk; it hadn't required much deduction to conclude that about him, or to learn that for years he'd drifted from one publishing house to another on a steadily downward course. Yet Wally had contrived to keep me on the Horton payroll: clerical work, filing, codexing, but he'd nab editors in the hall and introduce me to them, obtain galleys for me to read, encourage me to submit reports on them, write sample blurbs, things like that. And on the frequent mornings that he was late and the coffee wagon was moving on, I'd buy a container for him, black, no sugar, which, when he hoppity-hobbled in, I'd deliver to his shaking hands and . . .

Finnerton's, winked the neon sign over the bar at Forty-eighth. I wiped at the dripping window and peered in at the dim, moist, jukebox-pulsing interior, looking for Wally Pfeiffer. I didn't actually know which saloons he favored, but since this was his neighborhood, the likelihood was that . . .

Looking for who?

I turned away from the window, the jukebox suddenly loud and crashing in my ear. *Who was Wally Pfeiffer that you'd . . . ?*

I continued walking up Second Avenue, past the rooming house on Forty-ninth. For two days Wally hadn't shown up at Horton's; each of those days and again this morning, I'd kept the container of coffee waiting for him . . . *why*? So that when he raised it to his quavering mouth,

I'd hear him say, "Thanks a heap, son. Can't get the motor going without my morning java. Couldn't get by without you, nossir, son." Still couldn't reach him on the phone this afternoon, so I'd raced out of the office in such concern that I'd even neglected to . . .

Wait, you forgot your coat.

I stepped from the curb, *plink* went a puddle as my shoe hit it. I crossed to the other curb, kept on walking, following the flickering shadow of myself cast by the street lamps over the wet-splashed pavement. I didn't bother with the street signs any more, just kept on walking, the rain streaming in rivulets from my chin.

Back to Gray's tomorrow . . . why? Why back to Gray's?

A traffic light flashed green, I pulled back from the curb, caught in a bobble of umbrellas. Fifty-seventh Street . . . doormen were shrilling their whistles for taxis while in the canopied apartment entrances ladies and gentlemen stood in evening clothes, bound for dinner and the theater. I remembered the doorman at Max's apartment on Central Park West, calling the duplex to announce my presence, when I'd gone there after Mrs. Tredder had called, "Bye!" and gaily departed for Yonkers. I'd sat alone in the dressing room, scared that if I didn't do something, go somewhere, talk to someone . . .

The traffic light flashed red again, I joined the bobble of umbrellas across Fifty-seventh Street. The rain swept down in hard, slanting sheets, obscuring the lights of the Queensborough Bridge ahead and the curving ramps that disgorged traffic onto the congested streams of Second Avenue. I faltered to a halt, tried to collect my scrambled-up, loused-up thoughts. B.M.T. at Lex and Fifty-ninth, subway to Queens, Richmond Hill, home, but where was home?

I stepped from the curb, *plink* went another puddle, then the scream of brakes, glare of headlights, skidding to a sickening slippery . . . "Crazy? You gone crazy?" a truck driver shouted, leaning from his cab, purple with fury. "Jesus, pal. Another inch there and . . . move it. Jesus, get the legs going."

Horns were honking, lanes of traffic streaked past; on-lookers gestured, shouted instructions, warnings, deprecations, from the west side of the avenue. I darted between the lanes of traffic, staggered onto the curb, clutched a phone booth for support, breath in ragged gasps.

I was angry more than frightened. Shaky-legged and in need of support, but it was anger that raged through me, blotting out the various lectures I was receiving from a small group of safety-minded citizens.

Anger, hot and coruscating, and unsparing: *Tomorrow will not be Gray's again. No idea what else, but it won't be Gray's. Finished, goddammit. Over with. Tomorrow goddammit will not be Gray's.*

I let go of the phone booth, slicked down the wet tangle of hair, tugged the sodden jacket into a semblance of orderliness. Ignoring my critics, and with what dignity I could muster, I turned the corner and proceeded along Fifty-ninth Street.

The rain was letting up, making for easier passage. Fifty-ninth between Second and Third was cheerful with shops —fruit and vegetables; butcher's, hung with salamis; Italian grocery stores laden with pasta, pannelone and gallon tins of olive oil. From the doorways of the shops flowed a bustle of housewives and office workers, juggling packages and umbrellas. And from among them, as I hiked along, keeping to the curb, I heard called out a name I hadn't answered to in nine years.

"Christopher Kerry!"

I spun around, as a tiny, vivacious woman bore down on me. She was waving a polka-dot umbrella, lest she escape my attention. Twin discs of rouge enlivened her face, along with India-ink bangs that frizzed from under her hat. "Oh, no, you don't, not a second time," she cried, seizing me by the arm.

"I shouldn't even speak to you," she chastised, dragging me into the doorway of an upholsterer's. "What's the matter, you didn't say hi at the Garrick that night? Before we go any further—"

"Rose." I raked at my streaming, tangled hair. "Rose Weintraub," I said in stunned disbelief.

"Don't give me those pussycat eyes. There's only one answer I want from you," she declared, pausing to brush disgustedly at the sopping jacket. "Max has been waiting for years to holler and shout and make up with you. So when you going to give him the chance?"

On an afternoon three weeks later I turned another corner, from Broadway onto Forty-fourth Street. Despite Rose's avowals of the peace pipe Max yearned to extend, he had twice canceled appointments with me. He was casting a road company of *Anniversary*; auditions were his excuse for backing out of the first appointment; and last week he'd pleaded—wrong word, unless you could plead while furiously issuing rebukes—a flying trip to the Coast.

Trench coat reclaimed, herringbone and flannels newly pressed, I hiked past Sardi's, Shubert Alley and the play-houses that were clustered along the street. It was a clear, cold afternoon, the sun was out, glistening on the fresh-painted house-boards of the Majestic, which advertised the April opening of Mary Martin and Ezio Pinza in *South Pacific*. The opening was a month away, but already a line snaked out from the box office—doubtless a vexing sight to Max when he peered from his lair in the St. James across the street. Max was domiciled in the rabbit's warren of producers' and press agents' offices tucked under the St. James's roof.

I dawdled for a moment on the sidewalk outside, experiencing mixed emotions. Cash was right in saying I owed Max an apology: I'd blamed him for something that wasn't his responsibility. However, it was unlikely I'd be allowed the opportunity of opening my mouth . . . and to enter his office was to go back again to the past.

I rode up in the minuscule St. James elevator, once more embarked on that familiar journey. I hadn't gone back to Gray's, I reminded myself. I'd sent a deposit last week to the University of Wyoming for summer admission; what's more, I'd found a job related to books. It was only part-time, indexing a cheap-operation encyclopedia, and was due to end in June, but I'd be headed west by then.

The elevator wheezed to a halt; I went down the lozenge-tiled corridor to the frosted-glass door with the inscription fanned over it: *Max Jacobs Productions.* I opened the door and entered.

The small, nondescript outer office was besieged by actors; some were seated on the hard-backed benches in attitudes of gloom, stoic determination, or devil-may-care insouciance; others were storming the wooden rail that protected Rose Weintraub from them. She was at her desk, attempting to deal with several ringing phones, the persistent buzz of Max's intercom, and the onslaught of actors.

"Look, take my word, the road company is cast," she kept repeating to them. "The tour is cast, anyway we only see people through agents, so everybody out. Hi, doll." She waved to me at the door, while lunging for another phone. "Grab a seat, he's expecting you. Everybody else, thanks for dropping by, but *out.*"

The appointment was for three o'clock. At three-twenty Rose ushered me into the inner sanctum. In a vain effort at comic relief, she imitated the blowing of a trumpet, which elicited no response from Max. Nor did I; apparently I was a nonpresence in his chamber.

He sat enthroned behind an ornate Louis XV desk, relic of some departed production, as were most of the room's furnishings. The size of the desk emphasized the round dimunitiveness of Max's form, although his stance indicated that he dominated *it,* by virtue of sheer dynamism. Ruby cuff links flashing, a host of expressions playing on the round, cherubic face, he was engaged in a duel on the phone. In classic style, it shifted from thrust to parry to *en garde* and back again. By not so much as a glance did he acknowledge my advent.

"Sidney, that I don't argue," he argued into the phone. "Bigger than Janet Gaynor someday. Bigger, who's to say, than Lillian Gish, Mary Pickford, but at the moment the general public is unacquainted with your Tilly Jones. *Maggie,* I stand corrected, and you, Sidney, if you'll permit me, are being ridiculous."

Not a glance in my direction, so I wandered among the exotic memorabilia of Max's office—a Chinese screen, a red-plush banquette suitable for a night club, a Victorian chaise, an antler coat tree, a pinball machine, all masked from daylight by thick brocade draperies at the windows. Dusty play scripts were piled on a gilt table, waiting to be returned to their agents, probably unread. Strewn across these were photographs of a young girl, an actress whose fate would be similar to the scripts. I drifted over to the collection of photos, citations and plaques that took up an entire wall of the office. It was at this point that the eminence at the desk more or less addressed himself to me.

"Sidney," he said into the phone, "excuse me while I consult with a stranger who just barged into my office." He clapped a hand over the receiver. "You, stranger, I'd like an opinion. The name Maggie Jones is familiar to you as a moviegoer?"

Before I could reply, he'd uncapped the phone. "Forgive me, my dear Sidney, but he never heard of her, which makes it unanimous. So please, why are we quibbling about salary?"

The photos on the wall starred Max in the company of various notables. Max with Eleanor Roosevelt, Max with Bernard Baruch, Gertrude Lawrence, Moss Hart, Cardinal Spellman. It was a photo of Max, his arm draped paternally over the shoulders of a young boy blowing out the candles on a birthday cake, that prompted me to move to the windows. Max continued on the phone: "Sidney, I'm offering this girl stage experience a fortune couldn't buy. How can you make salary demands? Explain." I stared down at the ticket line at the Majestic, thinking what a mistake it was to have come. I'd wait until Max was off the phone, present my apologies for having pulled out of the tour, then I'd leave and it would be over with.

Over with. Over with.

I swung away from the window, paced restively among the clutter. I halted at the table of manuscripts, and it was as if some blow to the body had arrested the breath in me. For a moment I stared at the photographs that spilled over the scripts, then slowly reached for them.

They were standard 8 × 11 glossies, duplicates of the same shot of a girl posed in a patio. Behind her were palm trees and white graceful arches; daisies grew at her feet, brushed at her gown. It was white, high-necked, tiered flounces of skirt . . . an old gown, with a quaintness about it that contrasted with her fashion-magazine looks. Her face was in three-quarter view, as though the camera had caught her by surprise in the act of turning. The dark silk-spun hair fell in wings, strands of it brushed at her face from the motions of turning. But it was not her face that so riveted my gaze.

It was her eyes, the look in her eyes that held my stare. Caught by the camera, taken unawares, she'd turned, chin uplifted, and the look in her dark eyes was . . . I could not define it, other than to say that I'd seen it before in some-one else's eyes.

Two things happened then. "Tell me, Sidney," I heard Max on the phone. "A girl I read on the Coast last week, a nobody, how has she turned into a valuable property?"

This was the girl, I speculated, about whom they were fighting. The girl in the photograph, and the eyes that gazed back at me from the California garden, the look in the eyes caught by the camera . . . Aunt Cash would have called it the look of the candy-bar club.

"So." The click of the phone diverted me back to the present. "So the prodigal returns." Max glared at me for what is known as a stage pause. He rose from the kingly desk, invoking as much majesty as his short stature, snazzy tailoring and built-up heels would allow. "So the ingrate actually dares to—" He interrupted the diatribe to cross to the door. "Mrs. Weintraub, airmail the contracts for the Jones girl immediately to the Coast," he commanded.

"The original figure. Some movie mogul! Unfortunately I knew him when he was Sid Hermanski, furrier.

"It's cast, the road company's set, I see no one without through an agent," he hollered and thrashed his hands at the actors in the outer office. He closed the door, and I was certain, fairly certain, that at least one role in the touring company had been set.

"Ingrate. Traitor." He advanced across the Bukhara to the wall of photos, singled one out for scrutiny. "Ah, yes, *The Pumpkins* . . . what was the occasion? A birthday party, yes, that I gave in honor of a boy in the cast. Off the streets, I took him, practically."

"It wasn't off the streets, Max," I pointed out. "Lifted from a Theater Guild show."

"Off the streets, a complete unknown," he waxed on, unperturbed. "Biggest boy's part since Tom Sawyer. We won't go into the salary I paid him. He was special to me, not merely for what he brought to the play." Skillfully he orchestrated the wrath in his voice. "More, much more, he was to me."

I cut in on him, not without skill myself, "Max, I came today to apologize."

"Much more." He pivoted around to confront me. "A son, he was, the son I never had, that was denied me." He broke off. "Apologize?"

"For backing out of the tour."

"A son, a son! Is that how a son rewards a father?"

"The other incident—I shouldn't have blamed you for it."

The avenging upraised hand froze. "What incident? To what do you refer?"

I looked at him a moment, posed like some Old Testament prophet. "The Saturday I came to your apartment," I said, "and you told the doorman you weren't at home. After all, you weren't obliged to see me."

"Out of this office," Max thundered, neatly sidestepping the incident. "Out, and take your apologies with you."

I remained standing at the table of manuscripts, the idea

forming, taking hold. "Part of why I reneged on the tour was to pay you back," I said to Max. "All these years later . . . maybe I have a chance to make up for it."

Max's eyes narrowed, sensing a shift in course. He took refuge in verbal abuse. "Half-drowned, Rosie said you looked the other night. A bum, you're turning into? Throw away your life, is that your ambition?" he raged.

I waited for the rage to subside, then said, "I walked out on you on one tour, Max. Give me the chance not to fail you again."

He gaped at me, as if I'd taken leave of my reason. "What nonsense are you talking? What tour?"

"The *Anniversary* tour. I realize there isn't a part for me except the delivery boy in the third act, but—" I forced myself to keep talking, lest the infusion of boldness dry up. "But he'd double as assistant stage manager, wouldn't he? I'd be good at that. You're right, Max. I'm turning into a bum, throwing my life down the drain. Why, the night I ran into Rose . . ."

It dried up at that point; I stood there while Max regarded me with almost a defeatist air. Another stage pause, less theatrical, closer to real. "The Saturday you refer to . . . important dinner that night," he said. "Guest of honor on the dais, I couldn't be late."

"Anyway, you weren't obliged," I said, and my voice shook slightly. "It was more my doing than yours . . . the father-and-son routine."

"Afterward, the change in your attitude . . . it crossed my mind that perhaps you saw me leave the apartment, a few minutes later."

"It doesn't matter. It's over with."

He puffed out his cheeks, as if in affronted protest. "Over with? I say when it's over with. Me, Max Jacobs, a string of hits I'll match against Sam Harris. John Golden." He strutted to the Louis XV desk, flicked the switch on the intercom.

"Mrs. Weintraub, prepare a contract, standard Equity minimum," he bellowed into the instrument. "What do you mean, who for? Have I got in my office Eddie Cantor?"

Then I was at the door, privately declaring myself certifiably insane while nodding and listening to Max's instructions. Rehearsal was in two weeks, April fourth; take home a script, arrange with Rose for a pass to the show, get familiarized with it.

"I will, Max. Yes. Right."

"A young man uncertain what to do with himself—a tour is a helpful experience. Different places, different people, different situations—it affords a whole new perspective."

"Right. I'm sure it will."

"But please, I beg you, Christopher." He thrust out a ruby-flashing hand. "Don't rob me in the bargain," and relieved me of what until then I was unaware I had appropriated.

"Little girl from Kansas. Harmon has her under contract." He bore the glossy of Maggie Jones over to the manuscript table. "But can she act? Soon we will see." He shrugged and tossed the glossy onto the others that spilled over the dusty accumulation of scripts.

April fourth was a Monday, and waiting at my breakfast plate that morning was a good-luck gift from Cash, placed there before she'd galloped off to Macy's.

It was a shiny red apple, tied with a red satin bow, and with a note in her impetuous slapdash scrawl. *Here's to happiness, kiddo, full steam ahead.*

Usually, apples were exchanged in the theater as good-luck tokens on opening night, but Cash had jumped the gun to the opening rehearsal, so convinced was she that I was aimed, or re-aimed, in the right direction at last.

But it was of something else that I thought, as I lifted the apple from the plate. I listened to the clatter of pots and pans in the kitchen: Soon, my mother would be without hearty breakfasts to prepare. I was leaving, but not in any of the ways I had anticipated. I ran a hand over the shiny red of Cash's apple and remembered Amos Feather's gift at the bus terminal the day I'd come home . . . and all at once the two apples made a link; they linked together the days in between, the days of going nowhere.

Linked them together, much as a line drawn between random points on a map traces out a route hitherto unseen —so that each moment of those days, each person and happening, Gray's and Mr. Ferguson, the temporary jobs, the city, Horton's and Wally Pfeiffer, the rain and Rose Weintraub . . . each had been a connecting link, leading me somewhere.

My mother accompanied me down the vestibule stairs, in a kind of prelude to my leavetaking. She kept to the bottom step and plucked at her apron, as held-back as ever.

"Well, I managed to get a few extra pounds on you. Off you'll go again—not a new adventure, exactly—"

"It will be," I said. "It will, Mama."

"Mustn't be late." She sounded a familiar echo, extricating herself from my arms. "Off you go, Christy. Go now."

"I'll see you tonight. It's not goodbye."

"No, of course."

I walked across the porch and down the steps, down the street, away from the cream-painted house. I rode the El to the city and made notations in the script in preparation for rehearsals, but at frequent intervals my glance wandered to the window and lingered there.

How could it be? How could you feel you knew someone whom you'd never seen before or met?

PART TWO

Maggie
1949

CHAPTER **4**

The rehearsal call was for ten o'clock; since my duties as assistant stage manager included setting up the stage for rehearsal, I was at the Garrick by nine-fifteen.

Willie, the stage doorman, recognized me the moment I came in from the alley. "Why, by Jove, look who's here. Taller, a' course, and not them big shoulders on you, but . . . how many years it been?"

Willie was as loquacious as ever, wore the same outfit of knitted vest, suspenders and pot-bellied pants. "Nine," I said. "Nine years, Willie."

"Why, say, you walkin' back in here makes it seem like time never passed."

"But it has, hasn't it?" I went along the passage to the fire door and onto the stage; memory steered me through the narrow clutter of the wings. I stowed my coat jacket on a stool at the light board, took a look at the clipboard list I'd made out of things to take care of. I then prodded myself onto the stage I'd sworn never to set foot on again.

Just a stage, really: a stage in an empty theater, and what theater did not include its share of ghosts? I moved in and out of the shadows cast by the naked work light, taking the muslin sheets from the furniture of what purported to be *The drawing room of the Prestons' townhouse in Gramercy Square*. It was a conventional set—center arch upstage, with stairs leading off; bay window at right, mantel at left, bookcases, tables and a good deal of chintz. The center arch was designed for grand entrances; a glazed mulberry chintz sofa was placed conveniently downstage left for intimate scenes, and the mantel would permit the actors any number of posings.

I folded the muslin sheets into a bundle and listened for the padded thud of the fire door that would signal the next arrival. The actors, like children intent on proving themselves the first day of school, would arrive early, but not this early. Anyway, get your mind off it. I carried the bundled-up sheets into the wings at stage right, halted at the soft thud of the fire door. I stored the sheets in a trunk designated for that purpose; from stage left, some affable cursing, then the border lights switched on, expunging the Prestons' drawing room from its shadows.

"Hi. How ya doing? When'd you get here, dawn?"

The owner of this voice, Chip Barrett, was maneuvering a battered kitchen-type table through the mask curtains at the left. He was stage manager for the tour; we'd met on one of my trips to Max's office. Chip Barrett was trim, kinetic, in his mid-thirties, and possessed of an easygoing manner, irreverent eyes and a ruined choirboy's face.

"Chris. Christopher. Which they call you?" He positioned the table—it would function as the prompt table—down left of the set. "What you'll get here is 'Kid—hey, kid, go get me a—' "

"I don't mind."

"Why'd you hold out on me?" From a briefcase he unloaded onto a table the tools of his trade: stopwatch, legal pads, pencils, scripts. "Rosie told me about *Pumpkins*. First show I saw in New York—you were damned good in it."

I was conscious of my voice floating in the empty theater. "That was a long time ago. After it closed, I—I left the business."

"Yeah, don't we all." He breezed around the set, inspecting the solidly constructed mantel, the columns that flanked the arch, the carved valance that curved above it. "Jesus, we'll have to cut the weight in half to travel it," he groaned. "Jesus, I swore I'd never go on the road again."

"Don't we all," I quoted back at him. It would be agreeable, working with Chip. "The itinerary's ideal—couple one-nights, then Boston, then Chicago for a run."

"Easy, you think?" He'd mosied into the wings, reappearing with another table. I helped him carry it to downstage center. "We've got problems already. The girl."

I felt my hands steal into my pockets. "Maggie Jones? The girl Max hired on the Coast?"

"Typical Hollywood name, twice as phony for trying not to be. Actually, she's only a problem because of Joel Baby."

Joel Lieber was the stage manager of the New York company of *Anniversary*. He was directing the road company, but the program credits would not list him as such. Stage managers were like understudies, forever champing to be unshackled from the anonymity of the wings.

"It's the usual gripe." Chip placed a water carafe and bottle of digestive tablets on the table. "Max won't give him billing, so he's playing it by going after the girl."

"Refused cast approval, that type of thing?"

"Bitching like hell she hasn't got a dime's worth of experience. Dumb Hollywood broad."

I heard myself defending someone I didn't know. "She might surprise him, turn out to be good."

"Not if Joel Baby can help it. He's out for her hide." Chip lit a cigarette, surveyed the progress we'd made so far. "Listen, I'm gonna hop over to the Piccadilly for coffee. Plenty of time yet, think you can carry on?"

"I made a checklist. Away for so long, thought I'd better."

"That's the stuff." He jumped neatly into the orchestra, snaked through a row of seats to the side exit doors. "This swearing off the road—it's the same with Arlene."

"Who's she?"

"Waitress at the coffee shop, incredible knockers." He unlatched the exit door and gave a wry shake of the head. "The minute I nail her, though, it'll be who's next. Why can't I settle down?"

With a grin, he sailed out into the blast of traffic noises. "Joel gets here, you'll know where to go for me."

Go for, Gofer. "The Piccadilly. Right."

The door shut behind him, wafting a current of April breeze toward the stage. The rows of empty, silent seats climbed in the shadows from the orchestra to the upper reaches of the balcony and the nymphs that chased one another across the painted ceiling. I went into the wings, where I'd left the clipboard list on the stool with my jacket. The pocket of the latter betrayed a slight bulge—emergency rations in the event that we broke late for lunch. Well, emergency Oh Henrys and Clarks is what they were. I resisted the urge to grab a munch and focused on the clipboard instead.

Breakables. I toured the set, removing the figurines and assorted bric-a-brac to the prop tables behind the flats. *Chairs.* Ten were needed for the ten actors, including understudies, who made up the cast of *Anniversary.* From the wings I hauled on the chairs by ones and twos and set them in a semicircle facing Joel's table. *In which would Maggie Jones sit?* A chair at the side, if I knew anything of her from the photographs.

What nonsense, what utter absurd poppycock. Jesus, but I took the cake. I mean, who could top me for fantasy trips? It was the story of my life. This morning, Cash's apple linking the days together, forget it, it's merely your rationale for the latest fantasy, the topper of them all.

Mouth a grim line, I set the last of the chairs in the semicircle on the stage, then heard, muted by the fire door, a salvo of greetings in the backstage entry.

The actors were arriving.

It was nine-thirty. I hurried back to the wings for the clipboard list, flicked the pages to the cast sheet. In Chip's absence, I prepared to greet them and check off their names as they appeared.

The bright talk wended closer, punctuated by the thud of the fire door; there were giggles and exclamations at the obstacle course of the wings.

"Mind the light cables, darlings. *So* musty and cramped, but isn't it heaven?"

"Otis Skinner opened the Garrick, you know. Dear Otis."

"*Here* we are, lambs. Lovely."

The mask curtains were parted by a tall, statuesque woman, who came toward me, swathed in silver fox. Her black hair was coiled in a chignon, a tiny veil hid the crow's-feet that marred the otherwise creamy complexion, and her smile asked only that she be adored, or failing that, kept ignorant of it.

"Hal*looo* . . . so pleased," Irene Vail, our leading lady, murmured throatily, in wafts of Shalimar, and turned to a patent-leather-haired Malibu-tanned gentleman in a polo coat, who was approaching. "Jack, sweet, come say hello to this charming young man, whoever he is. The bone structure of a Donatello, isn't he divine?"

"Delighted, old chappie. Dreadful bore, rehearsals." Jack Millet executed a nautical salute, two fingers to brow, which befitted the sailboats that skimmed across his necktie. Irene and Jack were film luminaries of the 1930's, the *early* 1930's; for several seasons they had devoted themselves to the road and summer stock, where they were said to be a draw. Jack was married, but not to Irene. They were a celebrated couple.

"But where is darling Max?" Irene inquired, while taking quick, expert inventory of the set. "I'm not sure I'm wild about the mulberry. What, Donatello?"

I repeated the information that Max was at a League meeting, which she at once relayed to the actress, small and round as a pincushion, who was advancing from the mask curtains.

"Not at rehearsal?" Grace Marsden had something of the startled look of a pincushion as well. "What a pity. Max has such wonderful authority," she proclaimed. Translated, this meant that the cast was to be spared Max's interference for the present. "Tony Ives, it can't be you," Grace cried, as a dapper, loose-jointed young man slithered through the mask curtains. "I haven't seen you since when, Skowhegan?"

"Ogunquit, the week Tallulah had to be restrained from going onstage nude," he replied.

Singly and in pairs, the road company of *Anniversary* assembled on the stage of the Garrick. I checked off their names on the cast sheet: the loose-jointed young man was Tony Ives, and close up he wasn't that young; Diana Knapp was crisply attractive, midway between ingenue and leading woman, which explained why she was an understudy. "Hi, I'm Scott Andrews," said the second male lead, built like a halfback, and he presented me with a card that read, *Hi, I'm Scott Andrews.* "Nice gimmick, huh? I distribute 'em by the hundreds. Till the movies grab me, I've got to do my own promo, correct?"

Like guests at a house party, the actors strolled the stage, explored the nooks and crannies of the Prestons' drawing room. To what degree they had schemed, plotted and agonized to win their current assignments was not evident in their behavior. Illusion was the actor's medium, and this superanimated house-party talk was his language of illusion.

"Go up?" went the swirl of chatter. "My dear, she went up every night out-of-town and couldn't be less bothered by it."

"Like it? Why thanks awfully. Hungarian chap on Rodeo Drive. Bill Powell put me on to him."

"Worlds improved. She found this marvelous chiropractor, you see, and—"

"Can you wait for Boston? I played *Apley* there and every night smack in the audience—"

Theater talk, the language of illusion: I'd never been adept at it. I circulated among the actors, provided ashtrays, distributed copies of the itinerary, a silent wrong note. There was another more fatal difference: I had never wanted beyond all else to be here on a stage.

"Is it who I think?" smiled Vi Henry, a slim, petite woman in her sixties, with fluffy white hair, sparkling eyes and a knitting reticule slung over her arm. "You're so very tall and grown-up, I wasn't sure at first."

"No, it's me." I checked off Vi's name on the list. She had joined *The Pumpkins* for the final weeks of the run and the tour. It was nine-forty-five; one name remained unchecked on the sheet.

"Did you get to Ireland that summer?" Vi Henry asked. "I remember you talked of nothing else."

"No, I didn't," I said. "The war broke out in Europe. It was the summer the war broke out."

"Egad, was *Pumpkins* that long ago?" boomed Ben Forbes, the stout, ruddy character man who had come in with Vi. "Good grief, how many years?"

"Nine. Nine years," I said, and excused myself to go over to Irene Vail. She was waving a chiffon handkerchief at me from the sofa, where she and Jack Millet were holding forth for a group.

"A little Hollywood person, I'm told," Irene was confiding to the group. "Selznick has her under contract, or is it Sidney Harmon? In any case, her very first role. Oh, Donatello, would you be a lamb?"

"Yes, Miss Vail?"

"Irene. You must call me Irene. Is that the property man's refrigerator I spied in the wings?" She unclicked a small, fitted Vuitton case and handed me a silver thermos and oilskin sandwich packet. "Our special Poland Water and pâté and watercress for lunch. It must be kept chilled."

"Certainly." I took the thermos and sandwich packet and escaped gratefully to the wings. The prop man's ancient Kelvinator was crowded up behind the flats at the pipe wall. The sandwich packet was tied with a red ribbon, like Cash's apple. The links of days leading somewhere . . . or nowhere, all over again.

The fire door whooshed open and Joel Lieber stalked in, looking put-upon. He combed a hand through his untidy wisps of fuzz and refused to be mollified by Chip, who followed at his heels.

"Max respects you. There'll be other shows, other credits," Chip attempted to soothe, to which Joel bleated, "Director? I'm a goddamn traffic cop, moving actors around. Cast approval? A laugh." He stalked past me, script under his arm, and onto the stage to an effusive chorus of welcome.

"Kid? How's it going?" Chip sidled over to me in the musty shadows. "Everybody check in?"

"Yeah. About."

He observed my hand, which was twisted around a pipe, and nodded at the hectic babble onstage. "That'll go on for another half hour. Scoot out and take a breather. Look as if you could use it."

"Thanks." I unwrapped my hand from the pipe. "Maybe I could."

"I recommend Arlene at the Piccadilly. Knockers like cantaloupes, I don't exaggerate."

Willie was sorting the morning mail in the key rack pigeonholes. "Yessir, by Jove, the minute you walked in," he eulogized, as I went slamming past him.

The stage door wheezed shut, and I stood on the iron-rung steps, at one end of the little cul-de-sac that was formed by the backs of the Majestic on one side and the Royale and Golden on the other. The rear of the Lincoln Hotel rose at the opposite end, and there the alley made a right angle past the Golden, tunneling out to Forty-fifth Street.

Alleys, blind alleys . . .

I slammed down the iron-rung steps, hurried past the peeling backs of the theaters, each with its shantylike stage entrance and cone-shaded bulb overhead. At night before curtain time, with the musicians tuning up, the stagehands jousting, and the dressing-room windows aglow like jack-o'-lanterns, the alley took on a gaudy magic. In the cold of morning, with the wind chasing bits and scraps over the pavement and rattling the fire escapes that hung above, its magic was in short supply. A dearth of magic, you could say.

I hunched my shoulders against the wind, fists jammed in pockets; I made the turn at the Golden up the remainder of the alley, and as I did, at the other end, a girl veered in from the street.

CHAPTER 5

More than veered—she burst upon the alley, a person dedicated to maximum haste. She was running, her face lifted, raincoat flaring out. In her arms she clutched a script and a leather pouch bag, held dangling by its straps. Her haste was causing a silk scarf to slip from her head; she was reaching to catch at it when she saw me. The thin hand lowered hesitantly.

"Excuse me," she said. "Excuse my ignorance, that's what it amounts to, but would you happen to know—?"

"The Garrick stage door?" I halted halfway up the alley. "The alley turns," I said, gesturing behind me. "You go left at the—"

"I asked the man in the box office—"

"Left at the turn," I went on, with gestures. "And there it is. The Garrick."

"Oh. I see."

That completed the dialogue for the moment. We looked at each other and, raising a hand, she untied the scarf from under her chin. "Well, I actually *got* here," she laughed nervously, shifting the pouch in order to fold the scarf. "Listen, when it's your first time in New York and—"

She gave a cry as, due to her juggling activities, the script went flying from her grasp. We both made a dive for it, hands colliding. The face, the incredible primavera face, raised itself to mine, inches away, and the dark eyes regarded me questioningly.

"I think it's always like that, don't you?" she said. "I mean, the first time with anything is usually the same."

I was gaping at her in the most awful calf-eyed manner that ever was. "The same what?" I asked, kneeling opposite her, wrestling with my gaze.

She quickly collected the script and stood up. If a similar paralysis had afflicted her, she'd recovered from it. "I mean, take New York," she rushed on, brushing at the wings of hair. "The moment I spied it from the plane yesterday—"

"It happened." I got to my feet, cuffed at my trousers. "Either it does or it doesn't, is what you're saying."

"The very first time, instantly." The eyes mirrored for an instant the same questioning look as in the photograph, then she was off and away on a description of her arrival in the city, replete with dramatic arm flingings, exclamations and astonished sighs. "The skyscrapers, the sheer profusion of them, reaching up to practically touch the plane! The drive from the airport, well, I wouldn't call that part thrilling—"

"Nobody does," I interjected. "What we call it is Queens."

"But then all at once you see it again, the city, only much closer, and you can't believe any of it! Fifth Avenue, Rockefeller Center, the Waldorf Astoria! You don't know which way to look! It's all you'd expected—no, it isn't, it's more—and so much that you didn't expect, such as the houses."

"Houses?"

"Across from my hotel, the Barbizon—know where it is? East Sixty-something—well, right across from it is this row of houses, the most darling little—" The recital, portions of which had been addressed to the street, the skyline, the alley and the posters slabbed along it, was abruptly cut off. "I'm sorry," she said, turning to me. "I—I tend to rattle on."

The calf-eyed stare was threatening again, like a nervous tic. "Uh, probably you're referring to . . . brownstones," I offered.

"Yes, but wouldn't you think, considering all the movies

with New York scenes, that at least one would show—" She gave a rueful laugh, as if catching herself at an old game, and flopped back against the alley wall. "See? Didn't take me long." She shook her head.

"I don't—?"

"Even yesterday, with the plane right over the city, my immediate thought was, Will they have *Waterloo Bridge*?" She folded the silk scarf, slipped it in the pouch bag. "Naturally, you've seen it."

"The bridge?"

She laughed and the wings of hair swung as she glanced up at me. "No, the movie. Vivien Leigh, Robert Taylor, MGM?" she clued. "World War I, she's a dancer, they meet in an air raid?" She paused. "Not only haven't you seen it, you've never heard of it."

"Sorry."

"To me, it's the all-time champ. Also the bane of my existence. Nome, Alaska, and I'd go."

"You keep tracking it down, you mean?"

"To put it mildly, except it always shows up too soon or too late. For instance, yesterday when I left L.A., what did I spy in the movie ads, starting Wednesday at the—" She broke off again and in her eyes was the look in the photographs, of being caught unaware. "Rattling on, and I haven't even introduced myself," she apologized.

My voice had a rough edge, like stone scraping over glass. "I think I know who you are. You're Maggie Jones," I said.

"The prize, isn't it? A whole studio, an entire publicity department to name me, and I wind up as—" The primavera face registered belated surprise. "How did you know?"

"I'm the assistant stage manager for the tour. Your name's on the cast sheet."

"Oh." She nodded, then another thought prompted her to check her wristwatch. "Rehearsal's at ten, isn't it? I didn't get it wrong?"

"Ten, which it isn't yet," I said, to ease the quick leap of distress.

"They didn't send you out looking for me? Listen, it's okay." She backed up the alley, a hand thrust out. "You can level with me. In this life—I'm quoting my mother—the good is mixed with the bad and—"

"Look, I absolutely—"

"I'm a strong-minded person able to deal with both. Also, if I keep backing up—" She glanced over her shoulder. "I'll end in the street under a truck. Oh, terrific."

I remember that I sprang forward, hearing again the scream of brakes on Second Avenue the night in the rain. The sudden lunge startled as well as puzzled Maggie Jones; then a smile, clear as spring water, broke over her face.

"You too?" she asked. "I mean, trucks grinding over people—you tend to expect the worst?"

"Well—"

"Listen, so do I, but I have this formula I developed against it."

"I could use it," I said. "I tend to think I could use it."

She nodded and gave a wave of her hand. "Well, apart from a truck, what's the worst that can happen to me right now? See, you have to ask yourself that—and the answer, in my case, isn't that I'd get fired from the play."

"No?"

"Supposing I did—I'd still have the contract with Mr. Harmon. What if he dropped my option—the worst?"

I was mired hopelessly in staring. "Er, you could get another contract," I lobbed a reply.

"And if not, I'd have money to keep me going. If that ran out, I could get a job. The point is, there *is* no worst, so why get into an enormous tizzy? See?"

"I see."

"Naturally, like any formula, you have to work at it," she qualified, with a shake of her head. "Which, if you want to know, is what I've been doing for the past hour, at the drugstore on the corner."

I looked at her. "You've been in the Astor drugstore for the past hour?"

"Timing was part of it. Look a fool to show up a whole hour early." She sighed and pulled at her raincoat. "Plus I had qualms, large ones, about my dress."

"What's wrong with it?" She buttoned the coat over the dress, the yellow dress that peeped from under it. "It's a lovely dress."

"A summer dress, really. Why I picked it to wear is beyond me. Totally beyond me." She buckled the belt firmly, brushed at her hair. "What I'm saying is it took a while to get the formula working. Five cups of coffee, in fact."

It was inconceivable to me that, given that face, she could worry about her appearance. But then she glanced past me at the alley, to where it turned, and her eyes might have been estimating the location of a guillotine or a hangman's noose. I thought of what Chip had said about Joel Lieber and his number-one gripe.

"Well," said Maggie Jones, slinging the pouch bag over her shoulder, with a nod at the alley. "Turn left, is it?"

"I—I came out for a breather, that's all," I told her. "I mean, I'm going back in . . . and I'd be glad to show you the way."

She clasped the script to her. "All right."

I stepped back and she went ahead of me down the alley. She didn't speak until we'd made the turn at the Golden, into the cul-de-sac. "You haven't told me your name," she said.

"That's right, I haven't. Casey. Christopher Casey."

"It's sort of reversible, isn't it. You could be Casey Christopher just as easily."

"Most of the time I'm not sure who I am. I mean, a certain confusion seems to exist."

We were approaching the iron-rung steps. She stopped suddenly and rummaged furiously in the ample pouch bag. Much searching and clinking of objects, but at last she extracted a safety pin to which was attached a small gold medal.

"My friend, Joe Scully, gave me this in L.A. before I

boarded the plane," she said. "Maybe that's who you are."

I took the medal which she held out, and examined it. *Papa, wait, you forgot your coat.* "I'm afraid I'm not related to Saint Christopher," I said, and handed the medal back to her.

"He protects travelers, doesn't he?" Maggie Jones rejoined. "Well, I'm a traveler, and look what you've done for me." She turned and faced the iron-rung steps. "Without you I seriously doubt I'd have made it through that door."

And with that, and a fine assertive nod, she went up the steps and in the stage door of the Garrick . . . to what was to be for her that day a guillotine.

Affecting an airy disregard, she preceded me through the fire door onto the stage. She stood in the musty dimness, gazed up at the fly ropes that dangled high overhead, and the gallows aspects of it did not elude her. Her gaze strayed down to the tentlike structure of flats that comprised the *Anniversary* set, from which sallied laughter occasioned by Joel Lieber's preliminary remarks to the cast. The rehearsal was about to get under way.

"As I say, it's a question of getting the formula going," Maggie Jones espoused her creed. "What's the worst that could happen? Fired? Wrong."

She listened to the onstage comments for a few lagging moments, then took charge of herself. She crossed downstage, plunked bag and script on a prop table, and took off the raincoat.

Her dress was made of sunlight. "Filched from wardrobe," she confided to me. "It was designed for Gene Tierney—*Obbligato*, this movie the studio just finished shooting—wrapped, as they call it, and—"

She was intent, as she spoke, on the remarks that could be heard from the other side of the flats. "Everybody quieted down? Scripts open?" inquired Joel Lieber. "Despite the absence of one or two of us, why don't we begin?"

I started toward her. "Second day in New York—we'll tell him the taxi took you to the wrong theater."

"*No*." The refusal was sharp and incisive. She looked at me, her eyes declining assistance. She took a comb from the bag, ran it through her hair. Then, gathering her script, raincoat, she crossed behind the flats to the wings at stage left. She stood in the wings at the mask curtains, and out on the stage, heads turned in unison from the semicircle of chairs, to note her arrival. Joel was slouched at the director's table. He stood up, beckoned to her.

"Ah, Miss Hollywood and Vine," was his greeting. "Where you going in that outfit, honey, on a hayride?" and the blade sliced down.

Throughout the morning, to the embarrassment of the other actors, it sliced down on her with what became predictable regularity. Each time she was responsible for a lapse in the cast's reading of the play, Joel's refrain was "Hear that, folks? Miss Hollywood and Vine is sorry again. So am I, honey, so am I."

It was stupid behavior on Joel's part, and self-defeating, but the stage manager who was content with his lot was a rare specimen. The job brought with it the headaches of a production and few of the rewards. Nobody clapped for a stage manager; he didn't take bows. He might get to direct summer stock productions and college groups, and for a few hundred dollars the road editions of a Broadway success. But he was seldom credited with his work in the program: The billing was reserved by the original director. The typical stage manager either acquiesced to this, or he gnashed his teeth, and acquired ulcers, along with a thickening residue of anger. Joel was permitting his anger to spill loose on an ideal ready-made target for it. The principal effect of his anger, however, was to bog down the rehearsal.

"Cue for Miss Hollywood," he screamed, over and over, as the cast toiled through what he had intended to be a preliminary reading of the script. "We're waiting, Miss Hollywood. What goddamn page you on? Lost your place again?"

"Here it is. I'm sorry."

"She's sorry again. You and me, baby, you and I both.

Chip," he bawled at the table where Chip and I were stationed. "Throw her the goddamn cue."

Maggie Jones sat out to the side in the semicircle of chairs, devoutly willing invisibility upon herself. That she was inexperienced as an actress was glaringly evident in her faltering reading of lines, dropped cues, and in the faint wisp that had replaced her voice.

"Can't hear, can't hear." Joel pounded the table. "Christ, what were you doing on the Coast, picking oranges?"

"Opening supermarkets," she volunteered, back. "I mean, that's the terrific extent of it so far." If her role was to be that of company idiot, she seemed to be saying, so be it. "Van Nuys, Sherman Oaks—I don't even get Beverly Hills," she contributed further comedy. "Strictly the valley."

"How boring and trivial," responded Joel, with a yawn. "Take it again from your entrance."

"You mean, when I—?"

"Your *entrance*. Your goddamn entrance in the goddamn first scene in the goddamn first act."

She took it again from her entrance, and since invisibility was not conferred on her, nor the floor going to open to ingest her, she compromised: she kept hanging on to where she was. She did not collapse in a faint or flee in tears. Pale, taut, despairing, yet uneradicated, she hung on while the reading, and the morning with it, dragged along.

There might not have been a lunch break, if at two o'clock Willie Olsen had not shuffled out from the wings. "Mr. Jacobs on the phone," he informed Joel. With a groan, the latter stalked across the stage; he paused, looked at his watch. "Shall we send Chris for sandwiches, gang? It'll have to be a quickie."

The actors stampeded the prompt table like victims rescued from a shipwreck. The orders flew, I struggled to copy them down.

"Dr. Brown's, if it's iced, otherwise Pepsi."

"*Seeded* rye, heavy on the mustard."

"Do you suppose they'd have Stilton? If not . . ."

I jotted down the orders, in my capacity as gofer. I took the bills that were being waved at me like flags, noted the amounts; and through the waving bills, the crush at the table, I took note of the lone dweller in the semicircle of chairs.

Her sole bid for invisibility was the raincoat, which she'd pulled over her shoulders. She betrayed no other evidence of her recent ordeal. The script was propped on her lap, and she was using it as a writing board on which to get some postcards on their way, like any tourist new to the city. She plied her fountain pen and not once did she glance up from her task.

It was from consideration, not indifference, that the actors had left her to herself. Given the beating she had taken, they too would have chosen solitude. She looked as alone and somehow as defenseless as anyone I had ever seen.

I collected the last dollar bill, scribbled the last *White, no mayo,* and I then went over to the semicircle of chairs. The pen continued its travels, launched upon another card, a view of the Stock Exchange. Behind us the actors were strolling about and chatting, house-party guests once more.

"Probably, if I ventured a guess," I said to Maggie Jones, "I'd guess you were the cottage-cheese type. With maybe pineapple."

The pen wavered, but she didn't reply. "That's the Stock Exchange." I nodded at the postcard in her hand.

"This?" She held it up, her hand trembling, and laughed. "What on earth can I write about the Stock Exchange?" She lowered the card to her lap. A silence, then: "Listen, instead of cottage cheese, make it a Baby Ruth."

"A what?" I stared incredulously at her.

"On second thought, change it to an Oh Henry."

I made every effort to sound as if I were participating in an ordinary conversation. "To the connoisseur," I said, "there's a subtle but decided difference between Oh Henrys and Baby Ruths."

"The chewiness factor, as with Butterfingers," agreed

Maggie Jones, and swung around in her chair. "Of course, Walnettos are the one unpardonable. The total dregs."

The words leaped from me. "You know about Walnettos?"

"At the movies, every slot in the machine can be empty," she elucidated. "Raisinets, Milk Duds, even the Jujubees."

"Even the Fruit Chunkys," I put in.

"But never the Walnettos. I used to swear to myself that someday . . ." She gazed up at the dark, empty balcony and let the sentence trail away.

"Someday what?"

"Well, I'd get about two dollars' worth of dimes and feed them in the Walnetto slot, on the chance that . . ."

"What?"

"Sounds so stupid." She fiddled with the postcards, shuffled them on her lap. "On the chance that a Milky Way got in by mistake . . . which, all things considered, isn't very likely."

I looked at her and all of it added up, my instinct hadn't been wrong, not from the moment I'd spied the photographs. "To club members," I said, "it's a definite likelihood, not to be discounted."

"Club?"

"Sort of a club. I'm a member, not always in good standing, but—"

It was as far as I got with the explanation. Irene Vail was signaling me from the center-arch stairs, where she was fetchingly encamped with Jack Millet. "Do be an angel, Donatello. Poland Water, so beneficial for the tum-tum."

"Right away, Miss Vail."

I went rocketing to the Kelvinator in the wings, but when the thermos and sandwich packet were delivered, there were still the take-out orders to attend to. Before loping to the delicatessen, however, I delved in the herringbone jacket and made a brief detour to the semicircle of chairs.

She'd drawn the raincoat over her shoulders, retired to some private place within herself, as she steered the fountain pen over another of the postcards. *Mrs. Ida Belton, 140 Dakota Street, Clarion, Kansas,* she wrote; then under the message, which she'd forgotten to sign . . . *Janya,* she inscribed.

She did not look up or acknowledge my presence, and I contented myself with depositing the orange-wrapped Clark bar on the chair alongside her. "Not a Milky Way, but adequate till one turns up," I said, and hurried off to the deli around the corner on Eighth Avenue. There, as I stood at the counter waiting for the orders to be filled, I tried to puzzle out the riddle of what in Maggie Jones's life could have qualified her for the candy-bar club. It was hard to imagine that primavera face consigned to the ranks of so tattered a band of outcasts . . . how could it be?

It wasn't, I learned before the week was out: She had been happily spared any incidents to qualify her for membership. From what she told me of her placid growing-up years in the small Kansas town of Clarion, the strongest epithet that could be leveled against it was, "uneventful."

Except for one event, that is, which appeared to link us startingly together . . .

By Thursday, rehearsals had settled into an orderly and productive routine, due to certain changes in attitude.

On Tuesday, to the company's surprise, the rebellious, foul-tempered Joel Lieber had been replaced by a notably agreeable Joel, dedicated to assisting his actors in their difficult chores.

Chip's theory in regard to the change was that Max, having gotten wind of Monday's stormy debacle, had summoned Joel for an amicable chat, to wit: Do the job or get out. Tuesday morning Max was conspicuous by his presence at the Garrick, rather than by his absence; and after a round of hand-kisses for the ladies of the cast and fervent hand-clasps for the men, he'd graciously turned the stage over to Joel.

The gist of Joel's opening remarks that second morning was that he'd set one goal and one goal only for himself:

the sending forth of the best company ever to take to the road.

"So how about it, folks? Shall we roll up our sleeves and get to work? I'm ready if you are."

This was received with admirable equanimity by the cast, but at the prompt table Chip had grunted to me, "Poor stupid sonovabitch. Max must've really shafted him. Oh, brother"—he nudged me—"look what's going on with Miss Hollywood and Vine."

Joel, a protective arm shielding her, was promenading the stage with Maggie Jones. Back and forth in gentle conference, she listening in dumbfounded astonishment—and when Joel had commenced rehearsal by getting the actors "on their feet" to block the first act, and Maggie was late on her entrance cue: "Not to worry, sweetheart. Take it again, and remember, I'm here to help you."

"Oh, brother," whistled Chip at the prompt table, and as an afterthought: "Listen, I'm thinking of taking a crack at Diana Knapp. Nice ass, yuh notice?"

By Thursday Joel was into blocking the third act of *Anniversary*, and his revised treatment of Maggie Jones was beginning to pay dividends. Gone was the wispy treble of the first day, replaced by a clear, rushing brook of a voice, refreshing to the ear; the careful, drama-coach diction was edged with a prairie flatness that lent it an appealing naturalness. She had yet to learn projection, and her lack of stage technique continued to be apparent; she was tentative, awkward, unsure of herself; she didn't know how to sustain or build a scene, allowed the other actors to take it from her. Yet despite these limitations the glimpses of an actress were to be seen; and were it only the barest glimpse, there was the compensation of her looks, the extraordinary primavera face that exerted its own special magnetism . . . and was, in other respects, off-putting.

Off-putting to the company, none of whom appeared to know, beyond the standard interchanges, quite what to do with Maggie Jones. Her pluckiness the first day had won their respect but not their intimacy. She was the outsider among them, an unlikely creature materialized from a

Hollywood dream factory, ephemeral and unreal, in their midst temporarily; on loan, so to speak. They were polite and friendly enough, but they did not invite her to join them on lunch breaks; no one cozied up for a chat with her in the wings between scenes.

Or was it the reverse? Was it she who maintained a distance from them, under the guise of preoccupation with rehearsals, the novice intent on learning her craft? Off in a corner she'd sit, the wings of hair fanned over the ever-scrutinized script . . . so quiet and unobtrusive that she might almost not be there.

And with me . . . what was she with me? I could not make sense of it. Friendly, you couldn't call her unfriendly. Each morning before rehearsal, a friendly stop-off at the prompt table to relate her latest New York discovery —the antique shops on Third Avenue, the film collection at the Museum of Modern Art. "You can't guess what they're showing next Tuesday. Bette Davis in *Dangerous*— it never turns up in L.A. Never!"

"I—I've been checking *The Times* for *Waterloo Bridge*. No luck so far."

"It's fated, I tell you—the day after we get to New Haven, bingo." Shifting the pouch straps: "There's Mr. Lieber. Well, better run over my lines . . ."

Since the Garrick stage was required for a performance every night, rehearsal broke up not later than six. Another friendly stop-off at the prompt table, before departing for the alley.

"Ever heard of the Cosmopolitan Club? Miss Breal's taking me there for dinner and some sort of lecture."

Miss Breal was Sidney Harmon's New York representative; a formidable lady with a Bryn Mawr accent and terrifying poise, she'd collected Maggie backstage the first night and borne her away. "Dear, it wants only an egg basket to go over the arm," said Miss Breal of the yellow dress. "You'll have to change it." Miss Breal and the Barbizon for Women: Sidney Harmon was keeping an eye on his property.

"It's a woman's club, I think," I told her.

"Fancy?"

"It's not the Y, you could say."

"I'll be a wreck."

Friendly exchanges, but in them not a trace of the impact that had chimed and reverberated between us the first day, before either had spoken a word. Perhaps it was only I who had felt it, and assumed it to be so on her part. I thought no, then yes, and did not know what to do about it, whichever the case was . . . and when Maggie Jones whisked off for an evening at the Cosmopolitan Club, she betrayed no hint of what had admitted her to a less fashionable, considerably more ragtag association.

There was only my instinct to go by, but on Thursday I was granted a clue, or what in open-mouthed shock I interpreted as such.

I was the last to quit the Garrick at night, for the same reason that I was the first to report in the morning. If the stage had to be set up for rehearsal, it had also to be restored to its proper state before the evening performance. One bibelot not returned to its appointed position, one delinquent coffee container left on a table, and there were screams from the Property Master.

It was six-thirty by the time I said good night to Willie—"By Jove, Christy, it's like old times havin' you around"—and shuffled up the alley to Forty-fifth Street. With nightfall the string of playhouses—those that were tenanted: the Imperial, Music Box, Plymouth, Booth and Morosco—were stirring to life in a shimmer of marquee light, brightly bathed lobbies and the jingle of box-office phones, impatient with ticket requests. By eight-thirty the street would be a hopeless, horn-blaring tangle of traffic, the pavements solid with theatergoers, but this was its children's hour, the quiet before the uproar. I went past the Booth and Shubert Alley, headed toward Broadway and the eternal B.M.T. (No, I'd be bidding it goodbye in two weeks), and as I neared the Astor Hotel on the corner I felt my steps slow.

Maggie Jones was standing outside the Astor drugstore.

She was backed up against the windows, out of the sidewalk jostle, and was consulting a map. A tourist map of New York, I saw it was, as I laggingly moved closer. The wail of a police siren on Broadway pulled her eyes from the map; she glanced up, straight into my path.

She looked at me a moment as she had in the alley, then smiled and called over the din, "Just found out that Broadway's crooked."

I went up to her in a curious rubbery gait. "You mean, geographically or in spirit?"

"Undoubtedly both," she laughed, explaining that she'd gone to the Harmon office in the Paramount building to meet Miss Breal, only to be told to proceed instead to the Plaza Hotel. "So I was trying to figure how to walk there," she finished, with a plaintive nod at the map.

"Well, the Plaza's up at—" the map was spilling its accordion folds "—at Fifth and the park." I caught hold of the folds and pointed at the location. "It's right there."

"Oh, yes."

I stood close against her, our heads nearly touching, and was peculiarly short of breath. "So what you want to know is the best route by foot."

"Yes."

"Well," I said, clearing my throat. "Well, several routes, and although it's true that Broadway angles west . . ."

"It does, doesn't it." She pointed at the errant, caterpillar path.

"Still, if you haven't strolled up Broadway at night . . ." A last final clearing of throat. "I'm headed in that general direction. I could walk with you, if you'd like."

She kept her eyes focused on the map. "I wouldn't be taking you out of your way?"

"No. Absolutely. I guarantee."

She folded the map, returned it to the pouch. "All right, then." She swung the bag over her shoulder, we moved from the drugstore windows, and whether it was shyness that had caused her to hesitate, or reluctance—whatever her reason—it vanished at the spectacular sight that loomed before us.

Broadway at night was a blazing bonfire, a brilliant conflagration of electric signs and movie marquees that raged out of control from the juncture at Times Square up through the canyons to the Fifties. The huge illuminated waterfall over Bond's cascaded down in a torrential flood; its neighbor, the Camel sign, blew gigantic smoke rings out over the surging crowds. The giant electric signs—Coca-Cola, Benrus, Gillette, Canadian Club—made their own constellations in the night sky, and from the Criterion at Times Square to the Hollywood at Fifty-second, the movie palaces strung a glittering necklace of lights, jeweled crowns, diadems, competing for the hordes of entertainment shoppers.

Confronted with this spectacle roaring and blazing down at her, Maggie Jones was struck silent with awe, like a pilgrim at a shrine reached after a long and arduous journey.

We turned at the corner, started up through the dazzle, past the Astor and Victoria theaters, Childs' restaurant and the Automat. Some thought of pigrimages must have occurred to her, for, clasping the *Anniversary* script to her, she said, "First night in L.A. I went walking along Hollywood Boulevard—can't compare with this, naturally, but I'd never seen anything like it before."

She lifted her face, and in the garish neon whirl of that carnival midway it was carved crystal, flawlessly cut, set with the dark, brilliant stones of her eyes, the rose marble of her lips. "Went gawking past the Egyptian and Grauman's Chinese," she went on, the Kansas flatness stealing over the careful diction. "And I said to myself, 'Janya, you've sure come a long way from the Alhambra.' "

"The Janya part I know—it's what you sign on your postcards home—"

"Short for Virginia, with about a hundred flat *a's*."

We walked past a phonograph store, from which blared a recording of Frank Sinatra crooning "That Old Black

Magic." "But what's the Alhambra?" I asked. "Wait, I bet I can—"

"Correct," she laughed. "Clarion's one and only movie house. Two shows daily, three on Saturdays. Change of feature twice a week."

"Sounds like you were a good customer."

"The leading customer in town. Easily." She glanced down at her moccasin-shod feet moving along the sidewalk. "Of course, you have to take into account there wasn't a large variety of amusements."

We went past the Strand, which was displaying giant blowups of Doris Day, as well as her name in foot-high lights. Across the street were the B.M.T. stairs, which I was pleased to let recede behind us. I wasn't, as in the months past, alone; I was with Maggie Jones, and my steps were light and buoyant, in no haste to reach the Plaza.

"I guess you always envy what you don't have," I remarked. "I'm strictly a city kid, from the cradle on up—"

"Also, which you fail to mention, the finest child actor on Broadway."

I turned to her. "Where'd you hear that?"

"Miss Henry told me about the play she was in with you."

"She did?" It was out of proportion, the elation I felt at having figured in her conversation. "Anyway, I went through this phase where I yearned to live in a small town."

"Was it before or after you read *Huckleberry Finn*?" she laughed.

"I own up to it. Shortly after. In fact, during."

She smiled, her gaze cast downward, hair dipping over a cheek. "There's really not much to tell about Clarion," she said after a moment. "Houses. Main Street. Everything the same every day. Our sole distinction—" she brushed the hair from her face—"is that we're on the main line of the Santa Fe. The big Sunday activity was to go down to the depot and watch the Chief go by. You know, the famous Coast train."

"Trains," I said, gesturing with unusual sweep. "Train whistles calling across the countryside—you don't get any of that in a city."

She nodded, silent and pensive, the crowds carrying us past the theaters and restaurants, Keeno arcades, Pina-Colada stands and second-floor dance-hostess halls. "That's what a small town is," she said quietly. "It's listening to a train whistle at night and thinking how different it'd sound if you were on it."

Her words seemed to echo up the light-bedazzled canyon, lonely and haunting, like a wind from the prairie, but then her voice was lilting with excitement. "Imagine being on a train like the Chief," she said. "Imagine the dining car! The silver gleaming on the white cloth, fresh flowers, the scenery rushing past the window—oh, I'm sure nothing can equal it!"

"I take it you've given the matter thought."

"Well, as I was saying about Clarion, every day the same —no, I have no right to complain. It was a pleasant place to grow up." She gave a firm assertive nod. "Neighbors, church socials, picnics, books and books in the library—and Mama." She lifted her face to the blaze of lights, illumined by it. "Best mama in the world. Always raced home after school, couldn't wait for the sight of her! Plain little house, but with an azalea tree out back, and in the spring I'd sit under it with a book . . ." She gestured for emphasis. "No, I have no cause for complaint."

There was something as yet left out, omitted from the cozy, homespun picture, and I waited for her to supply it. The crowds had thinned out now that we'd reached Fifty-third Street, past the movie theaters and restaurants. Ahead, Broadway veered west, populated with automobile showrooms and dingy hotels.

"Every day the same, but one day you're suddenly graduating from high school," she continued animatedly. "I remember thinking, as I went up to receive my diploma, how fortunate I was, on the whole. Eighteen years, and I couldn't single out any real hardship or . . ."

She paused, as if to reconsider the last statement. "That's not exactly so," she amended. "There was one terrible blow we had, but even then I was spared the brunt of it."

"What?" I asked, a ringing in my ear. "What happened?"

"Spared in the sense of age, I mean."

"What was it?" I asked again.

She continued at her musing, pensive pace, the script hugged to her. "When I was five, not quite five, a few months short of it," she said, "Mama and I . . . we lost my father."

I stood rooted to the sidewalk, struck as if by a hammer blow. "Funny word for death," I said, the ringing louder in my ear. "*Lost*, as though you'd misplaced him, left him by mistake at the A&P."

She swung around, several lengths up the sidewalk. "Your father died?"

"When I was older than you. Seven."

"I'm so sorry."

"Listen, it happens." I shrugged awkwardly. "They used the same word, *lost* . . . at seven it can put crazy notions in your head."

She looked over the dark pavement at me. "Lost, so go find him again?"

I was shaking; no reason for it, none. "Thankfully, I grew out of such notions," I said. "Imagine if I'd kept on looking for him. Swell kettle of fish—a candidate for the couch."

She looked at me, and her expression was unfathomable. "Being so little . . . you see, I have no memory of my father," she said. "Or didn't after a few years. It was like—" she groped for an analogy "—like a snapshot that kept fading, until finally it was blank."

"Yes, well . . ." There was a strange, elusive shift in her, a drawing away, though she stood unmoving, chin lifted. "In the long run you're better off, not remembering," I said.

She shook her head, gestured helplessly. "A blank where my father ought to be? I doubt how good it is. Except," she added, after a pause, "that's *how* it is."

Then, with a gasp, she lowered her eyes to her wristwatch. "Good grief, it's seven-thirty. I'm supposed to be at the Plaza—fifteen minutes ago." She turned, scanned the four corners of Broadway. "Is it much farther? How far?"

It had returned, the distance between us that during the brief walk had magically lifted. "If it's a question of late"— I flagged the Checker that was rounding the corner— "you're best off with a taxi."

"Really? What a nuisance. I was having such a nice—" The taxi pulled up; I held open the door while she got in. "Can I drop you? You didn't say where you're going, but—"

"Subway. Down a few blocks, but thanks." With an ache, I shut the taxi door. "Don't forget to be careful of trucks."

"Scuse me?" Then she remembered what she'd said in the alley. "Oh, that, yes, I'll be careful."

"See you tomorrow. First-act line call." I swung away, hands in pockets, back down Broadway toward the electric bonfire.

"Christopher?" Her hand gripped the taxi window, the dark eyes watched as I retracked to the curb. "Just wanted to tell you . . . I liked our walk. You're very nice, a very nice person."

"Yeah," I said. "Kind to animals and help old ladies across the street."

"I . . . see you tomorrow." The hand left the window; she leaned forward to the driver, and the taxi, releasing a snorting plume of exhaust, was gone.

But not her, not Maggie Jones.

On the subway ride to Queens, the swaying car plunged and racketed through the tunnel and the image of her face flickered like a candle flame on the grimy window before me. It flickered there, as haunting and far-off as the cry of the train whistle she'd listened to at night on the prairie.

Maggie Jones.

Janya.

The more I knew of her, the less I seemed to know of her. Only this could I not be dissuaded from believing: that somewhere a link existed between us, and that when I found it I'd find her. Then there'd be no distances any more.

New Haven. Two weeks. The train wheels clacked in the sooty tunnel, and I wasn't alone: the candle of her face shone before me, lighting the way.

CHAPTER 6

The tour of *Anniversary* opened at the Shubert in New Haven on Tuesday, April 26, and the wonder of it was that it opened at all.

I rode up from New York at dawn in the scenery van. This was at the behest of Abel Klein, company manager for the tour, who wished to discourage the drivers from leisurely stopovers en route. Unhappily, it did not discourage a carburetor breakdown five miles south of Stamford; as a consequence, it was closer to noon than to ten o'clock by the time we chugged off the parkway at the New Haven exit.

The question, as we drew up to the Shubert on College Street, was *Where is everybody?* The marquee duly announced the coming night's event, but the box office wasn't open yet, nor was the house porter in evidence. The reception committee outside the theater consisted solely of a child, a girl of seven or eight, who returned my queries with stubborn silence. A little sparrow of a creature on matchstick legs, homely of face, with spikes of hair protruding from a pulled-down knitted cap, wearing a droopy skirt and a bulky, ragamuffin sweater that threatened to capsize her spindly frame, her only reply was to stare belligerently and insert a thumb into the thin little wedge of a mouth.

"I just thought you might have seen them," I explained once again. "The men, the crew that's supposed to be here to unload the scenery. They're supposed to be here, you see, and—"

For a moment the flinty gaze of her rabbity eyes wavered, but then, thumb corked firmly in mouth, she turned heel and made off down the sidewalk at a demon speed, to vanish, reeling, around the next corner.

Where was the crew? Why, in a luncheonette down the street, from which they presently ambled and shuffled forth. This was the local crew, but they were led by Frank Merkle and Eddie Ruick, property man and electrician, respectively, for the tour. Completing the ensemble was Frank's wife, Edith, our wardrobe mistress, who took upon herself the role of spokeswoman.

"Where the bloomin' dickens you been?" she demanded, with a show of temperament for which her sisterhood was not unnoted. "Chrissake, we been hangin' around for hours. Where's my bloomin' costumes?" She barged up to the van. "I don't want nobody layin' a finger on 'em but me."

The logistics of all this, as plotted by Abel Klein, had the scenery van arriving by nine A.M., to be met by a crew instantly alerted to unload the Prestons' drawing room (its grandeur modified for purposes of travel) and set it up on the Shubert stage. The logistics called for the set to be up by the time the actors were on hand for a runthrough at one o'clock.

They'd arrived by train from New York at noon, as scheduled. However, what with confusions over luggage and checking into the Taft Hotel, combined with the state of their nerves and the need for sustenance—no food had been available on the train—they did not actually troop into the Shubert until one-forty-five.

That's what my watch read when, turning from the pandemonium on the stage—the crew hoisting flats, lashing ropes, wheeling on packing cases and stacked dollies of furniture—I observed the subdued procession migrating down the aisle.

"Mauve," cried Irene Vail, spying the mulberry chintz

sofa. "Why couldn't Max have given me mauve with lavender accents? It was naughty of him."

"Great thunder, the set's not up by half," boomed Ben Forbes, a muffler wound theatrically round his throat. "How in heaven are we to do the runthrough?"

Maggie Jones offered no comment. She stood slightly back from the others, looking pale and tense and beautiful on the eve of her professional debut as an actress. She gazed at the stage as she had at the alley the first day—a guillotine.

"Okay, everybody." Chip Barrett urged the group back up the aisle. Joel Lieber had been felled by an ulcer attack following yesterday's dress rehearsal. He was to be denied the New Haven launching, where he could have played the role of director to his heart's content, despite the lack of program credit. "Why the moans and groans?" Chip jollied the actors. "You've had the New York set for three weeks. We'll do the runthrough in the smoking lounge. You're in great shape. Besides, it's only to keep you busy until tonight."

Onstage, as the actors repaired to the lounge downstairs, there was a stream of oaths and curses from Frank Merkle.

"I don't believe it," he screeched, gesturing at the strip of carpet he'd unrolled. Below him at the footlights Eddie Ruick, scampering over the lowered boom lights, was also blistering the air with obscenities.

"They sent the wrong effing carpet for the stairs. It don't effing match the rest," howled Frank, and I hastened over to pacify him.

Between emergency forays to New Haven carpet dealers, phone calls from Max Jacobs in New York firing off fresh instructions for the party he was hosting at the Taft after the performance; between racing out to the diminutive derby-topped Abel Klein, in the box office, with names to be added to Max's guest list; between making up the dressing-room assignments and rushing to settle disputes among the crew, I did not glimpse the actors again until five, when they surfaced from finishing the runthrough in the

136

lounge. Spirits perking up, excitement battling with nerves, they journeyed next door to the Taft for the refreshment of naps, baths and a light repast before the half-hour call.

I'd yet to check into the hotel, and did not have the opportunity to do so until six-thirty. The set was up by then, but not dressed. Eddie Ruick had progressed to the balcony grids when I exited with my suitcase and zippered canvas bag for the Taft. The suitcase was newly purchased, a gleaming cowhide two-suiter, fitted with shiny buckles and straps to lend me a swagger I did not possess. Cash was coming up for the opening—"What, miss the thrill of seeing my feller tread the boards again?"—but she wouldn't be getting to New Haven till nearly curtain time. I could have done with a helping of her dauntless cheer as I signed the Taft register and followed the bellboy and cowhide into the elevator.

Quick shower, fresh shirt, then I was once more in the elevator, hurrying down for a hamburger before reporting back to the Shubert. As I entered the coffee shop a group from the cast—Tony Ives, Grace Marsden, Diana Knapp and Chip—were in the process of rising from a table of half-eaten sandwiches and assorted beverages.

"Have you seen her? Where could she be?" Chip shot at me as the others made for the cashier.

"Who?"

"Jones. Nobody's laid eyes on her since the runthrough. Room doesn't answer." He bolted to catch up with the others. "Get a chance, give her another buzz, will ya?"

I wasn't, I confessed to myself as I wolfed a hamburger at the coffee-shop counter, in the proper go-get-'em mood to check on the whereabouts of M. Jones. Since the walk up Broadway two weeks ago, I hadn't contrived a moment alone with her beyond backstage encounters. The nearest I'd come to it was last Sunday, when, Jesus H. Christ, I'd deposited myself on a corner across from the Barbizon for Women, on the chance that she would be among the parade of girls trotting into the April sunshine from the lobby. Stood there like a dope for approximately one hour, then had slunk away, mortified by my staggering lack of derring-do.

It was seven-thirty when I plunked a tip on the coffee-shop counter, paid my check, and started out the door onto College Street. *Nobody had seen her since the runthrough?* Wherever she'd been, perhaps she was upstairs in her room now, steadying herself for the trip up the stage alley.

I went back into the fustily ornate Taft lobby, with its marble pillars and balcony-railed mezzanine, and its quota of Yale students to enliven the ponderous potted-palm atmosphere. Sorry, the hotel operator informed me, but 515 did not answer. I fished out my room key as I hung up: 608. The floor above, the floor below . . . at least that much proximity existed between us.

The Shubert presented an appearance startlingly altered from its dreary morning garb. The marquee lights shed a warm glow on the pavement in front; the *Anniversary* posters and cast photos were on display and being studied by a sizable throng, while a goodly number of others were lined up at the box office in the lobby. We were booked for three nights at the Shubert, and the veteran Abel Klein had said of the advance sale, "Put it like this, I'm not doing handsprings."

I went up the alley, in the stage door, and my immediate glance was toward the dressing-room key rack. Key No. 4 was not on its hook, indicating that M. Jones was on the premises.

Of her whereabouts since the runthrough, I did not learn until I went to call half-hour. (Later, weeks later in another city, I was to have the identical thought: that I should have known at once where she'd taken herself.)

Hysteria was not an inaccurate description of the climate that prevailed backstage at the Shubert when I made the dressing-room rounds to call half-hour.

Flowers and telegrams were arriving every few minutes at the stage door. From the stage itself emanated, not the tranquil quiet that usually obtains before a performance, but a ceaseless din of hammers, thuds, straining ropes, carpet being tacked down, feet tramping, and other sounds of the frenzied efforts to get the set finished and lit by curtain time.

"Half-hour, Miss Vail." I tapped on the door of Dressing Room No. 1, in the corridor off the stage.

"Donatello!" The tour's leading lady swung around from her dressing table and its armada of Elizabeth Arden jars, bottles, tubes, unguents, lotions and creams. "How is the house? Sold out?"

"Spotty in the balcony, but almost."

She looked imploringly at me, tautened by panic as well as a chin strap. "You must promise to give me the truth, Donatello. The brutal, unvarnished truth. Leora?"

Not waiting for a reply, she turned to the large, placid black woman who was arranging costumes on a rack, her one concession to maidhood being the frilly apron tied over her slacks. "Darling Leora, *would* you go ask the crew to stop that dreadful hammering. It's as maddening as voodoo drums."

Leora, imperturbable as an African veld, blew at the feathers that bedecked Irene's second-act evening gown. "Honey," she said, "when you ever hear any voodoo drums?"

"Fourteen days straight, on my last picture," replied her mistress, blending spit in a tin of mascara. "*Voodoo Island*, for Monogram—a horror. Can it be wondered I fled back to the stage? Where were we, Donatello?"

"Brutal, unvarnished truth."

"Oh, yes, of course." Irene put aside the mascara, clasped my hand, and trained her large, soulful, thyroid orbs upon me. "About my performance—I realize I'm getting the comedy, but what of the pathos underneath?" she asked.

As a good deal of Irene's comedy was unintentional, it was difficult to detect any deliberate pathos in it. "The quality I get from it," I said to her, "is its humanity."

"How sweet. The humanity, yes." She breathed an intense sigh of relief. "Now run next door and comfort poor Jack. I'm able to take openings in my stride, but they're perfect torture for him, you know."

Next door, in Dressing Room No. 2, Jack Millet reclined under a portable sunlamp, renewing his Malibu tan, nerveless as an eel. "Come in, old chappie, and have a gossip," he invited. "Silly business, all this, never could take it seriously. Old Puss a wreck, is she?"

Oscar Clovis, husband to Leora and valet to Jack, was applying spirit gum to the toupee that, apart from the sunlamp, was Jack's only preparation for going onstage. He switched off the lamp and bounded up with the spring of Douglas Fairbanks. "Well, Oscar, shall we slap on the old rug? Strange, how the Prestons could be Puss and I . . . minus benefit of clergy, et cetera," he was reflecting as I went into the corridor.

I collected the flowers and telegrams that were accumulating in the entry, and went up the iron stairs. Dressing Room No. 4 was on the second floor; I worked down from the top.

"Half-hour, please, Ben. Western Union for you." "Half-hour, please, Grace. Flowers." In the drab cubicles, made vivid by the splash of costumes, the spill of makeup boxes—rouge, liners, eye shadow, pink base, grease sticks—on the tables, the actors crouched half-dressed before their bright-lit mirrors, alternating between dread and elation. This was what it was for, the plotting, intrigues, anguish to secure a part: these moments that led to the rise of a curtain and "going on."

"Thank you, Christopher," they sang, exclaiming over the flowers and telegrams in a mixture of high wonder and tough-eyed appraisal. "To think that Howard remembered to wire! He used the night rate, I see." "Flowers from Lucille? As she gets ten percent of me, she might have done better than gladiola."

They received their tributes, daubed on juvenile pink, guided pencils, and called to one another through the open doorways.

"Vi, you will cover for me if I get stuck on that second-act change?"

"Scott, I've been thinking—if you'd come in a beat sooner on my Picasso speech, it'd help the laugh."

"It's not that the cross doesn't work beautifully, ducks. It's that unless you end up below the sofa I can't see you."

I knocked on Dressing Room 4. There were roses for Maggie Jones, the box cut at one end to accommodate the long stems. She took the box from me with quaking hands and attempted to admire the dark crimson blooms.

"From Miss Breal . . . they could be weeds for all I'm able to tell." She relegated the box to a chair and sat at her mirror. A white linen towel, tied back at the nape, sheathed the raven hair; her face was shiny from the cold cream that had wiped it clean for the makeup she had yet to apply. She stared at her reflection in the mirror as if it belonged to someone else.

"Listen, I've been apologizing to everyone for my disappearing act," she said. "I guess I should've left word where I was."

"It was the subject of a certain amount of speculation." Pause. "Where were you?"

She laughed and seized a jar of foundation cream. "Right across the street at the movies," she said, unscrewing the jar. "It's the only place I could think to go to quiet down."

Loew's Poli was directly across College Street from the Shubert. "I'll make a note of it for the future," I said. "Did it help?"

"Well, a nap was obviously beyond me. I might have dozed off for a couple minutes, but—" She stared at the mirror, her hand idle on the jar of cream. "Do you ever have that happen?" she asked. "Where suddenly for no reason you wake from a sound sleep?"

"I . . . generally I get some clue as to the reason."

"Well, I don't," Maggie Jones said, with something akin to defiance. She applied a daub of foundation cream to her face. "Some nights, bingo, I just simply wake up." She

141

blended the rose-tinted cream into the alabaster skin. "It can really be sort of pleasant. If it's still dark I switch on the light and read, or else I lie there and . . ."

"And what?" I asked.

"Dream, just drift away and dream." She laughed again, applied more cream, deftly blending it into the alabaster. "Of course, today I had a reason—pure blind panic at ever thinking I could be an actress. Well, listen, I've got only myself to blame." She dabbed rouge on her cheeks, blended it into the pale rose. "It's what I asked for, when I climbed on that bus for L.A."

"The fatal bus." She'd told the story of it at lunch one day, the final week of rehearsals. She'd become more at ease, relaxed with the other actors and they with her. Ralph's, the poor man's Sardi's, across from the Garrick, was the cast's favored haunt for lunch, and to a group of us one day she'd related the tale of her adventures in Hollywood. Two years of working in a bank in Clarion to save money, then a bus ticket to L.A. . . . and the typical aspirant's routine. Bread-and-butter jobs, salesgirl at Bullock's, waitress at Frascati's, making the rounds of the studios, never getting past the gates or the casting-department receptionists. A year of that, then, untypically, the classic Hollywood Cinderella wand had waved o'er the head of Virginia Belton.

By then she was working part-time at a camera store on Ivar Avenue, Saturdays only; into this store one providential Saturday had come Joseph V. Scully, A.S.C., two-time Academy Award recipient for his cinematography . . . and from this meeting had come the luminous photographs of the girl in the garden, face swung toward Scully's Leica. From the photographs, a screen test for Sidney Harmon, to whom Joe Scully was under contract. After weeks of *will he, won't he*, Harmon had signed her, and after that the Cinderella aspects of the tale had dimmed somewhat. The contract was standard minimum, seven years with options; the salary was $125 per week, $50 raise each option period. She was rechristened Maggie Jones and after a year at the studio had yet to step before a camera. Teeth capped, drama lessons, publicity stints opening supermarkets, and an appearance as Miss Yuletide in the annual Hollywood Boulevard Christmas parade, but not until Harmon had arranged the reading with Max Jacobs had she been given work as an actress.

"Entirely my own doing," she avowed, reaching for an eyebrow pencil. "A case of pure and simple insanity, solely myself to blame."

No ground for complaint, she'd said of her Clarion years. I watched her trace the pencil over the arched brow of the face she regarded as if it were someone else's. It was unaccounted for, the fear that ruled beneath her random chatter and observations. *"Does it ever happen . . . where suddenly for no reason you wake?"*

It was time to call fifteen minutes. Carefully she traced the pencil over the other brow, and I took from my pocket the purchase I'd made earlier at a fruit stand. I placed the apple on her dressing table, among the pots and jars of cosmetics. A link to join the days together, hers and mine, a linking-together somehow.

"In the theater—good-luck token," I mumbled as she turned from the mirror, once more caught unawares. "And though you haven't a notion of it, you're going to be very good tonight," I said. "A very good actress."

I hurried away then, back down the stairs to call fifteen minutes.

The opening performance of *Anniversary* went off with comparative smoothness, revealing a number of facts, few of them unforeseen.

One fact was that the play itself was less than a jewel. It was formula comedy, slick and contrived, dealing with the vicissitudes of Laura and Keith Preston—she a famous best-selling novelist, he an equally famous news commentator—on the approach of their twenty-fifth wedding anniversary.

It was a play that rested on a gimmick, this particular one being that Laura and Keith, owing to some improbable legal technicality, are not actually married. The omission is predictably rectified by the final curtain, with the intervening time devoted to assorted foolish subplots. Laura has a flirtation with a *Life* reporter assigned to cover the anniversary, and Keith cozies up to the naive young girl he's just hired as his personal secretary. Mixed up in the action are a rival network tycoon out to topple Keith, and Laura's droll spinster aunt, who unmasks the tycoon as the long-ago Harvard beau who'd once attempted her seduction. By the third-act curtain the *Life* reporter has paired off with the secretary, the tycoon has proposed marriage to the aunt, while Laura and Keith, in the guise of repeating their vows over national hookup, are at last united as man and wife.

Anniversary was that sort of play, and its one claim to distinction, at least in the Broadway production, were the Laura and Keith of Marion Sykes and George Bradshaw, two of the best comedy actors in the theater. Alas, the next fact gleaned from the New Haven opening was that Irene and Jack were not Marion Sykes and George Bradshaw.

They resembled, with their glides, hand-kissings, bows and pirouettes, ballroom dancers on the order of Veloz and Yolanda; it was as if they'd wandered by error into the play and were valiantly attempting to cope with its demands. As for the rest of the cast—Ben Forbes as the tycoon, Scott Andrews as the *Life* reporter, and Grace Marsden and Tony Ives in minor roles were professional and competent. If the road company could boast of distinction, it was in Vi Henry's playing of the aunt . . . and in the person of Maggie Jones.

I watched from the wings, from my station at the sound-effects table at stage right; watched her prepare for her entrance in the first act, climb the scaffoldlike steps to the platform above the center-arch stairs. Stand there, breath suspended, eyes wide with alarm; yet the lift of her chin, the erectness of her stance, suggestive of someone who has ascended to a mountaintop . . . *a mountain, climbed from what dark valleys below?* She listened in a kind of trance to the dialogue onstage, gripped with white knuckles the platform rail . . . and then her eyes swerved to where I stood, flashlight beamed on the script. I signaled her entrance cue and, with a shuddering intake of breath, she went down the stairs into the white-hot arena glare of the stage, there to bestow her radiance on it.

I watched each of her scenes from the wings, saw the initial awkwardness and uncertainty give way to confidence as the play progressed and she began to respond to the audience rather than retreat from it. There is a communication that can leap between an actor and an audience. It is not explicable, other than in terms of personality, chemistry, a special, ineffable interchange that occurs and is felt by both parties, each responding to the other. Untrained as she was, unskilled in technique, Maggie Jones was possessed of that gift, though she might be ignorant of it, or at this point not know how to use it to her advantage.

The curtain swept down, the applause rose up, breaking upon a dazed, astonished Maggie Jones as she took her position with the cast for the calls. Up and down swept the curtain on the lineup of bowing, hand-linked actors, her astonishment that she'd survived as marked at the final call as at the first. She carried it with her to Max Jacobs' party afterward, and back to the Shubert with her on Wednesday for the first matinee.

It was the astonishment of a person not simply rescued from drowning but washed up on an enchanted shore . . . and two days later, Friday morning, an hour or so before we were to leave for Hartford and the next performance, venturing forth from the Taft Hotel I stumbled upon a clue to what might lie behind Maggie Jones's astonishment.

The face that she had regarded in the dressing-room mirror as if it had not belonged to her—didn't, at least not in her private estimation.

A van was parked outside the Shubert and the scenery was being reloaded when I jounced down the hotel steps, bound aimlessly for a walk. I watched the men load the van for a moment; then, glancing across the street, I saw Maggie Jones coming out of a shop next to the Poli.

It was a children's shop, and someone was with her, whom at first I did not recognize.

"Maggie?"

I waded straight into the shuttle of traffic. She stood in the shop doorway, her companion doggedly entrenched behind her. Betrayed by eagerness, I dodged a rear bumper, skirted a fender, and landed on the curb, where further initiative deserted me.

"Shopping?" I asked—which was superfluous, as she was holding a bag with Jack 'n Jill, the shop's name, printed on it.

"Nothing very much." The soft heather-tweed suit accented the ivory face and raven brows, gave an amethyst sparkle to the dark eyes. She smiled, tugged at the silk scarf that tethered the wings of hair. "Originally I was just wandering around—the soul of a tourist, I'm afraid."

I shifted my feet, doomed to gawking. "Who's your friend?" I said, by way of diversion.

"Louella, you mean?" She turned to the little girl who had wedged herself in the doorway and was focusing us with a wary gaze.

"Oh, Louella and I met each other outside the theater before," Maggie said. "Watching them load the scenery . . . didn't we, Louella?"

The child hedged back farther, sparrow-thin, a plaid skirt drooping below her knees; but it was the thumb that went sliding into her mouth that identified her for me. The thumb and the oversized sweater: she was the little girl who'd been outside the Shubert Tuesday morning when I drove up in the van. Flinty-eyed, thumb in mouth, she was as uncommunicative now as then.

Maggie, however, appeared undaunted by it. "Louella, this is Christopher," she said, with a step toward the doorway. "He's with the show, too."

The little girl dug in her toes and gave me a sharp, measuring look. "So what?" she tossed.

146

"Well, it's always better to know who somebody is," Maggie said, and went up to the doorway. The two made a painfully divergent pair: Rose Red and the Little Match Girl. "Anyway, you don't have to worry about him," Maggie went on. "He's very nice, Christopher is."

"Says who?" Unprepared to yield a scrawny inch of her pride, Louella coolly appraised us, first one, then the other, and apparently reached a conclusion.

"Well, time to shove off." She moved sharply from the doorway.

"Don't you want to wave goodbye to the scenery first?" Maggie turned at the retort of the van's doors shutting, across the street. "It's leaving, I think. Come, Louella."

The latter, registering elaborate indifference, permitted herself to be conducted to the curb, where she stood with her feisty bones wedged against Maggie. Her outfit had acquired a new addition since Tuesday: perched atop the chopped-off hair, in lieu of the knitted cap, was a sailor hat of shiny new straw, with grosgrain ribbons floating entrancingly down the back.

Louella gave the ribbons an angry poke, and Maggie, other half of this odd, disparate pair, reached down to smooth them. As I watched, she rested her hands on the stiff, bony shoulders and spoke in a manner different from any I'd heard before.

"Listen, I wouldn't have understood about the scenery, either," she said to Louella. "Where I grew up, nobody heard of anything *but* movie houses. Real yokels, take my word for it."

Over at the Shubert, the derbied, pint-sized personage of Abel Klein had materialized and was checking the truckers' bill of lading. He circled the van, tested the chain-bolted doors, signed the worksheets. Up front, the driver revved up the motor.

"Ever been to a county fair?" Maggie asked Louella as they watched the van back from the curb. "Ever watched a fair close down?"

Louella shook her head. "No, I ain't," she said. "Who'd take me to a fair? Name one."

"Me. I would," came the answer. Maggie smoothed the mousy hanks of hair that protruded from the hat brim. She nodded at the van, which was swinging into traffic. "After the fair's over, they fold up the tents and booths," she explained. "Down comes the Ferris wheel and merry-go-round . . . and it's just an empty clearing again. Not a trace left—like the theater over there."

She gestured at the denuded marquee, the vacant photo cases and bare house-boards of the Shubert. "On a road tour they packed up the scenery and costumes . . . and today we move on, with nary a trace."

Louella swiveled around. "So?" she demanded. "You go away today, so what?"

"Just that—"

"*What?*"

"To leave nothing—" Maggie knelt down, unmindful of me, and grasped Louella by the shoulders. "New Haven's the first place I ever *did* something," she said. "Acted in a play, something worth doing. This morning I went out looking for . . . a way to remember it, I guess . . . and found you."

Louella's gaze was tough and unsparing. "You really an actress?" she challenged.

"It could be argued." Maggie laughed and fussed with the hat brim. "Definitely, you could argue it."

"Don't let her fool you, Louella," I put in, thinking of opening night, Maggie's terror. "She's the kind of actress, someday you'll see her name in lights."

Having none of this, Louella leveled the flinty gaze on her benefactress. "Then why," she asked, with a sudden quaver, "if you're all what you say, so gorgeous and swell, why'd you buy me this hat?"

Maggie frowned. "I've made trouble," she ventured. "You'll go home and they'll ask where you got it, is that it?"

"Know what I'll tell 'em?" Louella threw back, her pent-up anger unloosed, spilling out. "I'll tell 'em this beautiful actress seen how ratty I looked, like out of a garbage can."

"*No.*" Maggie's eyes widened. "Is that what you think of yourself? You mustn't, do you hear?" She shook her scrawny charge, and in that moment the disparity between them no longer existed. "Look at me, Louella. Listen to me."

Pale, rabbity lashes fringed the downcast eyes. "I'm sorry," she said. "I know you meant to be nice."

"Promise never to think of yourself like—" Maggie broke off; she glanced at me, then stood up. "Someday you'll grow up and forget you ever had such foolish thoughts," she said quickly, ending the exchange.

But Louella had a different ending in mind. She flung the grosgrain ribbons over her shoulder. "You won't make trouble with the hat," she said, looking up at Maggie. "If my mama asks . . . I'll tell her I happened to run into this lady who happened to like me," she said. "How can she carry on about somebody liking me?"

Maggie clutched the paper bag. "Oh, Louella," she said. "Louella Meggs, you'll get along fine, I bet."

"When's your train leave?"

Maggie consulted her wristwatch. "That's right—haven't checked out yet."

Louella hesitated, pulled at the incongruous hat. "I got this method of goodbye where you make a bargain," she said.

"You do? What?"

"Neither person looks back," said Louella, with another hesitation. "And one of 'em has to go first."

Maggie looked at her. "That's a hard bargain."

"Yeah." Louella yanked at the hat, patently a delaying action. Maggie remembered the bag—it contained the former chapeau, the knitted job, which provided further delay, as Louella stashed it under one, then the other, arm. A tug at the droopy skirt, then, "Guess it'll be me first."

Surrendering delay, Louella Meggs performed a last appropriate gesture. Lifting a sparrow hand to her lips, she implanted it with a kiss, then touched her hand to Maggie's cheek. She turned then, clamped the hand on the sailor hat, and took off blindly down the sidewalk, matchstick legs churning the pavement. "No looking back," she hollered behind her, the yellow grosgrain ribbons flying . . . yellow as the daffodil dress worn on the first day of rehearsal.

"No looking back," hollered Louella, gaining the next corner at full gallop. Maggie, faithful to the bargain, confined her gaze to the lilliput dummies in the shop window, the curly-wigged, dimpled plaster girl in ruffled organdy, the stalwart plaster boy in Eton suit and collar . . . images that were about as real as placid tales of small towns and uneventful growings-up, where one day was like another until suddenly you'd graduated from high school.

"Bargain's kept." I gestured at the now-vacant corner. "Louella's quite a person."

The primavera face turned from the window. "What time is it?"

"A person to be prized," I went on. "Awarded medals for spunk."

She glanced over at the Shubert, as though I hadn't spoken. "Three performances and another tonight," she said. "Despite the nerves and sick stomach, I can hardly wait."

Stop pushing, I thought. Let her tell you of Clarion in her own time.

She slung the pouch bag over her shoulder. "We'll be leaving for the train. I haven't checked out of the hotel."

"Oh, you mustn't ever worry. I'd never let you miss your train," I announced, with no idea of what I meant by that sweeping statement. "Just . . . it's part of my job."

Maggie smiled, as if the meaning, along with the emotions that had prompted it, were clear to her. "It's as I said," she joked. "The patron saint of travelers."

"On a very minor scale—but I'll try to do my best."

"Yes, I'm sure you—" She turned, stepped from the curb. "Still, hadn't we better get started?"

We crossed back to the Taft, the conversation left unfinished; and what with queuing up to pay our bills and check

out, and my arranging for the company luggage to be collected, it was time, in no time at all, to leave for the station.

In my capacity as gofer, I hustled up the platform ramp
from the station refreshment canteen below. It was eleven-
twenty-five; as yet the Hartford local gave no sign of its
approach on the rails, but only one member of the company appeared to be awaiting it.

She stood at the south end of the platform, gazing at the
avenues of the tracks that converged in the distance. The
wind rippled the scarf tied under her chin; I thought of
Louella Meggs's hat with the yellow streamers, and of the
yellow dress the first day of rehearsal . . . a link, and how
many steps separated us now?

Twenty, thirty, I measured the length of platform between us, surely within my ability to traverse . . .

But first, I went up the platform to where the rest of the
company was gaily congregated on benches. Lively with
talk and laughter, they didn't appear to be waiting for a
train or any other event. It was as if one among them had
suggested, "Let's go hang around the station," and off
they'd traipsed accordingly. The opening was behind them,
the New Haven reviews had been favorable, if not raves,
and ahead was the pleasant prospect of two weeks in Boston,
with only one-nighters in Hartford and Providence to get
through beforehand.

I went up to Jack and Irene, who sat amid a quantity of
aged Vuitton luggage, creating the impression that they
were embarking on the *Queen Mary,* at the very least.
Irene's hat was a huge pouffe of tulle; Jack was natty in a
Savile Row houndstooth, circa 1935, and they were engaged in one of their rare but spirited disputes.

"But, Puss," said Jack.

"It's no use, I'm adamant," said Irene. "Mildred and the
twinnies shall have Malibu this summer."

"I needn't remind you, old Puss, of the tidy rental that
beach shack of yours fetches."

"Nevertheless, Mildred shall have it. She shall, she shall,

she shall," declared Irene, and who among the local passengers, if eavesdropping, could have hoped to grasp that Mildred, the recipient of Irene's largesse, was none other than Jack's wife, the twinnies being his sons, Edward and Theodore, also referred to as Neddie and Teddie.

"Oh, very well, darling, bless you for it," Jack acquiesced, splashing Poland Water into cups from the silver thermos. (It was Polish, all right, Chip had remarked during rehearsal: ninety-eight-percent proof. "Notice how by afternoon they've got a slight buzz on? What the hell, if it helps.")

"Darling," Jack toasted his beloved, with a joining of cups, and I interrupted to advise him that the station canteen did not stock Craven A cigarettes.

"What, no Craven A's?" It astounded him, but he accepted the Chesterfields with admirable grace. "Never mind, Boston will have them. Thanks awfully, chappie."

Twenty steps, thirty . . . I looked down the platform at the slim, solitary, heather figure at the end, and cursed my laggard's feet. "Hey, kid," rasped a froggy voice from the platform edge, further thwarting me.

I went over to the derbied, gnomelike individual who was pacing restively up and down. "Yeah, Abe?"

"The eleven-thirty to Hartford—" he removed the unlit cigar from his mouth, hauled a gold pocket watch from his vest "—is presently the eleven-thirty-two." He returned the watch to the vest pocket, the chewed-up cigar to the mouth, and meditated on this pronouncement. "In other words, don't count on schedules. It don't pay."

From the tip of his derby to his pearl-gray spats, from the sparkle of his diamond tiepin to the shine of his bulbous-toed shoes, Abel Klein epitomized a fast-vanishing branch of the theater. He was of a select but dwindling breed, the traveling manager who, year in and year out, shepherded troupes of actors across the United States, in and out of a hundred and more towns and cities from Trenton to San Francisco, Duluth to Galveston, Portland, Oregon, to Portland, Maine . . . wherever a curtain still rose on live actors in a show. The road was Abel's home (*where's home?*); his family was ever-changing, made up of the crews and casts placed in his charge. Abel professed a scorn of actors; his appraisal of them, like the glint in the shrewd, wrinkle-pouched eyes as he rendered it, was sharp and unsparing; yet his treatment of them, from what I'd observed, belied his scorn.

"Abel, darling," Irene Vail trilled throatily from the mountains of Vuitton, "do you think the funny little train has forgotten its way?"

"Should've hired mules, sweetheart. They'd be faster."

She lavished a smile on him, but in it could be glimpsed anxiety, the seeking of reassurance. "New Haven, all told, was pleased with us. The advance in Boston *is* building nicely?"

"What else, with draws like you and Jack?" Gallantly, he doffed the derby in tribute, then, sotto voce to me: "So far a lousy two five. It's like touring a waxworks. Some menagerie I'm saddled with, eh, kid?"

He indicated Chip and Diana, who'd strolled up the platform, engrossed in conversation. "That Chip, I heard about. Skirt-chaser, strictly wham, bam, thank you, ma'am —so why's he go after a girl like Diana, with a kid in Jackson Heights and no father to speak of?" The steely glint focused on Ben Forbes, who sat on a bench holding forth to Vi Henry and Grace Marsden.

"Him, I'll be bailing out of night court before I'm through. Puts up at the Y. Cheaper, he says." Abel removed the cigar. "Yesterday I spotted him with a fellow resident. Listen, to each his own, but this kid was sixteen, tops. As for *them*," he gestured at Eddie Ruick, the Merkles and Leora and Oscar, who formed a separate contingent at the front of the platform. "Classy bunch, eh? Look like they're planning a bank heist. Like I say—" he reinserted the cigar "—all in all, some menagerie."

How many steps—twenty, thirty? "Abe . . . you wanted me for something?"

"Appreciate it, we get to Hartford—" he chewed on the

cigar and scowled at the idle tracks "—you'd check that the scenery got to the theater. A foul-up like New Haven, we don't need."

"Sure. I'll go over from the station."

"Appreciate it, kid." He clamped the cigar in his mouth and contemplated the rails. "Unless you got something else on the agenda."

"Me? Why, no, I—I just planned on—" He turned to me, the glint in his eyes one of amusement; he nodded at the solitary figure at the platform's end, and answered the question of why he'd called me over.

"Hey, Romeo," inquired Abel Klein, with another nod down the platform. "Nobody's crowded around Juliet, so what's holding you back?"

The teasing glint forestalled any additional protest. "Funny," I said, and glanced with a deep, baleful breath at the southbound platform across the rails. The platform had been dark and deserted the night of the opening, when I'd taken Cash to catch the one A.M. train to New York. "Funny, somebody else recently compared me to Cyrano," I said to Abe. "I mean, as opposed to Romeo."

"A surefire crowd-pleaser, I don't knock *Cyrano*—" Abe's smile was like cracked leather splitting "—but about the plot, I got questions."

"So had my aunt."

"Here's a man surrounded by pals. They're crazy about him, so how come one of 'em—"

"Abe—" I backed away as he grabbed my arm. "Now Abe, listen, let me—"

"—don't give him a little push?" he finished, swiveling me around and applying the required pressure.

I heard his dry chuckle behind me; was conscious of a sudden break in the gay chatter from the benches, a diverting of attention to this momentary drama—the company gofer dislodged, pushed from his moony yearnings in the wings.

I started down the platform, thirty steps, twenty-nine, -eight . . . and it was Cash, more than Abe Klein or the

154

company's gaze, propelling me forward. Cash, the former Kitty Lorraine, who'd come to cheer the opening and had flung a warning at me before she'd left.

Twenty-four steps, twenty-three . . . unloosed from her switchboard at five, my aunt had changed to niftier attire in Macy's washroom, then negotiated a mad crosstown dash to Grand Central and the six o'clock New Haven express. "Places," Chip had been calling on the Shubert stage, "first-act places," when from the curtain hole I'd spied a bedizened first-nighter—bugle-beaded jacket, gold lamé skirt, ostrich-plumed, jet-sequined hat—being ushered to her third-row orchestra seat, which she had amply and joyfully filled.

Throughout the performance I'd heard Cash, when not able actually to view her. The loudest, most appreciative laughter had emanated from the third row; so sustained was her applause at the calls that it had inspired Irene Vail to curtsy in that direction, while speculating on which of her old-time fans had surfaced to give homage.

"Hurry out front, Donatello. Find her, bring her to me. We will weep, we will embrace."

It was unnecessary to hurry out front: My aunt had led the vanguard of visitors backstage. Ablaze in her bugle beads and lamé, she was gripped with shyness, once past the stage door . . . a shyness that was the product of broken dreams and talent not possessed. She'd hung back while the other visitors surged past her.

"Aw, Christy, it's great seein' you in harness again. Listen, you've got some celebratin' to do. If I hurry and catch a cab I can . . ."

I'd insisted that she not only tour the dressing rooms and meet the cast (she was struck dumb by Irene's impassioned embrace), but that she accompany me to Max Jacobs' party at the Taft. It was in the Cafe; she'd nabbed an Old-Fashioned for herself, a corner table, and waved me off. "It's your shindig, sweetheart. Get going, enjoy yourself."

Sixteen steps, fifteen, fourteen . . .

It was during the course of Max's party that my aunt's mood had drastically shifted. Trays of drinks and canapés, orchestra, dancing . . . I'd wandered among the groups, in and out of the bright volleys of talk; watched Max presenting an astonished Maggie Jones to his Shubert Alley cronies. "Quit hoverin'," Cash had complained when I went to check on her drink. "I can get my own goddamn refills. What the hell's the hour? Instead of a refill, get me a cab."

In the taxi to the station she'd launched on a mordant, rambling account of favorite shows from the past. "Listen, maybe I never made it out of the tank towns, but I sure saw the greats," she asserted. "Laurette Taylor in *Peg*, incredible. Jane Cowl in *Smilin' Through*, not a dry eye in the house. *Romance*, with Doris Kean . . . and let's not forget Walter Hampden in *Cyrano*."

"Hey, Kitty Lorraine," I'd joshed uneasily, "why the sudden tour down footlight lane?"

The taxi cranked up to the station and she'd responded by raising a fuss about getting out. "Watchit with the door, you'll rip my gorgeous lamé from Milgrim's. Of course, I never could swallow the plot of *Cyrano*," she carried on, haughtily gathering up her skirts, as if an ermine train swept behind, and clomping into the station. "I ask you, a lad who can take on whole armies single-handed, and he can't make a pitch for the dame he's nutty about?

"On account of a nose problem, of all things," she continued her ranting, toiling up the ramp to the southbound platform. "I ask you, who'd fall for that bale of hay?"

"I don't know," I said, aware finally of her pitching. "Who'd fall for it?"

"*Who*, cookie?" She'd trudged up the ramp and along the silent, night-shrouded platform. Her ankles were swollen from the spiked heels; the dim lights of the shed flickered on the creased and wrinkled lamé plastered to her heavy, ballooning hips. "*Who*, baby?"

She'd turned and wiped at the tears that coursed down her rouged cheeks. "I'll tell you who falls for Cyrano. The millions like him, who could never speak of their love, for one reason or another."

I stared at the tear-stained Kewpie-doll face. Up the tracks a rustle went vibrating along the rails; a stab of light slanted over them, and I knew of whom my aunt spoke; knew of the love she had guarded, kept within herself, all these years.

"No, it's you we're talking about." She threw out a hand, as if sensing my thoughts. "Oh, God, Christy, I watched you with her," she said. "Watched your eyes keep following her—and you didn't go near her. Listen to me, Christy." A whistle shrieked up the tracks, wheels clacked over the steel lengths. "In the whole world, there's only one of each person," Cash said. "No duplicates, and sometimes it never comes again, that kind of love."

"Cash. Cash, what'll I do?"

"Only one of each person, and you've found her." She flung her voice against the onrushing wheels. "Nothing's in the way, Christy, except yourself, so be warned." The wheels ground out her words, the train windows flashed on her haggard, imploring face.

"Hear me? Hear what I say?"

"I hear, yes . . ."

I did not count the remaining steps to the platform's end, aware only that there were fewer of them.

Then, a foot or so from me, the slim, heather figure tensed, glanced at the rails, the flylike speck that had appeared at the point where the tracks converged.

I searched for the words to convey all that I perceived about her, all that I felt and hoped for her. "I—I wish it were the Chief," I said, and she swung around, startled.

"The depot in Clarion," I went on. "How you went on Sundays to watch the Chief go by."

She plucked at the scarf ends; behind her the flyspeck on the rails was becoming a train. "I'd forgotten I'd told you," she said.

"The night we walked up Broadway." Janya had been a

157

little girl like Louella Meggs, it was as simple as that. "I'm going to see to it," I said. "In my capacity of patron saint of travelers, I ought to be able to get you on the Chief."

She looked at me, and as though by a sharp tug of a rope, the emotions between us, there from the start, swerved together, converged, like the separate avenues of the tracks.

"Oh, Christopher, what am I to do with you?" she asked, a plea as much as a question.

"Tell me to stick around—or go away—or maybe a little of both," I said.

"I've tried," she said, "and can't seem to do either."

The Hartford local, a collection of battered coaches, swayed toward us on the tracks. "Then don't try either," I said, and seized her hand. "We'll let it work out by itself."

With that, hands linked, we raced up the platform, neck to neck with the incoming train, and of a sudden a vista of days beckoned ahead, shining with possibilities over the rails.

CHAPTER 7

Possibilities!

I awoke and the room blurred into shape, made from a thousand mornings. At the foot of the bed was a luggage rack, the cowhide tumbled with clothes. *Notice to Guests:* sign on the ventilated door . . . *Biltmore Hotel, Providence, R.I.*

I lay back, listening to the *rat-tat* of the rain on the window. Sunday, second straight day without a letup. The company was to leave for Boston today, but not until four; we'd hang around the hotel, then troop to the station to board another decrepit local, those Toonerville Trolleys we seemed to specialize in, with sunken cane seats and cracked green shades, swaying and bumping over the rails . . .

I lay listening to the rain, then next I was flinging off the covers, parading up and down the brown chevron-patterned carpet. Barely awake, yet already I was totaling up, like some doleful bookkeeper, the day's debits. Canceling it out, as it were, before it had a chance to get started. How many days had been thus affected, by my not concentrating on the possibilities?

I marched across the chevrons to my wristwatch, which lay on the night table. Ten-forty was not indecently early to call someone on the phone, even when that person—I steered firmly along the positive track—was not always blessed with undisturbed slumber . . . indeed was likely to be as awake as yours truly, C. Casey.

I picked up the phone on the night table and immediately the negative forces got to work. M. Jones had played two shows yesterday, climax to an exhausting week, and if Morpheus was kindly disposed toward her this morning . . . later. I'd try later.

I placed the receiver back in its cradle and made for the bathroom, shucking my pajama top en route. As I set foot on the tiles, the phone gave a sharp *brrnngg.*

"Yes?" I lifted the receiver.

"This is the hotel operator, sir. Apparently we were disconnected."

"Disconnected? No, I don't think, that is—"

"Your light registered on the board, then went out. Of course, you may have accidentally dislodged the receiver from the—"

"No, I didn't," I interrupted, aware of the return of positive forces. "No, as it happens I was about to . . . I'd like Miss Jones, please. It's . . . room eight-twenty-five, I believe."

"You wish me to ring?"

"Yes, yes, I wish you to ring." I listened to the *crrkk-crrkk,* then Maggie answered and I said, "Listen, hope I didn't wake you, but I got to thinking how terrible it is. What an easy trap to fall into," I said.

"You didn't wake me. I was doing my hair. What trap?"

"That's an example of it. You weren't asleep but I almost didn't call in case you might be—" The explanation was getting tangled up, but I blundered on. "An example, I mean, of negative thinking."

It took Maggie a moment to digest this garble, then she laughed. "Listen, the main negative aspect in all of this is my hair."

"Pardon?" I couldn't recall how hair had entered the conversation.

"That's what drove me out of bed. The prospect of having to wash and put up my dandelion hair. Be grateful you're a man."

"Has something affected my hearing?" I asked. "Where

did you acquire the notion that your hair in any sense resembles—?"

"I don't know. Anyway, it's washed and I was in the middle of drying it when you called."

"I see." What I saw, actually, was Maggie reclined on the bed in her robe, preferably not encumbered with undergarments. "So if I'd put it off till later, you might have gone out," I continued my thesis.

"This downpour? I doubt it."

"Well, granted the rain has some bearing on the negative mood I woke in—"

"Don't you like the rain? I do sometimes," she branched off. "Whenever I visit the Scullys in Azuma and it rains, I go down to the beach and walk for miles."

"You do?" Azuma was a beach town, with ranches in the hills above, several miles up the coastline from Malibu. She often went there to visit Joe Scully—plus his wife, Lourdes, and their six children, so it was nothing to worry about. "With me, the rain doesn't have terrific connotations," I said, totally off the track; then, hopping back on in a triumphant leap, "which is even further proof of the trap I was speaking of."

"I'm not sure I—?"

"Negative thinking—waking up and writing off whole days before they've had a chance to get started," I soared onward. "Like not calling you just now and maybe passing up the chance to ask—" I got the words out, dislodged them from my throat or chest or wherever they were stuck, like a chicken bone "—to ask if you might care to have breakfast . . . in the extremely nice dining room downstairs."

There was a pause, but only a slight pause, at Maggie's end. "Half an hour in the lobby be okay?" she offered. "It'll take me that long."

Room, I should have suggested. Stop by her room. "Half an hour. Lobby. Fine," I said.

"With this hair, better make it forty minutes."

"Forty minutes for that silk-spun anything-but-dandelion hair," I said, at which she laughed, then was off the phone. I hung up and crossed to the window, reviewing the little sequence in my mind. Probably I wouldn't have phoned her after the first bungled try . . . but the operator had intervened and thus had altered the day's course.

Possibilities!

I tugged at the cord of my pajama pants and gazed out the rivered window at my old implacable enemy. By what immutable law did I assume that the skies would not clear today? Or that the train to Boston must of necessity be another Toonerville Trolley? I gestured at the window, commanded blue skies forthwith, candles and flowers in the dining room downstairs . . . and if not the Chief itself to Boston, a reasonable facsimile thereof.

Possibilities!

I went into the bathroom, stood soaping myself in the tub shower. My hands moved soapily, then hungrily over my body, and I lifted my face to the spray, the nozzle, the ceiling, the floor above. Here it was I who was a floor below, the opposite of New Haven, but was it not within the realm of possibility—why should it not be?—that one day there might be one floor, one room, for the two of us?

Why not? the spray tingled down on me. *Why indeed not?*

I did not attempt to deny it. When, at about three-thirty that afternoon, the taxis with the *Anniversary* company prowed up to the railroad station amid great sluices of water, I admitted to a slight degree of discouragement.

Not that I'd actually expected my newfound attitude to influence the weather, but what of the other fiascos? The idiot farce that breakfast had turned into?

It was a Mack Sennett farce, commencing in the elevator en route to the lobby. At each stop someone from the company had boarded the car. "Going for breakfast, Christopher? Marvelous, we'll join you." A group of five by the time we hit the lobby; then as the other car landed, "Here's Esther," cried Tony Ives. He'd taken to calling Maggie by that name after she'd recounted her Hollywood experience; it was pure Esther Blodgett, he'd decreed, which was the character played by Janet Gaynor in *A Star Is Born*. "Come, Esther, we're having breakie together," Tony had invited, and we'd caravanned across the lobby to the dining room. Forget the flowers-and-candles stuff, forget those details: the dining room was closed.

Sunday-closed, and so was every respectable eatery in Providence—that, or not open until lunch—with the dismal exception of a rancid Greek diner, to which we'd trekked in the downpour. Greasy eggs and sausages, dishwater coffee, and forget any ideas about splitting from the group. "What shall we do until train time?" sighed Grace Marsden on the puddle-splashing return trudge to the hotel, whereupon Tony Ives had come up with, "We'll inspect each other's rooms and vote on the most hideous. Mine has a framed Airedale over the bed. Esther, we'll begin with yours."

The taxis sluiced to a stop at the station entrance, the women of the company ducked inside for shelter. While Abel went in search of a redcap, Chip, Scott, Tony and I unloaded the luggage, and I consoled myself with the fact that Jack and Irene were motoring to Boston with friends, thereby relieving me of gofer duties. Once aboard the train, Toonerville Trolley or whatever it turned out to be, I could devote full attention to M. Jones. That's it, keep thinking positive.

Ac-cen-tuate the positive, ee-lim-inate the negative, I crooned the lyrics of the Bing Crosby song as we transferred the luggage onto a cart Chip had wheeled up. In reply, a gust of rain hit me squarely in the chops, but coming toward me also was M. Jones herself. In her trim, belted raincoat, cloche hat and shiny boots, she qualified as a walking advertisement for inclement weather.

"Practically a squall," I shouted at her above the gusts. "You ought to be inside."

"I was, but I came back out," she shouted back, smiling, and hoisted a suitcase onto the cart. "It's absolutely glorious."

"Glad one of us thinks so."

"No, I mean the station—oh, and everything else, really." She clapped a hand to the cloche, whose brim curved round her face. "Breakfast was so awful it was wonderful. The way the wind blows the rain makes me think of New England seaports and whaling ships, and no'westers."

"Which movie was that in?" I grinned, neglecting the luggage operation.

"Don't mock—everything I consider worth knowing, I've learned from the movies," she stated unequivocally. "But wait, just wait till you step inside."

"The station, you mean?"

"I can only report that to a girl who regarded the Clarion depot . . ." She tugged at the cloche and smiled up at me. "Well, not only is it a proper station, but the mere thought that I'm to depart on a train, even the grungiest local—"

"Maggie." I took her arm and relegated the luggage problems to the others. This was Janya who spoke, Janya at the depot, and the luggage would have to do without me. I took Maggie by the arm and we moved through the jostle of arriving passengers and those exiting from the doors, into the Providence station.

It was, as she'd attested, a proper station, smaller in scale than a big-city terminal, but with the same grandiose sense of importance and purpose, as though it were a ruler of many destinies. Under the high-domed ceiling manifold activities were going on: clerks sold tickets at the brass-grilled windows; redcaps trundled carts of luggage across the marble and granite rotunda expanse, followed by passengers clutching tickets and hand cases. Others sat or milled about the rows of benches while a loudspeaker boomed announcements of inbound and outbound carriers.

The *Anniversary* company was assembled at the benches.

Abe had snared a porter and was dispatching him to intercept the luggage cart. The crew as usual formed their own group over by the gates. They milled alike, though separately, actors and crew, restless and bored by the rainy Sunday confinement, impatient for Boston and two weeks of not having to pack suitcases. But such was not the view of the creature alongside me.

Perhaps she had considered that it might behoove her, as an actress on tour, to affect a certain indifference—rail stations, after all, were a condition of life on the road, along with cheerless dressing rooms and provincial hotels. But if she deemed this a more suitable manner, she was not succeeding at it. She gazed upon the scene with ill-concealed excitement . . . in particular, the attraction across the rotunda, which was among the prime lures of a well-equipped station.

"Guess we ought to head for the benches," she said, pulling her stare from this insidious lure. "Guess we should wait with the company and all."

"Guess we should." From the train gates issued the chug of an engine, hiss of steam, clang of a bell. As yet the Boston train hadn't been announced. We could hear the loudspeaker from one side of the rotunda as well as the other. "Come on," I said, yanking her after me. "We've got ten minutes yet."

Newsstand did not describe the enterprise that was doing a flourishing, cash-register-ringing trade in its choice station location; decked with flags, bursting with merchandise, it merited a worthier appellation: *emporium*— for was there an item it did not carry for the beguilement of the customer? Arrayed on counters, shelves and in spotless glass cases was a prodigious assortment of wares. Dolls, Steiff teddy bears, jigsaw puzzles, coloring books, crayons, Old Maid cards for the younger traveler; Lindt chocolates, Robertson's toffee, Peake-Freane biscuits for the more discriminating; best-sellers, anthologies, detective novels, paperbacks for those who wished to read. Souvenir ashtrays and tea canisters, hostess gifts, cocktail sets, tobacco humidors, cut-glass decanters—the assortment was mind-boggling, and the effect was to arouse the urge to reach at once for the wallet or pocketbook, solvency be damned.

Of the dazzling array, it was the magazines, strung across the top of the newsstand like yachting pennants and stacked row upon row at the front counter, that drew Maggie helplessly forward. She said, inspecting the glossy tiers of publications, "Ever wanted, just once, to buy every magazine in sight and not think of the cost?"

"What's wrong with now? This very minute?"

"With the amount out of my salary that's—" She drew away her hand. "I suppose it's old habit more than anything."

"Today," I said, ranging along the counter, gathering up *Harper's Bazaar, Vogue, Town and Country, Mademoiselle,* "is for casting off old habits."

"Christopher, no, you—"

To the growing stack I added *Modern Screen, Screenland* and *Photoplay,* and presented her with the lot. "Compliments of a friend."

She looked down at the lavish armful. " 'The aristocrat of motion picture magazines,' it's called," she said, with a nod at *Photoplay.* "That's because it cost a quarter, as compared to a dime or fifteen cents. Wouldn't you know it'd be the one I'd want?" She smoothed a hand over the glossy movie-star cover. "The kind of money Mama and I had . . . it wasn't Rolls-Royces or world cruises I dreamed of," she said quietly. "Just that I'd have a quarter for next month's *Photoplay.*"

I looked at the curve-brimmed rain hat bent over the magazines, and it seemed to me that she had given unasked a glimpse of Janya unedited; but then she was holding the magazines out and refusing to accept them.

"I can't, Christopher. It's awfully nice of you, but—"

"Let me. Why not?"

"It's strictly my policy to pay my own way, so—"

"Yes, but that doesn't apply to today. It's special somehow, don't you feel it? A special day." I handed ten dollars and the stack of magazines to the newsstand attendant. "There'll always be money, but never this day again. Please, as a favor?" The attendant was slipping the magazines into a bag; I caught sight of a paperback among those that were displayed on a wire rack. "Wait," I said, on impulse, and pulled the title from the rack.

I turned to Maggie with it. "Didn't know this was out yet—the paperback edition, I mean."

She read the title. "*The Seven-Storey Mountain*—wasn't that a best-seller last year?"

"Surprisingly, yes." I handed the paperback to the attendant. "Surprising, in that you wouldn't expect the story of a monk, a young man who enters a monastery to be a monk . . . it's not your typical popular reading."

"Oh, I'm not so sure." She looked at me as I took the slithering bag of magazines from the attendant. "Joe Scully had a copy at the ranch—the part I read was fascinating," she said.

"Not that it's entirely unusual—every year hundreds go into monasteries. By the absolute droves, you could say."

"Really?"

I presented her with the bag of magazines. "Although very few, maybe one out of fifty, remain—or even know why they went in."

"Why did you?" asked Maggie Jones.

"*What?*" I gaped at her.

"If you want me to act stunned, okay, but I'm not." She shrugged. "It's the sort of thing I'd have expected you to do."

I was flabbergasted and less, far less, than pleased. "All this while I've impressed you as a screwball ex-monk?" I blurted.

"No, of course not—just idealistic," she laughed. "And if it wasn't the place for you, how else would you have found it out?"

I looked at her face, framed by the curving hat, the wings of hair tucked tidily under the brim. "I—I found out that for me it was an escape," I said. "A way of pushing the past behind me . . . and it's only been in these last few weeks that—"

The boom of the loudspeaker interrupted my uncertain discourse. "Arriving on Track One," it boomed, and I listened in astonished pleasure to its message. Across at the benches the *Anniversary* company was preparing to advance to the gates, in response to the blaring announcement.

"Special, did I say?" I beamed at Maggie. "Did you hear what train you're about to ride?"

"You mean, it's not just another—?"

"Arriving on Track One, the Yankee Clipper for Boston," the loudspeaker boomed again over the station. "Parlor car, lounge car, dining car and coaches," it grandly announced.

"Definitely not another Toonerville Trolley," I assured her, and the two of us took off on a wild dash across the rotunda toward the gates that were opening to admit the passengers.

What did the rain matter?

It splattered the platform edge where we stood and gusted down from the roof, but in the distance through the slanting sheets a headlight threw itself over the tracks. A sleek, bullet-nosed diesel charged along the rails, ignoring as inconsequential the torrents that lashed it. As it pounded nearer, the diesel harnessed its velocitous pace, while behind swung a string of cars whose lighted windows, I imagined, as Maggie looked on, were shedding their glow on a lonely Kansas prairie. As the car wheels clacked in tandem, a whistle pierced the storm-clouded afternoon; for a moment the Yankee Clipper appeared suspended in time and motion, fixed against the drizzled landscape; then by some alchemy it was upon us, clamoring into the station.

The cars rolled past us with magisterial aplomb, close enough to touch—the behemoth engine, followed by the baggage-and-mail car and, behind it, that sanctum of the elect, the extra-fare parlor car. The glimpse of ladies and gentlemen conversing over drinks in lounge chairs, attended by a white-jacketed steward, was brief; the next car had appeared, and at this, Maggie caught her breath.

"Christopher, look!" she exclaimed. "There really is one," and she gestured up at the alluring vision of tieback curtains and window tables that fled past. She frowned then, and I identified the cause: the tables at the windows were stripped of cloths and silverware, and were flanked by empty chairs. No waiters with trays navigated the aisle to set tempting delicacies before their clients. Tables bare, the dining car clacked past, empty and not in service.

"Well, it's four o'clock. By now they've finished with lunch," said Maggie. The coaches were rolling past; far up the platform the engine slowed; hissing clouds of steam from the pipes underneath its cars, the Yankee Clipper rested at its berth.

Closed, I thought, while passengers debarked from the coaches and those waiting to board pressed forward. Closed, like everything else on this New England sabbath— no, it didn't make sense: crack trains didn't shut their dining cars in obeisance to Sunday virtue. Who ever heard of that?

Abel Klein, the redcap and baggage cart in tow, positioned himself below the steps of a coach and thumbed the company past him, counting heads as we filed up the steps. Tony, Scott, Chip and I spent the next moments transferring luggage onto the car, and it was during this hectic operation that Grace Marsden, peering down the aisle, said, "What's going on in that car in the rear? Why, it's a club car and I do believe they're serving drinks."

"Club car? Where?" The rallying cry was sounded before the train had so much as budged from the platform. Off came rain gear, to be tossed on seats; out flew lipsticks and compacts, pocket combs, as a merry band formed in the aisle.

"Idiots," muttered Abe Klein. He sat rummaging in the worn, sturdy briefcase, fitted with lock, that was as much an appendage of him as the derby hat. The object of his rummaging was the booklet of rail vouchers by which the company was transported from one leg of the tour to the next. Here was Abe, readying the vouchers for the conductor, and there went his actors scattering to the bar car. Up at the front of the coach, Eddie Ruick was dealing out a pinochle deck for a fast game with the Merkles.

"Beastly Sunday. I intend to get utterly swacked," said Tony Ives, leader of the club-car group. He pulled open the door at the rear of the coach, called back as the others trooped past, "Esther? Chris? Come get swacked with your betters."

"*Alllboard,*" the shout echoed along the platform. Maggie had shed her raincoat and cloche; she sat on the maroon-upholstered seat, turned to the window to observe the ceremony of departure. I finished stowing the last of the luggage on the rack and the unerringly drawn line of her profile, held to the streaming pane, struck at me like a chord of music. The train wheels gave a tentative lurch, the platform dropped back a notch, and I steered determinedly up the aisle.

"Christopher, where—?"

"Wait. Be right back."

The heavy steel door of the next coach forward twanged shut behind me. I groped up the aisle, past the dozing, reading and window-gazing incumbents in the reclining seats. The Yankee Clipper, leaving platform and station behind, was picking up speed. Another coach aisle, then what? How, if a dining car was closed, could it be persuaded to open? By what marvels of persuasion could it be done?

Steadying for balance, I pulled open the door to the dining car and that, for several long moments, was my most forceful, indeed my only, gesture.

I stood in the little paneled entryway of the handsomely appointed car, and it was simple to envision it at the height of service: the tables immaculate with linen, agleam with china and silver in the rosy glow of the bracket lamps;

the contented hum of conversation from the well-fed patrons as they lingered over coffee; the traffic of the waiters artfully balancing trays. Oh, simple enough to imagine, but at present nonexistent. Stripped of patrons and amenities, the procession of empty tables rattled up the aisle to the galley at the forward end.

Not entirely empty, I corrected myself; though for all intents and purposes the table nearest the galley might as well have been unoccupied. Lounging there was a quartet of waiters. Well, two of them wore white jackets and black bow ties; the other two had changed to mufti, but I assumed them to be of the same fraternity. Not that it made the slightest difference, actually. I stood in the entry and the Negro foursome sat at their table, swapping talk and the Sunday papers, and gave no indication of having registered my presence.

The initiative was obviously up to me. Mindful of my new positive attitude, I pitched my voice up the length of the swaying aisle. "Excuse me," I said. "I realize it's practically the end of the run, and that you well might speculate as to why I'm even in here."

This was not wholly accurate, since no one at the table was engaged in any speculation whatever in regard to me. Not an eye shifted, not a glance was thrown. The empty tables rattled, the Sunday pages were flicked; by degrees I advanced up the burgundy-carpeted aisle and continued my forceful persuasion.

"Who'd expect lunch at this hour?" I posed the query to my nonlisteners. "What person of sense? Anyone with any sense or experience—" One of the waiters betrayed a flicker of interest, the merest shift of attention, so I concentrated on him. "All I'm trying to say," I went on, "is I appreciate your position. I mean, I come barging in here—"

A grizzled, lamb-shorn head raised up from the Sunday papers. Of the quartet, he was the oldest, the senior by several decades. "Whut?" he grunted, his thin shoulders hunched querulously under the starched white jacket. "Whut you 'preciate?"

"Uh . . . your position," I explained. "As I say, I fully realize—"

With a harrumph of exasperation, he turned his bony, betel-nut-brown face to the outskirts of Providence, unreeling past the window. "P'sition," he humphed. "What position be that?"

"Why, that you're closed."

"Who say we is?" He swiveled around, snapped the elastic bow tie, and bugged his protuberant eyes at me. "Who say that? So far, you doin' all the talkin', mister. Elucidate yourself," he proposed, at which rich dark laughter geysered from his companions.

"*You* say we closed. *We* ain't say we is." The old waiter hoisted his skeletal frame from the table. He moved as if hinged together by wire. Where a moment ago the galley entrance had been vacant, it was now filled by an immense personage clad in a Hawaiian sports shirt, chartreuse trousers and a chef's hat. The waiter went up to him. "You hear whut he say? He say we closed."

The cook's countenance was a black thundercloud of disapproval. "Louis Tilford," he growled. "What the hell's got into you?"

"Gettin' *ready* to close ain't the same as *closed*." The senior of the group betook himself to the lockers in the passageway alongside the galley. "Well, speak up. How many in yo' party?" he barked over his shoulder at me.

"What? Er, two," I said, and held up two fingers.

He opened a locker, helped himself to linen. "Sunday run, nobody much come in after Prov'dence—reckon that about describes you perfect. Two in the party, you say?"

"Two." I held up the two fingers.

From a drawer in the passageway he dug a fistful of silver. "Don't go expectin' no six-course lunch, cook ain't about to oblige. San'wiches an' ice cream be about it."

"Listen, anything that's available," I said. "You see, there's a young lady with me, and she's never—"

"My, my, that is a piece of news." He went creaking past me. "A young lady, my, I'm surely amazed." His right shoulder was inches lower than the left, his gait slow and effortful, but the stiff, rheumatic legs accommodated themselves expertly to the aisle's sway. "Walt, go tell Rollins we got customers. He be in the parlor car," he fired out, and one of the waiters hustled obediently up the passage. With a murderous glare, the cook slammed into his galley, but it failed to deter Louis Tilford. Ornery jaw thrust out, he surveyed the aisle of tables, as from a command post. Selecting a table for two near the entry, he creaked toward it, and there commenced to practice a wizardry that was the special mark of his calling.

He billowed out a tablecloth and brought it parachuting down in a faultless landing. Over this he billowed another cloth, draped so that it formed perfect V's at the corners. With a few deft motions of the gnarled hands, the napkins became tricorns.

"Louis . . . is that your name?" I asked.

He didn't answer for a moment. "Whut my name to you, or yours to me?" He heaped silverware on the white cloth, arranged it, knives, forks, spoons. "What you is, a hitchin' post or sump'in?" he asked, delicately switching on the bracket lamp above the table. "Go," he urged. We be in Back Bay, less'n you shake a leg. Go fetch the young lady."

"Yes. Yes, I'd better." I turned and started for the door, then watched as it opened.

The train swerved, and in the doorway Maggie braced a hand against the paneled wall. "I wanted to tell you it's all right," she said. "I mean, if it's closed there'll be—"

She saw the table then, the one among the bare tables in the empty car that had been transformed. The effect was that of illusion, like some resplendent corner of a bare stage, and Maggie stood looking at it.

"If it was closed, there'd be other times," she said, not moving from the entry.

Louis Tilford had removed himself to the galley. I held out a chair at the table for Maggie; slowly, as if not trusting any of it to be real—in a moment the curtain would fall, the house lights turn on—she crossed to the table and sat down.

I installed myself across from her. She unfolded her napkin, the guest of honor at a surprise party, attempting to cope with the surprise.

The steward had materialized from the parlor car and was hastily jotting an order check as he bowed toward us. "Louis has relayed your order, I've taken the liberty of—" He slipped the check behind the sugar bowl and withdrew.

"I—"

"It's—"

We both spoke simultaneously; Maggie laughed, swept back her hair, turned and glanced out at the rain-swept hills and fields that we were now passing through.

"The weather," I said, "continues to refuse to cooperate."

"No, it makes it more special. To be able to sit here and look out at the rain—" A clink and rattle of dishes drew her attention from the window. "Ah, look," she said as Louis Tilford piloted down the aisle.

He did not speak, but lowered the weighted tray from his teetering shoulder, and set upon the table a banquet of delicacies. The thinnest of bread, cut in diamond shapes, housed delicate chicken, accompanied by a sauceboat of mayonnaise, and a dish of celery and olives on ice. The silver bowls of vanilla ice cream were bedded in ice, and with them were a plate of thin cookies and one of mints and bonbons. Each was set on the table, and the seamed, betel-nut face disdained to comment, nor did it invite any comment from us.

Louis's sole utterance was "Pekoe need to steep," as he fussed with the teapot. He arranged the cups, saucers, then from the tray he lifted the final item and placed it at Maggie's plate.

It was a pink rose in a silver bud vase.

"Cook and me," he said, and swung the tray under his arm, "extends our compliments." The stiff legs had piloted back up the aisle before Maggie could reply. She did not take her eyes from him until he'd rejoined his companions at the end table. Then, with a bright, forced smile, she grasped the brown earthenware teapot.

"Let it never be thought—" she took my cup and saucer, tilted the teapot over it "—that acting lessons don't pay off. Miss Folger, the drama coach at the studio, assigned me this scene from a Van Druten play, where I had to serve tea and—lemon or milk?"

"Milk," I said, and unsteadily she reached for the pitcher of milk.

"Had to serve tea," she went on chattily, "and Miss Folger insisted we use props. *I* didn't see it was necessary, but according to Miss Folger . . ."

Chatting in this fashion, she poured herself tea, offered the plate of sandwiches, the celery and olives. With drawing-room formality she stirred her tea, raised the cup to her lips. "It's her theory that the closer you re-create the conditions of a performance—" Shakily she lowered the cup to the saucer.

I leaned toward her. "Maggie?"

"It's nothing." She laughed, swept at the dark, shining mane. "Thinking about Miss Folger brings that waiter to mind. Kindness. The people who are kind when they needn't be," she said, then added with a strange emphasis, "as opposed to the people who are cruel when they needn't be."

"I guess . . . those are the two main divisions," I said, conscious once more that it was Janya to whom I was speaking.

"Yes, but it's not always easy to tell which is which," she replied, and again raised the cup of tea to her lips. "Mustn't forget it's Sunday—every Sunday night I phone Mama in Clarion. The faithful daughter."

"I'm sure you're that—I can attest to it, from all the postcards."

"She's the original kind person, Mama is." She lowered the cup of tea reflectively. "After Papa died she went to work as a scrubwoman at Bates Hospital—no schooling past the eighth grade, it was the best she could find."

I remembered the cone of light above the dining table,

my mother talking of placing an ad for housework. "In the Depression—people had to take jobs they never thought of doing," I said.

"Scrubwoman, then they put her in the kitchen, carrying trays to the patients." She toyed with the teacup, turning it this way and that. "Worked her way up to R.P.N.— that's the lingo for registered practical nurse. All of it for me—someday I just hope I can pay her back."

"You will," I said to the face tilted over, washed by the light from the window. "You'll make it up to her."

She smiled, transforming the grave countenance, suffusing it with its own light. "You can't say I lack for plans. Sundays in L.A.—well, it's crazy what I do. Bananas."

"Tell me about it." I smiled back at her across the snowy cloth, the silver jiggling from the train's motions. "Most things could use a touch of craziness—tell me."

She hesitated, then plunged in. "Well, the outstanding crazy touch is that I, a two-year resident of Los Angeles, neither own nor can drive a car."

"Unquestionably outstanding. Sets you apart."

"Certainly does. The freak category." She paused for some ladylike nibbles of chicken sandwich. "Anyway, frequently on Sundays I go riding the red cars, which is the next crazy touch."

"I require filling in on the red cars."

"You also require more tea." She laughed, replenishing the cups, and described the network of Los Angeles trolleys, painted a bright red, that connected the city with the outlying districts and towns—Pasadena, Whittier, Long Beach, Santa Monica and the San Fernando Valley. "I love the red cars," she said. "Sundays I go tooting off to some neighborhood or section where I haven't been. Then I get off and have a look around . . . for a house for Mama and me."

The animation that suffused her face dimmed and she sought to restore it. "Her whole life, only the prairie to look at—when finally I can afford a house for us, it's to have a view," she detailed. "High in the hills or overlooking the ocean, like the Scullys' ranch, and the moment it's mine I'll go back to Clarion and . . ."

She put down the tea. "Dreams, always plenty of dreams," she mocked herself, then, as if to shrug it off, she turned and glanced out, almost defiantly, at the grove of bent, dripping trees that rolled past the window. "It won't always be dreams," she said, sweeping back her hair. "I may not appear it, but I'm a very determined type, and once I set a goal for myself . . ."

She swung around from the window, and her hand, reaching for the tea, knocked against the bud vase instead. She caught it from toppling, traced a finger over its slender stem.

"Red, not pink," she said slowly, and lifted her finger to the pink petals. "On each table, a vase with a single red rose . . . I can see it still."

I leaned toward her confusedly. "See what, Maggie?"

She stared at the pink rosebud. "Funny to think that everything I came to want," she said, "started because of a train."

I looked at her, tried to piece together what she was telling me. "The Chief?" I asked, and the dark, luminous eyes lifted to mine.

"It stopped once," she said, and the Yankee Clipper, clattering around a turn, shrilled its whistle. "This one Sunday when I was at the depot—I'd go there sometimes, all by myself," she went on, her smile gaining ascendancy over the troubled eyes. "This one particular Sunday, instead of roaring by . . . the Chief stopped."

"Banner event," I said.

"Oh, it was. I stood on the platform right below the dining car—never imagined such magnificence existed," she laughed, the glow returning to her eyes. "To top it off, Joan Crawford was one of the passengers. Till then I'd thought movie stars were pictures that moved on a screen, and when the movie was over and the screen went blank— But, no, there she was on the Chief, Joan Crawford in person. My fate was sealed, you see, then and there." She finished, paused a moment, then took up her cup of tea.

"Except for that, you wouldn't be here on this train. We wouldn't have met," I said.

"Christopher—"

"No, let me say it," I rushed on. "I don't know what, if anything, is in store for us—but I wouldn't trade today for any other in my life. For so long I've had nothing to want or hope for."

"Christopher." She put down her tea. "Before you go any further—"

"You don't understand. If there was only today, no more than that—it'd be enough. You don't believe me, but it's so."

"I—" She looked across the table, her eyes seeking to be gentle. "It's just that I know about wanting," she said. "Everyone wants more, not the same or less than they have."

"And you want . . . what you were just telling me of."

The dark eyes struggled for an answer. "I—I haven't let myself think of anything else." She looked down at the array of jiggling silver. "I don't know," she said. "I don't honestly know."

"Well," I replied with a grin. "I'd prefer that to your knowing absolutely and past all doubt. As for me, it's true about today." I turned, nodded at the rain-streaked landscape that was growing populous with houses and streets, laid out in neat suburban patterns. "Take when I was last in Boston," I said. "It was winter and war—waiting to ship out, weekend passes, stumbling in and out of bars."

"*Bars?*" Maggie looked askance. "It doesn't the least sound like you."

"Definitely bars—also burlesque shows at the Howard," I admitted. "Except I didn't have a knack for either—they always asked for proof of my age, despite the pea coat and uniform."

"That sounds more like you," Maggie laughed. "If I were running a bar I wouldn't have let you in."

"Why not? No, don't tell me." I put a hand over my face. "Innocent. Too damned innocent-looking."

"To me . . . it makes for rather a welcome change."

I lowered the hand and looked at her. "I felt so alone that winter—one freezing sub-zero day I was headed across the Common, couldn't take another minute of it, the whole smear, so I upped and . . ."

"Yes?" Maggie asked, her eyes upon me.

"I picked out a hill in the Common," I said, "frozen hill, gnarled bare old tree on it, hung with icicles . . . and I sat under the tree, numb with cold, and swore up and down to myself it was spring and that at any moment along some path . . ." I watched the rain strike the dining-car window, remembering who it was I had willed to appear on the path. "Hazy on that score," I said, watching the rain strike at the window. "Anything, so long as it wasn't winter and cold any more," I said.

It was a moment before I was aware that Maggie's hand had crossed the table and was resting on mine.

"You'll have to be patient with me, Christopher," she said. "Give me time to catch up to where you are, but even allowing for that—" her voice trembled "—I wouldn't trade today for many others."

I wheeled around from the window and for another long moment was incapable of speech. *Patience?* My God, you'll never see such patience," I exploded, folding my hand over hers. "In fact, after a time you'll be dulled by it—My God, look!" I nodded at the line of storefronts that whizzed past the window. NEWTON PAINT & HARDWARE, a sign reared up. FEDERAL SAVINGS OF NEWTON, came another. "It's Boston," I said. "Ten minutes, we'll be in Back Bay."

"Haven't touched our ice cream yet," Maggie bemoaned, gesturing at the silver bowls and the rest of the array. "We can't not finish it."

"Not Louis Tilford's banquet."

"I couldn't bear it."

Nor could I have, and by the time the Yankee Clipper

rolled into the outer sections of the city, we'd polished off the last of the sandwiches, cleaned the silver bowls of ice cream, and were making headway on the mints and bon-bons.

I took the check from the table, and Maggie waited in the entry while I traveled the burgundy carpet to the galley. The other waiters were in the passage at the side, ready to debark, and there was no sign of the steward. At the table where I'd first seen him sat Louis Tilford in mulish solitude.

He sat at the table, grizzled, knobby head propped on his fist, contemplating the line of tenements, auto dumps and trash—littered vacant lots that sentineled the approach to the railyards. He sat with averted gaze and ignored both the check and the money that I placed on the table.

I was about to turn away, then a thought occurred to me, in regard to Louis Tilford. "Listen, tell me—" I turned back to him "—when I came in here, was the dining car open—or was it closed, and you went ahead and opened it?"

I did not receive the favor of a reply. Louis declined to elucidate, but then a possible answer was suggested. The train slowed, preparing to shuttle under a viaduct, and on the rusty fire escape of a dilapidated tenement was implanted an iron-haired Negro woman, as bony and gaunt and fierce-jawed as Louis. She stood as motionless as an ebony carving, yet as though this were an accustomed vigil. As the dining car rattled past her fire escape she peered over the rusty rail, then slowly waved a red-checkered dishcloth; Louis's response was a brief inclination of his shorn-lamb's pate, after which he turned to me.

"Git 'long," he grumbled. "Git 'long, the young lady be waitin'."

But another aspect of the view from the window had presented itself—droplets still trickled down the pane, but fewer of them: I looked again to make sure, then hotfooted it down the aisle, a choir bursting out within me, to where Maggie waited at the door.

"What is it?" she asked, and in her hand was clasped the pink rose from the table.

"Never a day like this—come look!"

I opened the door and from the platform of the next car gestured up at the skies that had cleared, the rainbow that was arching over the railyards as we shuttled into Back Bay.

We came out of the Back Bay station in the festive procession made up of the *Anniversary* company, and the golden afternoon shimmered around us; the sky was as blue as Bristol glass, the streets glistened like cellophane after the rain, and spread before us was a green-budding city that I had known only in winter.

We queued up on the ramp for taxis, with Abe supervising the giddy proceedings. He parceled the crew off to the Avery Hotel, which they favored, since it was not where the actors were putting up. The latter, refreshed no end by their sojourn in the bar car, divided up into taxis for the Touraine.

"In you go, kids," said Abel, waving Maggie and me into a taxi with Vi Henry. "Okay, anybody left?" He scanned the ramp. Maggie sat next to me, holding the pink rose.

No one was left on the ramp, with the exception of Ben Forbes. The Y was on Huntington Avenue, which lay in the opposite direction from the Touraine. Ben stood twirling his mustache, a macintosh slung over his shoulder in youthful, undergraduate affectation, but looked as old and travel-worn as the scuffed, scarred Gladstone at his feet.

"Driver, wait," Vi Henry said as the taxi started from the ramp. "Ben, dear—" she leaned from the window "—can't we drop you at the Y? It's quite close."

He pulled at the walrus mustache. "Be taking you out of your way."

"Not irretrievably," Vi replied with a smile. "Or you can drop us if you prefer."

He made a show of hesitating. "Shan't crowd you? Quite sure?" But then he was gathering his bags, stowing them in front with the driver; Maggie and I switched to the jump seats, and Ben, much pleased, installed himself next to Vi.

"Much jollier, this," he chuckled. "For a moment there I felt like a boy at school, watching the others go off on holiday."

"Yes, you seemed rather forlorn," Vi said.

Ben twisted around and stared at her. "Good grief, it was here in Boston, wasn't it?" he said, and clumsily addressed the driver: "I say, old scout, would you mind terribly going by way of the Public Garden?"

The taxi made a left into Dartmouth Street, and springtime Boston parted before us, its squares and mews mantled in leafy green and the patina of age and history, the look of having played host to illustrious and significant events.

We turned onto the wide, dignified breadth of Commonwealth Avenue; Maggie-the-tourist took it all in with solemn eyes, the turreted Victorian mansions set on lawns that sparkled emerald in the sun, and behind us Ben said to Vi, "As I recall, your lodgings were hereabouts. Or more toward the Fenway?"

"The Fenway, if memory serves me." Vi laughed ruefully. "How long ago was it, the Year One?"

"The Sothern and Marlowe tour, 1913." With a chuckle, Ben leaned toward us. "Very first tour, a country bumpkin out of Euclid, Ohio—and strolling toward me in the Public Garden one afternoon was a bewitching creature whom I'd seen the night before in *Captain Jinks* at the Castle Square. Well, you know, I was dreadfully unsure of myself in those days, but somehow I mustered the courage to march up to the young lady and introduce myself."

"If he hadn't, I would have," Vi laughed. "You see, I'd been to a matinee of Sothern and Marlowe—and knew exactly who he was."

"The problem was, of course . . . the tour moved on the very next day, and when we met again . . ."

The taxi slowed for the traffic light at Arlington Street, and silently Ben stared out at the Public Garden directly ahead, spreading its bowered greenness behind the iron-picket fence. The sun poured a golden effulgence upon the flower beds and graveled paths, the proud equestrian statue at the entrance and beyond it the footbridge that lifted over the cypress-hung pond.

"Tour moved on, and when we met again . . . how many damnable years had elapsed?" he consulted Vi.

"More than a few—a score, would you say?" she fielded his question.

He settled back, attempted a jovial tone. "Always good chums, of course. Never gave off being chums, did we?" he chuckled, and I thought of the hotel room this morning, hanging up the phone, then the operator ringing back . . . if not for that, the dining car might not have happened. I looked out at the garden's paths, wondered on which Ben had encountered Vi. It sent a cold chill through me, to think how quickly it had ended. Or were there boys already, and it had never begun?

I closed my hand over Maggie's, vowing I didn't know what, except that it would be different for us. The light switched green, the taxi swung into Arlington, and as it did, a wondrous, improbable vessel glided from under the pond bridge, to Maggie's enchanted gaze. The prow was a graceful elongated S, the stern a ruffle of white metal feathers, as circumspectly it ferried its cargo of children across the mossy-banked pond.

"Swan boats—ride 'em every day, if you like," I said.

Two weeks to spend here, two spring-bedazzled weeks; it wasn't winter any more, I was no longer condemned to wander the howling streets alone with nowhere to go. The taxi made another turn onto Boylston, scudded past the rolling, meadowed expanses of the Common. No longer would I clothe out of despair the bare trees with leafy raiment, nor squat on a frozen hill and seek to conjure out of the icy nothingness . . .

"Is that it?" Maggie asked from the jump seat next to me. "Is that where you went walking that day?"

"It's changed so, hardly the same place at all." The trees were no longer bare scaffolds, but each a fiefdom thick with green; the grassy hillocks and slopes glinted gold in the sun, and the meandering paths were thronged with Sunday strollers, family groups, young couples with baby carriages, sedate elders, drawn outdoors by the rain's surcease.

As the taxi continued toward Tremont, Ben spoke up, with an elaborate clearing of throat and as much of an offhand manner as he could contrive. "D'y' s'pose," he inquired of Vi, "that Abel might arrange a single for me at the Touraine?"

Vi was attending to her knitting reticule, tucking in the skeins of wool. "I should think it possible," she allowed. "Why not stop off and ask him?"

"Thing is, it's far more convenient to the theater than the Y." Ben grinned and gave his thigh a resounding whack. "Very well, I shall pop out and have a word with Abel."

The Touraine Hotel (*Special Discount to the Profession,* read the weekly ad in *Variety*) was at the corner of Tremont and Boylston, and the sidewalk in front, as the taxi drove up, was a carnival of actors and luggage, reunions and embraces, played to the required complement of spectators.

The *Anniversary* actors—Tony, Chip, Diana, Scott and Grace—were simultaneously identifying their bags for the edification of a bellhop, collecting money to pay the waiting cabbies, and hailing the thespian guests who had appeared from the lobby to welcome them.

"Gloria Norris, *you* here? But, of course, the Gert Macy play."

"Tod Engle, as I live and breathe."

"Grace Marsden, my God."

Before all of us were quite out of the taxi, Vi, Ben, Maggie and I were swept up in this antic maelstrom, which then progressed into the Touraine lobby, where, with pauses to greet fresh recruits, exchange gossip and make cocktail dates, it converged on the front desk.

"Please, I beg you, sign the register," the harried room clerk beseeched the laughing, chattering arrivals. "I can't assign your rooms until you've registered—or distribute your mail," he wisely added, with a degree of asperity.

The latter did the trick. The Touraine was the first forwarding address given for the tour; seized with an urgent desire for news from home, the company formed a queue at the register. I stood behind Maggie in the line; the bellboy trundled in the carts of luggage; the clerk handed out mail and phone messages as he assigned each room. "What's that, Mr. Klein? A single for Mr. Forbes? I think we can fit him in." The line inched forward and, thinking of the day's bounty, I scouted the lobby for the newsstand, the Boston papers that—who knows?—might carry an ad for a certain all-time movie attraction.

The newsstand—Sunday again!—was closed, but a stack of *Boston Herald*s were on sale at the elevators. It was Maggie's turn at the register, and while she signed in I went over to invest in a *Herald*.

I clinked a quarter in the tin cup provided for that purpose, hefted a bulky Sunday edition from the stack, plucked out the supplement devoted to entertainment.

The lead page offered a large glamorous photo of Irene and Jack, with OPENING AT THE WILBUR bannered above them, but my interest elsewhere, I turned to the movie pages. I skipped the big, splashy ads for the downtown houses and concentrated on the columns that listed the neighborhood fare. A whole page of these, listed according to area—South Boston, East Boston, Dedham, Roxbury, Dorchester . . . I ran an eye down the columns, not really expecting to hit pay dirt—after all, what were the odds?— but considering the day's amazing beneficence thus far . . . reversing direction, I traveled back up to the Cambridge listing, the ad for the Harvard Square Cinema, the name *V. Leigh* in infinitesimal type.

I lowered the pages in disappointment. It wasn't the all-time champ, after all. The actor billed with Vivien Leigh was Ralph Richardson, not, as it should have been, Robert Taylor. Well, not every pin was going to go toppling down in a single shot, a single day.

I folded the entertainment section and crossed back to

the desk. Diana Knapp was signing the register, hampered by some kibitzing from Chip.

"Same floor as mine," he instructed the clerk, with a broad wink. "The lady's too shy to request it."

"Why not adjacent—or for that matter connecting?" Diana coolly parried. "Forget it, Barrett, the lady's not interested."

"The lady," Chip growled, nuzzling up to her, "seems to feel I lack serious intentions."

"She doesn't feel it, she knows it."

"Dinner, then?"

The clerk rang for the bellboy. "Sure, but don't expect the usual payment," Diana concluded the byplay, then turned to indicate her luggage to the boy, her heel crushing something down on the carpet.

She went off with Chip; I retrieved the matted pink rose, severed from its stem, and looked around the lobby for Maggie.

She was standing over by a cretonne sofa in an alcove opposite the desk. Her back was toward me, she was reading a letter gripped tautly in her hands and did not hear me approach. "News from home?" I asked, and she swung around, her face blank and uncomprehending for a moment.

She hesitated, then nodded at the scalloped lavender notepaper. "Did I tell you about Myrt Sample? Mama's best friend at the hospital—retired a few years ago, just when I was getting ready to leave for L.A. and—" She smiled, swept at the dark mane. "I didn't like for Mama to be alone, so Myrt moved in as a boarder."

"Company for each other," I said.

"Yes, and since Mama isn't the world's best correspondent—" she reached for the leather pouch on the sofa "—Myrt keeps me up on their doings." She slipped the letter into the pouch, and from the lavender folds a sheet of white paper drifted to the floor.

"Thanks," she said, as I picked it up, handed it to her. "Well, where did you go off to?" She stuffed the letter in the pouch, slung it over her shoulder. "I turned from the desk and you weren't there. Vamoosed!"

I edged the torn pink bud into my pocket; she hadn't noticed it and somehow I wanted to spare her the sight. "Thought I'd check the Boston papers—you know, for the all-time champ."

"You can't mean—?"

"Not the champ, perhaps, but—" I submitted the *Herald*'s movie listings and fought to rid my mind of what I'd seen scrawled on the loose-leaf paper. "Under Cambridge— regrettably it's not the culmination of your longtime search, but—"

"Regrettable? What nonsense is that?" Her face aglow, she gaped at the page of ads. "Do you realize how few movies Vivien has made? A mere handful, none at all lately. Listen, I'll tell you about her—"

The bell at the front desk *pinged* smartly. "I have your room if you're ready to go up, Miss Jones," the desk clerk called. "And if the young man would oblige me by registering . . ."

I signed in at the desk; the bellboy stood waiting with our luggage. "With Vivien Leigh," said Maggie, "you take what you can get. It's playing two days, let's go to both, shall we?"

"All day, every show."

"I guarantee, the close-up of her swathed in Russian sable is worth it alone." The bellboy bowed us ahead into the elevator. "Besides, the way to look at it is, if I may be pardoned for mangling some poetry—"

It was gone, the flash of panic in her eyes as she'd explained about the letter; washed clear, like the skies over the railyards. "*O wind*," she quoted as the grille slid shut, "*O wind, if Anna Karenina comes—*"

"*Can* Waterloo Bridge *be far behind*," I finished the quotation and the elevator rocketed upward.

She got off at the sixth floor. The bellboy went down the corridor with her bags—I was to wait and he'd take me to my room on seven. Maggie started after him, then slowly turned back to me.

"About dinner, I might send down for something," she said. "I could use a nap . . . and a nice long tub."

"Sure, especially with the opening tomorrow."

She smiled, not very successfully, and for an instant, fatigue seemed to drain her face a chalky white in the dim corridor. "Poor Christopher," she said, looking toward me.

"Why poor? Rich as Croesus. Easily."

"You mustn't worry about me. Good night's sleep and I'll be fine."

She went hurriedly down the corridor. I waited for the bellboy to return, and on the brief whir to the next floor, the journey down the corridor, it ballooned into monstrous proportions, the scrawl I'd seen on the sheet of loose-leaf. Grotesquely at variance with the notepaper's prim, tidy script, it had lurched across the ruled sheet, wild and out of control, incapable of hewing to the lines or any semblance of order.

I stood in the corridor while the bellboy fitted the key in the door. The window at the end framed a rectangle of violet sky, cloudless, tranquil, deepening into twilight above the rooftops.

"Sir?"

I turned away, followed the bellboy into the room, and who was there to warn me that the rain was the least of my enemies?

CHAPTER **8**

The shock waves, beyond that first, preliminary tremor, held back for the time being.

The next day, in its dazzle of sun, gleam of promise, was a heightening of the one before; or the start of it was.

By nine-thirty Monday morning I was on the stage of the Wilbur, substituting for Chip—"Rough night, kid." He'd rung my room. "Goddamn bitch is screwing me. *Isn't*, I mean. Cover till I get there, huh, kid?"

Packing cases, flats, fly ropes; Frank Merkle screaming at the local crew to keep away from his hand props; Edith Merkle carrying off costumes to her basement domain, as though rescuing them from a burning building; Eddie Ruick clambering over the grid lights—by noon, the canvas ceiling of the *Anniversary* set was hoisted like the lid of a giant cigar box over the jigsaw pieces of flats; the crew was lowering the arch into position; and in the midst of the bedlam the door at the rear of the orchestra opened, outlining in a patch of sunlight the slim figure who then was hurrying down the aisle.

"Pictures are out front," she called excitedly to me on the stage. "Line at the box office—fourteen, I counted them."

I jumped down from the apron, jogged up the aisle to her. She wore a boy's button-down shirt, sleeves rolled up, a denim wrap-around skirt, huge sunglasses, and looked approximately twelve years old.

"Obviously you enjoyed a good night's sleep," I said, grinning.

"Glorious." She swung a shopping bag onto a seat, tipped up the dark glasses. "Ran into Ben and Vi in the coffee shop and they took me to Filene's. "Can't tell you the buys." She dipped into the shopping bag. "Pringle sweaters for ten dollars. Liberty prints for five. How's this little item strike you?"

She slid an amber barrette through her hair, tautening it back from her forehead. A couple of stagehands were ogling her, which explained the self-conscious lift of her chin. "Real genuine amber, if you please. What I came to find out is when and if you'll be free for lunch."

"Did I hear correctly, or is that an out and out proposition?"

"See? A good night's sleep and I'm a new person. I can actually look at that stage—" she gestured with the glasses "—knowing I have to go out there tonight—and not break into a tremble."

She turned, flung an arm at the mezzanine rail, the balcony stretching above into the shadows. "I can actually think of an audience filling all these seats tonight, and not worry whether they'll hate me or that maybe . . ."

"Maggie, who could hate you?"

She stared up at the balcony, the climbing rows of seats. "It's going to be different, altogether different. You'll call half-hour, then first-act places . . ." She swung around to me, smiling. "Well, how about it? . . . Not available till Chip's here? Inform me."

She waved the glasses at the stage. "Is that Chip or his double who just wandered in?"

We walked up Tremont Street in the lunch-hour crowds and the brilliant May sunshine that glanced off the shop and restaurant windows and movie marquees, flashed on the buses and auto grilles. For as far as the eye could travel up Tremont, flags were unfurled over the buildings, medieval banners hung for a fair; the verdant expanse of the Common ran parallel, and beyond rose the aristocratic elevation of Beacon Hill, crowned by the dome of the State House that shone molten gold.

Declining to part with the shopping bag, Maggie glided along next to me, chatting of the morning's expedition. "The Boston accent is not exaggerated. You actually hear *caah* and *paak* all over the place. As for the people—"

"Excuse the interruption—" I indicated my jacketless, tieless condition "—but if you'd like some place fancy for lunch."

"That's the Ritz, where Jack and Irene are staying." She pointed out the elegant blue-awninged tower that spired above the Public Garden. "The official movie-star hotel, every big city has one," she chatted on, "but what I've noticed about the people of Boston—"

"Look, about lunch—"

"They're thinner on the whole. More thin types." The crowds that swarmed past were composed of a mix of office girls in cotton blouses and skirts, shirt-sleeved clerks, proper Bostonian men in seersucker and straw boaters, and their feminine counterparts in dowdy flowered hats and the obligatory white gloves. Weaving toward us was a disreputable stray from Scollay Square, watery-eyed, the gingery stubble on his jaw repeated in unkempt tufts and whorls of ginger hair. Maggie turned as he stumbled past, and followed his lurching progress until he melded into the crowd.

"No use wondering where he's from or what home or family he once had," she said, turning back to me. "Any ideas for lunch?"

"Fancy or strictly hamburger?"

"What about you?"

We'd reached the Touraine, at the corner of Boylston. "If you'd care for a movie-star lunch at the Ritz I could zip upstairs and—"

"Sounds very tony, but on the other hand—"

"Won't take me ten minutes to—"

"What about the hill?" she asked, and receiving no answer: "The hill where you went when it was winter and cold and you were alone. Why don't we go there?"

"Maggie—"

"I—I've brought a picnic lunch." She patted the barrette, nodded at the shopping bag. "I thought we could find your hill and have our picnic there."

The traffic light switched green, releasing a wave of pedestrians, who flooded toward us. I took Maggie's hand, and the hammering in my ears muffled out the city noises, as in a dream we crossed over to the Common and stood at the confluence of paths branching off in all directions. Some tunneled under footbridges, others dipped and wound through the green, lifting trees, skirted over hills and down slopes.

"What'd be great, really neat," I said, as we viewed this wide selection of avenues, "is if I couldn't find the hill."

"You will. I have the utmost confidence."

I chose a path at random, set off upon it. I made a game of it, reconnoitering the terrain for landmarks—the bandstand, the Soldiers and Sailors monument, the playing field that was a frozen tundra on my previous excursion, resounding now with the squeals and shouts of a girls' hockey match. The paths intersected, divided, rejoined; we ventured from one to another, past bicycling children, nursemaids with prams, ladies on benches reading Womrath books. I couldn't find it, had no recollection of its location—not that we appeared, from the gales of laughter, the stops at water fountains and for admirings of views, to have embarked on a serious enterprise. At some point, interrupting her laughter, Maggie halted and smote her brow.

"Clear forgot to phone him," she moaned.

"Who?"

"Zinder—publicity for the studio in Boston—supposed to phone him. Ah, well," she airily dismissed it, continuing along the path that turned, steered down an incline, and led to a small, gladelike enclosure.

"This it?" She pointed, and it was, I recognized it at once: not the hill but the huge, venerable oak at its crest, gnarled and thick-trunked, whose branches spread wide arms over the grassy knoll. Twisted skeletons they'd been in winter, but spring had weighted them with curtains of leaves and a twittering chorus of birds.

"Yes, that's it," I said slowly, plunged back to that other time, seeing the bare skeletons again. Maggie went clambering up the slope; she stood under the low, green-drenched branches and looked down at me.

"Well?" she asked. "You swore up and down it was spring—then what?"

"I couldn't decide exactly," I said, caught in old currents. "That's the thing. I didn't exactly know."

"If only we could. Oh, Christopher, if only we could know of the good days ahead." Emotion charged her voice. "Just a glimpse, to get us through the bad days."

"Yes, but—" I remained awkwardly below, in the path. "How could we bear the wait?"

"It's my personal theory—" She tilted up the dark glasses, appraising the landscape, "that someone was meant to happen along that path, while you brooded on your hill. A girl, possibly?"

"Possibly."

She knelt down under the low-dipping branches and placed the shopping bag in front of her. "Sort of a peculiar girl, but not without her assets." From the bag she unfolded a geranium-splashed cloth and spread it on the grass. Paper plates, napkins. "A girl who, each time she ventured to the Boston Common—automatically she brought a picnic lunch along. In the event she ran into a friend."

Still I remained on the path. "I see. A girl prepared."

"For eventualities." From the bag came a bottle of wine, waxed-paper packets, containers, French bread, golden pears, grapes. These she arranged on the cloth, then, brushing the wings of hair from her face, she directed her gaze down the slope.

"You *are* invited, you know," she said, and I climbed the hill, knelt across from her.

"I'm glad I didn't know a minute ahead," I said, not trusting that any of it was real, was happening. "I couldn't have waited."

"I—" She glanced down at the picnic paraphernalia. "On the train yesterday, luckily I'd rehearsed tea, but I haven't done as much with picnics. You'll have to bear with me."

"You flabbergast me. Totally."

"Why, for pity's sake?"

I thought of Louella Meggs and understood again. "I mean, if you could see yourself as you really are. Not just beautiful—my God, you must know that."

"They say—" she smoothed back the barrette and waved a hand "—it's merely skin deep."

"Maggie—"

"Are you starved? Collapsing with hunger?" She busied herself unwrapping the packets of ham, cheese, the containers of salad and pickles, watermelon rind. "I discovered this fantastic store, S. S. Pierce," she informed me. "Only you pronounce it *Purse* for some reason, and I won't attempt to—" She glanced up from her labors. "What's funny?"

"Nothing. Not a thing."

She studied me skeptically, burst out laughing. "It's famous, isn't it, a world-famous store, and guess my parting words?"

"What?" I smiled.

"I told the man I intended to tell everyone I ran into about it. What a hayseed I am! Yes, unfortunately it's true, and furthermore . . ." She paused, then reached into the bag. "The only item Pierce didn't carry—" At my plate she deposited an Oh Henry, a Baby Ruth and a Clark.

"In honor of the club, though you've yet to explain it," she said, and very quickly, the dark eyes wonder-filled: "You're perfectly right. I couldn't have waited, either."

"Maggie, you've given me so much, in so short a time." I took her hand. "It shouldn't scare me, I know, but—"

"Maybe it's that . . . we're not accustomed to things

working out." She looked at me with something close to distress, then smiled and sat back on her heels. "You are the invited guest and are not to lift a finger. No protests, please." She held up an imperious hand. "It's bad form."

"Far be it from me to go against form."

"Exactly. Well, the wine, perhaps," she laughed, surrendering the bottle.

The wine was a Beaujolais, light and skimming on the tongue; we made crusty French-bread sandwiches of the wafer-thin Smithfield ham and Jarlsberg cheese. The salad was tart with vinaigrette, the pears sweet, the exact degree of ripeness . . . I lay back in the shade of the tree, took a bite of Oh Henry, made a hammock of my arms; I gazed up at the blue sky through the thick-leafed branches . . . and they did not change to skeletons.

Maggie looked up from collecting the plates, containers, picnic remnants. "Very quiet, of a sudden," she smiled. "What are you thinking about?"

"That it's over," I said, staring up at the branches. "I mean, about my father."

"Over?"

"His death won't keep happening. That's what I tried to stop, you see."

There was a silence. "No, I'm not sure that I do."

"He's why I came here that day." I stared up at the sky, arms locked under my head. "Used to take Sunday walks together in the park . . . there was a hill we sat on. I came here to resurrect my dead father. It's what I'd tried to do for years . . ."

"You—" Her voice was faint, muffled. "You loved him very much, I gather."

"Too much." A squadron of birds flew over the tree in a flutter of wings; one swooped down, perched tentatively on an upper branch. It was to the bird I spoke, fighting the glistening blur of my eyes. "Too much, so that when he was gone, nothing was left except the dark and being afraid in it."

"Solution to that—turn on a light," Maggie said.

"Or pretend he was coming back. Unusually gifted at that. Explains why the acting came easily—I was at it twenty-four hours a day."

"Acting . . . allows you to be someone else."

"Does it?" I crooked fingers over my eyes. "The other part was the way he died. Of any of it, I was least able to handle that."

Silence, her hand ruffling the grass. "It does no good to talk of it—for your sake."

I pushed up from the ground: She sat down the slope from me, legs curled under the denim skirt, hand riffling the grass, her attitude tense and held back.

"I never have before," I said, after a moment. "Silence is reputed to be golden, but more often it's like iron or steel, encasing you . . . and I couldn't break through it, Maggie, until today."

"Couldn't you?" She raked the barrette through her hair.

"To be free of it—oh, God, don't you see?"

"How did he die? Tell me."

Here was the moment for it, and my mouth would not obey. Stammering, then not even that; I got up, went to the tree, flattened a palm against the rough, gnarled trunk. "Accident," I said, the word like a blow. "The Depression, looking for work—to save money he went without lunch. Printing plant, going up this outside stairway."

"He fell?"

"Dizzy from hunger. Two hundred feet to the concrete."

"How terrible. I'm sorry. Truly sorry."

I dug my nails into the bark, scraped till it peeled off in ragged chunks. "He died broken and smashed on the concrete, alone, with no one to help him, no one there who loved him. I couldn't take knowing of it, so I . . . made up a lie. A fiction."

"He'd come back."

"If not, I'd go looking for him. Some search!" A shudder went through me; I stared blankly at my raw-scraped fingertips, swung around to Maggie. "Coming up Tremont

Street before—the crowds, that old stumblebum you turned to watch?"

"What of him?"

"It's what I did for years, looked for my father in crowds. Train stations, every town, city, crossroads I came to—a fiction, but it didn't stop me."

She plucked at the grass, her eyes riveted on me. "You went on like that? What for, when you knew?"

Far off, the shouts of the girls at hockey floated over the trees. "When I gave up the theater—the jobs, the money, were for him, a lure to get him back, and I thought when I gave that up it was the finish of it."

"Wasn't it?"

"Not so I realized it at first, the only difference was that I looked for him in other ways. Other places and people, other guises."

"I see."

"That is, until . . ." I moved from under the tree a step, not sure why I hung back. "Case you don't realize," I said, "today's more or less an anniversary."

"Oh?" Her tone was neutral. "Of what?"

She knew what, but I told her anyway. "Four weeks ago today in the Garrick alley . . . when I met you. Real, not fiction, this time."

Her head curved down, the wings dipping; she kneaded the grass abstractedly. "I suppose I shouldn't be grateful but I am," she said, after a mulling pause. "What's it brought you? What, aside from pain?"

I frowned. "My father, you mean?"

She lifted the dark eyes to me, sat back on her heels. "I'm grateful I don't remember, or do so faintly it amounts to the same—look what I've been spared."

"Deprived of, too."

"*Deprived?*"

"The memory of someone's love."

"Well," she laughed, "if you're an example of that, no, thanks."

I saw it then, the circumference of torn, shredded grass

her threshing fingers had created around her. "I've upset you, and I'm sorry—it wasn't my intention."

She reached for the barrette she'd tossed on the slope. "Let's not go into it."

"I even thought—I'm not exactly sure, but by talking of it—"

"Really, I'd much rather—"

I dropped to my knees in front of her. "I met you before the alley—some glossies in Max Jacobs' office, of a girl in a garden."

She looked at me, then down at the denim skirt. "Oh, yes, the shots Joe Scully took at the Bel-Air."

"In your eyes, as you turned to the camera . . ."

Slowly, her face lifted, at war with the emotions that played over it. "Yes, what?"

"I felt I knew you, all about you, just from your eyes."

She glanced quickly away, fingers closing over the amber barrette. "Maggie?" No answer and, with pounding heart, I extended a hand and turned the primavera face to mine. "I still don't know why it is," I said, "the feeling that we're alike, sharers in some way."

She submitted to my gaze, my finger crooked under her chin. "You don't know anything about me," she said.

"I feel I do."

"*Think* you do."

It wasn't true: I knew about Louella Meggs and yesterday the grotesque lurching scrawl on the loose-leaf sheet; I knew the legacy we shared—loss, deprivation in one or another form.

"Funny Maggie," I said, brushing the shining hair from her forehead. "Hair like silk, not dandelions—already I dread the moment."

"What?"

"It'll hit you, the incredible array of assets you have— where, I ask you, will it leave me?'"

She didn't react, just kept looking at me. "Well, where?" I laughed, after a moment. "Or is it that your thoughts have flown—" I scoffed at the tug of uneasiness "—to other realms?"

For a slow metronome beat she continued to look at me, then smiled. "Not entirely, but I confess to a slight distraction. The whole of the picnic—" She turned, gestured at the paper cloth littered with crumpled napkins, bits of cheese, pear cores, the empty wine bottle tilted on its side, staining the cloth with the last droplets that trickled out.

"It kept prodding at me the whole while," Maggie said, with a helpless shrug. "I suppose it's just as Vi said this morning—not a thing to do about it."

Another slow metronome beat; I leaned back, arm braced in the grass. "What did Vi say this morning? Regarding what?"

"In the theater, when you're in a play—" She knelt forward, pulled the littered cloth over the ground. "In the theater, Vi says, half-hour begins when you wake." She dragged the cloth to her, the motion harsh, abrasive. "I can only report it starts sneaking up on me at breakfast." She seized the cloth, caught up the ends. "Performance tonight, performance, like some awful echo." She made a bundle.

"Strange." I watched her twist the ends, tie them in a knot. "At the Wilbur earlier you were holding forth on not being nervous any more. The new you."

"Ah, that." She placed the bundle in front of her and surveyed the slope for any leftover litter. "*That* was to try and jolly myself along."

I put out my hand. "Maggie—"

"Omigod." She dove in the leather pouch and, after considerable searching, extracted a Touraine phone-message slip. "Best keep it in sight—" she laid the slip next to her "—lest I never return Mr. Zinder's call."

"Starting now, a pact, Maggie." The face swung up, and I was conscious of the edge to my voice, the effort to reverse the change in her. "A pact, never to mention the past again," I said. "We, I, get bogged down in it, always going back to some event or other, some stupid memory—"

She swept at her hair, smoothed the denim skirt. "Christopher, you really mustn't be so serious," she said.

"It's just—"

"So intense and serious about everything, at the drop of

a hat." She ran the barrette through her hair, drawing it taut. "I mean, I thought a picnic would be fun—wasn't it?"

"Maggie, don't. Not like this." She started to object. "Just say it straight out. No embroidery."

"Embroid—?" She laughed in protest. "Whatever are you—?"

"Easy to say it." I stood up, brushed the bits of dirt and grass from my chinos, took hold of the clanking, bundled cloth. "Picnic was fun, but what . . . it's over?"

"Over! Really, you're the limit." She scrambled to her feet indignantly. "What's changed? Everything's the same as it was. I refuse to have you look like that."

"Like what?"

"As if . . ." She frowned, slid on the dark glasses, and turned away. "Shall we go?"

She started ahead of me, then drew back; took off the glasses and stared up at the tree. "It's gone," she said, gesturing with the glasses at an upper branch. "Did you notice it there? Birds are such silly creatures—the least little thing frightens them away."

Then she slid the glasses back on and proceeded ahead of me, slim and silent and beautiful, down the hill.

We walked under the colonnades of the trees, out of the Common, and across to the Touraine; rode the elevator together to the rooms a floor apart, and I did not see her again until that night at the theater.

It was a Maggie whose existence I would not have conceived of and could scarcely believe, despite the witness of my eyes, the numbed membranes of my hearing.

At the hotel, in the room that narrowed at the airshaft window like a slice of pie, I sorted out the week's accumulation for the luandry; wrote to Agnes Theresa (*As Cash will have told you, New Haven went quite well, and with three more performances to iron out the kinks . . .*); I showered and dressed, tried Maggie's room at six-thirty; it didn't answer, and I went to the Childs on Boylston Street for baked beans and brown bread, then in the blue twilight to the Wilbur.

The scalloped-glass marquee lights of the handsome red-brick theater glowed brightly, and I paused to inspect the cast photos and newly painted house-boards.

MAX JACOBS
presents
IRENE VAIL   JOHN MILLET
in the Broadway Comedy Success

ANNIVERSARY

by
Hal Stein and David Compton
with

| Ben | Violet | Scott |
| Forbes | Henry | Andrews |

and
MAGGIE JONES

I waved at Abel Klein, who was in the lobby, gabbing with the box-office man. Evenings, Abe sported a carnation in his lapel, to go with the black, versus brown, derby, and from the wide grin as he waved back I took it that sales were going well, better than he'd calculated. Full houses and good notices in Boston would hypo the advance sale in Chicago, maybe provide the impetus for a long run.

The Wilbur stage door was around the corner on Stuart Street. It was seven-thirty; the stage doorman peered up from his tilted chair and evening *Globe*. Most of the dressing-room keys were in the pigeonholes, but two who had claimed theirs were Grace Marsden and Tony Ives; breathless as Alpinists, they toiled up the stairs to their nooks.

"I insist on an hour's quiet contemplation before a performance," Grace was declaring. "I simply require it."

"Sweetie, you've got eight lines in this show," Tony

pointed out. "It's not like you're going on as Mrs. Alving."

"Ah, but those eight lines *are* my Mrs. Alving," said Grace as they rounded the stair-turn and a burst of melody cascaded down the passage from Dressing Room 1.

"*Ah, sweet mystery of life at last I've found you,*" sang Irene, spirited if off-key, and accompanied by the swish of a scrub brush. "It's you, Donatello! Isn't Boston divine? Has your day been bliss?"

Garbed in an old robe, with a bandanna to protect her coiffure and rubber gloves her manicure, Irene was scrubbing her dressing-room floor, having piled its contents on a wicker chaise pushed to the side. "Naughty Leora swore to come early and didn't," she explained, her ample behind working toward the doorway. "We're sold out tonight! The muses are encouraged!"

"Naughty Leora and naughty Oscar were very much in evidence at the track today," contributed Jack from Dressing Room 2, across the passage. Toupeeless, he was jotting contentedly on a racing form. "Glorious double in the fifth. Old Puss, of course, was at Arden's."

"Somehow—" Irene extended a hand and I assisted her to her feet. She peeled off the rubber gloves. "Somehow I never feel wholly secure in a city that hasn't an Elizabeth Arden's, and when you throw in a Ritz as well!" She took some silver-framed photographs from the chaise and set them on the dressing table—Jack and Irene paired with Marion Davies and Hearst; a Madonnalike study of Mildred Millet gazing into a lacy bassinet.

"Taken in Montreux, where the twinnies were born," she reverently informed me. "The three of us stashed for weeks in a wretched chalet." The soulful orbs turned upon me, frowning. "Donatello, you seem less than gay this evening. Problems?"

"No. I'll empty this for you."

As I turned in the passage with the scrub pail the stage door opened and in tumbled Vi Henry and Ben Forbes, arm in arm and in high good humor.

"Entire afternoon at the Gardiner." Ben glowed at me.

"Favorite museum in the world, I do really think, eh, Vi?"

"That and perhaps the Frick. Tell us, Christopher"—Vi's summer-blue eyes had an extra sparkle; for once the knitting bag was absent from her arm—"how was the picnic? The child was beside herself with plans."

"Child" was Vi's name for Maggie. "Great, absolutely great," I enthused, and proceeded down the stairs to the basement. Above me, the stage door opened to yet another happy duet—Chip and Diana, glowing about dinner at Locke-Ober, in contrast to this morning's acrimony. I entered the low-ceilinged room that extended beneath the stage and was reserved for the pit men when a musical was at the Wilbur. Its present mute occupants consisted of Edith Merkle's ironing board, sewing table and machine, and the racks of costumes that hung from their packing cases. In the shadows the women's gowns glimmered like phantom butterflies, and as I carried the pail to the laundry basin at the back, some ghostly refrain seemed to echo, faint and scratchy as Cash's Victrola: *Still . . . not out . . . of the cellar . . . yet.*

The soapy water gurgled down the drain, then a clang as the pail slipped from my hand. Silence was not golden, it was sheet metal, cast iron that had welded itself around me, sealed me off, and when finally at the picnic today . . .

What were Maggie's secrets that she could give them no utterance? Today, tomorrow was what counted, nothing else.

I rinsed out the pail, crossed back to the stairs, heard the creak of the stage door as I started up. Then, as my level of vision ascended with the stairs, I saw the polished black gleam of a man's shoes, the swirl of a chiffon evening skirt.

The man wore evening clothes and was holding the door open for Maggie. "Nonsense." He smiled at her. "I hadn't expected my committee duties to be nearly so agreeable."

He turned to the startled audience in the passage—Ben, Vi, Irene, who'd ventured from her doorway—and gave them a polite, acknowledging bow. He was tall, acquiline, as well-mannered and correct as the cut of his evening clothes. He turned back to Maggie. "Call for you here at eleven?"

"Eleven-thirty. To get out of my makeup."

"Loads of time—the raffle's not till midnight." Another faultless bow and he exited to the street. Eyes glittering, face upraised from the velvet folds of her cloak, Maggie leaned against the stage door, and from the dressing-room stairs a long, low whistle issued from Tony Ives.

"Upon my word, Esther Blodgett, who was that?" he demanded. "If it wasn't a Cabot, it was a Lodge or a Lowell, or a combination of all three."

She leaned against the door, looking, in the black velvet evening cloak, jewel-clasped at the throat, the personification of everyone's concept of a young actress—illusory, romantic, unreal. The gown that swept from under the cloak was flame-colored; she clutched a beaded gold evening purse, matched by gold kid slippers that peeped from under the flame skirt.

"Borrowed," she laughed to Tony, with a gesture at her costume, avoiding the lower stairs where I stood. "It's been madness, since the moment I phoned Mr. Zinder. Tore off in a cab to the Copley Plaza. He's handling the publicity for this enormous charity ball tonight and—"

"Esther, who was the gent?" Tony indicated the door. "Surely it wasn't anybody named Zinder."

"No, that was, let me get it right—Cabot Olcott."

"Dear God."

"Who's on the ball committee and arranged for this outfit to wear to pick the winning raffle ticket—"

"You're to appear at the ball tonight?"

"Lord knows where else—dancing tomorrow night, some country club or other on Sunday." She smiled, the words spilling pell-mell from her. "I mean, with Cabot, not Mr. Zinder, though he's responsible for it. He represents the studio in Boston, publicity and so forth—"

The spill of words stopped abruptly, the glittering eyes swung toward me. "Apparently the papers give the ball a lot of coverage and—" Again she stopped, then laughed. "Listen, is there actually something called the Myopia

Hunt Club? Is that where Cabot actually said he was taking me?"

I didn't hear any more of her narrative. There was a flurry of embarrassed glances from the group of listeners. Irene looked on with so mournful an expression that sobs appeared imminent; I pushed down the passage, through the fire door to the stage.

In the wings I groped over the tangle of cables to the lectern at the light board, from which Chip would cue the show. I flipped on the gooseneck lamp, located my script in its binder, and went onto the stage.

The curtain was raised, as it always is before a performance, for reasons I never could determine. At the rear of the auditorium, red exit lights picked out the marching rows of seats, and from its iron stance, the muzzled work light threw shadows across the *Anniversary* set: the bay window that looked out upon the painted drop; the doors that opened in instead of out. As at the first rehearsal, I went about the set, unfurling the dust sheets from the furniture.

Up behind the set, the fire door thudded; then Maggie was standing in the center arch, below the shadowed rise of the stairs. The velvet cloak was folded over her arm; the flame chiffon gown had a halter neck that bared her shoulders; the pleated skirt fell in layers sprinkled with brilliants. She looked across the stage at me, and I at her, and neither of us spoke.

She tossed the dark hair from her bare shoulders. "It's past seven-thirty. Have to be getting ready." She was silent while I tore a dust sheet from the wing chair at the mantel. "If you'd care to talk—"

"Yeah, sure. The Myopia Hunt Club." She turned, moved from the arch, and I crossed after her, shaking with anger and hurt.

"Jesus, how cheap. Tawdry and cheap. I wouldn't have credited you with it."

"I didn't start any of this." She turned in the arch, her chin jutting defiantly. "I tried to put you off, but you wouldn't be put off."

"Yeah, guess I wouldn't."

"Catch you looking, every time I turned."

"I was wrong, see."

"The damned candy bars. Knocking yourself out about the dining car."

"I had this mistaken notion," I went on, flat, toneless, "that you needed somebody, just as I did. Couldn't dope it out, though. How could Miss America the Beautiful need anyone?"

Her hand tightened on the velvet cloak. "Christopher, it's no—"

"How could it be?" I looked at her from below the arch. "A beautiful will-o'-the-wisp, never quite there. Turn, and you were gone, vanished on the wind. So beautiful, yet so lacking in self-belief. I couldn't fit it together."

"Couldn't you?" She crossed down to the chintz sofa, folded the cloak over the back, tossed the purse on the cushions. "What about when you saw me with Louella Meggs?"

The silence was mine then.

"It's all right." She rubbed her bare arms as though she were cold. "I realized you realized."

"Maggie, listen—"

She paced back and forth, the brilliants flashing in her skirt. "Like her," she murmured to herself. "Like her."

"It doesn't matter." The knot in my stomach was untwisting; the hopelessness I'd felt, stronger than the anger or hurt, was lessening. "It doesn't matter. I'm the one who dragged up the past today."

She stopped her pacing. "You're right," she said.

"I could never talk of my father. Finally I did. I can put it behind me now—"

She shook her head. "I don't mean about that."

"We'll make a pact, never to—"

"It hasn't to do with that." She gathered her cloak, purse, from the sofa. "What matters, the only thing that really matters," she said evenly, "is that you're not what I want, Christopher."

I stared at her, and when I didn't answer, she folded the cloak over her arm, started back toward the arch. "I don't believe it," I said slowly.

"It's the truth."

"How would you know the truth from a lie?"

She paused in the arch, gestured. "Here it comes, folks. The accusations."

"So many lies, how would you know any more?"

"Step right up and guess the little lady's lies, folks."

"Stop that."

"Round and round she goes, where she stops nobody—"

"*Stop it.*" She turned, started from the arch, was blocked by my shoving in front of her. "I don't believe it," I said.

"No one ever does." She made to move past me; I caught her by the wrist. "It's getting near eight. I have to make up. Let go."

"Maggie."

"Let go. You're hurting."

"You lied. It's not true. You do want me."

She twisted her arm, the cloak slipped to the floor. "You're hurting me. Is that what you'd like? Let me go."

I gripped her struggling arms, pinioned them to her sides. "This morning when you came here to the theater, didn't you want me?"

"No! Only not to hurt you!"

"The picnic, the wine, the hill—wasn't that wanting me?"

"You'd been kind. Been of help."

"Maggie." I held her wrists in one hand, raised the other to the shining hair. "What terrible things were done to you? How could you think I'd add my share?"

"Please."

I swept the hair from her face. "If only we could glimpse the good days in store, you said. To get through the bad."

She looked up at me, not struggling as fiercely. "The good, yes, I said that, didn't I," she repeated, in a murmur. "The good in store."

"We're so close to it, can't you see?"

"Close." She looked up at me.

"So close. Almost there." I tilted up her face to mine. "You feel it, too. I know you do."

Her eyes shone. "Almost there?"

I trembled and brought my mouth down to hers. "I love you, Maggie," I said.

"Yes? Really?"

My mouth moved on hers, softly, then in a hungry grinding. She tensed for a moment, pressed closer. "Like this?" she asked, opening her mouth under mine. "This?"

I was shaking, lights spinning like catherine wheels, exploding, bursting inside me. "Jesus, Maggie." My mouth closed over hers, I slid a hand to the bare shoulder. "So long so alone. Jesus, Maggie."

She thrust close against me, darted her tongue in my mouth. "This? Like this?"

"Christ." I rubbed the bare shoulder, slid my hand down the smooth, supple arm, up the flame bodice, cupped the small, full breast.

"Nothing counts," I moaned, grinding my mouth on hers. "Nothing else, just you, being with you."

"Being with me." She pulled her mouth away, looked up at me. "By that do you mean going to bed with me?"

"I—" I reached with my mouth again.

"I'm willing," she said, "if it will help get rid of you."

It was the flat even tone that I heard first: the flat, detached, matter-of-fact tone, and only after did the words themselves register. I stared at her and like automatons my arms fell away from her.

"Well?" she went on in the same even tone. "Strikes me as a fair exchange. I've made that type bargain before. Is it a deal or isn't it?"

I stared at her and she swept at her hair. She reached down, gathered the velvet cloak from the floor. "Borrowed, like everything about me," she said, and moved down from the arch. She shielded her face with a hand, lowered her hand in slow deliberation, and looked out at the dark auditorium.

"Choices," she said. "It's what it's all about. Sooner or later, everything comes to a choice."

"Oh?" I said dully. "And you made your choice?"

"Only thing happens . . . I keep on making it." She gazed out at the climbing rows of seats. "When I took the bus to L.A.—most I thought I'd get was extra work. Crowd scenes. Then one day Joe Scully came into Nemiroff's and—"

"Bam. Hit the jackpot."

"It's ending, Joe says." She stood motionless, looking out at the empty rows of seats. "The big studios, Metro, Warner's, the long-term contracts, the bosses like Louis Mayer and Mr. Harmon—Joe says count the television antennas on any given street, that'll tell you."

She hugged the velvet cloak to her. "The end, but I wasn't too late for it. For once, I didn't miss out." She raised her head, the vision of her stunning on the empty stage, and gazed up at the gold-fringed curtain suspended above her. "At the movies, when the picture's over and the screen goes blank . . . I far prefer a curtain falling, don't you? Never dreamt I'd be part of this either."

"Choices."

"Yes." She took the cloak and swirled it around her bare shoulders. "You didn't say if it's a deal or not."

I didn't grasp what she was referring to.

"The free fuck, if you'll keep away afterward," she said, and when there was no response, crossed up to the arch. I didn't move to go after her; stood where I was at the right of the stage.

"The little girl, she'll still be there," I said. "Janya won't ever let you go, no matter who you pretend to be. It's her you'll always see, in every mirror you look in—not what you are, only what you were."

She faltered as she reached the arch, wavered there in the shadows. "You can't hurt me," she said. "Anything you think to say, worse has been said."

"And the secrets you hide, the lies—"

"I've lived with them up till now. Not so badly."

"It's honestly on the whole a shame." My voice broke; I clamped my jaw. "I'd have been good for you, Maggie. For nobody else, maybe, but—"

"Which?" she spat, gripping the newel post. "Which secret would you like dished up?" She laughed, waved a hand, dismissing it. "Win some, lose some, that's how the game goes. You'd be surprised, how little your losses really amount to."

"I—"

"Because when you get right down to it," her voice cut savagely, "I'm no one, Christopher. No one at all." Silence, then her hand sweeping back her hair. "It's half-hour, Teach. Can I go now? Huh, can I?"

But she was already gone, vanished into the shadows of the wings. I listened to the fire door close on her; finished removing the dust sheets and stored them backstage. I deposited my script on the sound-effects table positioned behind the window drop, angled to provide a sight line to the stage. I tested the door slam, which was placed off right of the arch, complete with doorknob and padded frame.

I opened the door, clicked it shut, opened it, slammed it, again, once more, again, hard as I could, harder, slamming it over and over, ignoring the tears on my face.

Then, wiping my face, I went out to make the rounds of the dressing rooms, calling half-hour.

"Half-hour, Miss Vail."

"Fifteen minutes, Mr. Millet."

"Ben, first-act places, please."

On stage, Frank Merkle set the first-act hand props in position, and the actors, vivid in costume and makeup, otherworld creatures, paced in the wings. Irene, attended by Leora, stood above the stairs, poised for her entrance; below stood Maggie Jones, waiting to climb to her mountaintop. She did not glance at me as I went past, nor I at her.

At eight-forty I came back from the lobby with Abe's nod to go up, and Chip cued Eddie Ruick at the dimmer. *"House down . . . house to half . . . house dark."* I took up my post behind the window drop; a hush fell out front. With a rush the curtain rose on the lighted stage and the play began.

Two weeks later, backstage after the final performance in Boston, the long-distance call from Clarion was put through to Maggie.

The days had become rudderless again, as in New York, the hours empty and drifting, occupied with meaningless pursuits. The mornings were disposed of by sleeping till noon—not difficult, since I'd joined the regulars who congregated in the bar up from the stage door each night after the show. This landed me in bed by three or four A.M., sufficiently liquored for sleep. Then up at noon and out of the hotel, so as to avoid elevator-lobby encounters with M. Jones. It was unnecessary, since she didn't loiter around the premises herself. If Cabot Olcott's vintage Bentley was not parked in front of the hotel, the likelihood was that the couple had already roared away for the afternoon's diversion. The photo of Maggie drawing the winning ticket at the charity ball had garnered prominent space in the papers. It was followed by society-page photos of Maggie and Olcott dancing at the Ritz, attending a hunt breakfast, polo match, art exhibit.

I spent the afternoons tramping the city. Long hikes along the Charles or the Fenway; museums, libraries; by foot over the Harvard Bridge to Cambridge and the secondhand book shops crowded along Brattle Street. Browsing among the crammed, musty shelves, exploring the books stacked like miniature villages on the floor, disposed of several afternoons, and the walk back to Boston brought the hour to six or seven. Supper, then to the theater by half-hour, curtain up, curtain down, and over to the bar with the regulars. To bed by three, awake by noon, the room blurring into focus . . . made from a thousand mornings.

The days were becoming lost again, I could see no means of repairing the break with Maggie, and by the second week I'd sought out Abel to talk to him about giving my notice.

I bagged him between the Wednesday matinee and the evening performance, in that most favored of his reserves, the box office. Derby pushed back, cigar mashed between his teeth, he was studying last week's statements, which he went right on doing as I stammered out my decision.

"I—I just think it's the better thing for me," I said. "I haven't any real reason to stay on—and you might as well replace me here in Boston."

"Why, kid?"

"It'll save Max a fare to Chicago." I shifted uncomfortably. "Y'mean, why give in my notice? I figured you knew."

"I mean," he slapped at the sheets, "why, after we did twenty-three thousand last week and ninety percent capacity this week—"

"Abe, I've made up my—"

"Terrific reviews, phones full blast, lines at the window —why won't Max hold over a third, a fourth week here? Why is he so hot on Chicago?"

"Abe, I'm handing in my notice. Official."

He pulled down the derby, flicked at the cigar. I'd yet to observe him take a puff.

"So answer me this." While he spoke he eyed the ticket buyers at the grille. "These dates she's been having with the Beacon Hill guy—it don't strike you she's overdoing it?"

"If so, it's only to make clear that—"

Abel chewed on the cigar, meditating. "Quiet girl, for such a looker. Hardly a peep from her, but I get the impression she's taken it on the chin a lot. Correct me if I'm mistaken."

I hesitated. "No, but it doesn't change the situation."

"The situation—you're positive you know what it is?"

"Enough to realize—"

"Tell you how it strikes me, kid." The shrewd eyes rested on me. "The ride's gotten bumpy, so you want to get off."

I was quick with annoyance. "Abe, I have to say I resent—"

"In New Haven, remember, I gave you a push." He shoved the cigar back in. "Permit me to repeat the gesture. No, I don't accept your notice."

"But—"

"Skip the buts. At least hang around long enough—" he clapped a hand on my shoulder "—so I get the opportunity not to have to call you 'kid' any more." Wiggling around in the phone-booth dimensions, he returned to the box-office sheets. "Meanwhile, I'm busy. Scram."

That night after the show, in a letter to Max, I formally submitted my notice; yet what Abe had said of my behavior lingered in the pie-shaped room, not easily dismissed, and I tore up the letter.

It was after the curtain calls on Saturday night, as Maggie came off stage, that she was informed of the Clarion operator's efforts to reach her.

The performance was sold out; the box-office man, when I went to check the curtain time with Abe, was hanging up the S.R.O. sign for the benefit of the line at the grille. Arriving by taxi and limousine, a festive Saturday-night audience, many in evening clothes, swarmed into the Wilbur's lobby.

"Who is she? Isn't she lovely?" murmured the arrivals inspecting the lobby photos of Maggie, while others remarked of Irene, "You must hand it to her. Always a lady, even when she played a murderess on the screen."

They pressed toward the ticket takers, "Who is she, isn't she lovely," streamed up the balcony stairs and into the orchestra level, an audience such as actors are wont to savor later on, for sustenance to tide them over lean periods.

What with the standees, we didn't ring up until eight-fifty. *"House down . . . house to dark,"* Chip cued, and the curtain rose on Jack posed at the mantel. He was greeted with solid applause, as was Irene when she glided down the stairs. Momentarily startled, she spoke her first line and

213

was further startled by the laugh that had previously eluded her.

It was that sort of audience. From her mountaintop, Maggie Jones flew down the stairs into the white-hot arena glare, and the stir out front was audible in the wings, where a performance independent of the one on stage was being enacted.

Behind the flats, the crew crouched in readiness. The packing cases had been transported up from the basement. Each prop, as its use in the play was over, was snatched up, instantly wrapped for packing. The actors came off stage and Edith Merkle fell upon them, reclaimed each costume as it ceased to be required. While the laughter rolled in from out front, the physical properties of *Anniversary* were being dismantled for the scenery van parked outside for loading.

The performance ran over by eight minutes, due to the volume of laughter. Exiting after her final scene with Jack, Maggie was dumbstruck: The audience was giving her a hand. They were applauding her, and when at the calls each actor stepped forward for his bow, the waves crashed thunderously over her. A final company call, the curtain made its final triumphant descent; the actors, makeup perspiring, filed off stage, undoing collars, hooks, zippers as they went, and colliding with the crew that herded on to strike the set.

For once Frank Merkle suffered my assistance with the hand props, and it was several minutes before I came off stage to a puzzling scene in the dressing-room entry.

Maggie was at the pay phone across from the key rack. Abel stood nearby, and grouped in a tableau about them were the actors. No one spoke, and when Edith Merkle clattered down the stairs with a pile of costumes, she was silenced by distressed glances.

"Long distance?" Maggie said into the phone.

"I decided better you finished the show," Abe explained gently. "The operator said urgent, but different people interpret it differently."

"Hello, Myrt?" The heavy stage makeup streaked down Maggie's face; the back of her dress was unhooked. She pitched her voice against the noise on stage. "Is that you, Myrt? It's me, Janya. Are you at the hospital?" She listened a moment. "It's all right," she said into the phone. "You can tell me about Mama."

The next morning at six A.M. Abel escorted Maggie from the Touraine and waved a taxi to the curb. He had arranged her transportation: the flight to LaGuardia in New York, the ten o'clock direct flight to Wichita. But Clarion was seventy miles from Wichita, there was no one to meet her—and how would she get there?

The taxi drew up, the night porter loaded her suitcases in the rear. I stepped from the entrance with my cowhide and zippered canvas bag. Across in the Common the trees were cobwebbed in morning mists, through which the lamps on the paths cast blobs of light pale as the dawn sky. Ida Belton was in a coma in Bates Hospital; her condition was listed as critical.

"Don't worry about the show," Abel said to Maggie. "Enough to worry about the Mama. Diana can go on for you if she has to."

He opened the taxi door. "The Daphne Hotel in Chicago—we get in Monday morning. I gave you the number?"

Maggie turned to him at the curb. "Yes, I have it."

"I'll notify Harmon," Abe advised her. "Any help I can give, ask."

I moved toward the curb, handed the cowhide to the porter. "It's seventy miles from Wichita to Clarion," I informed Maggie. "You don't drive. You'll need a car, someone to drive you."

No reaction from her, but Abel, with a grunt, stuffed some money in my seersucker jacket. "Don't argue," he said. I told him I'd get a Monday flight from Wichita. "It'll get me to Chicago by five."

"Good," Abel said. "That's good, kid," and pushed me into the taxi with Maggie.

The taxi prowed through dawn streets as deserted as if some alarm had sounded a mass evacuation. The driver swung into North Street, the approach to the tunnel to Logan Airport, and Maggie fixed her glance ahead.

"You have no one to drive you," I said. "Someone has to get you there."

The taxi steered into the tunnel. "I suppose it's time to fill you in," she said, expressionless. "Mama's first stroke was two years ago."

"Instead of—"

"Shortly after the baby episode . . . and not long before I took the bus to L.A."

"Maggie—"

"Causing a good deal of comment," she went on, and the taxi rocketed up from the tunnel into the rose-pearl light. She rummaged in her purse; Joe Scully's medal pinned to the inside made a dull glint of gold. She took out the sunglasses and said, "No way to prevent it, is there?"

"Prevent what?"

She glanced down at the dress, the yellow dress she was wearing. "No way to keep you from finding me out," she said, and slid the dark glasses over her eyes as the taxi turned onto the road for the airport.

CHAPTER 9

The baby was the climax of the story that over the next twenty-four hours was unfolded to me.

What Maggie did not tell of it, in blunt, unsparing terms that asked for no sympathy, was supplied by the town of Clarion itself, the prairie and the railroad tracks that cut across it a path of escape—a story of dreams and make-believe, of people who were kind and those who were cruel, and the choices that were bred from these factors.

Choices: It was most of all a story of choices, as I was to discover by the actions it led me to take . . . which bore out what all along had been expected of me.

But before any of this, before Clarion or Miss Gilmore, or the strange reception committee at the hospital, there was the prairie to form the backdrop for the story—the highway that traveled over the unending flatness of wheat and sorghum, a monotony of land and sky and the white, ever-pursuing ball of the sun, endlessly repeating itself until, after two hours at the wheel of the car, my throat grew parched and constricted and my vision glazed over in stupefaction.

Unfamiliar with the quirks of the rented Plymouth sedan, I steered along the two-lane asphalt, grateful when the flatness was relieved by the thrust of a water tower or granary, or a farmhouse roof poking up from a grove of cottonwoods. I loosened my tie, pulled at the sweat-damp shirt—the seersucker jacket had been shed after a few miles —and alongside me on the sticky-squeaky seat Maggie yawningly stretched her arms.

"Mighty silent, pardner," she remarked, in the exaggerated corn-pone twang that was among her present affectations. "What's ailin' yer? Speak up, pardner."

"*Pardner.* That's more Texas than Kansas, isn't it?"

She tilted her head back on the seat, removed the sunglasses, and traced airy patterns with them. "Reckon it is, reckon it is," she laughed. Since Boston her mood had swung between antic playfulness and bored distraction. She'd avoided any direct references to her mother or the latter's condition. During the stopover at LaGuardia in New York, she'd amused herself at the gift counter while I'd phoned Bates Hospital. She was examining a toy panda when I came out of the phone booth.

"Couldn't get through to the room," I reported, "but her condition is still listed the same."

"Pandas, you know, belong to the raccoon family. You'd assume bears, but not so. Still critical?"

"I said we'd get there by three."

"A rare species of raccoon, found only in China." She set the animal on the counter. "Did you know that I once visited a Chinese fortress? Not real, of course. Pretend."

"If you want, I'll phone again from Wichita."

"Is that our flight on the loudspeaker? Essentially planes are dumb, don't you think?"

On the DC-3 to Wichita she'd declined the stewardess's coffee and rolls and requested a split of champagne. "On second thought, it wouldn't do to arrive tiddly. Might we have a deck of cards?"

We'd played gin rummy. "Absolutely blitz you," she crowed, scooping up her cards. After a few hands, flinging them down. "Card games are ultimately boring. Take you on at movie titles."

"How d'you play that?"

"Alphabet—I name a title begins with A, then you do, on down till one of us gets stuck."

"You'll really blitz me at this."

"Ready? *As Thousands Cheer*."

"Er . . . was *Arrowsmith* made into a movie? I'm not sure, but—"

"Yes, yes. Ronald Colman and Helen Hayes. On to B. *Bringing Up Baby*, Hepburn and Grant."

"Uh . . . *Beau Geste*."

"Ha, book title again. C. *Castle on the Hudson*." She leaned back, gazed out at the clouds. "Did you know I once lived in a castle?" she asked, her voice strained and wondering. "Pretend, of course, but to me it was realer than anyplace."

The highway continued its flat, interminable unwinding. A gas station loomed in the distance, as starkly isolated as on a desert. The towns were like that, distant smudges on the horizon, materializing into a huddle of roofs, church steeple, storefronts, then snuffed out again: little towns snuffed out like candles by the unending prairie vastness. I looked at the speedometer and gauged from the mileage total that we'd covered close to seventy miles. No signposts yet, but Clarion would be soon.

"My, my," said Maggie in her corn-pone twang, as a lone billboard shot past. "The Kansas Four-H is havin' theirselves a jamboree." She might have been returning on idle whim, for a high-school reunion or the wedding of a girlhood chum, a whim that on the whole she regretted. With a bored sigh, a furnace-blast of air whipping at the primavera face, she regarded the railroad tracks that were again running parallel to the highway, as they had done intermittently since Wichita. Rather than overwhelmed by the vastness, the shining bands of steel appeared impervious to it, liberated from it, charting their own separate and unmired course.

"Never the least real, either," Maggie said, contemplating the tracks, the freight cars moored here and there on sidings. "Not the slightest real, till that Sunday with the Chief," she said, then straightened up abruptly on the seat.

Several miles ahead, what had appeared as two faint,

vertical pencil strokes on the horizon were materializing into the towers of two granaries, toward which the tracks, departing from the highway, now veered. To the left, a mile or so on, blown aslant by wind or cyclone so that it could not be deciphered until we were upon it, a rusted, paint-chipped signpost reared up: WELCOME TO VILA COUNTY. CLARION, 5 MI.

"Here we are," I said.

"Yes, here we are." She sat up very straight, corn-pone accent discarded, eyes leveled on the town that was taking shape in the distance, emerging out of thin air. Only once did she turn her glance away, to nod, a few miles farther, at a rutted dirt road that straggled through a tangle of weeds and brambles to cease its weary efforts at a ramshackle collection of rotted planks that teetered over a dried-up gulley.

"The drawbridge," she said almost fiercely, "to the Chinese fortress," then refastened her gaze on the swiftly materializing town. To the right the Santa Fe tracks sheared across the prairie toward the towering hulks of the granaries; sharing the horizon beyond were a clutter of roofs, chimneys and steeples, silhouetted low against the sky. Houses, streets, fences, yards—all at once it took shape; churches, schools, a depot, strung together by a cat's cradle of telephone wires, set back from the highway, isolated from it by a mile-long road.

"It's not true," Maggie said in a low voice as I turned onto the road to Clarion. "It's not true that you can't go home again. Mostly, you can't do anything else."

In moments the road was behind us and we were entering the town proper, through streets so sparsely populated that a Sunday edict might have forbidden all excursions save those for divine worship. I drove through the dozing afternoon quiet and the bang of a screen door was like a thunderclap. A woman sat rocking on a porch; in a driveway a man washed a 1930's Ford; some children frolicked under a sprinkler on a lawn, the liveliest show of activity. I followed Maggie's directions, turned left, right, left again, past rows of modest houses, the line broken by vacant, weed-choked lots; some were implanted with weathered FOR SALE signs that looked like announcements for a Depression, or were grim reminders of one.

"Well, what do you make of the old place?" Maggie asked. "That was Mrs. Dites rocking on her porch. By now she's in at her phone, spreading the news."

The streets, dusty-paved and almost bare of trees, extended flat as ironing boards for a distance of a few blocks, then terminated, dropped off sheer as cliffs, where the prairie resumed its dominion. No new houses were to be seen among the weathered rows; it was the height of the postwar building boom, but not here in Clarion. It looked more than anything like a town that had been relegated, unfinished, to some bankrupt chapter of the past while its founders moved on to more profitable ventures. A town that had been passed over, left behind years ago, to ruminate on its failure and inadequacy.

"You can see what I meant about nothing changing, every day the same," Maggie said, eyes focused on the dusty, sparsely shaded streets. "It *was* the same, though perhaps not ideally so, not entirely." She nodded at a maize-colored brick building on the corner. "District School Five," she identified it, as did the paved yard outfitted with swings and basketball hoops. "Went there kindergarten through eighth," she said. "What I remember about it today especially is the class poll we conducted, sixth grade, I believe it was, to elect the ten most outstanding—"

I slowed the car for the first traffic light we'd reached. There, spread out beyond the dust-streaked windshield, was Main Street, sprung from the pages of Sinclair Lewis or Sherwood Anderson. The low line of storefronts— hardware, J. C. Penney, a corner pharmacy with a mortar and pestle sign over the entrance, a corner bank pompous with stone pillars and brass plating—was pinned under the enormous tent of the sky. The street itself, wide enough for half a dozen horse wagons to pass abreast, was fronted at one end by a columned courthouse and at the other by the steep-roofed depot of Maggie's Sunday walks. On this May Sunday afternoon, Clarion's principal thoroughfare was drawing a fair number of strollers; a portion of them stood outside that other Main Street fixture, in the orange-and-blue dazzle of the Alhambra's marquee, inspecting the posters and stills.

Extravagantly, the Alhambra's marquee winked on and off in the sun's glare, but Maggie's attention was elsewhere. Across the street two bobby-soxed teenagers had taken notice of the Plymouth. The traffic light switched green, I drove toward the two girls, who commenced to nudge each other and gape open-mouthed. Fumbling in the pouch, Maggie slipped on the dark glasses.

"Guess the news has already circulated." She stared ahead, chin upraised, as we drove past the girls. "Hospital's up two blocks, then left. What was I tellin' about? Oh, yes, the class poll."

She glanced down at her lap; her speech, no longer a mocking exaggeration, was reverting to the flat cadences of Kansas. "Had a summer dress this color once," she said, smoothing the yellow folds. "Would've wore it to shreds, and almost near did. It was the one thing in creation made me feel pretty. Left. Go left here."

I rolled onto another somnolent street of dated houses and front porches with hammocks. "Mama used to swear I was pretty as any flower that bloomed, but she was the original kind person. The class poll—I'm gettin' to it, no fear—was to elect the ten most outstanding men and women of the U.S.A." She paused, shielded her face a moment. "Well, nobody had to tell me who was the most outstanding of men *or* women, so at the very top of my list—right. Turn right here."

I made a right and she lowered her hand, like a dropping barrier, as the red-brick building, white curtains masking its windows, swerved into view. "Wrote Mama's name at the top of the list," she said with a shudder. "Mama, whom I haven't set eyes on in two years . . . a matter, I guess, of choice."

I drove into the adjacent parking lot, which was marked off into areas for staff and visitors; from the number of cars in the latter section it appeared as if those townspeople not astroll on Main Street were all engaged in visiting the sick. I nosed into a space, rolled up the windows, since the rear was piled with luggage. Maggie took a comb and mirror from her purse.

"It's better that you talk about it," I said. "You haven't since we got on the plane at Logan."

She combed her hair. "Haven't I?"

"I understand why you haven't and what an ordeal this is."

She studied her face in the mirror. "Why, thank you for being so understanding."

"Maggie, look at me." She daubed her mouth with apricot lipstick—the face that didn't belong to her. "I came because I wanted to—couldn't not," I went on. "It wasn't, as you put it, to find you out."

"No, of course." She dropped the lipstick in the pouch. "I just don't want you regretting your good deed."

"Is that what you think of me?" I caught her arm as she turned and reached for the door handle. "What have I done to make you think that? Tell me, enlighten me."

"I—sometimes it pays to be wary." Her voice trembled but she kept her eyes steady on me. "Sometimes you think you can't wait to take on someone's troubles, but when opportunity knocks—"

"I'll stay as long as you need me. I won't fly back tomorrow. I'll stay here."

She looked at me, then shifted her gaze to the parking lot. "Used to wait out there for Mama after school," she said. "It scared me, going home to that empty house."

"Did you hear me, Maggie? I'll stay. Nothing's changed. I still feel—"

"Scared because of Papa," she continued evenly. "Alone in that house I'd get to thinking about him, as if he'd come back."

I stared at her with a dulled jolt of comprehension. "But you told me—I thought—"

"Lies, you said. Lies and secrets." She looked at me and shook her head. "Poor Christopher, I wish you could have been wrong."

She got out of the car, strode in the harsh afternoon glare across the parking lot. I grabbed the seersucker from the rear seat and went after her. A white cement path led across the hospital's front lawn to a bed of red zinnias speared by a flagpole and, above this, the white stone steps of the entrance. As Maggie turned at the zinnias, a figure in starched nurses' white bustled from the varnished oak doors. The two regarded each other in silence for a moment, the tension between them crackling the humid air.

"Why, Janya, as I live and breathe." The smile that had fled from the woman's round, plump face now returned, ready for disbursement. Dimpling, she advanced to the edge of the white steps and exclaimed, "Or should I say Miss Maggie Jones of Hollywood? Gracious, but I'm atwitter."

Maggie slung the pouch straps over her shoulder. "Hello, Miss Gilmore," she said, chin upraised. "I've come about Mama. How is she doing?"

"Myrt said you was flyin' in—town's agog, as you'd 'spect. Perfeck'ly thrillin', it is."

"I asked about my mother."

"Perfeck'ly thrillin', yes indeed." The dimpled smile fairly danced by itself down the stone steps, yet with a hint of stone in it. "I declare, Janya, it's like your dreams come true. A Hollywood movie contract, and what's this I hear tell—?" the button eyes under the starched white cap slid in my direction "—about a stage tour? Land's sake, how glamorous."

Maggie shifted the purse straps. "It's all right, you know," she said. "I haven't come back for the purpose of causing trouble."

"Gracious, honey, I should hope not." Only now did Miss Gilmore descend the steps, armed with the smile that was like alms for the poor. "Trouble, with your Ma so critical?" A plump and dimpled hand gestured at the seriousness of it. "Barely hangin' on, poor soul. When Doc Bates looked in on her this mornin'—"

Maggie drew back, her eyes flaring in anger. "I don't want him near her," she said. "He isn't to touch her. My mother is Dr. Everett's patient."

"Why, course she is, and it's only natural that you're upset," soothed the nurse, extending the dimpled hand in sympathy. "Only natural, so I'll overlook the aspersions you cast on that dedicated man—"

Maggie laughed. "Dedicated? Yes, I daresay."

"To whom I've proudly given my years of service," the other continued, and fastened the dimpled hand on Maggie. "I'll overlook your insinuations . . . 'specially since you have no evidence to back 'em up," she added softly.

Speechless, Maggie looked at the hand that gripped her in a dimpled vise, then at the round, plump face. "No, I'll simply urge you to hurry on up to Ida while she's still with us," Miss Gilmore went on. I took Maggie's arm, escorted her up the steps, but the nurse was not to be deprived of a final salvo.

"That's it, hurry on up to her," she called up the stone steps from the blood-red triangle of zinnias. "But, honey?" The voice paused as I opened the heavy varnished door. "Don't matter fudge about me . . . but spare a friendly word for the folks waitin' to greet you inside."

Maggie froze; she turned, saw the starched white figure march virtuously down the walk. Through the door that I held open she beheld the circle gathered in the hospital lobby; her hand tightened on my arm, she drew in her breath, then moved forward to meet them . . . and I remembered the circle of chairs at the first rehearsal and how she had gone forward toward them.

"Miss Carberry?" she said as she moved toward the gathering. "Mr. and Mrs. Buell, how're you?"

With the exception of a squirming captive male or two, the circle was composed of women, small-town matrons in fussy mail-order Sunday hats, girls of Maggie's age, one hefting a babe in arms—a circle such as might gather sociably on a church lawn after services. So intent were the ladies on their chatter that not a head turned to note Maggie's entrance, not an eye glanced up until she had spoken; after that, not a glance could pry itself from her.

"Hi, Betty Lou. That little Chuck you got in tow?" She advanced over the octagonal floor tiles and, the buzz of talk suspended, the circle broke, disbanded, parted to make way for her. Hasty smiles and nods were fetched; greetings were self-consciously extended.

"Janya. Nice seein' ya."

"Lookin' great, Jan. Surely are."

"Sorry 'bout yer Ma. Don't come finer than Ida."

The circle made way for her and behind the bland homespun countenances emotions flicked, of envy, spite, resentment—what else? The drama of the situation, the beautiful, errant, Hollywood daughter summoned to the stricken mother's bed, was obviously a potent lure, yet why would the ladies have massed together like this, rather than operating from behind their parlor curtains and backyard fences? Some other powerful emotion had drawn them here in defiance of decorum—*vengeance*, but for what? Pride stiffened and pricked at them, the raw festering pride of left-behind people in a left-behind town, confronted by one of their own who had contrived not only to get away but to flourish, which was well nigh unpardonable. Maggie moved among them, her very greetings a rebuke and hence an added offense—could she not have the decency to cower in shame? No, she walked with head held high, and as a consequence, hatred barely concealed flicked back at her from the assembled.

She was not wholly without allies, it proved. We'd reached the admittance desk, whose custodian, a gaunt, spinsterish female, had viewed our approach with increasing unease. Stringy-necked, hair skewered in a bun, she kept darting nervous looks at the other women, as if conscious of their weighing scrutiny; but as Maggie reached the desk, her fluttery approbation was overtaken by another factor.

"Janya," the woman said in a high, flutey voice. "Janya, how pretty you are." The sallow, pinched features took on a glow. "The prettiest sight, I always said, this town was ever granted."

Maggie flushed. "How are you, Miss Alma? It—it's been a while."

"The postcards! I've saved every last one, they go clear around my bureau mirror."

"We used to talk about places to travel, remember?"

"Do I!" The thin voice acquired a note of defiance now that Miss Alma had declared her position. "Why, I used to call you in from the parking lot when you'd be waiting—" With a murmur of dismay, she laid a gaunt, spidery hand on Maggie's. "You're not to fear, Janya. Doctor Ev was here twice today. Critical, but your Ma's holding her own."

"He said that? Really?"

"Gettin' the best of care, moreover. If we at Bates can pay back a token of what Ida gave this institution—" Turning, she favored the onlookers with withering scorn. "Least the town's in accord on *that* issue," she snapped.

Maggie forced her attention from the bronze tablet— *Harlow V. Bates, Physician, Humanitarian, Friend*—that adorned the wall behind the desk. "Is Myrt with her? May I go up?"

"Certainly can—402, and bear in mind the coma don't mean she won't know you've come." A bell clanged loudly, reverberating on the upper floors as well. "It's just she can't tell you of it," Miss Alma counseled, then turned once more to her audience.

"Four o'clock, visiting hours are over, case anybody needs reminding," she trumpeted, to little effect. A few decamped, the males eagerly, and the babe in arms had commenced to bawl, eliminating his mother from the scene. The rest of the gathering, a posse of five or six tight-lipped matrons, remained planted where they were. The hospital elevator, an ancient caged contraption, was housed in the oak stairwell that rose like a rampart at one

end of the lobby; we stood watching the cage crank downward, spiderlike, and Maggie said, "I'd rather go up by
myself, if it's all right."

"I'll wait here for you."

"It'll be quite a wait."

I felt my jaw tighten at the undefined, undeclared, un-
relenting contest between us. "Nice friendly crowd." I
jabbed a thumb at the studiously conversing group of
women.

The elevator landed with a plop of cables. "Stick
around, you're liable to get an earful," Maggie laughed,
and stepped back as the visitors herded from the car. Raw-
boned farmers in Levi's and Stetsons, their women in out-
moded sewing-machine finery, they trooped past, the
townsfolk among them identified by their goggle-eyed reaction at seeing Maggie. Impassive except for the lift of her
chin, the erectness of her stance, she waited for the elevator
to empty.

"You'll let me know how your mother is," I said as she
boarded the car.

"I'll have Myrt come down." She stood alone at the back
of the cage. "Gets to suppertime, Jezbo's is good for ham-
burgers and fries. It's on Main."

"Jezbo's. Right."

The attendant slid the gate shut, the bars rolled in front
of the yellow dress, sealing her off. Always we were parting
in halls and elevators—I wanted to get on, not be separated
from her. With a twitch of cables, the elevator cranked
upward. It seemed as if my coming here was resulting in a
worse estrangement—I wanted to turn it around, make the
reverse happen. I wanted—but what did Maggie want?

The elevator ascended through the stairwell and was a
signal, apparently, to the women in the lobby. The in-
censed and frustrated posse wasted no time in descending
upon Miss Alma at the desk.

"I marvel you didn't gift her with a bouquet," har-
rumphed one schooner-shaped worthy. "Our leadin' citi-
zen returned in triumph." Another preached, "For shame,

Alma Pruitt, toadyin' up to that girl after what she done to Ida."

The torrent was unleashed and I, pacing at the stairwell, was no deterrent to it. Accusations swirled unchecked, indeed seemed to be meant for my benefit, lest I be tricked by a Jezebel's charms. The ladies were not to be denied the settling of scores, the rendering of a verdict. I listened, could not but listen as together they pressed their charges . . . centering on the stroke that Ida Belton had suffered two summers ago, and the abrupt departure, a week after Ida's release from the hospital, of her daughter for points West, via a Greyhound bus.

"Selfishness, 'twasn't naught but that," went the seething chorus. "Head stuffed with movie nonsense, till finally she upped and abandoned her helpless, bedridden ma, hang the cost in grief."

"She didn't abandon Ida, now you know plain well she didn't." Miss Alma's flutey treble was not suited to oratory, but she made up for it in spirit. "She did no such thing, Emma Lowndes. Left her in Myrt's good care—and not a week gone by since that she hasn't sent money."

"Judas money, I call it."

"How can you be so unfair, Garnetta Sims? No daughter was ever more devoted than Janya."

"Walked out, didn't she?"

"Ask yourselves why she left. What made her do it. *Why?*"

I turned away from the shrill, indignant exchange, went up the oak stairs to the landing. This was what Maggie wanted, to leave me with her accusers, as though I belonged among them, was one of their number. This was her response to the impulse that had propelled me on and off planes, thousands of miles across the country and along that bleak, forsaken, endless highway—so that I might be further affronted.

"Hypocrites!" pronounced Miss Alma at the desk. "Don't your memories go back beyond a few summers? Janya had a normal ideal childhood, I suppose. Nothing

229

untoward befell her and Ida, is that what you prefer to think?"

I turned to the mullioned window on the landing, which looked out on the parking lot. The visitors' section was emptying rapidly—a dusty caterpillar of vehicles wound out toward the street. I picked out the rented Plymouth in its space. Serve Maggie right if I . . . *what*? If I what? I stared down at the car, imagined myself at the wheel, steering back along the—how could I want that? I pictured her upstairs, the sad and silent bedside reunion that was the price of the bus ticket to L.A. The baby, what had happened to her baby?

From the admittance desk floated the thin treble of Miss Alma, castigating the posse of women. "Why not George Belton, if you must point the finger of guilt?" she challenged, not without a certain dramatic flourish. "Isn't he to be blamed for any of this? Have you forgotten how that child worshipped him?"

I jerked around from the window, to learn from Alma Pruitt what it was that Maggie and I shared, were sharers of.

"The Sunday walks and Janya clutching his hand so proud—you've forgotten?" she chastised the woman. "Tell me," she exhorted them, "how did George repay her? What was his reward for the child who loved him past all else?"

The spiderlike cage did not descend with her until eleven that night. Fatigue washing over me, I was nodding off on a bench in the deserted, sepulchral lobby. The swish of the cleaning woman's mop blended with the tick of the clock over the desk; then the creak of the elevator startled me awake.

She stepped from the cage, the yellow dress a shaft of sunlight in the dimness; fatigue was written in the smudges under her eyes, the drawn tautness of her face. I got up as she came toward me; her face bore traces of something other than fatigue; a little flame kindled the tiredness.

"How's your mother?" I asked. "Myrt spoke to me, and Dr. Everett when he was here earlier."

"She's alive," Maggie answered, as though the realization was just occurring to her. "Mama's alive," she said, the little flame burning. "The doctor's encouraged. Myrt too. He said her life signs are stabilizing."

She smiled—"It sounds like talk about the economy." Then she went out the entrance, down the steps, repeating as though she could not speak it enough, "She's alive. Mama's alive."

Save for some staff cars, the parking lot was as empty as a football stadium after a game; above it, above the rooftops of Clarion, was stretched the vast, dark, moonless canvas of the sky. I unlocked the Plymouth, held the door open for her.

"It's good to feel hope come back," I said, and went around to the driver's seat.

She said as I switched on the ignition, "It's Mama who gave me hope. Well . . . it's no less than she always did." The little flame of hope in her flared. "She looks frightful, of course," she went on as I backed out into the street. "Tubes in her, mouth all twisted, and that awful, ragged breathing. The coma made her seem so far away, at the bottom of the sea . . . but I sat by the bed and took her hand. She couldn't speak, but I didn't let it stop me."

The dark shapes of the houses rolled past; here and there in the dense shadows a porch light glinted, or a light in an upstairs window; the shrouded night silence was loud with crickets. "I did the job for us both," Maggie continued. "All the brave things Mama once spoke to me—I said to her. I held her hand and whispered, 'Don't be afraid. Don't be feared. It'll be morning when you wake and the Lord will help us get by.' "

In the pitch-darkness the vacant tumbleweed lots were like the prairie sprung up, stealthily encroaching upon the houses while they slept. I turned at the next corner, Third, the route I'd walked to Jezbo's for supper. "I comforted her, as she did me so often—and she *heard*, some part of her did," Maggie said. "I held her hand and kept speaking to her, and she seemed to answer that I mustn't give up, either."

We were approaching Main Street. She sat up straight. "She's alive, it means there's a chance for her . . . and for me as well," she added after a moment.

"I ran out on Mama, took off for L.A.," she said. "Expect you've already heard it discussed."

"The welcome committee."

"Used to envision the high-school band at the depot, maybe a speech from the mayor." She laughed wryly, twining her fingers in her lap. "Still, I didn't leave Mama for the reasons everybody thought. I got on the bus and wiped it from my mind, like an eraser on a blackboard, everything that happened."

The motor thrummed in the silence. "Including your father?" I asked.

Silence. "Including my father."

"How could you think—" I heard the edge of resentment in my voice "—you could erase any of it?"

"Papa was what made most of it happen." Main Street swam out of the darkness, the store windows nicked at intervals by the pale pools of light from the street lamps. "If you want, we can pull over," she said. "This is where we came on our Sunday walks, Papa and I."

I pulled to the curb, switched off the headlights. "Isn't that Myrt something?" she said. "Couple hours' sleep and she's back on duty with Mama, wouldn't hear otherwise. You're to have her room, you know."

"Yes, she said it wasn't the Waldorf, but the bed's comfy."

"Well, that's not telling you about Papa, is it?" She looked out at the low line of buildings crouched against the sky, like old prairie dogs huddled close for warmth and commiseration. The courthouse columns rose spectrally at the north end of the street, the steep-gabled depot at the south, and in the whole shrouded expanse between, one edifice battled the night.

"The game of pretend ended up but didn't start over

there." Maggie nodded at the orange-and-blue twinkle. "Alhambra," she pronounced the proud name. "A castle in Spain, it said in the dictionary, which was exactly my feeling about it . . . a castle, with pictures that moved on a magic screen, more real, more beautiful than anything I'd known before."

She looked across at the movie theater and the marquee that spelled *J. Garland & V. Johnson in THE GOOD OLD SUMMERTIME*. "More real than anything . . . till eventually it got all mixed up," she said, with a tug of weariness. "But where it all started was with Papa, on the Sunday walks . . ."

The Alhambra's marquee had switched off as she spoke; now the gaudy circus doors were pushed open by the scattering of patrons who'd attended the nine o'clock show. They blinked, dazed by the abrupt transition from Judy Garland and Technicolor to the desolate tundra of Main Street; they lingered a moment, then made off like fugitives into the shadows. Earlier, the establishment next door, Jezbo's, had played host to the preshow soda crowd, when I'd gone in there for supper.

The proprietor himself had slapped a burger on the grill for me. Up front, Mrs. Bozeman had waited on the candy, magazine and greeting-card customers, and both had greeted me with friendly gusto.

"You the feller come with Janya?" asked Jesse Bozeman, squeezing his mammoth bulk behind the soda fountain. "Dif'rent! That was always the thing about her." He prodded the sizzling burger. "Coke with this? Shyness denotes a sensitive nature, but it was more than that with her. Somethin' special there, back even when she was homely as a mud fence." He fizzed up the Coke. "Growed up like nobody woulda dreamed. Used to knock the breath outa me, her comin' through that door. Well, if you want to earn the malice of folks, can't think of a better way. Kicked up a storm when she lit out for Hollywood— blamed her for leavin' Ida an invalid, but 'twasn't that, nossir."

He'd flipped the burger onto a plate, garnished it with potato chips, a pickle slice, and set it before me with the ice-jiggling Coke. "Gets back to the same thing—Janya's dif'rent. Let her wind up famous and smilin' on the Alhambry screen and they'll brag how she lived next door, but they'll never forgive her for it." He folded his melon arms across the gargantuan chest. "It's the same as what makes folks laugh at a fat man. Dif'rent! Now tell Janya I'm right sorry about her Ma, will you do that for me?"

The dashboard light threw a faint amber reflection upward onto Maggie's face, emphasizing the cheekbones. She watched the last of the Alhambra's customers slouch off into the shadows. "It started with Papa, the secret game we played on the Sunday walks . . ."

Her voice shook, a hand went to her face, was forcibly lowered to her lap; when she spoke again, to describe the Sunday game, she was back in those times she had erased from her memory.

" 'Where to?' Papa'd ask, and I'd answer, 'Scotland,' or, 'China, to visit the fortress,' and off we'd go. Papa was wonderful at the game. He could change Main Street into the Champs Elysées or Jezbo's into a—a Parisian cafe. It was his escape, you see, because Papa hated Clarion. He hated most everything about it."

She glanced down, her fingers made nervous pleats in the yellow dress. "He hated the bank and Mr. Carewe— funny, how I wound up working there. He hated the house on Dakota Street and the neighbors and the Depression. He hated the weeds that grew in the sidewalk cracks, hated the vacant lots and the dust that flew from the prairie. He hated the prairie for making him feel no bigger than a cricket. He hated Clarion for trapping him like it had—all that, he hated, and the Sunday game was his escape . . . till it became mine too."

She shook her head at the memory of it. "The difference was that the places we pretended to go weren't any more real to me than . . . than the picture shows at the Alhambra. The Sunday walks were a game of make-believe and would've gone on being just a game if it weren't for the Sunday that—"

She listened in wonder as, in the silence that enveloped the streets, the buildings, houses, trees, lamp posts, sky—far off on the prairie, in the vast, encompassing silence, a train whistle sounded a lone, piercing cry. It hung in the air, a siren call to other places, then dissolved in the night stillness. It dissolved, but Maggie went on listening as though she could hear it still.

"If Mama doesn't die," she said slowly, "if I can make up for what I did—Papa won't have won." And, turning to me in the amber dashboard light: "Shall we go down to the depot? Might as well tell you about it . . . at the scene of the crime."

I gunned the motor, shifted gears, and made a left onto Main. In that six-Conestoga width, the Plymouth traced the only moving course. "Really," Maggie laughed, and swept back her hair as the steep, shingled roof of the depot loomed closer. "The line between what's real and unreal . . . can sometimes be exceedingly thin. A thin, thin line, such as when you're going to have a baby, then suddenly you're not. With the Chief that Sunday, the unreal turned to real, then back again."

I drew up at the depot, she got out, went ahead of me through the grimy-paned door. She was standing in the musty, stale-smelling waiting room when I came in. A clock ticked in the shadows, and from the tracks outside, a signal light glimmered in the grime-coated window, faintly picking out the pot-bellied stove in the middle of the plank floor, the ticket window with its frosted glass pulled down. "A thin, thin line that can be a chasm as well," Maggie said, and the floorboards creaked as she stepped out onto the platform.

She moved up the rough-planked platform and the moon came out, floating from behind a drift of clouds. It poured its pale light on the rails that ran alongside the platform, then curved away across the prairie to the distant towers of the granaries.

"It was part of the game," Maggie said, the moonlight bathing her as she moved up the platform. "The Chief wasn't real, just a blur rocketing past, till this one Sunday when it rounded the bend at the granaries as usual, then slowed, as if it were going to stop."

The moonlight streamed on her as she gazed across the dark prairie, at the granaries, as though at any moment the great train would thunder into view. "It stopped, it actually did," she went on. "The Chief stopped, and I learned that Papa's game wasn't all just make-believe. The beautiful places he'd described—I saw it turn real on the Chief."

She shook her head, gestured at the tracks, as though the fabled train were there. "Beautiful ladies with jewels, snowy tables with roses and silver, Joan Crawford, who I thought was just a picture on a screen . . ."

She stared out at the moon-glinting tracks. "The Chief was as real as a picture show, I wanted to get on with Papa and ride away to someplace beautiful, where he wouldn't think any more that I was . . ."

She turned away from the tracks, as if the gloried train had resumed its journey, vanished into the prairie darkness. "Real, then it was unreal," she said. "Exactly like a picture show when it was over, and you were back where you'd always been, which was nowhere."

"Maggie." I moved toward her up the platform. The moonlight shining on the fear in her eyes. "Nowhere was Papa's name for Clarion. He made up names for things. Cruel names, sometimes."

"I didn't understand," I said. "I didn't understand about him."

She swung away, moved toward the rear of the platform. "I couldn't bear for the Chief to be gone. I ran to the end of the platform and waved goodbye till the last light in the last car flickered out . . . and when I finished with that and turned back to Papa . . ." She nodded dully to where I stood. "He'd gone, he'd left, I ran after him out of the depot, but I knew . . . I knew that . . ."

"What?" I asked, remembering about the dandelion hair. "Knew what?"

"That it was no use, I could run after him till my legs wore out and—" She hugged herself, glanced up at the dark-spreading sky. "Moon's hiding again. Never liked hide-and-seek." She turned away, kept her back toward me, hugging herself as if she were cold. "I knew it was no use hiding from it," she said. "Knew it wouldn't ever change, I'd always be 'Miss Mouse' to Papa—no, even worse. The way he'd look at me, like I was no one, no one at all."

She swung around to me. "How can you go on if you're no one?" she asked, the tears wet on her face. "You can't just be no one, what else can you do but pretend? What else?"

She wiped at her face, hesitated, then slanted past me into the waiting room. "I ran after him," she said, pulling open the door to the street, gesturing out at the silent, deserted expanse. "He was up by the bank. I ran after him as if it were part of the game. I took his hand and pre-tended I was—was Virginia Starr, a little girl walking home safe in the dark with her father who loved her."

She slumped tiredly against the door; then, rousing her-self, pulling erect, she went out to the car and got in. She sat silently while I slid behind the wheel.

"I haven't understood—any of it," I said, and her chin jerked up.

"You're to have Myrt's room, did she tell you? We—Dakota Street—up two blocks, turn at the bank."

I made a U-turn, drove back up Main Street. "Papa's how come I was taken on at Title Guaranty," she said as the bank pillars appeared at the next corner. "Mr. Carewe said that seeing as he'd been denied the privilege of a daughter to guide, and I the counsel of a father—" She laughed. "Talks sort of formal, Mr. Carewe. Sort of preacherlike . . . even when he wasn't behaving too father like."

I turned at the bank; the shadow-wrapped houses and lawns ebbed past, the occasional dimly illumined, vine-clad porch. Her voice braked sharply; she put a hand to her mouth for a moment, forced it down.

"Nine," she said as the houses filed past, like the pages in a memory book. "I was nine. It was August, heat spell something fierce. Papa was to go on vacation startin' noon Saturday. Title was open Saturdays till noon. He collected his pay on Friday, as usual, then Saturday morning as usual —*no*," she amended sharply. "Not as usual, you could say. He went on vacation but failed, you could say, to advise us of his whereabouts. Not then or later. *Right.* Turn right here."

I turned right onto Dakota Street, with its gap-toothed rows of houses. She indicated a dwelling on the next block, visible in the pool of light from a street lamp. I drew up at the curb and she got out, slamming the door behind her. She moved unsteadily up the walk, stood below the steps of the narrow, shingled, one-story house whose roof pitched downward, pinioning it to the ground.

"Save enough money . . . was going to send for Mama," Maggie said, eyes lifted to the house. "Buy a place on a hill somewhere, Azuma or the Palisades, and even though Mama was incapacitated . . ." Her voice trailed off, then: "Goddamn him. Goddamn him forever," she cried, and lurched from the walk, flung herself into the driveway at the side.

The shadows closed like a curtain over the yellow dress, swallowing her. I groped up the drive to a shed and into a back yard, where she stood.

A light from the kitchen at the rear of the house shone on the worn patch of grass and on Maggie. She was staring at a corner of the yard, back toward the slatted fence, where a shriveled tree stump twisted up from the ground.

"Stupid azalea tree," she said, with a shuddering, convulsive intake of breath. "Stupid worthless tree, not a blossom to its name"—gesturing at the stump. "I was twelve and still having nightmares. Waking up scared, running to Mama's room—*Miss Mouse! Miss Mouse!*" She gasped for breath, pushed the hair from her eyes. "One Saturday when Mama was at Bates I came out from the kitchen . . . over here to the azalea tree. Damn him. Goddamn him."

She sprang forward, thrust out a hand. "I ripped at the branches. Ripped, tore." Her hands were machetes, slashing, clawing, knifing at the air. "What I couldn't tear loose I hacked at with a saw from the shed. I kept on, I didn't stop. The goddamn tree was my goddamn father, and when no branches were left it meant I'd killed him, he was dead."

She swerved away, hands to her face. She was crying and did not want to be crying. "I killed him and when I was finished I went in the house. I took a bath, a nice long bath with cologne water, and put on my blue georgette and pumps and—" With a scream of rage she tore at the yellow dress, kicked her shoes flying across the yard. I looked on in horror, and did not have to be told where she had gone that Saturday.

"Can even tell you the movie," she laughed, and stabbed at her tears, ridding herself of them. "*Camille*. Beautiful and romantic and sad, and when Garbo died at the end— buckets!" She laughed, mocking her tears. "Absolute buckets. I went back the next day, luckily it was still on . . . and after that . . ."

She glanced distractedly around the yard, spied the kicked-off shoes lying near the shed. "After that I didn't live in Clarion any more." She went over and picked up the shoes. "I lived at the Alhambra," she said, frowning uncertainly at the shoes. "Where no one could hurt me . . ."

She shrugged, sat down on a turned-over fruit crate at the shed. "The thin line—I crossed over it, you could say. Oh, not entirely, but it did get awfully mixed up."

I looked over at her. "How do you mean?"

The look that she gave back seemed almost to be taking my measure. "Well, when I was fifteen, for example, and started attracting a certain amount of attention," she went on, with a deprecating laugh, "in history class or assembly, when I'd catch the boys sneaking looks, or the men when I walked down Main—well, it wasn't the least real."

"I—I can see how it wouldn't be."

"Can you?" She bent over, slid a shoe on her foot. "It was like I'd gotten into a movie, one of those ugly-duckling movies, except with me it didn't come off."

"Why was that?"

She glanced up at me. "Maybe in real life it never does. Everybody can see the change but the duckling. Ugly too long—looks in the mirror and can't see the swan."

I was silent and she bent over to tend to the other shoe. "However, irregardless of ducklings," she ventured, her tone light and bantering, "there's another question you'd sort of like to get to . . . *n'est-ce pas?*"

"You're tired. Exhausted," I said, disliking the glib solicitude that I was affecting.

"*Le bébé.*"

"Up again early tomorrow, listen, best thing we can both do—"

"*Le bébé*, translated, the baby." She looked up at me. "Isn't that what you'd like to ask about? Inquire into?"

"What makes you think that?" The unerring instinct, I realized with a jolt, that allowed her to read my thoughts, gauge my reactions. "Look, I don't know about you," I said, going over to her, "but I've just about had it for—"

"Not a single question in regard to *le bébé?*"

"Maggie—"

"*Quel* surprise." Her eyes flashed in the shadows. "Apologies for the Kansas high-school French, but I got this feeling it had priority—the baby episode, top priority."

"Only in the sense that—" I turned away, hands plunged in pockets. "Only in the sense of what became of it," I blurted, appalled at myself.

Silence across the yard. "And not who the proud father was?"

"Christ, Maggie."

"I suppose actually I already told you who, more or less."

I wheeled around, confronting her. "An old man, some dirty old man—Christ, to let yourself go to bed with him."

"*Let?*"

"How often, how many times? Enough to have a goddamned baby by him."

She stared at me from the crate. "Didn't," she said evenly. "Pregs by Mr. Carewe, but did not have *le bébé.*"

I stared at her. "What, then?"

She got up from the crate. "What's your guess?" And she made for the back steps.

"Got rid of it? Did you?"

She whirled around on the steps. "Got very well paid to get rid of it."

I looked at the fury blazing in her eyes. "The money for L.A.," I said, unable to stop. "At least be disgusted by it, not proud."

She turned to open the screen door, pulled the handle, let go of it tiredly. "I came off the elevator at the hospital," she said faintly. "All those hours, but you were still there."

"If I sound hard, even cruel—"

"You hadn't gone, when I'd given you every cause to."

"Maggie, you haven't leveled with me once, about anything—"

She looked down the steps, into the shadows where I stood. "Yes," she said, nodding slowly, abstractedly. "Yes, I see"; then the screen door twanged and she was gone into the kitchen, leaving me to wrestle with a bewildering, incomprehensible set of emotions. I could not sort them out, get to the source of them, except for the moment on the stair landing at the hospital, when I'd looked down at the Plymouth and . . .

She was in the kitchen, standing at the refrigerator; the screen door twanged, but she gave no indication of hearing it.

"Maggie, I . . . I'm sorry."

"Hungry?" She took a plate of cold chicken from the refrigerator. "Myrt said she'd leave some supper, you were sure to be hungry."

"Everything coming at me at once, and the fatigue on top of it—"

"I understand." She carried the chicken to the table, crossed to the glass-doored cupboard next to the sink. "You'll want to make plans for the morning," she said, getting down plates, cups and saucers.

"I told you my plans." A cone-shaped bulb hung over

the oilcloth-covered table. The stove—iron, claw-footed, white porcelain oven door—was like the stove at home. "I don't necessarily have to fly to Chicago tomorrow. I told you that."

"Did you? I must've forgot." She laid the rosebud plates on the table. "Mama never knew about the baby," she said. "The stroke, and when she came home from the hospital there was no baby." She set out the cups and saucers. "With the profits, so to speak, I arranged for Myrt to look after her, then took myself off to L.A."

"Maggie, what I said about it—"

She filled a kettle with water at the sink.

"I walked out on Mama, which makes me no better than Papa," she said, turning off the tap. "But now I'm back."

Choices, she'd said on the Wilbur stage: sooner or later it came to that. "I'll phone Abe in the morning," I said. "Tony knows the sound cues. I ought to be able to stay . . . until Tuesday."

She struck a match under the kettle on the stove. "Dr. Everett says to always have hope for the living."

"I'll bring in the luggage."

"And while Mama's alive—" she lit another match, held it flaming in her hand "—then maybe there's hope for me."

"Of course. I'll get the luggage from the car."

She blew out the match, stood looking after me. I went into the hall, like the hall in another haunted house . . . and as I went down it, the same blind impulse seized me by the scruff of the neck. The impulse, as it happened so often, to be somewhere, anywhere else.

With needless haste, I went out into the night that enshrouded the rows of houses that were not unlike others known to me. I went out to the rented car, in a night silence broken only by the brave chirp of crickets, and brought the luggage into the house.

I sat with Maggie in the cone of light at the kitchen table, at the cold supper, chicken, beet salad, Jello, that Myrt Sample had provided.

The people who were kind and those who were cruel . . .

242

We talked little at the table. Exhaustion catching up, we agreed. I helped with the dishes, after which Maggie conducted me to the middle bedroom of the three that opened off the hall.

The bed was as narrow as that in my child's room. I fell asleep the instant I hit the pillow, a deep and bottomless sleep with no dreams to shatter it.

I slept in shorts, I remember, and did not unpack the cowhide, only the zippered canvas bag.

And in the morning, early the next morning, I remember . . .

CHAPTER **10**

The phone rang, muffled, far away, jabbing through the layers of sleep. I lunged around in the bed, not wanting to let go of the thick, soft, woolly blanket of unconsciousness, deep and encompassing as an anesthetic . . . the phone, quick steps in the hall, and with a groan of protest I flung off the covers.

She was at the table in the hall, the phone to her ear, when I padded out, stuffing yesterday's shirt into my chinos.

"Hospital?" I asked.

"Yes, I will," she said into the phone. "No, not till I get there."

"Your mother?"

"Thank you. Yes, I know." She hung up the phone, stood at the doilied table. A cotton twill robe was knotted at her waist; her hair looked freshly washed, tied back in a ponytail with a twist of ribbon. She looked at the morning light that filtered through the net curtain on the front door; seven-thirty and already it burned with a summer intensity.

I asked again, "Was that the hospital?" and she moved slightly, turned her gaze to the small, square living room that lay beyond the slid-back doors.

"Maggie. Was that the hospital?"

"No."

"Is everything all right?"

"It was Dr. Everett. From the hospital."

I waited a moment. "He's there this early?"

"Myrt called him at five. Mama showed signs of a crisis—breathing, pulse rate." She turned and went into the living room. "A crisis, so she called Dr. Ev and he hurried over."

She stood in the middle of the small, overstuffed room, her back facing me. "And?" I stepped toward her. "What is it? Tell me."

"I'm trying to. It's just so—" She ran a shaky hand over her face, then swung around. "It's so unexpected and incredible," she laughed. "The crisis went on until seven, transfusions, oxygen, a heart machine, practically no pulse—"

I looked at her, relief sweeping through me. "She came through. Your mother came through the crisis."

"Yes! Came through! Isn't it incredible?" Her eyes shone, she shook her head, hand to her cheek. "Barely any pulse, then she started to rally. Breathing stronger—hasn't regained consciousness, but—"

"She will. That'll be next."

"The chances are doubled, Dr. Ev thinks." She went past me to the doors, looked across the hall at the front bedroom. The shades were drawn, but in the dimness was the white glint of a hospital bed and alongside it the chrome gleam of a wheelchair. "I might be bringing her home one of these days," Maggie said. "Not straightaway. She could still take a bad turn—careful not to get my hopes up too much."

"You've earned it. The right to hope."

She looked at me a moment, came back into the living room. Horsehair sofa, Morris chair, faded carpet, framed sampler over the mantel . . . preserved as in a museum. "Hope!" She laughed, crossed to the other set of doors, which opened onto a small boxlike dining room. "I just haven't been well-acquainted with it," and slowly, very slowly, she slid the doors shut.

It was a curious gesture, with no motive or purpose to it. "Maggie?" I said, and was rewarded with a flashing smile.

"At least the wait is over. For the time being, that is."
She pushed the doors open. "For you as well as me."

"Me?"

"I looked up the flight schedule. One o'clock plane—get
you to Chicago by five."

"I don't have to leave."

"Mama's out of danger. I won't budge till Dr. Ev says
it's safe. We can't both stay out of the show." She turned,
went into the hall. "Told the hospital I'd be over in ten
minutes. Nurse problems."

"I'll go with you."

"Fine, yes." She started down the hall, untying the twill
robe. "You can drop me off on your way," she said, then
paused at the doorway of Myrt's room. "Why, you can be
ready as soon as I can." She nodded at the shiny-buckled
cowhide at the side of the bed. "Easily as fast, just look,
you haven't even unpacked," she said, and continued
down the hall.

Fifteen minutes later, when I swung the Plymouth into
the parking lot of Bates Hospital, she was adamant that I
not go in with her.

"It's a long drive. You have a plane to catch."

"Not till one. Even with delays I can—"

"No, really." She got out of the car. "I'll be busy arranging for nurses. Myrt's not going to work another
double shift."

"Maggie, I—"

"Goodbye, Christopher."

"Not goodbye. You'll be in Chicago in a few days."

"That's right, I will." She hesitated, looked through the
window at me. "Be sure and wish Diana luck for me tonight. Tell her I hope the costumes fit . . . and not to
bump into the furniture."

"I'll phone you when I get to Chicago."

She stepped back from the car. "I'll be with Mama. No
calls put through."

"Then after the show, at the house."

"Yes, all right." She stood alone in the marked-off expanse of concrete, then turned, was striding across to the entrance. The last glimpse I had of her was in the rear-view mirror, as I angled into the street. Head erect, she moved along the cement walk, skirted the triangle of zinnias, was climbing the entrance steps, the sun white and glaring on her.

She was out of the mirror's range then, gone from it . . . and within scant minutes so were the streets of Clarion. The town receded behind in a cat's cradle of roofs and chimneys as I turned onto the highway, past the granaries and then the rusted signpost skewed aslant at the side of the road.

The United flight for Chicago, with stops at Kansas City, St. Louis and Indianapolis, left Wichita on schedule. The seat-belt and no-smoking signs flashed on, the door was bolted shut; the stair ramp was rolled away, clearing the runway . . . *the run, run runway.*

Motors roaring, propellers like whirling knife blades, the DC-3 taxied down the field, lifted, swayed, climbed. I saw Maggie on the hospital steps again, the blood-red zinnias below her. The plane gained altitude; below was the earth of Kansas, the unending monotony of landscape, unending miles of highway stitched now into a pleasing patchwork quilt. The clouds were like cotton batting, the sky serenely blue.

But all that I saw was Maggie.

On Thursday morning of that week I came out of the Daphne Hotel on Rush Street in Chicago and went out to Midway Airport to meet Maggie's plane.

I'd spoken with her twice since Monday, both calls tense and difficult; she'd made no pretense of wanting to speak to me.

"How's your mother?"

"The same. I must go, Christopher."

"I'm in a bar next to the theater. I figured after the show was too late to call. Seven, you'd probably be home from the hospital."

"I—Miss Alma's coming over tonight. I have to get ready for her."

"Call you tomorrow, tell you how the opening went, okay?"

Pause. "I'd just as soon you didn't."

"Yes, I—I know." I poked at the stack of quarters I'd lined up on the phone ledge for the operator. "I failed you, Maggie. Ran out, plain ran out on you, and I have no excuse."

"I don't want to talk to you."

"Scared—if I said I got scared, what excuse is that? None whatever, but I'm going to try to make up for it."

"I have to go."

"Can I phone tomorrow? By then you might know what day you'll be back. Maybe it's no use and there's no way to undo harm—"

At the other end of the line the phone clicked, severing the connection.

On Tuesday I'd phoned her again, from the same booth in the bar on Clark Street. The same lineup of quarters, feeding them into the slot, then the *crrkk* of the operator ringing. I counted the rings, saw the narrow hall that sliced the house on Dakota Street in halves, the phone on the table near the sliding doors—eight rings before she answered, her voice toneless, knowing that most likely it was me.

"Maggie? Listen, please don't hang up. Hear me out, just this once."

"Christopher—"

"I'm coming back there. Back to Clarion—I mean, if you can't leave Saturday, I'll fly down after the show."

"No."

"I can get a late flight to Kansas City, connect to Wichita."

"*No,* I don't want you to."

"I'll come anyway. If you refuse to see me, well, then you will, but I'm coming."

"Can't you understand? Don't you *ever?*" Her voice

shook. "I don't want you here. I'm not interested in anything you have to say."

"The baby—it was Dr. Bates who performed the abortion. Was Miss Gilmore there? No evidence, she told you in front of the hospital." I gripped the phone, seeing in ghastly detail how it must have been. "Did Carewe send you to him? Tell you it was just for a routine examination? Dear God, Maggie, did they get you on the table and— ether, chloroform?"

There was silence at the other end. Flat dead silence. "It's no use your coming," Maggie said dully. "I won't be here."

"Your mother's improved enough?"

"They . . . Dr. Everett was able to make tests today. He won't have a prognosis until tomorrow, but he thinks, is almost sure—"

"You can rejoin the show? When?"

"Barring setbacks—Thursday, probably." Some of the dullness went from her voice; she sounded more herself again, rueful, a touch mocking. "Doubtless you can't be persuaded not to meet the plane. Hope has its limits."

"No," I said. "I won't, if you tell me not to."

"Sure, like elephants and water holes—or me and the movies. I'll wire you, how's that?"

The operator broke in to request fifty cents for another three minutes. I clunked the quarters in the slot, tensed for the click at the other end. "Maggie, you there?"

"I'll wire you the flight, soon as I know."

"You don't have to. I'll phone again tomorrow at the same—" I heard the click then, but not with the ache of despondency, the gnaw of futility, of it's being no use, over with, that had drilled through me yesterday.

She was coming to Chicago and not opposed, if only because it spared her the wear of argument, to my meeting the plane.

It was at least a starting point, which was more than I'd thought I'd be given.

With a buoyancy I hadn't felt in a long while—when

last? the picnic in the Common?—I swung out of the bar and up the alley of the Erlanger Theater next door. *Anniversary*, glowed the marquee lights, and the glow was reflected within me, somewhere in the rib cage, in the vicinity of the heart . . . *Maggie was coming back, she wasn't lost to me.*

Abel Klein posted a notice on the callboard: *The mama is on the mend—our girl is coming back.* Diana Knapp, it must be confessed, wasn't thrilled: since Monday she'd been subbing for Maggie, very credibly too. "Oh, well, I'll get to play the dickens out of it in stock," she'd said, bowing good-naturedly to her understudy's fate. By way of compensation, Chip had treated her, after Wednesday night's performance, her last before Maggie's return, to a champagne supper at the Pump Room.

Wednesday night the telegram was in my box at the hotel—ARRIVING TWA FLIGHT NINE DUE CHICAGO TWO P.M. I didn't sleep much that night, tossing and turning, sitting up in the Murphy bed. The Daphne featured this type of sleeping accommodation, along with "cooled air," a euphemism for electric fans. I couldn't sleep, so I lay thinking about Maggie and sleep. *Sometimes in the middle of the night for no reason . . .*

She wasn't lost to me, I'd never fail her again. Somehow I'd become what she needed, a shelter against the wind, the shield she'd never had to protect and guard her. I was far from being that now, but I'd become it, *be* it for her . . . till the bad times faded, a nightmare forgotten, exorcised.

The plane wasn't due until two, but I left the Daphne well ahead of time, noon, though the ride to the airport was only half an hour.

In the Daphne's pink-and-black lobby I left a beaming Abe Klein, who had finagled Mr. Theopolis, the manager, into reserving a choice corner room for Maggie—not only at the minimum rate, but including the discount accorded to persons of the theatrical profession. A corner room for Miss Jones, high on the sixteenth floor, with a view (if you craned enough) of Lake Michigan . . . and waiting in a vase, sprays of dogwood from the company, to welcome her back.

I was at Midway by twelve-thirty. I checked the arrival board—three Wichita flights that morning, TWA 9 was the fourth, and listed as due on schedule. I went up to the observation deck that overlooked the airfield and watched the procession of planes land and take off. The day was warm and balmy with May, enlivened by a frisk of a breeze that fluttered the pennants atop the hangars.

I stood watching the movements of the planes from the deck: toys, they seemed, flashing silver in the sun; intricate battery toys discharging and receiving toy passengers on toy ramps, refueling, loading freight, soaring into, winging down from a sky that was bluer than Bristol glass.

I watched the toy planes and stole only occasional peeks at my watch. Twelve-fifty, one-ten—at one-thirty I'd take up my post at the arrival board, not before.

I revised this plan by a few minutes—flights, after all, had been known to arrive early. Not often, but every now and again. The main floor of Midway was astir with the business of aviation—staplers banging away at reservation counters, conveyor belts trundling off luggage for loading, dumping it into carousels for claiming; porters, flight personnel, passengers, those waiting for same, like me, and sightseers wandering around, taking it all in.

I joined the small group collected in front of the arrival board. If TWA Flight 9 were delayed, it would already be noted on the board—the space alongside the flight number was blank. I strolled up and down, kept an ear cocked for the loudspeaker announcements.

At one-fifty-five, "TWA Flight Nine, Salinas, Topeka, Wichita—" it blared; *Gate 4* was chalked on the board, and I was tearing in the direction indicated by the sign, the little vari-pointing arrow, out to the wire fence that enclosed the airfield; grasping hold of it, straining up at a sky that was bluer than that over Boston when the Clipper had rolled into Back Bay . . . enemy routed, or so I'd naively fancied.

I strained up at the sky, caught sight of the sleek silver bird plummeting downward, jouncing as it landed, skimming the airstrip, turning off the runway.

The run, run, runway.

I waited in the group clustered at the gate; watched the plane taxi to a halt, the ramp rolled forward to the hatch door. The passengers alighted, descended the ramp, and filed toward the gate.

I waited at the gate until I was alone there and the flight crew disembarked and threaded past me.

I intercepted one of the stewardesses, who checked, rechecked the passenger list. She asked for a description, which in a spiraling of dread I gave to her.

Maggie wasn't on the flight.

Not that one, at any rate.

CHAPTER **11**

The desk clerk at the Daphne glanced up from his newspaper as I came into the pink-and-black lobby.

"Miss Jones here? Good." He plucked a key from the
rack, was about to ring for the bellboy. "She's not with
you?"

"Mr. Klein around?" I asked, the fear knotting again.

"Coffee shop. Look, I'll have to know about Miss Jones,
whether to hold her room."

"You will, soon as we hear definitely."

"But—"

I made a line for the coffee shop across the lobby, trying
not to hurry. It was ten of three. The day was just getting
started for the Daphne's clientele, a raffish sampling of
whom were distributed around the coffee shop—show girls,
musicians and comics from the Rush Street clubs, bookies,
entrepreneurs. To my relief, only Abe was on hand from
the company. He was in a booth, hunched over coffee and
a bagel; the hooded eyes observed my approach, expressionless but making tabulations.

"Sit, kid," he invited. "Take a load off your feet."

I slid into the booth. It wasn't happening; none of it was
happening. "Some coffee you drink—three parts milk," I
said.

"I drink the milk. The coffee's to flavor it." He signaled
the waitress to bring me a cup. Abe looked tired and over-
worked, which he was. The Chicago reviews of *Anniversary* had been mixed, to give the kindest interpretation.
Not of a quality to inspire a stampede at the box office; so

Abe was out doing leg work every day, contacting lodges and club groups for theater parties, arranging publicity tie-ins, promotion stunts, so far with discouraging results.

And I was now about to add critically to his problems. I waited until the waitress had poured my coffee; I forced a swallow, hot and bitter, down me.

"Guess it's a question of habit," I said. "We were tea-drinkers at home, so it wasn't until I was grown that I started—"

"If she wasn't on the plane," Abe cut in, leaning forward, "and she hasn't contacted the hotel, which she hasn't—what gives?"

I put down the cup; the panic slashed like a knife. "When she wasn't on the two-o'clock flight . . . I made inquiries at the airport."

The hooded eyes flicked over me. "And learned?"

I pushed the coffee away. "She arrived on a Continental flight, eleven-thirty this morning. Under her own name, Virginia Belton."

A cigar was produced from the vest, the cellophane unsheathed. Abe shrugged. "To switch flights is not unusual. Not to get in touch, notify, that's unusual."

I choked back the panic. "She's in Chicago. We—we just have to find where."

Abe deposited the cigar butt in an ashtray. He chewed a moment, stirred the beige mixture in his cup. "Tell me, kid," he said, "you got some idea, some personal theory of why she'd do a thing like this?"

"I—"

"It could be serious, so level with me."

I looked across the table at him, and the answer seemed to come from someone else. "I—after I learned about the flight, I made a long-distance call," I said. "To Clarion, the hospital there." The next words seemed to balloon over the coffee shop, as in a comic strip when distress, a crisis, is indicated. "I—yes, Abe, she has a reason for it," I said. "And I've got to start trying to find her."

"We," Abe corrected, sliding the coffee toward me.

"Make that *we*, kid, and don't go ringing the alarm yet, not till I've made some inquiries myself. Come on, get some java down you."

"But—"

"Maybe it's not so serious. Who can figure what a dame might do, that wouldn't occur to you or me in a million years?" He winced as I drank the coffee. "Black with no sugar—an insult to the lining of the stomach. Okay, shall we start our inquiries?"

Chuckling, dispensing such remarks, joking with the cashier as he paid the check, waving to various colorful acquaintances as we made our way out, Abel succeeded in getting me across the lobby in a reasonably controlled state. He pressed the elevator button with a flourish and confided, sotto voce, "For the moment we'll keep the situation to ourselves. Especially, we don't want anybody from the company getting wind of it. Never forget who it was that shot Lincoln. A goddamn actor is who."

At which the elevator doors sprang apart and out bounded Scott Andrews. "Hi, where's Mag?" He grinned at us. "She here yet? Hey, I'll go give her a ring."

"Slight delay. Changed flights," Abe said with a twinkle, steering me onto the elevator, motioning the operator to start.

"She can relax about tonight, with me to carry the ball," grinned Scott, a simian paw detaining us. "Ball, hey, that's a hot one—the *Trib* comparing me to a linebacker an' all."

Abel closed his eyes. "It said you played with the subtlety of a linebacker, not the impact."

"Well, gosh, what's the dif?"

The doors mercifully shut, the pink-and-black car shuddered upward, and Abe intoned, "Don't ever forget who shot Lincoln." He fished some message slips from his pocket. "Remind me to head off Levitt—Harmon's local publicity flack, been after me about when's she getting in. Listen, you okay? No panic?"

We got off at nine and he proceeded down the corridor. "This reason you mention . . . it's got to do with you?"

"Some of it."

"You flunked in Boston—what was it, you flunked again in Kansas?" His steps slowed when there was no response, and he turned slowly around. "Well, kid?" he prodded softly.

"Abe, her mother was buried yesterday."

The shrunken gnome's-face stared at me. "But when you came back Monday—"

"She was already dead when I left." Like ice blocks in a flow, the words slammed together. "Maggie didn't tell me, but something in her behavior should have. It—it could have been that I preferred not to know. Her mother's dead and she's blamed herself for it."

Abe stared down at the carpet, a ruminating old man. "The Mama dead," he echoed. "Blames herself . . ."

The panic mushroomed up, but with it some other emotion, born of the last days, the failure and defeat. "Jesus, Abe," I said. "Always thinking we want somebody to love —it's the last thing we want. Always looking and searching, then someone comes along and the minute we see what's truly there, the pain that's hidden there—one glance at it and we run."

My leg, the left leg, out of old custom, was shaking, but I paid no attention to it. "I know about running," I said, "the sorts of places you go, and I'll find her wherever she is, I'll find her."

Abe regarded me silently. He chomped on the cigar, turned, plowed down the corridor, and his embattled stride was not that of an old man. "Come, I'll help you find her," he said, and went charging into his room.

It was a large corner room, compliments of Mr. Theopolis, and similar to the one Abe had wangled for Maggie. It was furnished as an apartment—sofa, chairs, the Murphy beds tactfully concealed in a wall, and a kitchenette at the back. The kitchenette looked as if Abe had yet to set foot in it. The whole room held few emblems of his occupancy —a littered desk, a boutonniere wilting in an ashtray, a copy of *Variety* on the bureau. The latter was joined by the derby hat, which he sent scaling through the air as we entered.

"So," he said, removing his coat, tossing it on a chair. "Some queries on the subject. The name she used on the flight?"

"Virginia Belton."

"Her real name?"

The real and the unreal. "Yes."

"It was safe to use on the plane, no one was looking for her, but now . . ." He moved to the desk, took out his gold pocket watch. "Ten past three—almost four hours, she's been here."

"We've heard nothing—that's good in one way."

"A condition, kid." He set the watch on the desk. "We give ourselves one half-hour, then I contact a certain connection in the police department."

The panic gave a leap, like an exposed nerve in a tooth when the air hits it. "All right," I said, nodding, then Abe was rolling up his sleeves, expounding on his general philosophy as a means of bolstering me up.

"Half-hour—my favorite time in the theater! The actors are putting on their makeup, out front they're getting ready to open up—a time when it's all coming together, the whole idea of theater. Listen, we could be unduly concerned. Yesterday the funeral, tonight the show—it could be she wanted a breather, nobody around, to pull herself together."

He reflected on this theory, was not persuaded by it. "The point is to get hold of her, let her know she's got friends if she needs them. Kid, you're in luck." Eyes agleam, Abel gestured at an article on the desk which, alone of the furnishings, proclaimed his occupancy of the room. Such was his passion for this apparatus that he'd had a second one installed as an auxiliary on the table at the sofa.

"Belasco, I'm not," said Abel Klein, seating himself at the desk, as at a Wurlitzer. "Sam Harris, Al Selwyn, even that mensch Max Jacobs, I'm not, but on the telephone—"

he flexed his wrist, a virtuoso reaching for his instrument "—I'm Jascha Heifetz."

Plucking the receiver from the hook, he led off with some swirling arpeggios for the hotel operator. "Hello, sweetheart, you get the chocolates? My pleasure. You picked a night yet?" On the pretext of arranging for free tickets to the show, he likewise arranged that any calls for Maggie—"Partic'ly a character goes by the handle of Levitt"—be routed to him, and that his own calls be held. "Unless somebody wants to get through urgent, sweetheart. An emergency, put him right on. Thanks, you're a doll, sweetheart."

He hung up, sat with hooded eyes probing, estimating. "Girl at an airport, she don't know Chicago from Walla Walla, what's she do?"

"Gets in a taxi."

Abe got up, stood at the window. "She don't know hotels, except she wants to steer clear of the Daphne, so what's she ask the cabbie?"

"To recommend a hotel," I said, but it sounded wrong, not what Maggie would do.

"And being a typical Chicago hack, sizing her up as a tourist—where would he take her?"

"The Loop," I said, unconvinced.

"Okay." Abel grabbed a classified directory from the desk, sent it arching toward me. "The following hotels, make a check mark. Morrison, Sherman, Bismarck."

I flipped the pages to *Hotels*, put a check by those he'd specified, which were located in the Loop. Any other girl might do as we'd outlined, but not Maggie.

"Add the Congress, Palmer House, Stevens," Abe continued, warming to the challenge. "Each hotel, you inquire for both names, Jones and—?"

"Belton. Virginia Belton." She hated the name for summoning everything she was afraid she was, unworthy, without merit.

"They don't have either name registered, speak to the desk," Abe went on. "A looker like that checked in today, the room clerks aren't gonna forget it." He frowned. "What's the matter, it don't hit you right?"

"No, but . . . don't mind me. I just want to find her."

"Then *look* it," Abe coaxed with a smile. "Don't look like the world is already kaput—close, maybe, but still a couple of innings yet. Agreed?"

"Agreed."

He consulted the gold pocket watch on the desk. "Three-fifteen. What d' you say we get going?" He lifted the phone from its cradle, wiggled his eyebrows at me. "What —if I can be Heifetz," he demanded, "you can't be Yehudi Menuhin?"

I lifted the receiver from the phone on the table by the sofa, opened the directory alongside it. "Sure, I can," I said.

"So tune up, make with the bow," gestured Abe, jiggling for the hotel operator. The phone on the desk was connected to the Daphne's switchboard; I was using a direct-dial phone. The *bzzzz* sounded in my ear; I thumbed the directory pages to the first check mark and dialed the Bismarck Hotel.

"Bismarck Hotel? Could you tell me, please, if you have a—"

"Jones. Maggie Jones," rasped Abe into his phone. "You don't? What about Belton, Virginia Belton."

"Sorry, we don't have a Belton," the Bismarck operator informed me, and I asked for the front desk. "Hello, is this the room clerk? I wonder if you could help me . . ."

"A family situation," said Abe into his mouthpiece. "The Papa forbid the marriage, she's run away in a snit, probably under an assumed—"

"Dark hair, very beautiful—sometime around noon today."

"Sweetheart, give me the LaSalle Hotel. You're a doll. LaSalle? I'd like to inquire you got a Miss Jones registered. Maggie Jones. No? Then what about—"

"No one by that description? Thanks." I hung up, dialed the next check mark. The way we were going about it was wrong, from what I knew of Maggie. She'd have gotten in a taxi at the airport and . . .

"Morrison Hotel, may I help you?"

The real and the unreal, and always she had sought—"Yes, operator. Have you a Miss Jones, Maggie Jones, registered?"

"No one by the name of Belton? You're positive?" Abe barked into his phone, the virtuoso air less evident. "Okay, let me talk to the front desk."

It took longer than half an hour. Between us we phoned every hotel in the Loop, spoke with the operators and room clerks, to no avail. It was getting close to four when I finished with the last check mark. We had not found a trace of Maggie.

I lowered the receiver to the cradle and closed the directory. The real and the unreal . . . how would she have crossed the thin line today, by what manner of make-believe? The unreal was her escape: if ever we were to find her . . .

I looked over at Abe, who sat at the desk, shoulders slumped dejectedly. Among the litter of ticket stubs, message slips, ad proofs and clippings was the morning *Tribune*, folded to the entertainment section. Instead of hotels, we ought to check . . . how, when there were literally hundreds of movie theaters in Chicago. Yet it was what she would do, something of that kind . . .

Abe sat kneading the chewed-up cigar; he was too old and tired to have this ordeal required of him. The hooded eyes flicked up at me, but he didn't speak. I waited a moment. "Half-hour's more than up," I said. "You mentioned contacting the police."

The eyes didn't flick, but stayed on me. "I already contacted them," he said. "Detective Bureau, Lieutenant Mullaney, a friend from previous occasions." Pause. "He put it on the wire."

The fear dug at my stomach. "Anything?"

"No incidents . . . involving her description." He sighed, got up from the desk, and stood at the window. "I asked Mullaney to run a check at the airport."

"Abe?"

He rubbed at his back. "From the flight number, the taxi dispatchers can check the fare sheets."

"Maybe she didn't go to a hotel in the Loop," I said in a rush, then as Abe turned, "at least, not the type we've been phoning."

"Christopher, I want you should listen." Abe came toward me. "Five hours since she arrived, we've got to—"

"Some other girl would go to the Sherman or Morrison, but not Maggie."

He placed frail, speckled hands on my shoulders. "Five hours at some hotel, under a made-up name so nobody finds her. Thinking what thoughts?"

"Abe," I interrupted, "which hotel are Jack and Irene at?"

"Thinking of her Mama and how—"

"The Blackstone. Aren't they at the Blackstone?"

He peered up at me. "You're saying that she told a cabbie, 'Take me to some fancy ritzy—'?"

"Or the Ambassador East—isn't that another of them?"

Abe cocked his head, a touch annoyed. "Another what? Christopher, what is this new—"

"Movie-star hotels. That's where she'd go." I turned, made for the table by the sofa; Abe looked on, bewildered, as I flipped the directory to *Hotels*, reached for the phone, and dialed.

"This, I don't follow," he sputtered. "I don't follow this nonsense. Christopher, put down that phone and—"

"Ambassador East," chimed a dulcet voice at the other end. "May I help you?"

"Yes," I said. "I'd like to check an arrival, please."

"The name, sir?"

"She arrived today, sometime after—"

"You'll have to give me the name, sir. What is the party's name?"

I shifted the phone and for an agonizing moment could make no reply. What name, what make-believe name would she use? I couldn't think of any. Janya, playing the Sunday game, crossing the thin line—what name?

"Sir, unless you can give me the party's name—"

I held on to the phone, as to a lifeline to keep from drowning. Opening night, the look in Maggie's eyes . . . Janya drowning in her.

"Are you there, sir? If you can't give me the name—"

I spoke then: spoke the name by which Janya had called herself so that she could be someone rather than no one; the name she'd imagined for herself at the depot that Sunday when she'd run alone and frightened into the darkness of Main Street, calling, calling to her father. I spoke the name, but it wasn't until the next hotel that I found her.

"Actors!" bewailed Abel Klein, pacing nervously and flailing the air. "Crazy actors! Don't ever forget about Lincoln." Then, shaking his head, he suggested that I try the Drake Hotel.

Brrkk. Brrkk.

"Drake Hotel. Good afternoon. May I help you?"

"I want to check an arrival, please."

"The party's name?"

I gripped the phone and said, "*Starr*. The party's name is Starr." I waited while the operator checked the guest rack, and then the lifeline unraveled.

The operator came back on. "We have a Miss Starr registered, sir, but I'm afraid I can't connect you with her suite."

"Why not?"

"She has a do-not-disturb on her phone."

The waves crashed over me. Abe hissed from behind, "What is it? She there or isn't she?" I gripped the phone, told the operator to put me through.

"I can't, sir. It's against our policy. You'll have to speak to the manager."

"All right, put me through to him."

"What's going on?" Abe rasped. "What's wrong?"

"Operator? No, wait." She was ringing the manager's extension. "I'm coming over," I said. "Tell the manager a friend of Miss Starr's is on his way over. Please, would you tell him that?"

I hung up the phone. There wasn't time to explain to Abe—I'd call him from the Drake, I said, already out the door, hurrying down the hall.

No time, other than to flag a taxi on Rush Street, speed the few blocks north to the Drake, and pray that time had not run out.

"Really, Mr. Casey." The assistant manager of the Drake tipped back in his swivel chair and made a tent of his fingers. "Do try to compose yourself."

It wasn't happening: Mr. Darlington, in morning coat, striped trousers and boutonniere, had not escorted me into his office as though to discuss arrangements for a banquet. I was not seated opposite him, attempting composure.

"Okay, no hysterics," I said. "Just let me very calmly ask you to—"

He reached for a registration card with Maggie's handwriting on it. "Attractive young woman, Miss Starr. I was—"

"It isn't her name."

"—at the desk when she checked in. Her mother is joining her in a few days and she felt that a suite—"

"Her mother was buried yesterday."

The barest pause. Mr. Darlington placed the card in a drawer. "She felt a suite would be more comfortable."

I stood up. "Look, what if we compromise? Instead of taking me to the suite, go yourself."

"Mr. Casey, we respect the wishes of our guests at the Drake. If they don't wish to be disturbed—"

I gestured at the phone. "Call the suite. Will you do that much?"

Mr. Darlington's glance took in my appearance, the shirt with no tie, the seersucker pulled over it. "Casey—Irish, isn't it?" he said. "So many of our chambermaids are Irish."

I leaned over the desk. "They make excellent chambermaids," I said. "Also saloonkeepers—and cops. Excellent cops."

"Put down that phone," said Mr. Darlington, pink with anger.

"Ask for the Detective Bureau, Lieutenant Mullaney. Tell him the girl who was reported missing as Virginia Belton—"

"Young man, if you don't immediately—"

"Tell him we've located her at the Drake under an assumed name." I shoved the receiver at him. "Tell him she's got a do-not-disturb on her phone and that the goddamn stupid moronic idiot assistant manager refuses—" I paused to gulp for breath "—to interrupt her privacy. Tell him, will you, Mr. Darlington? Okay?"

His mustache twitched. Glaring at me, he removed a ring of keys from the bottom drawer.

"Should this prove unwarranted, I'll lodge nuisance charges against you," he said, getting up. "Follow me."

He led me back out into the lobby of the Drake. The paneled walls were hung with old tapestries, lamps glowed over Chinese vases aburst with exotic flowers; in the cool, expensive hush a fountain plashed and guests moved about with the easy assurance of those guarded by luxury from ordinary workaday harm.

I learned from the Chief . . . that Papa's game was real . . . beautiful places really existed, he hadn't just made them up.

I followed Mr. Darlington into the handsomely fitted elevator, which spun upward with a soft, almost inaudible whir. He led me down a gray-carpeted corridor, where the only sounds were the murmur of voices behind doors, the tread of my shoes on the broadloom, and the hammering of my heart.

How can you go on if you're no one? You can't just be no one, what else can you do but pretend?

The corridor turned, Mr. Darlington halted before the doors of a suite. Suspended from the delicate fluted-bronze knob was a do-not-disturb sign. He waited a moment, then tapped softly on the door.

"Miss Starr. It's the management."

He tapped again, less softly. "Miss Starr. I do apologize for the intrusion, but it's the management."

No response, no sounds from within, only silence. He knocked more loudly. "Miss Starr, it's the management."

I seemed unable to breathe, as though adrift in some high, treacherous altitude. "Don't wait," I said. "Go in. Please."

Mr. Darlington inserted in the lock a key from the ring. "She could be out shopping and simply have neglected to remove the sign."

"*Go in.*"

The lock clicked, the door was not bolted from behind. A foyer, black and white squares; to the right a living room, ivory and gold, splashes of chintz reflected in the mirrors. A copy of *Photoplay* on the gold brocade sofa shrilled a silent alarm; the crystal tears of the chandelier tinkled faintly as Mr. Darlington advanced toward the bedroom.

"Miss Starr," he sought once more to announce himself, then glanced into the bedroom and froze.

He could not propel his legs forward, and I plunged past him into the silk and satin of the room. A quilted satin headboard curved ornately above the twin beds, joining them. The bed to the left was made up, undisturbed, but the satin spread on the other bed was thrown back; protruding from the rumpled blankets was an inert, lumplike . . .

It was a pillow, the sheets twisted over and under it. I tossed it back on the bed, turned, glanced around the silken room. In the doorway Mr. Darlington snapped his starched cuffs with glacial precision.

"If you're quite satisfied," he said, as I prowled the room. Maggie's luggage was on a rack against the wall. The smaller of the two suitcases was opened, the other locked; TWA baggage checks were tied to the handles. Across the room, a window gave a magnificent panorama of the lake and shoreline, and in front of it was a room-service cart, set with linen and china.

"Simple to reconstruct," said Mr. Darlington from the doorway. "Sent down for lunch, then a nap and out for a tour of the shops. Now if you will kindly . . ."

I went over to the cart. A chair was drawn up to it, facing toward the lake. A pink napkin was discarded on the pink linen cloth. Lunch had been left unfinished; a cup of tea half-filled, half a club sandwich on a plate. Alongside it was a morning *Tribune*, which I picked up from the cloth.

"Young man," cautioned Mr. Darlington as I crossed to the night table at the beds. "If you so much as touch a single article in this—put that down."

I'd taken a note pad from the night table. It was embossed with the Drake crest and on it Maggie had scrawled a phone number, along with the jottings *4:10, 6:25*. The explanation was in the newspaper, the *Tribune*, folded to the movie ads. As I'd done in New York, then Boston, I scanned the long columns of ads, which were grouped according to neighborhood—Loop, Near North, Lincoln Park, Glenwood . . . ONE DAY ONLY, screamed a small box ad midway down the page. I reached for the phone on the night table.

"Very well," said Mr. Darlington, heading for the living room. "If you want the police, indeed you shall have them."

I gave the operator the Daphne's number. "Abe? It's the kid. I'm at the Drake. She's all right, everything's all right. Yes, I mean, no—not at the moment, she isn't, but I know where she went from here. Listen, have to go. Say a prayer, will yuh? A large prayer."

I hung up, went diving past Mr. Darlington, who was summoning reinforcements via the living-room phone. I ran out into the corridor, past the doors and the polite murmurings behind them. The elevator was closing its door—I signaled wildly for it to wait.

Fifteen minutes later, by my watch, the Checker cab I was in turned off Sheridan Road onto Bryn Mawr Avenue on the North Side.

It was a neighborhood shopping street—bakery, fruit market, butcher's, haberdasher's, Kroger's supermarket—that conveyed the look of a small town in its homey details. The El that bisected it, the shuttle of trains to and from the Loop, sounded the only big-city note; and among the commercial establishments was one indigenous to Main Streets everywhere, harking back to the days of the nickelodeon. The marquee, as I crossed the street toward it, shed a fairy glow, announcing the feature presentation.

Last Day
V. Leigh & R. Taylor
WATERLOO BRIDGE

I moved through the jostle of housewives, baby carriages and children toward the Bryn Mawr theater. An El train rattled over the tracks, blocking the marquee from view; the cars went clattering away and I saw, emerging from a Whelan's drugstore up at the corner, Maggie's slim, heather figure, the pale face and dark sweep of hair. She started walking in quick, resolute strides, then glimpsed me coming toward her in the crowd of shoppers.

She halted in stunned disbelief and something in her face warned, as I continued toward her, to take care, the peril wasn't over.

CHAPTER **12**

It was she who spoke first.

Affecting a grin and a breezy, ambling gait, I covered the remaining span of sidewalk and she said, "Well, appears I was wrong about the all-time champ—bagged it at last."

"Phenomenal. Incredible," I said. "We were waiting for you at the Daphne—"

"I took an earlier flight—switched hotels while I was at it." She brushed at her hair, quick, darting. "Decided to splurge on a suite at the Drake, no less."

"*That's* where you went." I shook my head, as if glad at having the mystery solved. "Abe kept asking, 'Where is she?' and I hadn't a clue. Then I spotted the ad in the *Tribune*—"

"Always too early or too late, but there it was, finally." She smiled, gripping the purse straps, her face chalk-white. "Finally made it . . . Last day only."

She gave the words a light, playful stress that sent a chill through me. "I—I haven't asked about your mother," I said. "Coming along all right?"

"So I immediately hopped a cab," she went on. "Only I didn't want to walk in in the middle"—a small boy on a tricycle bore down on us in the stream of shoppers; she moved up against the drugstore window, out of his path. "So I went in here for a Coke . . . my mother's out of danger. Is that the term for it?"

I looked at her leaning tiredly against the drugstore window and its marching rows of lipsticks, Fire and Ice. "No, let's not talk about it, shall we," she cut in as I started to speak. "Mama or any of it, okay?"

I waited a moment. "You seem terribly tired—not that you shouldn't be."

"Tired? Yes, I suppose so, but what's that compared to seeing the all-time champ?" She pulled herself erect, moved to go past me. "You're in my way," she said.

I stood between her and the fairy glow of the marquee down the pavement. "Maggie, listen, what I said about myself on the phone—"

"May I please go past?"

I stepped aside and she joined the stream of housewives, shopping carts, baby carriages, children—the housewives on their way home to prepare supper while, at the front window, the children kept watch for their fathers to come along, turn in at the walk. The heather-tweed suit too warm for the May sun, Maggie moved toward the marquee of the Bryn Mawr, fatally out of step, and I knew with overwhelming certitude that I must not let her go.

"It's futile, don't you realize?" I called after her. "How can you be rid of me, when I'm pinned to your purse—the other Christopher, remember?"

She wavered, then continued along in the jostle, and I sprinted over the sidewalk, swung her around, indifferent to the stares I was attracting. "The medal in your purse—I said I wasn't related to that Christopher, but you disagreed. You said—"

The dark eyes looked up at me, the look of Janya drowning in them. "You said you were a traveler and that I'd done well by you," I plunged on. "So if I keep showing up all the time . . . you have yourself to blame, for assigning me the job.

"Only yourself," I repeated, and while she didn't speak, neither had she turned her back on me. I took off on another tack, improvising, lest the infinitesimal headway be forfeited. "As for the present instant, you really ought to consider my plight," I said, gesturing at the Bryn Mawr marquee. "The all-time champ—when is it likely to turn up again? If it does, how likely am I to know of it?"

"Christopher—" Her voice trembled and she gripped the purse straps "—for your own sake . . . it's better that you go. It's no use, don't you see?"

"*Go?*" I huffed, ignoring the thin, cold trickle of fear. "Go, when it's my only and undoubtedly my last chance at *Waterloo Bridge*? I refuse, outright refuse. Can't you feel at least a twinge of pity?"

I turned from her, crossed the sidewalk to the Bryn Mawr, gestured at the lobby posters and cards, the framed stills. "A complete novice, who in his entire misspent life has seen but one movie twice—excluding *Springtime in the Rockies*," I qualified, by now drawing stares from the passersby, "which doesn't count, as I was trapped on a Coast Guard cutter, plus it rained the entire week they showed it. Totally ignorant about movie-going. For instance—" I went up to the poster of Vivien Leigh and Robert Taylor, depicted against a flaming background of war-torn London. "Do you check this kind of thing before you go in—or after you come out? I'm ignorant of the simplest procedures."

Maggie hesitated, then moved under the fairy glow. "Depends," she said, as though calling upon some inner core of strength to compensate for the obvious exhaustion. "Usually you look over the lobby cases, a fast check, but with an all-time champ—"

"What?"

She nodded up at the poster for *Waterloo Bridge*. "With an all-time champ, you long ago memorized every poster and still. By remote chance you might find one you never spotted before, but usually—" She turned from the poster, with that same exertion of will over exhaustion.

"Usually you go inside," she said, and stood quietly while I presented myself at the ticket window, behind which, like a doll in a shooting gallery, sat the blond cashier. *Adults, 50¢, Children, 25¢,* read the sign, and I slid a dollar under the opening, was supplied with two tickets coughed up from the register.

I turned to Maggie, who stood against the backdrop of the bustling street. The aproned butcher enjoying a smoke in his doorway, the delivery boy whistling as he loaded his cart, the flow of housewives and children—it was such an ordinary scene and we were part of it, about to indulge in the most ordinary of diversions, the great American pastime of going to the movies.

"Think of it," I smiled at her, the awful fear of the past hours diminishing, receding, "first time out for us at the picture show."

She raised her chin. "It is, isn't it?"

"And *Waterloo Bridge* at that—I don't know an iota about the plot."

"War, ballet, Tchaikovsky—it's got everything," she said, looking at me. "It's a—a love story."

"The only kind, really." On this day when surely she had need of someone, I was with her. It suddenly seemed as if I hadn't known before who I was: I was Christopher who had found Maggie, who had need of me.

I opened the gaudy circus door to the outer lobby. "Shall we go in?" I handed the tickets to the grizzled elderly who was on duty, outfitted in a soiled, braided usher's jacket and baggy gray trousers. He tore the tickets in half, returned the stubs, pulled open the inner door.

We stepped inside and the daylight closed behind us.

The darkness took adjusting to after the bright sunshine of the street; for a moment we stood at the doors, eyes gradually tuning to the dimness.

The lounge we'd entered had duplicates in a thousand neighborhood movie houses, a thousand Gems and Grands, Jewels, Rajahs and Avalons. In the marinelike dimness the wavy-patterned carpet receded to the heavy portieres that masked the aisles of the auditorium, from which drifted tantalizing snatches of the sound track. Dim, marine rays of light picked out the rest rooms and phone booth, the drinking fountain and fire extinguisher mounted like fishing trophies on the wall. The lure of the lounge lay elsewhere, however: it centered on three items of equipment, each sending out a phosphorescent glow, without which no movie house was complete. The soft-drink dispenser, with its undulating lights, resembled an undersea grotto; the popcorn vendor was a calliope; but it was toward the third of the triumvirate that Maggie nodded.

"There," she indicated the candy machine. "Think you can name the choices without looking. A member of the club, after all."

"Observe." I advanced across the wavy carpet and it echoed with the herding gallop of children on countless Saturday afternoons, thundering over this same path to the rays of chrome that emanated from the mirror set above the glass selection panel and row of shiny brass knobs. Back turned to the glass panel, I groped a hand over the knobs, counting them. "Six selections," I pronounced, seerlike. "Any particular order?"

"However it comes to you."

"Very well, I'll lead off with—" I frowned in deepest concentration, hand clapped over my eyes, and allowed for a sufficiently dramatic pause. "The Great Waldo, wizard of the unknowable, makes his first prediction. Milk Duds."

"A cinch for Milk Duds."

"Secondly the Great Waldo sees . . . Jujubees!" I held my hand over my eyes, saw again the rainy Saturdays in Richmond Hill and F. X. out of work, a stranger to his old self, getting me out of the house to the movies. A dime for admission and a nickel, always a nickel for . . . "Thirdly, the Great Waldo sees—Raisinets."

"Oh, invariably."

I lowered my hand, not wanting to continue the childish game; felt a prickle of fear, like the jab of a needle. Maggie was leaning against the wall, her head tipped back; she straightened up as she saw that I was looking. She straightened her shoulders, smiled, and moved through the underwater dimness. She came over to the candy machine; her hair swung down as she checked out the glass panel.

"So far, the Great Waldo is batting four hundred. After Raisinets, what?" She laughed, ran her hand over the knobs. "Walnettos? Surely Walnettos."

Her face up close was smudged with fatigue, as though with charcoal. Ought to get her back to the Drake. "Maggie—"

"That was another of my lies. The biggest, probably." She twisted at each of the knobs. "Feed enough dimes in the Walnetto slot . . . and that's what you'll come up with." She laughed, pulled her hand away from the knobs. "You see, I never belonged to the club."

"More than anyone."

"Not true." She shook her head, moved toward the portieres, the muffled blast of the sound track.

"It's you that—" I hesitated, as so often I had; but then I went over to her. "It's you that's enabled me . . . to attest to the Milky Way," I said.

She stared at me, expressionless. "I wish—" She turned away, her eyes restive and darting. "Noticed?" she asked, glancing around the lounge. "No one's come in or gone out. No one seems to be here at all."

"We're here. *Us.*" I glanced at the phone booth that was wedged between the doors to the rest rooms. "I promised to call Abe," I said. "He's worried about you. Just let me ring him, then—"

"Sometimes in the middle of the week at the Alhambra—" She stood looking through the marine dimness at the portieres that cloaked the aisles. "Sometimes I'd be the only one there," she said, gesturing at the portieres. "Imagine having a castle all to yourself! Wherever you go, in nearly every town—a castle! She turned to me. "And today—you've come."

"You're so tired, Maggie. Let me take you back to—"

"No, I'm all right. Hear that? Listen!" She held up her hand as from the auditorium the sound track of *Waterloo Bridge* swelled with the lilt of violins playing a waltz. "It's where Roy brings Myra home—the ball to announce their wedding," she said, listening a moment more, after which she swung around to me.

"I'd call it a perfect time to go in, wouldn't you?"

I went toward her, and everything else—the panic, the phone call to Abe, the lateness of the hour in regard to tonight's performance—was forgotten, dissolved in the shine of her eyes, surrendered to the very quality that, even as I drew close, made her seem beyond reach, a will-o'-the-wisp.

"Well, then," I said, awkwardly offering my arm. "I'm a novice, so you'll have to instruct me as to behavior."

She smiled and took my arm. "Such as?"

"Serious matters—whether to scrunch down in the seat, talk in whispers or not utter a sound."

"Whispers," she said, "are allowed."

"Especially since I don't know the plot."

"A love story—I told you."

"Which naturally means an unhappy ending." I sighed and pulled back the heavy portieres, and followed her into the pitch blackness.

Dark as any night, pitch black, it closed around us, filled with the suddenly amplified blare of the sound track. We stood at the back and the arc from the projection booth spliced the darkness, disclosing here and there among the empty rows seated figures given over to reverie. There was a moon shining in this night, and it was toward it that we went down the aisle.

Silver-white, its glow flickered over the rows of seats, offering another world, a magic shadow world in which to dwell. It was a movie screen and on it, twenty times larger than life, Vivien Leigh danced with Robert Taylor, shadow creatures, gigantic, luminous, dancing in a ball-room to a multitude of strings; gazing at each other, unaware of our approach.

"The fabled Myra and Roy?" I queried, groping down the aisle after Maggie.

"The very," she said, selecting a row down front. The seats squeaked as we pulled them down, while on the screen Vivien Leigh and Robert Taylor continued their waltz, unperturbed by our traffic or the fit of coughing that erupted at the back.

The empty row conferred a royal isolation on us; we sat together, guests at the ball. "Needless to inquire," I remarked of the waltzing couple on the screen, "if they fell instantly in love."

"Instantly."

"Obstacles to overcome?"

"Barrels." Maggie leaned her head back, her gaze focused on the huge screen, where the scene had cut from the ballroom to an upper corridor of presumably the same house.

"That Roy's modest dwelling?" I asked, indicating the ducal hall. "It could pass for Blenheim Palace."

"M.G.M. likes to do it in style." She settled back and the screen was filled with a gigantic close-up of Vivien Leigh, raven-haired, alabaster-skinned, gazing out upon the dark rows.

"She's going to Roy's mother . . . to tell her the wedding can't take place," Maggie explained.

The scene cut to a bedroom, Lucile Watson at a dressing table. "Why can't it?" I asked, as a knock sounded on the bedroom door.

"Too much . . . in the way of it," Maggie answered, sliding down in her seat.

"Scrunching's allowed?" I followed suit, the two of us leaning back, nearly prone. On the screen, Vivien Leigh was engaged in a tense exchange with Lucile Watson about the forthcoming nuptials . . . and in the silvery moonlight wash, details that the darkness had hidden were being revealed in the rows around me . . . the torn upholstery of the seats, some of them oozing wads of stuffing, the sloping floor littered with candy wrappers, popcorn containers, a pint whiskey bottle.

Maggie whispered something as the silver luminescence exposed a fat woman across the aisle, dress pulled up, feeding herself chocolates, attention fixed raptly on the screen.

"Mustn't look," Maggie whispered, and when I turned to her: "Not too closely."

Down in the front row at the side, in the sulphurous red glow of the exit-door sign, a man lay sprawled asleep.

"Look too close, the castle isn't real any more," she whispered, head turned to me.

"Ah, Maggie." I took her hand and leaned toward her. "Whose castles are real? That's the thing about them . . . the wonderful thing."

"Is it?"

"We're leaving," I said. Her head was slumped to the side, as if she could not support the weight of it. "I'll take you to the hotel. Come," I said.

Her eyes focused on me in the dark; I felt the faint pressure of her hand. "The baby was real . . . then it wasn't," she whispered. "Mr. Carewe promised . . . take care of me. Sent me to Dr. Bates. Legs in the stirrups . . . and when I woke from the chloroform . . ."

"I know." The voices from the screen blended with our own in an eerie, ghostly mix. "Let me take you home, Maggie," I said.

"Chris'pher?"

"What?"

She looked at me, her voice faint as mist. "In New York . . . frightened to go to rehearsal . . . said to myself each morning, 'Christopher will be there.' "

"I'm here now." I took both her hands, clasped them in mine. "I always will be."

She struggled to lift her head. "You were real . . . moment I saw you in the alley."

"It did happen—just like that—for both of us." I rubbed at her limp hands, alarmed at the rag-doll slump of her. "Why did it take me so long?" I said. "Why couldn't I have been more for you than I was?"

"Not your fault . . ." She struggled once more to raise her head.

"But we've won out." I gathered her in my arms, there among the empty rows, the torn seats, the carrion litter of peanut shells, Crackerjack boxes, candy wrappers. "Wherever you'd gone, I'd have found you today," I said. "No matter where, nothing could have stopped me. I'd have found you."

276

She lifted lusterless eyes to me. "Always trying to figure the worst . . . it was there, all along."

"I'm taking you out of here."

"The worst . . . is being afraid." She turned, the thin mist of her voice evaporating. "Just being afraid," she said, and her hair spilled back as she nodded up at the screen. "Myra knew. She knew."

"*Maggie!*"

I looked up and the screen was enveloped in mists. Foghorns bleated on the sound track, boat whistles, the *clip-clop* of a carriage on Waterloo Bridge. A gas lamp shone on a slim figure posed alone on a parapet, Vivien Leigh, staring down at the river. Turning, staring at the convoy of trucks rumbling over the bridge. Headlights flashed on her face, flashing as well on Maggie's, as the trucks rumbled closer. *The rainy night on Second Avenue, the rumble of trucks coming off the Queensborough Bridge, the shriek of brakes.*

"*Maggie!*" She slumped forward against me, arms dangling. "*Maggie!*" I shook her until the glazed eyes slit open, stared blankly, closed, and her head lolled back. "*Maggie!*"

The projector arc sliced off, the sound track went silent, the giant screen turned blank. I lifted her in my arms, and the pathetic gaggle of moviegoers watched stricken, like the mourners at my father's funeral, as I carried her up the aisle.

Outside, the housewives turned from their shopping carts and baby buggies to stare as I bore her under the twinkling fairy marquee to the curb.

A station wagon was going past; the woman at the wheel took a shocked moment to react, then reached to the ignition, the door. I got in, Maggie cradled against me. Her face had a waxen pallor, her lips were tinged blue, the breath trickled from her, shallow and labored. On the seat alongside, the woman's two children, a boy and a girl, looked on, struck silent. The little girl cowered back, her face twisting up.

"It's all right, don't be frightened. You mustn't cry," I said, and the car shot around a corner.

At seven that evening I jumped up from a bench in a corridor of Cumberland Hospital, a mile south on Kenmore Avenue. The doors to Emergency were swinging open, and I prepared once more to be obstreperous.

The doors swung forward and a nurse came out, one who had been on duty when they'd wheeled Maggie in. (Lifted her onto the stainless-steel table, tore at the heather suit, slapped the comatose face, hard and stingingly. Stomach pump and, as they'd curtained off the table, a spew of vomit.) The nurse fixed me with a stern and embattled look.

"See here, young man, any more tricks from you and—"

"Is she responding any better? That's all."

She took a count of the patients lined up for treatment on the benches. More were at the admittance clerk's desk at the entrance. A man with a dish-towel bandage on his head, a young woman in the throes of an asthmatic attack, waited while the clerk filled out forms in triplicate.

"Miss Belton hasn't regained consciousness yet," the nurse said. "Her pulse rate has improved. The doctors are working on her," and she went off to attend to the clamoring, gesticulating line-up.

I sat down again on the metal bench that was nearest to the Emergency doors. It was my vigil post, the vigilante's perch, much to the annoyance of the staff. After the stomach pump, they'd ordered me out of the treatment rooms. I waited on the bench, then barged back in, Maggie lying naked and spread-eagled on the steel table, catheter between her legs, IV tube in her arm, bloated face bruised and swollen from the pummeling. Unseeing eyes, the pupils dilated, as an intern pried them open and . . .

I picked up the leather pouch from the bench. Someone —the theater manager?—had shoved it at me as the car drove away, and subsequently it was the cause of yet another skirmish between the staff and me. I'd refused to let

anyone—interns, nurses, admittance clerk—touch it.
Handed over the empty phenobarbital bottle—100 mg's
was the estimate they'd pumped from her—supplied her
name, as requested, but nobody, repeat nobody, was going
to lay a finger on her purse, enough violation was being
done. Abe would be here soon. I'd called him after the
stomach pump. "Turned out like we were afraid of, huh,
kid? I'll get Mullaney on it. Don't answer any questions
you can help. If the papers get wind of it . . . listen, what's
the address, I'm coming."

I opened the pouch, not for the first time. Joe Scully's
medal, still pinned to the lining, made a small gleam of
gold. Not for the first time, I took out the letter written on
Drake stationery. My name was scrawled on the envelope . . .

Christopher—
Beautiful here. I've ordered lunch. I'll have them put the
table at the window so I can look at the lake. Then I'll lie
down, as if for a nap, and . . .
I didn't want it to be in Clarion. Too many sad things there
already. Buried Mama yesterday. Too many sad things. The
house is to go to Myrt. See to it for me?
Started on the plane but don't feel drowsy yet.
I think of us and a part of me hopes you'll find where I am.
Does St. Christopher find lost travelers? But what would that
change? Not who I am or what I did.
There's the—

The letter ended there, unfinished. The room-service
waiter had probably interrupted her. Lunch at the window, morning *Tribune* courtesy of the hotel, and she'd
turned to the . . . I returned the letter to the envelope, put
it back in the purse, and got up from the bench.

I went down the corridor past the benches, whose
bandaged, bleeding, emergency-torn occupants glanced up,
thinking I might be their means of help, then glanced
away, knowing that I was not. The admittance clerk was
not too busy with her cherished forms to glare at me as I

279

neared the desk. I glared right back, waved the purse at her for good measure, and went through the entrance to the lobby.

There was something I had to do, someplace where no one would see me. The last time was in the dark of my child's room, the night after my father's funeral, when I'd spoken to the copperplate, asking him to come back.

A service hall opened off the hospital lobby; the door, when I tried it, was unlocked. The hall was used for storage—wheelchairs, stretchers, oxygen cylinders like giant bullets. I closed the door and switched off the light so that the dark would hide my tears, and then I repeated what I had offered once before, too late. If F. X. was dead, even if he was really dead, well, what if I—?

In the dark and the tears, among the wheelchairs and stretchers, emblems of suffering, and the oxygen cylinders that gave air to the lungs . . . I offered my life in exchange for Maggie's.

I stayed only a few moments, after which I switched the light back on and went out into the lobby—to see Abe, derby, spats and boutonniere, swinging in the doors from the street.

At eight o'clock he stood with me outside a room on the third floor of Cumberland Hospital. Abel had not been idle: through Lieutenant Mullaney, he'd secured a doctor for Maggie, removing her from the jurisdiction of Emergency and the necessity of police reports. At seven-thirty, when she'd regained consciousness, Dr. Barnes had had her transferred to a private room, and was to return in the morning to appraise her condition.

"Half-hour," Abel noted, hauling forth the gold pocket watch. "Listen, like I said, it's my favorite time. The actors are getting ready . . ." He glanced into the shadowy room, the figure that made the slightest of presences under the bed sheets. A tube was taped to her arm and attached to a glucose bottle. She was asleep, her breathing deep and regular.

"Tell her no more monkey business," Abe said. He went into the room, over to the bed. "Tell her she's been out of the show nearly a week, that's too long." He looked down at her, then plucked the red carnation from his lapel and placed it on the white coverlet.

"Tell her she gets docked for tomorrow if she's not back." He fished a fresh cigar from the pearl-gray vest, came into the hall. "You, we can do the show without." He jabbed the cigar at me. "Stay with her. Better she finds somebody when she wakes."

"Abe, thanks."

"What's to thank? You get docked same as anybody." He turned without further ado and, at a pace that belied his age, went churning down the corridor. He paused before making the turn to the elevators and said in his raspy croak, "You didn't catch it."

"What?"

"The switch," said the last of my surrogate fathers. "I haven't been calling you kid," and with a whack at the black derby he rounded the turn to the elevators.

It was quiet in the room. A nurse came in to take Maggie's blood pressure, check her pulse. Apparently she'd heard of my Emergency scuffles: a glare, but she didn't attempt to eject me. I opened the window, the night air stirred the white curtains. I pulled the armchair closer to the bed. My head sank back of its own volition. I listened to the slow, even breathing from the bed, and my lids did their own bidding, too.

I dreamed, a series of discordant, disconnected images. Telephones, taxis. Airports, toy planes. Movie lights, hotels. Had to find her, find where she was, quick about it, hurry, hurry.

I sprang awake and up from the chair, ready to be on the move again. I swayed unsteadily: it was morning. Maggie lay in the bed, face flat against the pillows. She was looking up at me.

I rubbed at my black-stubbled jaw. "Must've dozed off," I apologized. "Bad dream or something."

"It was me. I called to you."

I stared at her. "You did?"

"I wanted to hear your name."

"Really?" I shifted my feet clumsily. "Damned if I heard it. I mean, I hate to ask you to repeat it—"

"*Christopher*," she pronounced it. I leaned over the bed and, though the IV tube imprisoned her arm, she reached up a hand to my face and pronounced it again—"*Christopher*"—like the sound of bells.

PART THREE

Maggie and Christopher
1949

CHAPTER 13

She was released from the hospital the next day.

The dawn light stole across the room, a broom sweeping away the shadows. She drifted in and out of tides of sleep, and I don't remember that between these calm drifts we spoke very much.

"Must be hungry," she said to me, startled awake, her eyes relieved of nightmare and not fully comprehending it. "Hungry and so tired."

"There's a machine down the hall." In the corridor, the sounds of the morning routine, rattle of carts, low pitch of voices. "Peanut-butter crackers, Lorna Doones and Oreos," I recited.

A smile lit the bruised face. "Good selection."

Dr. Barnes, a rumpled, untidy man who looked as if his practice was largely made up of calls like that of Lieutenant Mullaney, came at ten. She would need clothes, if released, so while the doctor was examining her I went to the Drake to get her luggage.

"Ah, Mr. Casey." Mr. Darlington detached himself from a covey of matrons and hastened toward me. "Here to vacate the suite? The, uh, lieutenant was in touch with us. If you'll permit me to accompany you . . ."

Nothing had been disturbed in the suite. The *Photoplay* lay on the sofa in the sitting room as it had yesterday. In the bedroom, the bed to the right hadn't been made up. The note pad bore its jottings, the room-service trolley stood at the window, only the food was removed. As he had yesterday, Mr. Darlington remained in the doorway.

"With incidents of this sort, where there might be police activity," he said briskly, "our policy is not to touch a thing."

I went about, collecting the few possessions that were out. Robe and slippers, hairbrush on the vanity, toilet case in the bath. *This morning the maid would have knocked on the door, and failing to obtain a response . . .* I closed the suitcase, stared at the rumpled silken bed. *Failing to obtain a response, the maid would have entered the suite, and lying in the bed, twisted among the sheets . . .*

"Is something wrong?" inquired Mr. Darlington. "If you've finished with the bags, I can ring for a boy."

I swung the suitcases from the rack. "Don't bother. I'll carry them."

Downstairs, Mr. Darlington escorted me to the cashier to attend to the bill. Maggie had paid for the suite in advance; the only charges were for phone calls. *No debts left behind, so that when her body was trussed and blanketed and carried to the morgue wagon . . .*

"Dear me, I haven't asked if . . ." Mr. Darlington smiled as the cashier stamped the bill paid. "I trust the young lady is . . . ?"

"She's alive," I said, and moved with the suitcases across the plush sanctuary.

The taxi followed yesterday's route up Lake Shore Drive. It turned off at Sheridan Road, as it had yesterday. The nightmare unreeling. I carried the luggage up the steps of Cumberland Hospital. A guard forbade me the elevator until I'd obtained a pass. The elevator stopped at 2, doctors, nurses, attendants got on. I pushed off at 3 and the nightmare went faster, accelerating.

I ran down the corridor, suitcases bucking against legs, and burst in upon the room as though life depended on demon speed.

If it had, it did so no longer . . . and I halted in the doorway at what I saw.

Maggie was not in the bed, but grasping on to the bars at the side. The coarse hospital gown enveloped her as it would a child; bruises marred her face, her upper lip was swollen still, but in the light that fell on her from the window her face was transcendent.

"Christopher?" the notes ascended, inquiring into my name. "The doctor said . . . I can leave."

I lowered the suitcases. "When?"

"When you got back." She gripped the bars, her brow damp from effort. "Guess who phoned?"

"Abe." I nudged the door closed with my shoulder. "The redoubtable Abel Klein."

She laughed and flicked at her hair. "Very severe with me. Docked if I miss tonight's performance." She held on to the bars, guided one foot in front of the other. "Been practicing."

"So I see."

Another step, then she swayed, fastened her grip. "Bit on the wobbly side."

My jaw clenched with the effort to not help her. "Seen wobblier," I said thickly.

"All in all. Considering." She steered along the side of the bed, practicing how to walk instead of run. She reached the foot, let go, and stumbled forward, arms out-flung.

"There!"

I caught her against me, the thin, trembling length of her, and the nightmare was over.

At one that afternoon she stepped from the taxi in front of the Daphne Hotel. A scarf, dark glasses and pancake helped to conceal the facial bruises. I unloaded the luggage and she stood contemplating the wedding-cake hotel, where her fellow actors would have to be given some explanation of the preceding twenty-four hours.

"Abe's sure to have covered for you," I said, but she needn't have worried. If it was a jury she had to confront, she could have done worse than a jury of actors.

Indeed, such was their conduct that any responsible judge would have thrown them out for incompetence and failure to properly weigh the evidence.

Sal, the bellboy, an ex-hoofer in the tradition of Kitty

Lorraine, appeared to fetch the luggage and convey us across the pink-and-black rococo lobby; simultaneous with this a colorfully garbed individual sauntered from the coffee shop. He was attired in a cabana jacket, Bermuda shorts and thong sandals, the Daphne not ordaining any particular rules of dress.

"Esther! Abe told us," cried Tony Ives, hastening over solicitously. "Exhausted after the funeral, *of course* you stayed an extra day. The shock, the bereavement, has it been dreadful?" He clasped Maggie's arm. "Poor Esther! May I make a shocking confession?"

She blinked at him dazedly. "I—"

"It's not the occasion to go into it, but I adore funerals. Yes, Salvatore we're coming." He shepherded Maggie into the elevator, where Sal waited with the luggage and room key. "I'm forever dropping in at Campbell's in New York," Tony continued. "Perfect strangers, but I offer condolences and help with the flowers." The pink-and-black car jolted upward with a lively bounce. "Was the casket open? Promise you'll give me the details later. Heard about Irene? She's decided not to sue the *Tribune*."

Next, Sal was conducting us along the sixteenth-floor corridor, and Maggie had yet to utter a word, not that the opportunity had presented itself.

"The indignity of it—imagine being compared to an act of resuscitation." Tony outlined Irene's travail at the hands of the critics. "The poor darling had to look it up in the dictionary, after which she required sedation. Isn't Sal wonderfully sinister?"

Now Maggie was standing in the middle of Room 1604, admiring a vase of dogwood blossoms and pussy willow, and Tony was on the phone, alerting his confreres.

"Held up nicely since yesterday," he remarked of the blossoms. "The vase is from Jack and Irene, so don't give it to the maid. Hello, Grace? Tonykins. She's here, sixteen-o-four, and don't forget the gin."

The room that Abe had wangled for Maggie was furnished with a metallic-gold sofa, ceramic lamps shaped like pelvises, and gold-sprayed tables, among other choice pieces, but she hadn't time to either admire or disparage it before the door buzzer proceeded to ring and the rest of the jurors began to assemble.

Vi Henry, Grace, Scott, Diana and Chip—in they flocked to gather around and install her on the sofa, protesting that she must rest after the plane flight she had not taken. They plumped pillows under her head and opened the windows to catch any vagrant breezes that might waft in from the lake. A bottle of champagne, which had been icing in the kitchenette refrigerator since yesterday, was brought forth, popped, and paper cups of it distributed for a toast.

Tony gave the toast, his antic features composed and solemn as he lifted his cup. "To Mags, who's come back to us," he said.

"To Mags," chorused the others and, cups drained, they pulled up chairs or sat cross-legged on the carpet . . . forming a half-circle around the sofa, the third such that Maggie had faced, beginning with the Garrick stage, then repeated in the hangman's circle of women at Bates Hospital.

This one was to be her reward, a manifestation of what she had talked of at the picnic on the hill in the Boston Common: the good that lies in store to make up for the bad, which cannot be glimpsed beforehand.

This semi-circle of jurors now behaved in a style that would have expelled them from a court of law. Replenishing the paper cups with their combined supply of gin, bourbon and vermouth, together with bags of potato chips and pretzels, boxes of Social Teas and Fig Newtons for nibbling, they blithely ignored the prima facie evidence that was available to them.

Maggie's pallor and bruises, poorly disguised by the pancake, received not a comment. The adhesive tape over the puncture wounds in her arm was similarly overlooked, as was my unexplained absence from the show last night. Instead, her fellow workers set out to beguile and entertain her, which after all was an aspect of the vocation they had elected to follow.

Whatever they knew or surmised or had conjectured among themselves about yesterday, it was not evident in the laughter that commenced rolling into the hall from Room 1604. Jointly and to hilarious effect, the group re-enacted for Maggie the vicissitudes that had plagued the Chicago opening of *Anniversary*, starting with Irene's fatal entrance, when she had snagged her gown on a nail, mooring herself to the stairs.

"Pulled and tugged and could *not* dislodge herself," described Tony, leaping up to deliver a wicked parody of the mishap.

"If only she hadn't smiled out front the entire time," exclaimed Vi Henry. "The audience all but applauded when she disentangled herself."

"And when Jack spoke his next line, 'My dear, how wise of you to be unencumbered by trivialities—' "

"Dear God, the house exploded."

"Why do we laugh?" Grace Marsden gasped, amid the gales of mirth. "It was torture. When I went on in the next scene and saw that Jack's toupee was actually—"

Why did they laugh? They were performers, illusion was their medium. They performed for Maggie, infusing her with their warmth and camaraderie, thereby helping her return from whatever dark region she had been in. Behind the laughter lay a tough reality: Who among them had not, in one way or another, visited such nether regions and learned something of the struggle of return? The opening hadn't been funny while the mishaps were occurring; the reviews the next morning were distinctly unfunny, as well as being a threat to the life of the tour. Actors as a group are the least exempt from despair—what are they exempt from?—and so are quick to recognize its shape. Diana, as she related for comic effect the tribulations of going on for Maggie, was aware that tonight she would be relegated once more to the wings. Her son was not to join her in Chicago when school let out, as planned. Chip had vetoed it, and in an effort to secure their fly-by-night relationship, she had complied. And Vi Henry, enrapturing Maggie with theater tales—was Vi thinking of Ben Forbes as she spun her amusing anecdotes? Ben was not staying at the Daphne but at the Y, and after the show each night a muscular youth in a leather jacket waited for him in the Erlanger alley. "She possessed extraordinary charm—it was her passport, stamped in gold," Vi went on with her theater lore, and did not refer to Ben, nor permit her glance to stray to the adhesive tape on Maggie's arm. Vi had been there, so had the others; performers, they entertained her, it was their profession, and while a judge would have dismissed them as jurors, I was inclined to rank them high.

Maggie, on the sofa, responded in kind. Her lack of strength was evidenced by her willingness to remain lying there, yet it was nourishment she was receiving from her callers. She drank it from them like drafts of milk. At moments, as the gay tales of backstage adventure went on, her eyes were captive to other visions. Other, harrowing visions, and at these moments her eyes would swiftly seek mine, light up with the old resolve, directed now toward different horizons.

She had come back and was not the same person; nor was I. Together we had crossed some invisible boundary at last, into another land. Her eyes lit with eagerness to explore its strangeness.

"No, stay," she protested when the circle broke up, returning chairs to their positions, forming a tidy-up brigade to deal with the paper cups and bottles and cracker boxes. She rose from the sofa. "Don't go yet. If you think you're tiring me—"

"It's past three, child," Vi Henry laughed, coming back from the kitchenette. "You'll want to be fresh and rested for the performance tonight."

She stood at the door, would not hear of doing otherwise, bestowing a hug on each of her callers as, laughter still volleying, they filed into the hall.

"Christopher?" She closed the door, moved slowly, with

effort, across the room. "It's a nice room, don't you think? Not the furniture, just look at that sofa, but large and airy . . ." She stood at the windows at the front. "They knew, didn't they?"

The dirndl skirt hung on her, testament to the painful thinness. "Probably," I said. "But actors make a good jury —they're used to bum raps."

"Mama's gone." She looked from the windows, out over the jumble of rooftops. "You can almost see the lake. Do you feel it, too—that you're not sure where you are or how you got here?"

"Squeaky new," I said. "Haven't unwrapped the cellophane."

"I know this much. Wherever I am"—she touched the curtains, as though they held a secret message—"I'm terribly glad to be here and I—I intend to do well by it."

I went over to her in this strange new land we'd come to. The journey had worn her out—her eyes, though they shone, were sooted with fatigue. "You can start by taking a nap. Before you keel over."

"It's a nice tiredness. Really," she averred, but did not overly protest when I put an arm around her and guided her to the sofa. "I haven't unpacked."

"Later."

"Tomorrow, then." She lay back with a sigh on the heaped pillows. "Tomorrow I'll positively burst with activity, confounding one and all."

Sleep fell on her in no more time than it took me to draw the window shade. I finished with the other windows and in the muted light took a blanket from the closet and unfolded it over her. Her hands lay over her breast; dark lashes brushed the pale, bruised face.

I tiptoed to the door and, "Christopher?" the notes ascended drowsily, pulled from slumber. "Where is your room? Very far?"

"Fifteen. Down a floor."

She struggled from the pillows. "That's quite enough separation, don't you think? I mean, from what they said about the reviews—*Anniversary* won't close? It can't."

"Course not." I pushed away the specter of such a contingency. "We won't let it close."

"I don't intend to," said Maggie, lying back again. "Not for an instant." The lashes fluttered closed, like butterfly wings. "Come for me?"

"Six okay?"

Sleep stole her answer, swift as a stroke of a sword. I stood looking at her, then went out, clicking the door softly behind me. Later, much later, I would think of the scene as the first moments of our parting—but that was years later, when I was able to think of it at all.

Maggie's thoughts?

That evening at 8:52 at the Erlanger Theater she climbed once again to the platform above the center-arch stairs and gripped the rail, listening to the dialogue on-stage, for her cue. By what powers she had summoned back the full measure of herself I couldn't have said. She waited there, I signaled her cue, and she went down the stairs into the white arena glare and the launching of Maggie Jones as an actress.

It was a week later, June, and I was in the shower cooling off from the Chicago temperatures, which in a few days had soared from the tolerable 70's to the sizzling upper 80's, without regard for man or beast.

I was cooling off, but not wholly from the temperature. Yowling in debased frustration, man and beast in cohabitation, I switched on the cold full blast.

Teeth chattering, I poked my head from the shower, at what sounded like a knock on the door.

"Sal?"

Quick action was called for: I turned off the spray. I'd sent out a suit to be pressed on Monday, the Daphne's special one-day service, which didn't take Sal Finella into account. What with functioning as the hotel bookie, he didn't have time to spare for room deliveries.

"That you, Sal?" I wrapped a towel around my middle—HNE, it spelled across my groin—and padded dripping from the midget-sized bathroom. Not that the bedroom was much bigger—it resembled, with the Murphy bed folded up, the waiting room of a failed dentist, located over a store. It required about half a second to get to the door.

"Sal—"

I opened the door, then backed away, grappling with both towel and apologies. "Listen, excuse it. I, y' see, I was in taking a shower and—"

"You were? So was I," said Maggie from the hall. Very cool, she looked, with her slick-wet hair and face like hosed-down marble. Very cool and composed, in her pink shirt, wrap-around skirt, slim, bare marble-cool legs. "Listen," she said as I gawked. "With you in that towel, and this door wide open, not that the Daphne is fussy, but—"

Remarkably, she was no longer in the hall. She was in the room, sauntering to the combination desk-bureau (a leaf pulled out) at the window. "So this is your room," she said, having a look around.

"I thought you were Sal," I said, hitching up the towel. "I sent out a suit to be pressed and—"

"Well, no, I'm not Sal." She turned, sifted a hand among the objects on the pulled-out leaf. "What's this?" she asked.

"That clipping?" The conversation was acquiring a weird echo-chamber effect. "Oh, come on, you must have that review memorized by heart," I said. "If not, you ought to."

She tossed the clipping back on the desk leaf. "I still don't see why the fuss. I gave my usual performance on Monday. What was different about it?"

The difference was that Ashton Stevens had been in Monday night's audience. Stevens, the *Herald-American*'s critic, was the most widely read, most influential critic in Chicago. He'd been away for the opening of *Anniversary*, and sent an assistant to cover it. But Abe Klein's friendship with Stevens dated back over many years and many shows, and on the strength of this, he'd agreed to attend Monday's performance. The bait was a young unknown actress who'd been absent from the opening-night cast. *Radiant, glowing,* and *gifted* were some of the adjectives that had studded Ashton Stevens' column the next day.

"Well, it was the same performance." Maggie dismissed the subject, restively prowling the room. "But if it helps us keep open, terrific. So this is your room." She gestured around.

"Yes." I pulled at the towel, aware that I wasn't dripping any more—body heat, I supposed. "The way the thermometer's shot up, can't shower enough," I said.

"Isn't it awful?" She leaned back against the dresser, which resulted, from the particular distribution of her weight, in the upper part of her shirt pushing open. "I just had my third since this morning," she said. "What about you?"

I was having audio problems, a fade-in, fade-out effect. "Showers?" I said, deducing that a contributing factor to the condition of her shirt was that the buttons were open.

"Anyway," she went on. "There I was, spray coming down . . . and it made me think about you. You being on fifteen and me on sixteen . . ."

Not only were the buttons open—it was plainly evident that she'd neglected to put on a brassiere. "I can see where it would get you to thinking all kinds of things," I said, my voice thickening like oatmeal on a stove.

"Especially with the heat and everything."

"The floor above and the floor below—" I said, in an unexpected burst of oratory, complete with outflung arm "—every hotel on the tour, it's been that for us." Hastily, I returned the outflung arm to the task of holding up the bulging towel.

"Always a floor between us—"

I looked at Maggie and somehow it ended the need for oratory. "Both of the rooms," I said, "what they've been in a way . . . is waiting rooms."

Her hand lowered from the shirt. "I'm not good at poses like this," she said, "but I was afraid you'd think I wasn't interested."

"Sex. You're referring to sex."

"Yes." She nodded solemnly, as though taking an oath in court.

"Perfectly natural function, after all." I hitched up the bulging towel. "Like eating or breathing."

"Or walking," she agreed.

"Yes, precisely." I sucked in my breath. "Then, Jesus, why is it so complicated?"

"I don't know, but when you think of it, eating and walking haven't much to do with the heart. Oh, Christopher," she said, her voice trembling. "You've gone where I thought no one could any more, because I'd closed it up. You're as much in my heart as you're standing there on the carpet."

"Listen," I said, hiking at the towel. The room was dimming—the afternoon light was unchanged at the window, but the room had dimmed as though shades had been drawn, enclosing us. "Listen, you probably don't know much about Murphy beds," I said, with a gesture at the contraption that lay behind the room's odd-looking extra door.

"What?" Maggie asked. "Oh, yes. Actually, I know little about them."

I went over to this extremely peculiar door, whose function appeared dubious, not to say questionable. My left leg was shaking, asserting its ancient prerogative. "The Murphy bed is a Chicago invention, by a man named Murphy," I said. "Very clever invention, when you think of it."

"Very practical, with the need for extra space," Maggie commented. "Do they come in different styles?" Pause. "The ones upstairs have doors that open out . . . but yours . . . ?"

"Mine works on a pivot basis. You grasp the knob—" I suited action to word, then pulled, "and it just pivots around, like so."

I pulled the knob, the door opened and in what was certainly a magically easy manner, the trussed-up bed rolled by tractor belt into its appointed position . . . and then it wasn't trussed up but quite nicely in its intended state, which was to say, prone, legs planted squarely and securely on the floor. And I was moving through the golden dimness, from one side of the bed to the side where Maggie waited.

"I love you," I said, undoing the remaining buttons. "I love you."

"I bought a nightgown yesterday."

"There's so much so quickly—I get scared."

"Lacy black, to have ready. Lacy black—" She lay beneath me on the bed, eyes shining up at me, huge as stars. "I wanted to make it special for you. All the dopey things. Moonlight and lace and music."

I leaned over her, mouth on her throat where the pulse leaped. "I hear music," I said. "Don't you?"

"Yes!"

"Brahms?"

"I think, Brahms."

And for all that afternoon music played for us.

We were convinced that, like measles, it showed, and was instantly, embarrassingly apparent to the most casual passerby, what we'd been up to.

Usually Maggie had a light supper before the theater, but we went to Joe Miller's, up from the Daphne on Rush Street, and feasted on steaks. Maggie was ravenous, as well as conscious of what she felt to be the waiter's diligent stare.

"We can't actually *look* different. He can't tell from merely *looking* at us."

"Of course not . . . it's like the hatcheck girl when we came in. She might have *seemed* to be giving us the once-over—"

"Dear Lord, you noticed it, too. What'll we do?"

"Fool everyone. Behave like brother and sister—of extremely formal upbringing."

Throughout the rest of the meal we avoided physical contact, no sneaky touches or squeezes as the garlic bread or pepper mill was passed. In the taxi going downtown to the Loop we kept most of the seat between us—a brother and sister of paralyzing formality. We rolled down the windows to the hot, humid June night and the neon-flashing, sidewalk-jammed, marquee-blazing blocks of the Loop. The conflagration of lights reminded me of Broadway the night I'd walked up it with Maggie; the taxi swung onto Randolph Street and the gigantic new sign atop Woods Theater was a spectacular twenty-foot-high reminder of the first time I'd heard mention of her, the day in Max Jacobs' office. The current feature at the Woods was a Danny Kaye comedy, but the billboard above the theater ballyhooed in big, flood-lit letters the attraction about to open in July. SIDNEY HARMON PRESENTS . . . *OBBLIGATO* . . .

The giant sign loomed closer, a sudden sobering intrusion. Maggie acknowledged it with a wave of her hand as the taxi weaved past it in the traffic.

"If you look very hard in the night-club scene, you're apt to catch a glimpse of yours truly," she said. "Probably the one and only glimpse."

"Oh?" The contract with Sidney Harmon had been until now almost mythic in its remoteness. "You don't foresee big plans for you? Big studio buildup?"

"Let me wise you up on Mr. Harmon. For two years"—the taxi turned into Clark Street—"he couldn't think what to do with me."

"It's called potential."

"Not a clue, till he latched on to the tour."

I remembered Harmon's wrangle with Max over her salary. "Could be part of a master plan," I said, half kidding. "Wait'll he sees the Stevens review."

"A road-show review? Chicken feed, believe me." She turned and fixed a gaze on me that was distinctly unsisterly. "Absolutely," she said. "Any worries in that department—groundless!"

The state of my trousers was in flux, so to speak. I groped an unbrotherly hand over the seat. "Worries. Who's got worries?"

"Exactly my point."

"Erlanger," the cabbie bawled up front, pulling to the curb a few tousled moments later. "My fault," I said, unlocking from the torrid embrace. "Practically assaulted you."

"No, I started it." She whipped out her compact, one of the rare occasions. "Good grief, I *do* look different."

"Well, your lipstick, but aside from that—"

She repaired her lipstick, then as we got out of the cab in front of the Erlanger: "The company will be on to us in two seconds flat. Can't you just hear everyone?"

"We'll go in separately," I said. "That way they won't make the connection."

"Right." She looked at me, the raven brows knitted in distress. "We'll do it Louella Meggs style—'Me first,' remember?" With that, she turned and ankled quickly, and with a fine show of legs, up the stage alley. "Hopeless weakness of character." She turned back at the stage door. "I don't think I can."

"I'll follow in a minute," I said, and the length of the alley to where she stood was a thousand miles. Then she had vanished through the door and I was skulking along Clark Street, slugging through the movie and restaurant crowds. *Breathing and walking don't go very far inside you, not to your heart . . .*

I went into a cigar store down the street, bought some El Productos for Abe, and requested the change in quarters. I went into a phone booth at the back of the store, dialed long distance, clunked quarters in the slot. *Crrkk, crrkk,* then the ever-guarded tones of Agnes Theresa Casey, née Lenihan, came over the line.

"It's Al Capone," I informed her. "Me and Dutch Schultz gotta invitation to extend. We hereby would like to invite you and your swellegant sister to the Windy City, all expenses paid—for the purpose of meeting someone."

"You—you sound good, Christy."

"I want you to come, Mama. The invitation's for real— so you can see for yourself I'm not a problem any more," I said. "See that it's finally behind me, those days that neither of us could recover from, that came between us . . . Mama? You there?"

"Yes," she answered after a moment, "Yes, I'm here," and in her voice was more than she had been able to speak to me in years. "I—oh, you'll want to tell Kathleen," she said. "Let me put her on."

"This my feller?" sang the rough Rock-a-bye-baby-toot-toot-tootsie pipes of Kathleen Lenihan. "Hey, what news did you throw at Ag? She looks like a flock of angels just floated down from the ceiling."

"They did."

"Yeah? Well, how's about lettin' me in on it?"

"I'm calling in fulfillment of a promise, Kitty Lorraine."

"What the—?" A pause while my aunt recollected the promise. "Yeah, baby? I—I'm listenin'."

"Remember when the ice wagon delivered you and your Victrola and vaudeville trunk to our door? Or earlier, when F. X. took me for Sunday walks and it was so beautiful it hurt like a knockout punch?"

"Listen, maybe you better stop," said Kitty Lorraine. "I don't have a Kleenex. Oh, God be praised, let's hear you say it."

"*Cash,*" I gripped the phone and said, "I'm so happy I don't think I was ever alive before—not for the longest while."

Happiness!

After the performance that evening we didn't repair to Henrici's or any of the favored Loop spots for late supper. I waited at the foot of the dressing-room stairs while Maggie changed and got out of her makeup—waited at the stairs so as to watch her come toward me.

There can be love without happiness, Maggie and I and the world knew that . . .

Outside in the alley some high-school girls waited with programs to be signed, the first of the fans who were to cluster nightly from then on at the stage door. She signed the programs, apologizing for her lamentable penmanship, after which we set out for the hotel.

There can be love for a cause, an ideal, a belief; for a flag, a house, a garden, a book, a poem, the rise of a hill, the shape of a tree ...

We walked in slow, meandering fashion through the night streets, past the theaters and restaurants, the rattle of the El; over the Dearborn Street bridge, past the Chez Paris, the Medina Temple, to Rush Street and the Daphne Hotel. We rode up together in the pink-and-black elevator, and I did not get out at fifteen.

There can be love in infinite form, but without it there can be no happiness. Maggie and I, if not the world, knew it, for this was the strange new land we'd come to dwell in, for the time that remained.

Two nights later, two of the number left to us, the closing notice for the tour was posted on the call-board backstage at the Erlanger.

CHAPTER 14

Abel Klein called the cast onstage after the performance that Saturday night. The audience had cleared from the theater, but the ushers were still thumping the rows of seats back up. The crew looked on from the wings and a pin could have been heard to drop as Abe, positioning himself in the center arch, extracted a telegram from his pocket.

A pin could have been heard while he read the wire from Max Jacobs, and mournfully returned it to his pocket. The actors, makeup perspiring under the stage lights, exchanged woeful glances, but no one spoke.

"Effective June seventeen. That's the two weeks to comply with union regulations," Abe commented, fishing for a cigar. "The part about barring an upswing—depends how you interpret it."

Still no one spoke. In the wings Edith Merkle hissed at her spouse, "I told you we should've went with *Carousel*." Then Jack Millet smoothed a hand over his patent-leather toupee. "Abe, old chap," he drawled, "are we to understand that the closing is conditional? Not altogether final?"

Abel shrugged, as wretched as I'd ever seen him. "Depends what you call upswing," he said. "Tonight, for instance, we did five hundred over last Saturday. The take is up for the whole week."

It took a moment for this information to sink in; when it had, a brushfire of excited murmurings swept the stage. "Five hundred over last week!" "Why, that's very nearly capacity." "If we'd run some decent ads featuring the Stevens review—" "What about twofers? Why doesn't Max put us on twofers?" "Aren't we going to fight at all?"

"Darlings," cried Irene Vail as the murmurings grew in excitement and intensity. "Darlings, may I make an announcement that might be of interest? May I, darlings?"

The hubbub quieted, and Irene turned to Abe with a gesture appropriate to Joan of Arc, prior to being led to the stake. "I should like to wire Max immediately," she trilled, "that Jack and I—*may* I include you, lamb?—are prepared to go on Equity minimum forthwith."

Abel scowled in the suspense-ridden pause that awaited his comment. "To me, I don't close without a fight," he said, pulling at his ear. "Not without I try every trick in the book." He clamped his jaw in a fierce terrier scowl. "That, I would like to apprise our producer of."

The response to this embattled challenge was instantaneous. Seldom were a group of employees as agreeable, indeed as dedicated, to the wholesale slashing of salaries, Maggie and I included. But as they surrounded Abe, urging that he inform Max at once of the salary-cut proposal, I detected a glimmer of uneasiness in the hooded eyes. We may have taken in five hundred over last Saturday, but I thought of Abe's dictum about Saturday night on the road, which was that you could sell out a funeral. Nevertheless, Abe agreed to phone Max in the morning.

"We are not Pearl Harbor. We will not be torpedoed like the *Maine*," Irene sounded the battle cry, thus aligning *Anniversary* with two of history's important disasters. "Furthermore, darlings, as a demonstration of confidence," she finished, "Jack and I—wouldn't we, dearest?—should like to invite you all out for, yes, a victory celebration."

The invitation was rousingly accepted, the triumphant thespians marched into the wings. Abe called after them apprehensively, "Not to put a damper on it, but let's nobody forget—I still got to post the notice."

Useless to preach caution. Jack and Irene grandly ferried their guests to Gibey's, the late-night show-biz hangout on Monroe Street. Celebration was the theme of the gathering that sat at pushed-together tables in the rear of the noisy, hectic, piano-whacking establishment. Setting the tone of the festivities, Jack called for a jeroboam of champagne. Gibey's did not stock jeroboams, there not being a demand for that lavish-sized vessel, the waiter apologized.

"Very well, magnums then." Jack waved him away. "Splits if you've nothing else, and mounds of caviar."

Ben Forbes had come and was sitting with Vi Henry. Diana and Chip, Tony, Grace and Scott made up the rest of the party, and after the inaugural round of champagne—"To a year's run, darlings"—Tony betook himself to the piano, where he sailed into a repertoire of show tunes—Cole Porter, Gershwin, Rodgers and Hart, Dietz, Youmans—that had Gibey's entire clientele joining in boisterously, none more so than at our tables.

Caviar was duly brought forth and the iced champagne kept flowing, for what was to be the last time, other than at the theater, that the *Anniversary* company would be together, with all its members present.

"Amusing little dive," Jack remarked, glancing round at the cafe tables and posters on the walls. "Rather Parisian, Puss, don't you think?"

"The night we wound up at that bistro in Montmartre—you, Millie and I," supplied Irene.

"How extraordinary of you to remember."

"Darling, how could I not?" laughed Irene. "We danced the tango madly, and I in my fifth month."

They gazed at each other, as though the revelation weren't the least startling. With dashing, white-toothed aplomb, Jack rose to his feet, bowed, and extended his arm.

"May I?"

To the fascinated attention of the table, the two moved onto the patch of floor space reserved for dancing. "Did I hear what I think I heard?" marveled Grace Marsden, ever wide-eyed, as Jack conferred with Tony at the piano. "Her fifth month, did she say?"

"The twinnies," Vi Henry said. "Hadn't you guessed by now?" Tony swung into a slow and passionate tango, the cue for Irene to execute a spectacular backbend, as Jack slid an arm under her waist. "Seems to have worked out remarkably well, considering."

Ben Forbes gaped at the parents of the aforementioned twinnies, as they slithered across the floor. "Astonishing," he said, with a tug at the walrus mustache. "However did they manage it?"

"They . . . went on," Vi said softly, and next to me Maggie raised her glass of champagne. It was her fourth or fifth, and the wine had given a flush to her cheeks, a brilliance to the dark eyes.

"Us too," she said, clinking her glass against mine. "It'll work out for us too, you mustn't worry."

"I'm not. Slightly."

"More than slightly." Jack and Irene were reaching a sinuous climax to their tango, to the cheers of the crowd. "Did you know we haven't yet?" Maggie asked, downing her champagne. "Danced, that is."

I got up unsteadily and bowed in imitation of Jack. With each drink, the closing notice was acquiring a delightful haziness, till it had practically disappeared.

"If I may . . . correct the omission?" I said.

"You may."

I escorted her onto the patch of floor space, at the piano Tony lilted into a waltz, one-two-three, *one*-two-three. I held out my arms and for the first and last time danced with Maggie Jones.

She arched back her head and looked up at me. "You really think a contract could come between us?"

"No. Yes."

"The show closes, Mr. Harmon says back to the coast, and back I go—is that how you see it?"

I drew her close, one-two-three, *one*-two-three. "No," I said. "With the champagne, I see a whole different picture. Us going to New York, the whole thing."

"New York and then—" She moved light as thistle with

me to a waltz that was reminiscent of *Waterloo Bridge*. "I see college, most likely, and a little walk-up, where the rent is cheap."

"Books."

"Entire walls of them."

I scowled in mock gravity. "Never confided my ambition, but it's to be an editor of books."

She smiled, moved closer, one-two-three, *one*-two-three. "I see a publishing house and this extremely distinguished—"

"*Maggie*." I locked my arms around her, losing count of the beat, not keeping to it. "Mightn't be so simple, getting you to New York. Might not."

She laughed and brushed a hand to my cheek. "But it is—just get on a train and go."

In some back region of my mind a chime sounded, muted by the champagne. *Train, but which?*

"That easy, huh?" I said. "Get on and go, just like that."

"No, but—" Her eyes filled with concern, fiercely she burrowed her head against me. "We can do it, you mustn't worry, hear? I've got it all planned, I tell you."

She thought that she did—steps already taken, I was shortly to find out: a letter mailed off, even before she'd known of the closing.

By Monday, when we came to the theater, Abel had affixed a bulletin to the call-board, side by side with the closing notice. It was a report of his plea bargaining with Max Jacobs. Since this had occurred over the weekend and was immediately picked up by the grapevine, namely Tony, the bulletin was merely a bleak confirmation of the outcome.

Max, while thanking the actors for their noble gesture, had declined the generous proposal of salary cuts. He held to the two-weeks' notice, though not disallowing for a miracle at the box office . . . and should it happen, who would rejoice more than he, the producer?

Each actor, as he came in the stage door, made straight for the call-board. The bulletin was raptly studied, as though for some mysterious, unaccountable change in its message; then the closing notice, and helpless shrugs replaced Saturday night's bravado. To their dressing rooms then, to get into their costumes and makeup.

"Don't you just simply bet," mused Tony Ives, dawdling up the stairs, lobster-red from a day at the Oak Street Beach, "that as the *Titanic* was going down, the only passengers who swore it wouldn't were actors? Not till the water lapped over them, poor fools."

"Perhaps it didn't lap over them," suggested Grace Marsden, following in Tony's wake, who had neglected to change from her beach outfit of polka-dot pajamas and floppy straw hat. "Perhaps they kept thrashing about and, lo and behold, were spotted by a lifeboat."

The lifeboat for the actors at the Erlanger that Monday night was the performance they gave. Half-hour, places, please, house to dark, curtain—rail and kvetch as they did, the performance they lavished on the half-empty theater was brimming with spirit, a gallant defiance of their own depressed state. By the final curtain it was restored to them, the vivid ebullience and sparkle that made them actors. That something of it was communicated to the audience could be heard in the clamorous applause from the sparse audience. It wouldn't last, this high engendered by the performance, but it would last until morning, and who could ask more than that the night be gotten through so splendidly?

They came off the stage in a whirl of bright chatter and deliberation as to where, what particularly attractive place, to repair for drinks and a late supper. Up to the dressing rooms they bounced, scarcely recognizable as the glum creatures who'd eyed the closing notices so disconsolately . . . and waiting in Maggie's dressing room was a visitor whose purpose was not to entertain.

I hadn't seen Dave Levitt come backstage, not that night. Navy blazer and orange-striped Princeton tie projecting an Ivy League, as opposed to show-biz, image, he'd bobbed up several times last week to inform Maggie of various publicity coups. Interviews, her photo on the cover

of *Where*, the Chicago entertainment guide, Marshall
Field fashion show, big coverage in the papers—in New
York there had been Miss Breal; in Boston, Zinder; and
representing Sidney Harmon in Chicago, affable Dave
Levitt.

Affable, even engaging, if you disregarded the flat, hard
eyes that didn't match the super smile and ingratiating
talk, the eager-beaver enthusiasm he displayed for his
work. Young man on his way up, was the term for Dave
Levitt, and those who applied it to him were not, as I
learned, in error.

I waited at the foot of the dressing-room stairs, for the
pleasure it gave to watch Maggie descend, freshly scrubbed
of makeup and shiny from Pond's. Usually it was a minute's wait, then down she flew, but tonight . . .

"Esther not down?" inquired Tony, doing some stair-
flying himself, Grace scurrying behind. He hung their keys
in the pigeonholes. "That Princeton number must still be
with her."

"Dave Levitt?"

"How he yearns to be a Wasp. Now, Gracie, the Pump
Room's out, with that beach ensemble," he lectured as
they crossed to the stage door, "so shall we settle for Rick-
et's? Icy-cold draft beer and a yummy Welsh Rabbit?"

I waited a moment longer, then went up the stairs.
Maggie's dressing room at the Erlanger was the last in a
row of three, the door was ajar, and as I rounded the stairs
to the corridor I heard the affable, eager-beaver voice of
Dave Levitt.

"But why not? Give me a reason and I'll be happy to
leave," he was saying, with earnest sincerity. "One good
reason why you won't move to the Whitehall."

"I told you," Maggie answered. "I like it at the Daphne."

"Ah, but wait'll you're at the Whitehall. Small, discriminating—Hepburn always puts up there when she's in
town. Cooper, Myrna Loy—it's our real movie-star hotel."

"Not the Drake? I thought the Drake. Look, whatever
you say, I don't intend—"

"*Uh*-uh, watch yourself," Levitt playfully interrupted. "Who knows what I'm liable to say, on behalf of Mr. Harmon?"

Silence. "What do you mean?"

"Well, he might not like it that you're shacked up with the boyfriend at the Daphne." Another silence. "It could be why he wants you at the Whitehall, starting tomorrow."

From where I stood the door blocked the dressing-room interior and its occupants. I heard someone get up, then Levitt: "Arranged? Terrific. I made a reservation. They're expecting you."

"Well, really, they'd better not," Maggie said, which occasioned the longest silence yet, with the sound of a match striking in it, the exhaling of cigarette smoke.

"You're refusing?" Levitt laughed, followed by more exhaling. "Listen, seriously, you're in enough hot water as it is."

"Oh?"

"It was headstrong—no, I'll come right out and say it was stupid."

"The letter to Mr. Harmon?"

"Incredibly stupid. Why would he let you out of your contract? It's incredible. After all this preparation, he's going to let you ride off with Buster Brown into the sunset? Listen, if I ever was guilty of such incredible stupidity—"

"What preparation?" Maggie cut in. "What are you talking about?" she asked.

Levitt told her in detail, or as much as I remained to hear of it. He told her that Sidney Harmon was coming to Chicago to personally supervise the opening of *Obbligato*— "Sort of a break for me. Never had the honor of meeting the man face to face," he confessed engagingly. "Who's to predict what it could mean? Some good fieldwork, good solid interference, it could mean goodbye, Chicago, and hi there, Beverly Hills. And you—want to know what it could mean for you, Maggie Jones?"

He told her about *Anniversary* then: what was in the

works for it and why it wouldn't close, forget the date on the notice, until the end of the month, coincidental with the arrival of—was she getting it, putting the picture together?

I was halfway down the stairs by then and did not hear her reply.

I waited again at the foot of the stairs. "Hi, how's it going?" Levitt called a few minutes later when he breezed down and, not overlooking a friendly good night to the doorman, batted out to the alley. Then Maggie was on the stairs, smiling, breathless, the skirt of her paisley cotton flaring above the slim, bare legs.

"All this stuff about publicity." She brushed aside the talk with Levitt. "The cover of *Life*, naturally."

We walked home in the sultry, moonlit night, up Michigan Avenue to the white ramparts of the Wrigley Building and the gothic soar of the Tribune Tower across from it. It was prom time in Chicago—taxi loads of girls in organdy and corsages, slicked-up boys in rented Palm Beach jackets, went by us. They formed little parades all along the avenue, swept into the hotels with exaggerated nonchalance and what they took to be the requisite air of world-weariness. It wouldn't matter how the actual evening turned out: tomorrow, back in their classrooms, they'd weave a fantasy of it to keep pressed in their memories, a night to belong to them always.

It belonged to them, was theirs by right, not to be taken away—just as these days and nights of June, of spring passing into summer, belonged to Maggie and me. It was our time, as though by some royal proclamation, and nothing could take it from us.

"Come . . ."

"What?"

I clasped her by the hand, hurried us along Ohio Street to Rush, into the pink-and-black elevator.

"Christopher!"

"Hold still . . . there."

She lay with me in the royal bedchamber on the sixteenth floor of the Daphne, in ribbons of moonlight streaming through the windows. "There." I felt myself move in her. "Oh, God, Maggie."

"I know. Yes."

"You're my life. All of it."

In the morning, languidly, we fixed breakfast in the kitchenette—I, the orange-juice squeezer, Maggie, the toast and coffee maker—and if she was disturbed by thoughts of Levitt and the transfer to the Whitehall, she gave no sign of it.

Nor, sitting across the breakfast table from her, did I.

This was our time, belonging to us, and no one could take it from us, at least not for now.

The days went by and, in defiance of the notice on the call-board, we spent them in ordinary pursuits.

Room 1604 at the Daphne did not lose its tenant; when Dave Levitt showed up backstage again, a certain strain, a slight tensing of jaw muscles, were the only hints that he might have a quarrel with Maggie. "Publicity! No end to his schemes" was as much as she said of their meetings, and I was equally dismissive in the occasional comments I proffered.

We awoke each morning to happiness that was ever strange and baffling and wondrous as it presented itself to us, like a bank draft of unlimited credit made out in our names and bearing no restrictions.

Hoard it for future needs or squander it in reckless extravagance? Looking back on it, remembering, it wouldn't appear that we had a gift for extravagance. Ordinary pursuits, average-everyday-ordinary, yet endowed with a certain quality, as if suffused with a golden light, that rendered them extraordinary.

Some mornings when I yachted into consciousness in the double Murphy bed that jutted out from the wall like the prow of a ship, and reached for the warm, taut silken . . . Maggie would not be there. Had the king summoned her to the palace? Conspirators abducted her for the purpose of fomenting a revolution?

No, it was that we were out of milk or oranges or bread

and she'd dashed around the corner to Kessler's market. I'd listen for the clank of the elevator stopping in the hall, footsteps drawing nearer . . . and if they were not forthcoming, it meant that she had ventured farther afield than Kessler's. Up past Chicago Avenue to the French bakery she'd discovered on Bellevue Place, whose fresh-from-the-oven croissants melted on the tongue at first buttery taste. I'd lie in the Murphy bed, waiting, listening, the few minutes that transpired slowly acquiring a tremendous urgency, precisely as though a king had fetched her away irrevocably or conspirators dragged her off after desensitizing me with opiates. The elevator, footsteps—unable to endure another agonizing moment, I'd hurtle out of bed, grab for my chinos, to race in pursuit of her, at which instant there'd be the clank of the elevator, footsteps approaching, key in the door, Maggie surprised but not discombobulated in my arms . . .

In like manner, when we went shopping at Marshall Field's, the taxi bearing us to the Loop was a golden coach; unseen, liveried footmen attended to our every requirement. "Chicago's top attraction, second to none," was Maggie's opinion of Marshall Field's department store. "Plus, it's got the best air-conditioning in the world, like marvelous ocean breezes—and have you ever *seen* so many escalators?" She could not get enough of Field's, touring the fabulous acreage, riding the multitudinous escalators, wafting from floor to treasure-filled floor.

Marshall Field's, Carson Pirie, Peacock's, Kroch's Bookstore, Lyon and Healy, to listen to phonograph records in one of the booths. Old St. Mary's Church, candles flickering in the dim, burnished interior as we wandered in from the burning glare of the sun and the fearsome rattle of the El . . . Maggie hesitating, keeping to the rear, gazing at the immaculate white altar.

"You're Catholic, aren't you, Christopher? So are Joe and Lourdes. Once at the ranch I asked to go to Mass with them . . . well, it was disgraceful."

"How come?"

She stood at the back of St. Mary's. "I don't know what came over me, but I started weeping and blubbering . . . and out spilled the entire story of the baby. Joe said—he asked if—"

"What?" I asked softly.

She fiddled with the scarf knotted under her chin. "He said that my baby was in Heaven with God, and would I like to light a candle in memory of it."

"And did you?"

"I—" Her voice broke, she clapped a hand to her mouth. Lowered it, after a moment, and joked, "Did I light a candle? I lit about ten. I went on a candle-lighting spree, you could say, and it was the only time that—"

Hand to the mouth again. "The only time I felt my baby hadn't ended in a pool of blood . . . that there was something more."

I took her hand, but she would not go down the aisle. Instead, we conducted our transactions at St. Anthony's altar, which was at the side toward the rear. Maggie lit a candle for her baby, another for her mother; and the tallow that I held the taper to, the little flame that flared up, was for F. X.

Marshall Field's, the Art Institute, the Lincoln Park Zoo —ordinary everyday pursuits, and on matinee days when the temperature soared beyond endurance, when it was "egg-fryin' time," to borrow Saffrona's term for it, we went to the Oak Street Beach.

Saffrona Willets was the sixteenth-floor day maid, and was not averse to conversation while she plied her vacuum and duster. "Baby, skip Marsh' Field's today," she'd advise Maggie. "It egg-fryin' time. Scramble 'em on the sidewalk for sure. Ask His Highness to take you to the beach."

Saffrona disapproved of both me and my tenure in the room. She did not view with high regard the sex to which I belonged. "Some no-account be ever crossin' the path of womankind," was a frequently expressed sentiment of Saffrona's. "Hear whut I say, honey? Tell His Highness it's egg-fryin' time an' you wants to git some relief."

Those afternoons at the beach were the most leisurely, the least hurried and therefore the most deceptive of any. In the long curve of the beach, the wide, wide expanse of lake stretching to the horizon, time was encapsulated, held motionless. We'd lie on towels in the sun, Maggie toasting honey-brown, I a dark shade of umber. With interruptions for crazy twenty-yard dashes into the rolling breakers, laughing wild dashes back to the towels, shedding beads of silvery coolness on each other . . . and with excursions to the hot-dog-and-soda-pop stand, we spent the hours lying immobile in the sun, baking hot and languorous in its rays. I remember the afternoon when, head propped on elbow, I lazily followed for an interval the course of an iron-ore freighter bound for Duluth, far out on the blue rim of the horizon. It made no progress, followed no course, a cut-out ship pasted on blue cardboard . . . but when I next propped myself up for a look, the horizon was blank, the cut-out freighter was gone, no trace of mast or funnel. And the sun that had shone directly overhead had shifted position, too, was pasted over the skyline to the west.

"What time is it?" Maggie lifted her dark glasses in inquiry. "Can't be! It positively cannot be four-thirty. Only just got here."

"Right . . . and only just leaving."

"I can't conceive that a whole afternoon could pass in a trice!"

Sighing, brushing each other of sand, collecting towels and beach bag, Maggie slipping on her harlequin wrapper while I pulled white ducks over my trunks and a striped terry shirt over my umber chest, we'd head ourselves back down Michigan Avenue in the direction of the Daphne, and the night's performance.

Due to the untiring efforts of Abel Klein and the advent of several large conventions in the city, receipts at the Erlanger box office were gratifyingly improved. Not capacity, but healthily above the break-even figure; no word yet from Max Jacobs to rescind the closing date, but how could he not? What fool, confronted with such promising indications, would close a show?

It was with the approach of evening, of half-hour, that Maggie and I surrendered the time that was ours, belonging to us, and turned to the issue that was unendingly hashed over by the *Anniversary* company. The manner in which we talked of it, however, was curiously restrained and noncommittal.

"Oh, I haven't a doubt," from Maggie. "It'll be on the call-board tonight. Postponed indefinitely."

"Abe says once we get into the summer tourist trade and work some package deals with the agencies—"

"Can't imagine how not." Pause. "How many days to the seventeenth? Five, just five. It'll be on the board tonight."

"Postponed. It's a cinch."

"We can breathe again." Pause. "Of course, if we close on Saturday, it's not a total catastrophe. We've set that pretty straight . . . Christopher? Haven't we?"

"Sure. Absolutely." It was at this juncture that fiction took over the discussion. "Off to New York, first train out."

"Did I mention I looked up schedules?" Continuing the fiction, embellishing it. "There's one train, the Pacemaker, leaves at four every afternoon. All coach, but reserved seats *and* dining car and lounge."

"The Pacemaker's famous. It's the common man's answer to the Twentieth Century . . . or the Superchief."

Reinforcing the fiction. "We're not *positive* of the closing date yet, but maybe we ought to make reservations for the eighteenth anyway, just to have them."

"Yeah, probably should . . ."

The fiction that we were indulging in had its origin at Gibey's, the night of the closing notice. The waltz and *Mightn't be so simple, getting you to New York.* One-two-three, *one*-two-three. *Sounds it to me. Get on a train and go.* From there it had been taken up, developed, passed with the coffee over the breakfast table, woven in the rib-

315

bons of moonlight in bed at night—the fiction of a young actress grown bored with her career and deciding to chuck it in favor of going off to New York with a young man. The young actress was saddled with a movie contract, however, and her studio, rather than rejoicing at her decision . . .

It was an appealing tale of two young lovers who triumphed over every obstacle to ride off, as Dave Levitt had phrased it, into the sunset—a necessary fiction, if these two golden weeks were to be ours, belong to us, and so I had embraced it with all the fervor and some of the desperation of the arms that held Maggie each night, blind to the dwindling number that was left.

But as fiction goes, it wasn't altogether convincing—too many holes, inconsistencies—and for me it fell apart the night of Thursday, June 16, when we arrived at the Erlanger to find an excited group clustered around the callboard.

Abe had posted a communication from Max Jacobs on the board, amending the closing notice. He didn't rescind it, but instead extended the run for two weeks, to the end of the month, the July Fourth holiday weekend.

Two weeks more, the reprieve that the actors had vowed would come; and now they foretold a second extension that would follow this one, and a third, a fourth, culminating in the removal of the notice from the board.

It fell apart that night, the fiction of the two triumphant young lovers, and was replaced by the real-life story, which wasn't as triumphant.

The house was sold out on Saturday night, packed to the rafters with conventioneers and their wives, a noisy, jubilant crowd whose buzz of conversation rose and crashed against the curtain and could be heard, a muted din, on the stage as Chip Barrett cued Eddie Ruick at the dimmer, "*House down . . . house to half . . . house dark.*"

Owing to the tardiness of many of the conventioneers in getting to the theater, it was 8:51 when the curtain rang up. At 8:58 I signaled Maggie her cue and she went down the stairs into the hot arena glare and the audible stir out front that greeted her entrance. Then, as arranged, Tony took over the sound-effects table and I went out into the orchestra through the pass door to watch Maggie in the play.

Seen from the wings, a play is stripped of illusion. The batteries of lights constantly adjusting, dimming, brightening according to cues; the crew lounging behind the flats; the actors dropping in and out of character as they enter and exit—from the wings the mechanics show and the illusion the play seeks to create is all but nonexistent.

Out front, the experience is so different as to bear only the slightest relation to the goings-on backstage.

I stood at the back of the orchestra and looked over the hushed, attentive rows at the convincing replica of a Gramercy Park drawing room, and at Maggie, who sat on the mulberry chintz sofa, a newly hired secretary taking dictation from her employer. Jack Millet, dapper in his Sulka robe and favoring his left profile, stood at the mantel, outlining the hectic, glamorous schedule of a celebrated news commentator. I watched the scene unfold, waiting for a particular moment.

"Eleven-thirty, Scribner's, to go over the new book. Twelve-thirty, lunch at Pavillon with Dean Acheson," Jack dictated, and his naive secretary diligently transcribed it on her steno pad. "NBC at three, Sarnoff . . . cocktails five-thirty, but where? The Chatham? Lafayette?" She waited, pencil poised. "Or would you prefer some charming hideaway?" Jack asked, and the moment occurred.

There was a pause as Maggie looked up from her steno pad. She turned to Jack and said, "Prefer?" and in the space of that moment the slick contrivances of the play turned real for the audience. Suddenly the attentive rows felt concern for the girl on the stage, whose worldly employer was taking advantage of her innocence. Suddenly, it was manifest, the quality that singled Maggie out as an actress: a vulnerability that was at odds with her ravishing beauty. She looked at Jack and suddenly she was Virginia Belton, hireling of the Clarion Title & Guaranty, hungry for attention, wanting to respond, yet out of a knowledge of betrayal, mistrusting the offer of it. It was Janya, yearning for kindness, wanting to trust in it, who spoke on the stage and gazed out from the primavera face.

"Prefer?"

All this she conveyed in a single moment, such was this gift of hers as an actress, to make an audience feel what she felt, to catch them up, make them care about her. The scene over, she exited and I could feel the audience wanting her to come back. They would wait for her, and when she returned, the formula comedy of *Anniversary* would be touched with something authentic and real.

I started from the orchestra rail and there was a cough, a shifting of feet. Abe stood beside me in the shadows, the derby clearing the rail by not many inches as he contemplated the stage.

"Something, huh?" he murmured. "One in ten thousand, you get like her." He chewed meditatively on the unlit cigar. "Could be that's the explanation."

"Of what?"

"Otherwise, it don't add up." He scratched his ear, hooded gaze fixed on the stage. "In January when I saw Max, no mention of a tour. Gets back from the Coast and can't wait to put a company together. Why?"

"I don't know," I said, which wasn't true. "What's your guess?"

"Somebody on the Coast must've changed his mind." He frowned, removed the cigar. "I hear from Dave Levitt we can expect a big shot in the audience one of these nights. You hear rumors to that effect?"

"Sydney Harmon," I said. "Got a movie opening at the Woods."

"Sydney Harmon catches the show," said Abel, "and bingo, we close. Funny, if all these weeks we haven't been running a tour, like we thought, but a screen test." He turned away from the rail, clamped down angrily on the already mangled cigar. "Not so funny for the actors it puts on the unemployment line."

On the stage the first act was nearing its finish. The ushers were hooking back the lobby doors for the stampede at intermission. Abe, thin, frail shoulders squared defiantly, went into the lobby, leaving me with his speculations. I headed down the side aisle for the pass door. The curtain started its descent, swept down, as I went through the door, to a volley of applause that was like the clap of thunder before the rain.

"Wacker Drive," I said to the cabbie, climbing first into the white-and-green Checker. It was Monday afternoon, five-thirty, early to be leaving for the theater. The taxi pulled away from the Daphne, and Maggie, honey-cinnamon from two consecutive days at the beach, flopped back next to me on the seat.

"I ask no questions," she declaimed, with a sweep of hand, head tilted back. "If your desire is to dine in the Loop, so be it, milord."

The taxi made a left onto State. "Have to see about trains," I said. "Cash and my mother, for when they come out next week."

She sat up on the seat, a Javanese princess with her bare, tawny arms and gold-looped ears. "Trains, and you have not consulted the expert?" she protested, plunking a finger on my mouth. "Which do you require, pullman or coach?"

"Pullman—a bedroom." I nibbled on her finger, maintaining the fiction of the carefree young lovers. "Don't you think?"

"By all means, in style." She leaned over, brushed sun-warmed lips over mine; glanced out the window, the young actress wearied of her career. "However, I don't believe we want Wacker Drive."

The taxi nosed down the ramp to the traffic-congested drive that banded the river, following its turns and peregrinations. "The city of Chicago, rail center of the nation, boasts five major terminals," declared the young actress, grasping the taxi hand strap, lowering herself in an arch across my lap. "Of these five, the principal transit point for New York is the LaSalle Street Station, to which we are *not* presently headed."

"Adams Street," I said to the driver, "take the Adams Street exit." Frowning, she raised herself up. "How about Union Station?" I queried. "What's that the principal transit point for?"

The taxi swung off the drive. "Christopher, what are you up to?" she asked quietly. "Where are you taking me?"

I delivered the fiction its first blow. "To where you'll be leaving from soon," I said very quickly, and the taxi drew up to the great, block-long facade of towering stone pillars. I got out, paid the driver, turned to Maggie, who was staring at me from the seat.

"I can't let you, don't you see that?" I reached in to her.

"Let me what?"

"Throw away a part of yourself that—" She recoiled back in the seat, gripping the hand strap. I grabbed at her, hauled her onto the pavement. "I know about Harmon and the show," I said, dragging her after me toward the great, columned facade. "He's buying the movie rights and he's got these plans for it."

"What nonsense are you talking?"

"For it and for you. Big plans—" I yanked her after me through the doors of Union Station, down the stairs into the immensity of space from which a far-flung empire reached north, south, east, west, to every point of the compass, linking by rail and semaphore the boundaries of a continent . . . and of dreams, the countless dreams conceived at remote crossroads and dusty prairie depots, the dreams of the left-behind, bred of unutterable longing as they watched the trains go past and heard the whistles that called, *Come with me, come* . . .

"Big plans," I went on, hauling her after me. "Buying the show, which is why he put you in it, a sort of tryout—"

"Unhand me," she cried, halting at the foot of the stairs. "Let go of me at once." Her eyes flashed hatred, outrage, defiance, contempt, in lightning sequence. "I'll never trust you again, do you hear? Why are you laughing?"

"Don't you see? Are you blind?"

"*What?*" She swept at her hair.

"You're the most marvelous actress." Renewing my grip, I dragged her through the streams of rush-hour commuters, into the enormous forum of the station; past the rows of ticket windows that were dispensing coach seats, uppers and lowers, to Peoria, Sioux City, Omaha, Salt Lake, New Orleans, Galveston and all points between; past the redcaps trundling luggage carts, the engineers and brakemen in striped overalls, who strode, mythic figures, across the concourse—led her, the little girl of the left-behind depot, under the giant, illuminated logos—*Union Pacific, Denver & Rio Grande, Missouri Texas, Burlington* —that were mounted on the walls; down to the lower concourse, the green chalkboard on which the names of the fabled titans of the rails, evoking powerful images of distances conquered, were inscribed, along with their track numbers and departure times: *Empire Builder, Denver Zephyr, Overland, Olympian, El Capitan, Chief . . . Superchief.*

"I said let go of me." Eyes blazing, she tried to wrench free.

"All along you had a ticket, but you didn't know, couldn't see. The most wonderful kind of ticket."

We went down another ramp to the wide enclosure at the end that was ringed with train gates, each bearing its number and departure time . . . and there on the board at Gate 26 was the legend *Superchief*, with its list of Pullman car numbers. The train itself lay beyond the gates, not to be glimpsed, but its imminent departure had endowed this corner of the station with a glamour and excitement that were electric. Seated at a table in front of the gate were the conductor and his assistant, consulting Pullman diagrams, checking off space allotments, as the line of passengers moved forward to present their tickets for this westbound journey of the Superchief.

"See?" I jerked Maggie forward, nodded at the privileged line, the chic women, the well-barbered, well-brushed, well-tailored men, who carried so lightly the accoutrements of first-class travel—jewel cases, expensive cameras and binoculars—and treated the business of waiting as an amusing exception to their accustomed routine. "All along you've belonged to this," I said to Maggie. "Back in Clarion during the worst of it—all along you had your ticket to belong, which you still don't realize."

And I marched us through the gate and into the vast train shed, its iron-latticed glass ceiling as high as that of a ten-story building, its array of platforms and tracks tunneling to the yards that could be distantly seen, burnished gold by the final fading of the sun.

With furious intent, Maggie yanked loose of me. "If you'd explain what this gibbering's about."

"About us . . . the little play we've been acting." I looked at her, rapidly losing any will for the enterprise. "What job, when we get to New York?" I asked. "You haven't said, but I'll bet anything it's waitress."

"*So?*" She brushed at the mane of sun-streaked hair. "I've been a waitress before—forty dollars a week in tips alone."

"It'll have to be some job like that—Harmon can take you to court, get an injunction to bar you from working as an actress."

"*Let* him. Who cares? Certainly not I."

"Well, then I guess that leaves me." And before the will for it was entirely gone, I once more seized her by the hand, steered her down the incline to the silver leviathan that was berthed at the platform, its gleaming silver length extending into the shadows far down at the end, the central element in the memorable spectacle that was being staged on the platform.

On this one platform there seemed to be a raja's portion of the world's riches. Messengers hurried with flowers, baskets of fruit and candies, hampers of brandy and champagne. Porters wheeled carts heaped with the most opulent luggage, stickered with labels of the most opulent hotels and resorts. At the steps of each gleaming silver car stood a black-suited Pullman porter, to receive the casually chatting passengers as they approached, relieve them of packages, and assist them up the steps into the air-cooled, soft-carpeted luxury provided for their two-night journey on this supertrain. The Santa Fe drumhead on the observation car glowed purple on the jostling scene of passengers, messengers, redcaps, vendors with carts of magazines, books and candy, all converging on the silver cars.

"You shouldn't have brought me here," Maggie said faintly, pulling away. "You shouldn't have. It was cruel of you."

"But you have a ticket. Ask me about the ticket." I kept hold of her, led her along the platform, past the silver Pullmans whose names were etched on their shining flanks, proud Indian names, *Navaho, Oraibi, Yampai.* "I went out front Saturday night," I said. "Watched you from the audience, the effect you have."

"I don't want to hear. You're ruining everything. Smashing it."

"Very rare, one in ten thousand, Abe says, but what really does it, reaches out and holds them—" I pushed through the jockeying platform swarm. "It's Janya who's on the stage, reaching to the audience and making them care. This tremendous talent that was hidden in Janya all along." I pulled us toward a pillar, away from the jostle, and turned to her. "Don't you see? It was the ticket that let you travel to foreign lands those Sundays in Clarion, and make the Alhambra a castle—this gift you've always had but didn't know about."

Tears blurred her eyes as she looked up at me. "But I don't care about it, Christopher. Not any of it."

"Don't you?"

"Not any more. It—it just seems to have gone out of me."

"When I call *places* and you go down to the stage, do you care?"

"I—mainly what I think is that it's one less performance to give."

"Mainly, but there's another part of you that goes down those stairs and comes alive, in that special way."

"I want *you*, Christopher." She pulled at my sleeve. "You're what I want. Let's leave, let's not stay here."

"If I'm what you want—" I sucked in my breath "—you're in for a hard time, for a while. Both of us, it looks to me."

"No." She shook her head. "No, don't say that."

"What instead?" I shrugged helplessly. "That we'll go to New York, Harmon or no Harmon? You'll be a waitress to help me through college? We'll live in a cold-water flat, happy as larks?"

"We would be." She caught at my arm, fierce, urgent. "So happy! You know we would."

I dragged the words from me. "Yes, but you'd have given up a part of yourself you might never get back—and I'd have let you do it."

She bit her lip, stepped back. "Now and then a few moments of regret, is that so terrible?"

"Is the alternative? Few would agree." I reached out a hand to the primavera face. "Harmon's buying a play just for you. When he comes and sees you in it—he'll ship you to the coast, bound and gagged."

"It could be for nothing. A total fizz, when he sees the rushes—bounce me right off the picture."

"You'll take the chance."

She jerked up her chin, the fighting spirit resurging. "Mighty sure of yourself, aren't you? A whole continent between us—it's a chance you maybe oughtn't take."

"I'll have to risk it."

"Maybe you shouldn't." She swung her back to me, moved along the platform in the thinning crowd. Fewer passengers were clustered at the steps of the silver cars. Instead, they were to be seen at the windows of the satin-wood-and-silver-ash compartments and drawing rooms, the women freshening up at mirrors, the men settling on the cushioned sofas with books and cigarettes, readying for the *All 'board* of the journey about to get under way.

"Risk I'll have to take," I went on. "The cold-water

flat—that'll be mine, I guess." She moved off down the platform; I followed. "Night school probably, and a job in a bookstore."

"Bookstore clerk! This incredible movie star I'm apparently to become—why would I fool around with book clerks?"

"Disguises. A blond wig, for when you show up at the cold-water flat. Secret codes and messages—"

"You're not funny."

"Jesus, no. Agreed." I looked at her and something turned over in me, an idea ballooned in my head. No, I couldn't ask that. Clerk's salary and two cents' worth of prospects? I couldn't ask her for a long, long time. "Not funny at all," I fumbled on, "but we'll find a way."

"Oh, what does it matter?" She flared. "The studios and men like Mr. Harmon—according to Joe Scully, they're on their way out. The whole system. Nothing lasts, so what does it matter?" She gestured angrily at the silver cars. "Trains like the Superchief, all gone, so in the long run—"

The anger was startled silent by what she saw in the car above. Snowy tables agleam with silver, asparkle with crystal, and on each a silver vase with a red, red rose. She stood, as of long ago, gazing up at the dining car.

"Papa said . . . lobster was money, shipped on cracked ice," she said with a tremor. "Mr. Harmon is money, it comes to that—and I'm something he bought."

"No, it's your talent that counts. That's important."

"Really?" She swung around from the dining car and thrust up her chin. "Take me to New York with you?"

"If—" my heart gave a lurch. "If you'll tell me that the rest means nothing, isn't a part of you, like it or not."

She looked at me from across the platform, and her lips curled derisively. "What you're saying is no. All right, let's get it over with. Do it here, *now*."

"Maggie, I—"

"Leave me here. I want you to."

The clang of steel doors being shut reverberated up and down the platform. The stools were gone from the Pullman steps, the porters were on board, standing at the doors. From a car up front came the sharp bleat of the conductor's whistle.

"Just go. Right now," Maggie cried, and an answering whistle sounded from the observation car at the rear. "Louella Meggs style. You first. No fair looking back," she challenged.

"Maggie—"

"*All 'board.*" The conductor's shout rang mightily. "Well, do it. *Go,*" she bid me, and clouds of steam, hissing from the underbelly of the dining car, swirled about her like fog.

"Go. I want you to."

"*All 'board,*" rang the final warning, followed by a slow, tentative grinding of wheels. I turned and started back up the platform. Passengers waved from the windows that had started to glide past me. I kept on walking. More swiftly now the silver cars rolled past, and I fixed my attention on the proud names that were spelled on the silver flanks. *Oraibi, Yampai, Acoma, Navaho.* The wheels clacked faster, churning in rhythm. I could no longer make out the names in the silver blur that was streaking past. The purple glow of the drumhead on the observation car flashed by, and I heard from far up the tunnel the farewell salute of the diesel's whistle, and mingled with it was another cry.

"*Christopher.*"

I turned on the ramp leading from the platform, and framed against the rushing silver blur of the departing train, Maggie ran toward me, hand upraised, signaling lest I not hear her. Skirting baggage carts and pillars, the Javanese princess covered the platform in splendid, hair-streaming style.

"Well, anyway," she panted, breath pounding from her, at the foot of the ramp, "anyway, I didn't lie about the acting. For a person also gifted in lies—" she hauled for breath, tossed back the falling mane "—it's not a bad improvement, is it?"

"No." She was my life, all of it. "Not bad."

"Which only goes to show how overrated the truth is."

She sliced the air for emphasis, her eyes wide and desperate and pleading. "If that stupid acting junk means something to me—where does it leave us? What now?"

"There'll be something." My voice had a hollow ring. "We'll find a way."

"So little time—another week."

I nodded dully and we looked at each other, swallowed, overwhelmed by the vastness of the shed and the tracks that spelled distance, separation.

"The theater—better be going," I said, and she journeyed up the ramp to me. Arms entwined, we walked from the train shed.

Tuesday morning.

Six-ten, by the luminous clock dial.

I lay on my side, careful not to wake Maggie. I lay with my legs jackknifed up, as if I were cold, and listened to the tattoo at the windows.

Wait, you forgot your coat . . .

"Christopher?"

I mumbled groggily, pretending sleep, and burrowed under the coverlet. Beside me, Maggie shifted position. She sat up, got out of bed. I observed through slitted lids her movements across the room.

She pulled up the straps of the batiste nightgown, looking a child in it, but not a child. She yawned, swept back the tousled hair, stood for a moment, went to the window.

"It's raining," she said, and I burrowed down farther. "Was it the rain that woke you?"

Some more groggy mumbles, and for extra effect I rolled onto my right side.

"It was your enemy, you said. Is that why it woke you?"

"Thanks." I rolled back grumpily to the left side. "Verge of dozing off again, but thanks to you—"

"Your enemy, because not very terrific things happened to you in it." She parted the curtains, looked out at the downpour. "What things?" she asked. "What nonterrific things?"

I gave up any pretense of sleep and pushed myself up on

the pillows. "Look, if I said that, which I don't especially remember—"

"Providence, when you phoned my room."

"Okay, I said it, but just how—" I reached to the carpet for my shorts "—exactly how it relates to now—"

"It might, though." She turned from the window. "What if we've had the same enemy?"

Clutching the coverlet to hide my randiness, I pulled on the shorts. "Listen, I don't know what you're talking about, but—"

"Yes, you do, Christopher." She moved toward me from the window. "The same enemy stalking us still, this very minute."

"I was going to suggest—"

"Right on our trail, don't you see? And what are we doing about it?"

"Listen—" Some impulse was seizing her, some wild, unbridled streak I wasn't sure I appreciated. "We'll make some coffee," I said as she moved to the closet by the door. "Coffee, and if there're any of those sweet rolls left that you—Maggie, what in God's name?"

She took her raincoat from the closet and slipped it over the nightdress. Next, my raincoat came sailing over the Murphy bed.

"The same enemy, but we shouldn't let it—"

"You crazy? Bonkers?" The raincoat made a plop as I caught it. "If you're actually suggesting what I—we'll get arrested. *Jailed.*"

"For what, slaying our enemies?"

"Maggie, look at me." I gestured at my shorts. "Practically naked, so are you, and if you think I'm going to participate in this nutty, hare-brained—"

"It won't be—and at least it'll be doing something." Her eyes pleaded with me as she belted her raincoat. "Can't you feel it?" she asked. "We've given up."

I stared across the bed at her, then pulled on the raincoat. "Okay, but it's definitely hare-brained," I said as she rooted in the closet, on hands and knees. "Better get an alibi set, in case we're stopped."

With a shout of triumph, she dug from the closet the espadrilles we'd bought for the beach. "Alibi, indeed. We'll tell the truth." She sent a pair of espadrilles winging at me.

I caught them rather neatly. "Such as what?"

"We'll simply say," Maggie laughed, "that we're defying the elements."

And so we did, although it was difficult to attach any credence to it. Who were these creatures, collars pulled up, bare legs sticking out from raincoats, who boarded the Daphne elevator, rode to the lobby, and thence strode out into the rain? What madness afflicted the two, that at six-thirty on Tuesday morning, June twenty-first, in the Year of Our Lord nineteen hundred and forty-nine, they should be impelled to go leaping, chasing and puddle-splashing up that portion of Michigan Avenue known as "The Magnificent Mile"?

It was, too. At that hour of the morning the wide vista of avenue—emptied of crowds, shops closed, the usual clog of traffic thinned to a light skim of taxis, news trucks and a lone double-decker bus, solemn as a bishop—it belonged to us and was magnificent, as was the rain.

A summer rain, it plashed, flowed, streamed in cooling torrents on us. "Isn't it glorious?" Maggie cried, cupping handfuls of it. "It's glorious!" She went leaping over a puddle at the curb. "Well, isn't it?"

I ran to catch up with her. "It's fantastic. The best."

"Laggard." She turned to look back, wiping rivulets from her face. "Slow as a tortoise, I must say."

"Tortoise?" I took off after her. "We'll see who's the tortoise."

We made a contest of it, one outdistancing the other, only to fall behind, collapse panting in a doorway, then on again, the front-runner for a stretch, leaping over gutters and drains, to collapse at the next curb. At some point in the mad relay the espadrilles, sodden weights by then, were kicked off, discarded. The bare foot gripped the wet-splashed sidewalk with primal urge, a spur to the race, along with the gusts of wind from the lake, which increased in force until . . .

"Christopher?" We'd reached Oak Street, Maggie in the lead. She swung around, raincoat plastered to her body, and slicked back the wet skeins of hair. "What is it?"

I gulped for breath. "Nothing. Sorry to poop out."

"Oh, I get it." She blinked the droplets of rain from her lashes, nodded across the avenue at the Drake Hotel. "I went back there, you know," she said after a moment. "I made myself go in the lobby and sit there." She brushed at the rivulets. "So it wouldn't be an enemy any more."

The rain blotted my mouth. "The afternoons at the beach, I used to look over at it . . . and think how close it came to happening."

"But it didn't happen." Her gaze on me was steady and insistent. "It didn't end, wasn't like . . . the other."

I stared at her, wondering what she referred to. "Like what other?"

"I—" She hesitated, turned to the curve of beach and basin of rain-splattered, wind-whipped blue water that extended its mileage across the avenue, bordered by Lake Shore Drive.

It occurred to me, what she was getting at. "Maggie?"

She stepped from the curb, ran across the intersection, through the sparse threads of traffic, to the lake side of the Drive, and down the stair ramp that led onto the beach.

"Maggie?"

I rushed after her. The wind, unhindered by any buildings, swept at us from the lake. Running, both of us were running once more. I ran down onto the deserted beach, past the vacant lifeguard stands and the litter baskets that were like giant upturned stovepipe hats . . . ran after Maggie to the edge of the beach, where the breakers rolled in, crashing on the shore.

Not until she was at the foaming water's edge did she halt and turn to me. She braced her feet in the swirls of water, pushed at the wet tendrils of hair and began to speak, not of my father, but hers, as she had never done before.

"Used to look everywhere for him." She hurled her voice against the crash of waves. "L.A., New York, Boston —every night at the theater I'd think, Will he have seen the papers, found where I am? It wouldn't have made a difference, the whole world applauding or not—"

The rain lashed at her, the waves broke and clawed at her feet. "It was for him, to show him I was somebody instead of nobody, but he wouldn't have seen. He'd have thought as he always did. Be nice if I didn't care anymore, didn't keep looking for him, even these past weeks in Chicago."

I waded through the swirls of water to her. "You—you love him still."

"And hate him. Both." She backed from me in the foaming swirls. "It's worse for you, isn't it? You have worse to think about."

She was getting to it now. "Why worse?"

"Was it raining when he died?"

I didn't answer; she flicked at the wet tendrils matted to her head. "Did he kill himself, Christopher? Was that how he died?"

I heard my fumbled discordant denial. "Accident—fell from these—hungry, tired, not himself any more. Ghost of himself."

"He killed himself and you took the blame for it." The wind hurled Maggie's reply. "You hated him for it, too— why wouldn't you?"

"No. *No.*" The waves washed numbly at my feet and through the rain I saw the cemetery again, the coffin lowering in the ground, heard myself cry, "What good was I to him? Don't you see? No goddamn good."

"Christopher. Christopher." She steered toward me through the crashing, eddying water. "Listen. *Listen* to me." She grasped me by the arms, shouted against the wind. "I was hungry and tired—a ghost, a pale little ghost scared to go on, and you saved me."

I stared at the washed marble of her face. "You saved

me," she said. "Maybe that doesn't make up for it, maybe nothing ever can—"

"Maggie—"

"—ever, but what I know is—" she backed away in the swirling water "—I'll always look for my father." Her voice faltered. "I'll always wish Mama could've known before she died that I'd come back. My baby. I'll always wonder about my baby. Son? Daughter? I'll never know for the rest of my life, but it's all right, I accept it. Papa, Mr. Carewe, Dr. Bates—*everything*." Her hand slashed at the sheets of rain. "All of it, Christopher, if I knew . . . that at the end . . ." She looked at me, her eyes wide and imploring. "That at the end, there'd be you," she said.

A silence filled with the wind and the rain, the crash of waves. Neither of us spoke; then, "Links," I said slowly. "The good and the bad, links in a chain, which can you break? None, it seems."

"Seems not." She slicked back her hair, wiped at her face. "We mustn't get scared, give up."

I stood looking at her, the water eddying between us. "It's all extremely contradictory," I ventured. "At the station yesterday, I mean."

"Contradictory?"

"I mean, there I was, using every argument against it, practically pushing you onto the train, when all the while . . ."

"Yes?" she inquired.

"All the while—" To my astonishment, the words tumbled out of their own accord. "Maggie? Before Harmon gets here, or the show closes, before any of it . . . marry me?"

She blinked. "What did you say?"

"I'm crazy. Do you hear the craziness I'm actually proposing? Bookstore clerk, fifty a week tops. Cold-water flat, and half the time you'll be on the Coast—or what the hell, I will. After all, they have bookstores in L.A."

"Pickwick. Martindale's." She nodded. "And let's not forget Hunter's."

A grin seized my face, I flung out my arms. "What the hell, we'll work it out. What's to stop us?"

"Nothing," she grinned back.

"Today, tomorrow, the soonest possible—" I plowed through the foaming swirls to her. "Marry me, Maggie?"

"Well, finally," she said, a hand to her mouth. "I was beginning to think you'd never ask."

"Marry me. Marry me. Marry me." I circled my arms around her, the two of us crazy, knee-deep in water. "Isn't it terrific? No enemies left. Where'd they go?"

"Far away, where they can't get us," she said, and her arms encircled me, and the wind swept her words along the beach, up into the sky.

CHAPTER **15**

Friday morning, June twenty-fourth.

Sleep, a dream.

Sky was in the dream, strange and perplexing: a daylight sky filled with stars, how could that be? Whole galaxies, constellations flung across the firmament. Daylight sky full of stars, how? I strained for a closer look, closer, but they were dimming. Too much light for stars, too much light streaming in the . . .

I drifted awake, sleepily regarded the sunlight streaming through the curtains. Friday. City Hall today, department of licenses. Blood tests okay, then the wait for birth certificates, mine yesterday, Maggie's by special delivery last night, when we got back from the theater. License today, and *then*, then on Sunday . . .

I yawned, lazily stretched my arms, slowly lowered them. Strange to dream of stars in a daylight sky. Stranger that I should remember it; usually I didn't, I forgot dreams the moment I woke. Only nightmares hung around. I yawned, turned by careful degrees in the Murphy bed, so as not to disturb my wife-to-be. I slid a hand under the covers to the warm, smooth, silken . . .

Not there.

Had the king summoned her to the palace? Conspirators abducted her for a ransom in jewels? Milk—we were out of milk, or was it oranges, and . . .

The batiste nightgown was folded primly, chastely, on a chair. She wasn't kidding about chaste. Tomorrow, with the arrival of the Lenihan sisters via a swank bedroom on the Commodore Vanderbilt, I was to be banished from 1604. Kicked out, booted to some solitary cell and a life of celibacy till the Sunday nuptials—which, she'd ruled, were to be held in a church, under the personal auspices of God. Insisted upon it, so before the Wednesday matinee we'd gone to the rectory of Old St. Mary's . . .

I cocked a contented eye at the clock . . . 9:40. I lay back and listened for the sound of the elevator grinding to a stop in the hall outside. We'd sat in the rectory parlor of Old St. Mary's, unenthusiastically, for my part. The priest who bounced into the parlor—no other description for it, bounced—was a spry, pixyish man in a cassock shiny from wear, with steel spectacles that slid down his nose, and eyebrows that shot in quixotic amusement. An Irish Abe Klein, though he was distinctly his own man.

"I trust," he said, waving at a hideous oleograph on the wall, "that if I get to heaven I won't find a Christ with marcelled hair and a manicure. Now." He pulled up a chair. "What can I do for you?"

I spoke up with ill-concealed antagonism. "We're here to see about getting married."

"Are you?" said Father Driscoll. "Could've knocked me over with a feather."

"I'm a Catholic, was raised as one, at any rate, while Miss Jones—"

"Is not." He smiled at Maggie. "A mixed marriage, to use the unfortunate terminology of the Church. As though we were discussing hash or a stew." The spectacles over which he peered at Maggie were mended with adhesive. "I've seen you in church," he said. "Once or twice, in the back."

"I—yes, once or twice," she said.

I interrupted. "Father, I'd like to make it clear that if this is any sort of second-class arrangement—"

Paying no attention, he continued his peering. "Are you in love with this earnest, humorless, long-winded young man, as he so obviously is with you?" he asked.

"Yes. I am, Father."

"If I have an objection, Father, it's—"

He scratched his temple, flipped open a ledger, and asked, "When would you like to be married?"

"On Sunday," ventured Maggie. "Sunday afternoon, if we could. If you perform marriages then."

I'd watched him make a notation in the ledger. "Surely you want to ask us questions," I said.

"Sunday at four-thirty. For your music preferences, you can speak with the organist." He hopped to his feet. "Good day. God be with you."

"But you don't know anything about us," I said as he bounced to the door.

He turned and peered over the spectacles. "I believe I do, oh, yes," he'd said, and went bouncing from the parlor.

Nine-forty-five, by the clock hands . . . and the elevator hadn't cranked to a stop in the hall. Kessler's Market was around the corner on State, ten minutes there and back, unless she lingered to chat with Mrs. Kessler. I threw off the coverlet, swung my legs to the floor: Get shaved and dressed, gulp breakfast when she got back, make it to City Hall by ten-thirty. I padded to the bathroom, pulling on shorts en route.

Marry me! Marry me! Marry me!

I stood at the bathroom mirror, lathering up my bridegroom's stubble. After City Hall, million other arrangements. Wedding reception at the Ambassador, menu to check, flowers, combo. Announcements—through the intercession of Abel Klein we'd located a printer not averse to rush orders. Specialized in theatrical handbills, but could turn out high-class quality one-hundred-percent engraved work for all social occasions, upon request. No shopping for a bridal gown—Joe and Lourdes Scully were flying in from L.A. on Saturday, Joe to give Maggie away, and with them would be the gown Lourdes and her mother before her had worn in Mexico as brides, the white linen tier-skirted gown Maggie had worn in the garden, face turning, surprised by the camera . . .

I lowered the razor, gazed at the lather-jawed reflection

in the mirror. My mother had sent my baptismal certificate along with the birth certificate, and yesterday afternoon I'd rung the bell of Old St. Mary's rectory. Father Driscoll, the housekeeper had snapped, was in church hearing confessions. "If you can call it that," she'd grumbled. "I've no doubt the man'd let off a murderer with a few Hail Marys."

It wasn't what I'd intended, but I'd gone into the quiet, candle-flickering church and into the sour-smelling box that bore Father Driscoll's name above the priest's door.

The grille slid back. "It's me, Father," I said. "Christopher Casey. The wedding Sunday."

"Ah, yes, the enchanting Maggie."

"I didn't come for confession. The housekeeper said you were in here."

"The difference between a priest and a dentist is that nobody informs the latter he hasn't come about his teeth. Still, since you're here . . ."

"Maggie and I, we've . . . I don't regard it as a sin. Sleeping together, I mean."

In lieu of a rebuke or lecture, Father Driscoll delivered a meditative sigh. "Tell me, Christopher, do you love God?"

"I don't know." My voice shook suddenly; the thin-padded kneeler cut into my shins. "I—I spent last year in a monastery, trying to find God, I suppose."

"And didn't?"

"I don't think it was God I was looking for, only my father. Same thing all over again."

"I'm afraid I don't—"

"My father died when I was a child. No, that's not all of it. He committed suicide . . . and a question I could never answer about it was where God was when it happened."

"Close, I should hope," murmured the voice on the other side of the grille. "Close enough to take your father to heaven."

I wiped the unbidden tears from my face. "Took him from me, when I needed him. Loved him."

"But we must all go to God, Christopher. We are his creatures, we belong to him, like it or not." There was a silence, long and ruminating. "It's a mistake, you know, to imagine that we can ever comprehend a mystery. This young girl of yours, when I saw her in church . . ."

"She never said she'd come."

"What brought her here, though? Looking at her, I felt I was very close to the mystery." Dimly through the grille I saw a frail, worn hand push at the mended spectacles. "It seemed to me that happiness had brought her here, born somehow from sorrow."

"Father—"

"And you, Christopher." He leaned forward slightly. "Had sorrow no part in leading you to her?" He shook his head slowly, reflectively. "I don't pretend to understand why sorrow must visit each of us, but it's at the heart of the mystery. Without it, how could we grow nearer to a God who died on a cross between thieves? Or know joy, such as has been given to you?" Behind the grille the worn hand raised up, traced the age-old symbol of sorrow. "Let me give you God's blessing . . ."

I scraped the razor over the sharp ridge of my cheekbone, heard the elevator in the hall. Wiped off the lather, hurried into the other room, listened to the elevator clank to a stop. Footsteps approached, then passed the door. I stood listening to them, alone but not alone. I hadn't awakened alone. She was with me, filling each moment with her presence, so that when she walked in the door . . .

Five after ten, by the clock dial. I pulled on trousers, hunted for socks. Located one of a pair, fished under the bed for its mate. She hadn't gone to Kessler's, but to the French bakery up Rush Street on Bellevue Place. Croissants to celebrate marriage-license day. I jammed on loafers, stuffed shirttails in trousers. Six blocks to Bellevue, if I moved fast I'd meet her on her way back. I grabbed the seersucker jacket from the closet at the door. The yellow dress wasn't on its hanger: she'd said she wanted to wear it today—in memory of hard times overcome.

I pulled on the jacket, hurried out the door, straight into the personage of Saffrona Willets, day maid, stacking towels in her arm at the linen closet. Since the marriage plans, relations had improved between Saffrona and me. She treated me now with exaggerated mock scorn. Flinging a black hand to her face, she let out a howl of ersatz indignation.

"Pass from my vision and be *gone*," she cried, following this with rich peals of laughter. "What you doin' sneakin' off minus the sweet darlin' bride-to-be?"

"It's the bride who's done the sneaking off." For no reason, I thought of the dream again, the dream of stars in a daylight sky. "But I think I can find her, Saffrona."

"Buyed me a dress for Sunday, fuchsia an' orchid, an' hat to match with a bird on its crown!"

Looking for Maggie . . . I jabbed for the elevator and thought of the day a month ago when I'd waited in agony for this elevator. The Drake, then the Bryn Mawr—somehow I'd found my way to her, as though the looking had begun long ago, years before the morning in the Garrick alley, the rain-clad figure bursting in from the street, head raised, scarf slipping from her hair. Long, long ago, links in a chain, each leading to the next, finally to her.

"Down?"

The elevator stood with gate ajar and Hal, the operator, yawning at the controls. I stepped into the pink-and-black car, Hal slid the gate shut, and with a whoosh we trundled downward. I counted off the numbers painted between the floors . . . 16 . . . 15 . . . 14 . . . What could it mean, stars in a daylight sky? It was contrary to nature, the earth would have to slip from its axis, turned upside down by some awesome, cataclysmic . . . 11 . . . 10, I counted the floor numbers, and it was at 5 that the sound of a siren, police or ambulance, couldn't tell which, floated up through the shaft from the street outside.

The panic knotted as I listened to the distant wail. It wasn't tangible fear, reasoned apprehension, but a conditioned reflex dating back to . . . 4 . . . 3 . . . 2, the numbers descended. Six blocks up Rush to Bellevue, gone half an hour, by now she'd . . .

"The siren," I said to Hal. "Hear it? How far, would you say?"

"Sound close, to me." He braked the controls and shuddered to a stop at the lobby flor. "Sound to me it comin' a block or two up Rush."

"Two sirens now. Hear?" I stood at the back of the car, listening to the wail of the second siren, farther away but screeching nearer, blended in awful harmony with its twin. I looked out at the Daphne lobby, the pink plaster cupids that frolicked in the guise of lamps, attended by the murals of pink-turbaned blackamoors. I stared out at the lobby and didn't move. Stars at daylight meant cataclysm, the world turned upside down.

"Sound to me"—Hal nodded toward the street—"like they been a accident. That what it sound to me."

I didn't start to run until I was out of the hotel, going up Rush Street. Two blocks away at Huron, the revolving light on the police car flashed red in the sunlight; an ambulance gleamed white as it clanged down Rush from Chicago Avenue. Others were running, from stoops, shop doorways, office buildings, converging on the corner of Huron, where the police car and ambulance had turned.

Corners!

I felt my legs buckle, steps give out before I reached the corner. *Steps*, links in a chain, each joined to the others— break off, be rid of, destroy which, without destroying the chain? The prayer at Cumberland Hospital, whispered among the wheelchairs and oxygen cylinders—silently I screamed the offer again, my life for Maggie's, but I knew, even before my legs regained their function, that it was not to be.

Like a sleepwalker, I covered the remaining distance to the corner, knowing that I must if I was ever to move limb again. I reached the crowd of spectators and heard a woman beside me confide to another woman, "Saw the whole thing, a perfect tragedy. Poor girl hadn't a chance.

340

Still on the curb, she was, then from nowhere the car, out of control, straight at her . . ."

From the crowd, I gaped at the scene, surely from a movie, of police cars, uniforms, ambulance, interns, stretcher. A robin's-egg-blue convertible, blood dripping from its fender, tire marks tracing its wild zigzag course, was crashed into a lamp post. The driver leaned in nausea over the fender, while a policeman attempted to question him. The man, his face lacerated, kept staring at the broken, crumpled form that was being lifted onto the stretcher.

"Saw the whole thing," continued the woman. "Hadn't a chance . . . came from nowhere, out of control."

I pushed through the crowd then and stepped from the curb. In front of me stood a policeman, arms extended to block off the street. "Back. Everybody back," he kept repeating. "You. Back," he said, at my sleepwalker's somnolent advance.

Then he lowered his arms and allowed me past.

The ambulance attendants were lowering Maggie onto the shiny, chrome-wheeled stretcher. Blood seeped from the yellow dress, it streamed in a frozen river from her mouth and stained the white sheet that one of the attendants proceeded to draw over the waxen primavera face. At my slow, shell-shocked approach, he exchanged uncertain glances with the other attendant, after which they set the stretcher down and stood back.

I knelt before the stretcher, I remember, thinking there must be something I could do. The raven hair spilled from the sheet covering her face; I smoothed it back, then there was nothing more to do.

The police came over; I identified Maggie for them, told them who I was. Exclamations swept through the crowd, were hushed, as the attendants lifted the stretcher and slid it into the ambulance.

Nothing more to do? Nothing, ever again?

I climbed into the ambulance after the stretcher. I heard the retort of the doors being shut, the low, vibrating hum of the motor. The attendants rode up front with the driver, leaving me alone with Maggie in the rear . . . and I remember that, as the ambulance drove away in a cortege led by the police car, and the crowd surged forward, some jumping, craning at the windows, it was none of this I saw, or was conscious of seeing.

Instead, reaching out, I slipped the still-warm hand from under the sheet and held it in mine. "We made it through, all the way," I said to Maggie. "We won. Not as we thought, but we won."

Then I lifted her hand to my jacket, inside, to my heart, where now she lived; and as the ambulance drove away I saw the street corner as it had been moments ago, Maggie in her yellow dress hurrying toward me, as I toward her, having found each other across terrifying distances, for a time.

EPILOGUE

Christopher
1975

Back . . . back!

The door of the compartment swung open—the catch was loose, we were making a turn—and it wasn't the policeman who spoke, but the porter.

" 'Scuse me, suh?"

I lifted the still-warm hand to my jacket, inside, to my heart . . . the compartment door tilted crazily, the wheels screeched on the turn. "Yes?"

The porter steadied the door. "Speculatin' whether you hear me before."

Inside, to my heart and as the ambulance drove away, it was not the crowds I saw, but . . . "Heard you?"

"Dinner, suh." He was as old and grizzled as Louis Tilford, but of imposing girth. He balanced against the sway of the train with the same practiced ease, and pulled at the red Amtrak mess jacket, bulging at the seams, that was an affront to his dignity. "It soon be gettin' past time."

"Oh?" I turned and looked out the compartment window. Still daylight, but streaks of mauve crayoned the opalescent sky and the landscape had changed, greens instead of desert browns and reds. I wondered for a moment what day it was.

"Tha's Colorado you lookin' at," the porter supplied, after a pause. "We done left New Mexico back at Raton, an' it was way before that . . ."

It started again. The cool green Colorado spruce and

pine at the window changed to Rush Street, *the sirens again, people running, the robin's-egg-blue fender splattered with blood, and in the street the broken, crumpled . . .* I turned from the window; a reflection stared from the mirror that backed the door—shocking, a stranger's face, unshaven, lines carved deep at the mouth, nostrils, eyes. Bloodshot eyes. Charcoal hair flecked with white.

"Back at Lamy, so that make it over two hours—"

I reached for the bottle of Jack Daniel's, met the expressionless gaze of the porter. I put the bottle down, gave a laugh. "Sorry, guess I wasn't thinking about dinner."

"Nossuh." He tugged at the offending jacket. "Nor lunch, neither."

"Yes, well, I—" I nodded at the elaborate gift basket Ziegler had dispatched to the train, having failed to persuade me to stick to the friendly skies of United. "Cheese, fruit—as you see, I'm well provided for."

Tactfully, the basset-hound eyes avoided the near-empty whiskey bottle. "Yessuh, reckon so."

"Not many passengers this trip. Train seems empty." Maybe if I talked to him, it wouldn't start again, at least not the blood. "Only decided to come myself at the last minute. Business trip, figured I'd grab some rest."

Christopherrr!

A buzzer sounded down the corridor, prompting the porter to shake his head. "Old lady in J, when she not complainin' of the heat, be expirin' of the cold. 'Scuse me a moment?"

"Of course. Sure."

He went with solemn tread down the corridor. I sat waiting for him to return. Talk was the antidote. Keep talking. The seat was upholstered in orange and purple, of a synthetic fiber as unyielding as cement. Nubby purple carpet, plywood armrest in imitation walnut. From what I'd glimpsed of the other Pullmans and the vista-dome lounge car up forward, the train resembled a monstrous Howard Johnson's, all plastic, foam rubber, fake veneers, done up in violent hues that commanded, Smile! Perk up!

The *Southwest Limited,* it was listed as in the Amtrak schedule, service between Los Angeles and Chicago, a Howard Johnson's-on-wheels.

Chriistopherr!

I listened for the porter's steps, *heard the elevator in the hall the last morning at the Daphne, the footsteps approaching, going past the door.* I eyed the whiskey bottle, the paper cup jiggling on the windowsill, and the effort it took not to reach for either beaded my forehead with sweat. Dig in the gift basket, get some food down. Ziegler, the donor, was a Hollywood literary agent. Normally I did business with him over the phone, but a property as big as the Wilson book, million-six paperback sale and a complicated movie deal, ninety pages of clauses, subclauses, riders *. . . who was I kidding?*

I hunched over on the seat and the silent haunted cry tore through me. *Maggie! It's no use, I can't keep on any more. All the years and I think I'm over it, but I'm not. Yesterday, crossing Sunset Boulevard, the traffic light changed, but I kept going, praying, sweet Jesus, for a car to hit me so I could be with you.*

I seized the paper cup, raised the bottle shakily to it; there was a knock, the door clicked open, and the porter stood there, his chicory features impassive.

"Sorry, if I be disturbin' you, suh."

"No, I was just . . ." I sloshed amber into the cup, a little civilized drink before the dinner I couldn't get myself to. "How was the old lady in J?"

He grinned, black hand steadying the door. "Expirin' of the heat this time. Says to her, simple enough, turn down the valve."

I stared at the paper cup, drained of amber, crumpled it. "Guess old ladies is what you mostly get nowadays on runs like this."

"They be one type of passenger. Old folks with time on their hands, no hurry to git where they goin'." He paused as I capped the bottle, propped it against the armrest. "Sprinklin' of young folks too."

"Surprised to hear it." I stared out at the darkening Colorado hills. "I'd imagine trains for them would be as extinct as buffalo."

"Extin—?"

During the night the hills would be succeeded by the flat Kansas prairie that was Maggie's grave. "Vanished, nonexistent. *Extinct*," I spat out the words, the smear of blood bright against my vision.

The porter spoke quietly, with regret. "Mistuh, you the other type of passenger we get on this run."

I swung around. "Oh?"

"Ridin' on journeys past," he said, "that won't never come again."

"Wrong," I corrected. *Maggie! Maggie!* the wheels clacked. "Journeys that never happened. Missed trains." I turned back to the window, the spool of rails unwinding behind, and the cry started in me again. "It—it traveled this same route." I nodded at the rails. "At least, I think it did."

"The old Santa Fe, y' mean?"

I stared out the compartment window. "Same route, a train once. Never traveled on it, but I knew someone who was about to, except she—it turned out she didn't make it."

A silence against the clacking wheels. The porter shifted his feet. "Whut was that word you used in connection with buffaloes?"

I stared out at the imponderable sky. "Extinct. Gone."

He paused tentatively a moment. "Before Amtrak I was employed by the Pullman Company," he volunteered. "Twenty-eight years, all of 'em on the Santa Fe . . . which leads me to speculate," he went on, "that you might be talkin' about the Superchief."

I turned from the window. "You worked on the Superchief?" I was unprepared for his answer.

"Yessuh, still do, in a manner of speakin'," he said, then gestured at the purple-and-orange compartment. "Somethin' awful, the way they junked it up." He jutted his lower lip in disapproval. "Wouldn't ever recognize this car as the Yampai."

It struck no chord, then I remembered Union Station, the names flashing on the silver cars as they rolled past. "This was the Yampai?"

"Wuz and is." He tugged at the offending red mess jacket. On it was pinned a plastic name tag, *T. C. Davis.* "Them young folks we get on board, pesterin' me with questions about the old trains, like they was covered wagons or sailin' ships gone from the seas. *Extinct?*" He tugged at the jacket again, thrust out his jaw, imperious as Louis Tilford. "Tell you this, T. C. Davis ain't extinct, and as for the Superchief"—his voice lowered to a whisper— "mistuh, you're ridin' on it."

I looked at him, and in his eyes was an urgency. "So you didn't miss out on it," he said. "It's just that time's gone by, like for all of us."

"Gone by . . . yes," I said.

"Same as it's goin' by right this minute," T. C. Davis went on. "Dinner's whut you gonna miss less you git a move on."

Time fled inexorably, and each moment reiterated that which had passed, good and bad, sorrowful and joyous, and that to come. *You a lamp post?* Louis Tilford had remonstrated. *Less'n you get movin', we be in Back Bay.* I got up from the seat, remembering the people who were kind.

"Still serving in the dining car?" I asked T. C. Davis.

"Only till eight." Fretting, he shook his grizzled head. "When I made the last call an' you didn't come out . . ."

The solitary passenger locked up with the whiskey bottle: I'd given him the classic ground for alarm. "Sorry for making you worry, but . . . thank you," I said.

He nodded, turned, stepped into the corridor. "For sure, you'll take yourself?"

"For sure."

"Feel better, some food in your stomach." The buzzer sounded down the corridor, querulous and demanding, and his steps receded in testy answer to it. "Comin', lady. Where the fire? Huh, old lady?"

Steps . . .

I went into the shiny purple bathroom, unzipped the toilet kit on the washstand. I soaped my jaw with aerosol cream, lathered it up, brought the razor scraping down the gaunt, stranger's face . . . yet not a stranger, for someone had told me once who I was. *I was hungry and tired, and you saved me.* The beach in the rain, and she'd said of her life what had enabled me to go on with my own. *I'd accept it all, everything, if I knew at the end . . .*

And I had gone on, it was only that times it got hard, got out of control. Not often, but at certain times. *"Oh, Maggie."* I leaned over the washbasin, rested my face against the cool mirror. *"I'll live through it all, accept it all, if at the end . . . there'll be you."*

I continued shaving then.

Tie crisply knotted, navy pinstripe well-fitted, the proper editor, I stepped from the compartment, navigated the corridor of the Yampai, formerly of the Superchief, which therefore was not gone. The trains still ran, still covered the long distances, went on, as I would try to do.

I pulled open the door to the lounge car. It was rendered in fuchsias and reds with chrome highlights, authentic Howard Johnson's. Above the bar, futuristic stairs wound up to the glass dome, where I'd thought later to keep watch on the prairie, the dusty ghosts of depots and small Kansas towns that the moonlight, or the stars if they were out, might reveal.

If? If?

Look where for Maggie? She was not to be found in ghostly depots or passing towns; only the memory of her, and her grave, were there. Maggie had gone in victory to a place beyond, and death was not the enemy.

Threading my way among the cocktail tables, I negotiated the length of the lounge car. Death was not the enemy, no more than was the rain. We were the enemy, our own flawed vision, pinioned to earth, failing to see that the stars, even in daylight, are never absent from the sky.

I pulled open the door—doors opening, closing—to the next car.

We cannot know, ever, what the course of our lives is to be, nor even with certainty where the next moment will take us. It is subject to change.

But to know that, after all, is to know a great deal.

The heavy steel door thudded behind me, and I stepped into the lighted dining car that rocketed through the night.